PRAISE FOR ANDREWS & WILSON

"Action-packed. . . . Andrews & Wilson thrill with their imaginative world building, edge-of-the-seat plot, and deeply felt characters. Fans of Frank Peretti and Ted Dekker will enjoy this."

PUBLISHERS WEEKLY on *Dark Angel*

"A pulse-pounding thriller. Andrews & Wilson will capture you right out of the gate!"

JOEL C. ROSENBERG, *New York Times* bestselling author of the Marcus Ryker series, on *Dark Angel*

"A compelling story combining spirituality and the supernatural with tier one operators and hard-hitting action sequences, *Dark Angel* provides a front-row seat to witness the age-old battle of good versus evil in a way you likely haven't experienced before. The dynamic duo of Andrews & Wilson delivers a stimulating faith-based military thriller that will take you on a journey beyond this world where anything is possible, and light must stomp out darkness to maintain the fragile balance of today's society."

STEVE NETTER, Best Thriller Books

"Fans of Frank Peretti will enjoy this action-packed inspirational."

PUBLISHERS WEEKLY on *Dark Intercept*

"*Dark Intercept* is a fantastic blend of supernatural thrills, crisis of faith, and military thriller all rolled into one. . . . A unique crisis of faith novel that is sure to be a hit!"

MYSTERY AND SUSPENSE MAGAZINE

"*Dark Intercept* is a masterpiece of a military thriller with remarkable heart and depth. No one in the genre writes grittier and more authentic action than these two authors, and yet *Dark Intercept* also deals with the intriguing questions of spirituality and the human condition, making it a spellbinding page-turner that will leave you both thrilled and enriched by the experience."

MARK GREANEY, #1 *New York Times* bestselling author of *Relentless* and the Gray Man novels

"A blistering page-turner of a thriller . . . that effortlessly transports the reader from the adrenaline-filled highs of the battlefield to the soul-searching lows that follow."

JOSHUA HOOD, author of Robert Ludlum's Treadstone series, on *Dark Intercept*

"The characters are unforgettable and unique, promising a blockbuster Shepherds series. Andrews & Wilson write with the authenticity that can only be achieved through boots-on-the-ground downrange experience. Whether you're military connected or not, reading this novel will make you want to enlist with these spiritual warriors. Un-put-downable."

K.J. HOWE, internationally bestselling author of *Skyjack*, on *Dark Intercept*

"In *Dark Intercept*, Andrews & Wilson flawlessly weave a tale of spiritual and natural warfare as riveting as it is inventive. By combining the grittiness and veracity of their bestselling military thriller series with an unabashed focus on the eternal struggle between light and darkness, Andrews & Wilson inject a shot of adrenaline into faith-based fiction. Frank Peretti has company!"

DON BENTLEY, author of the Matt Drake thriller series

"A thrilling and gripping ride through the eyes of those who strap on the uniform and serve, [*Dark Intercept*] helps us see what true leadership looks like. . . . You'll enjoy this crackling adventure and learn some valuable things along the way."

DANIEL DARLING, bestselling author of *The Characters of Christmas* and *A Way with Words*

THE SHEPHERDS SERIES

DARK FALL

ANDREWS & WILSON

Tyndale House Publishers
Carol Stream, Illinois

Visit Tyndale online at tyndale.com.

Visit Andrews & Wilson online at andrews-wilson.com.

Tyndale and Tyndale's quill logo are registered trademarks of Tyndale House Ministries.

Dark Fall

Cover designed by Faceout Studio, Jeff Miller

Edited by Sarah Mason Rische

Published in association with the literary agency of Talcott Notch Literary, LLC, 276 Forest Road, Milford, CT 06461.

For information about special discounts for bulk purchases, please contact Tyndale House Publishers at csresponse@tyndale.com, or call 1-855-277-9400.

Library of Congress Cataloging-in-Publication Data

A catalog record for this book is available from the Library of Congress.

ISBN 978-1-4964-5144-6 (HC)

ISBN 978-1-4964-5145-3 (SC)

Printed in the United States of America

28	27	26	25	24	23	22
7	6	5	4	3	2	1

For Karen Watson and the incredible team
at Tyndale House who made this series possible.
We are in your debt.

★

NOTE TO READERS

We've provided a glossary in the back of this book to define the acronyms, military lingo, and abbreviations used in this series.

★

PROLOGUE

Dagan Meier stopped to catch his breath as he wove his way up the mountain. At fourteen thousand feet elevation, the air was thin . . . very, very thin. The rocky trail he took from the lower village, *Hatun Q'ero*, to the upper village, *Hapu Q'ero*, resembled a goat path. But so far he hadn't seen any goats. Only llamas.

Provided he didn't pass out and die from hypoxia in the next few minutes, he would meet with the village *paqos altumisayuq*, or spiritual leader. The spiritual leader resided in the upper village and was in conference with the tribal elder, or *paqos pampamisayuq*, who traveled regularly between the upper and lower villages. Together, they ministered to the spiritual needs of the villagers, listened to grievances, dispensed wisdom, and mitigated disputes.

Dagan couldn't help but smile at the thought: *Even here, in the most remote village in the world, bureaucracy is alive and well.*

That the elder was willing to meet with him seemed a good sign, though it didn't surprise Dagan. He'd found the Q'ero to be some of the most welcoming and accommodating people he'd ever met, more than living up to what he'd learned about them in his two months of training at Global Gospel Missions. Dagan felt joy and relief that God had led him here, to such a loving people, for his first assignment as a missionary spreading the gospel of Jesus Christ. He even felt a surge of confidence as he rounded the final switchback on the rocky path and the few scattered wood-and-mud huts came into view. The bulk of the Q'ero resided in the lower village, but up here the elders gathered in conference while the young men tended crops in rocky terraced fields with llamas. In winter, this village would be empty, serving only as a refuge for any traveling Q'ero trapped by snowstorms at the higher elevation.

Two young Q'ero waved to him from where they stood beside one of six structures surrounding a dirt courtyard. He smiled at the boy and girl and stopped to take several slow, deep breaths before waving back. When the heaviness in his head cleared, he said a short prayer for God to fill him with the Holy Spirit and guide his words as he shared the Good News with these people. Immediately peace came upon him, but there was something else, just out of reach. Not dread but . . . something.

You have done good work for the Kingdom of God. You have a pure heart.

The words were at once his but also not. He shook the strange feeling off and continued his trek to share the message with the two men inside the long hut, the only one with curls of smoke coming up out of the rectangular chimney.

"Hello, my friends!" he said in Quechua to the children, one of the few phrases he'd mastered in the ancient language, before adding, "How is the work up here today?" in Spanish.

Most Q'ero were bilingual, with children learning Spanish from a very young age. "How is the work," he'd learned, was a common greeting equivalent to "How are you" in English, and he liked using it.

"Hallo to you, Dagan," the older boy, perhaps ten or eleven, said in English, beaming with pride that he'd mastered the phrase, though he'd substituted a *j* sound for the *y* in *you* and softened the first vowel of Dagan's name.

"Hello," he said back, smiling.

The two children laughed, then skipped off together toward another hut, where a large woman called out to them. Dagan watched as she beat a lovely, colorful tapestry with a flat stick, clouds of dust billowing around her. The Q'ero were known for their weaving skills, a style that some experts claimed linked them to the Incans, and Dagan was struck by the beauty and intricacy of this blanket or carpet—though often it seemed the tapestries were used interchangeably for both purposes. He waved to her, then ducked through the equally magnificent woven drape hung over the open doorway at the front of the hut he was visiting.

The spiritual leader smiled with his large gray teeth and gestured for Dagan to join him and the tribal elder seated beside him on the wood floor atop a brightly colored carpet. As Dagan approached, the former rose with a fluid grace, embraced him, and just as effortlessly returned to the floor, cross-legged. The frail-looking elder beside him gave the faintest of smiles and a long, deep nod, gesturing with a hand for Dagan to join them on the floor.

As he sat, Dagan reminded himself not to assume too much about the faculties of the old man—who looked to be somewhere in the neighborhood of two hundred years old. After all, the old man had climbed to Hatun Q'ero from another village six or seven thousand feet below them and more than twenty miles away. Dagan rather doubted he could make that hike very easily—if at all.

"It is a joy to have you with us, Dagan," the man said—in Spanish, grate-fully—and placed a hand on his shoulder, squeezing it warmly. "Our *paqos pampamisayuq* is quite excited to speak with you about your beliefs, as we share many similar ideas."

Dagan bowed—unsure what else to do—and said a quick, silent prayer for guidance. When the elder did not speak, Dagan seized the opportunity. "It is both my honor and my duty to share with you the Good News of Jesus Christ," he began. "We believe that Jesus—"

"Ahhhhh, yes . . . ," the old man interrupted, smiling broadly with the teeth he had remaining and nodding. He continued in Spanish, "We know well your Jesus Christ."

The old man's words surprised Dagan at first, but then he remembered that missionaries had been visiting the Q'ero for decades.

"That is wonderful," he said, smiling back.

"After founding the city of Qusqu," the old man continued, "the Inkarri created Jesus Christ. Perhaps, when Inkarri returns, he will bring your Jesus with him."

The man smiled and patted Dagan on the knee. Dagan was amazed at the parallels to Christianity—a returning prophet, like a second coming, and the creation of Jesus from a god. Of course, this might be nothing more than the blending of religions. The first Christian Spaniards had encountered the Q'ero hundreds of years ago, and their missionaries had shared the gospel then before disappearing. Q'ero legend had it that the Spaniards had not been kind to the Q'ero, and their disappearance had been at the hand of the mountain gods, or Apus, who had buried the invaders in a rockslide caused by a massive earthquake.

"We believe," Dagan said, choosing his words carefully, "that Jesus Christ is not only the Son of God, but that He is God, who came to us in the form of man so that His sacrifice, by dying on the cross, would allow for our sins to be forgiven and our covenant restored with God. In doing so, we have a relationship with God, and by accepting Jesus as our Lord and Savior, we may have eternal life."

The older man leaned over, speaking rapidly to the younger *paqos* in their native Quechua. They conversed heatedly but without anger. Then the old man smiled at him again and nodded.

"We believe," he said, seemingly excited to give Dagan his spin on this, "that all things were created by Pachamama. It is to Pachamama we give our praise and who must certainly have created your Jesus Christ. By finding balance in all things we honor Pachamama and find peace and harmony with each other and all that exists—including your Jesus Christ."

Dagan nodded, wondering how to politely suggest that what the Q'ero called Pachamama could simply be another name for the one true God. He'd been taught to find commonality in both culture and religion while doing missionary work. Sharing new knowledge was easier if it didn't require others to abandon their tightly held beliefs entirely.

"If we can agree that God and Pachamama are names given by our different peoples to the one true God of the universe—"

A scream cut him off.

Then came a sound much like a muffled explosion, and the smell of sulfur filled the air.

Dagan was on his feet but a beat behind the elders. He fell in behind them, lunging for the door as his heart accelerated in his chest. The old man pushed aside the brightly colored tapestry over the doorway, which fell back into Dagan's face. When he pushed it aside, he froze in place, mouth dropping open and hands trembling.

Where the hut beside which the woman had been cleaning dust from the tapestry had been he now saw only a deep, scorched hole with flames coming up from the bottom like a firepit back home in Pennsylvania. The entire hut had been consumed, and beside the crater he saw a smoldering pile of dark, charred clay, perhaps two or three feet high.

With horror, Dagan realized the smoldering pile was all that remained of the woman. His brain refused to accept what the two smaller smoldering piles probably represented.

A high-pitched squeal made him turn, and he watched a streak of light stretch from the sky and a pillar of flame erupt where a man had been standing just fifteen feet away. A second hut caught fire, and a half-dozen villagers of all ages ran out screaming. Frozen with fear, he watched while yet another figure was incinerated from heaven, leaving behind nothing but a pile of char.

The spiritual leader and the village elder turned to him, their eyes wide with fear and condemnation.

Is your God doing this? their faces asked.

And then they were gone too, consumed by light and heat.

And Dagan was running.

All he could think of was the book of Genesis, where God destroyed Sodom and Gomorrah for their violence and hatred. He'd read that the destruction might have been from fiery meteorites impacting in and around the cities.

Is that what just happened here?

He turned his back on the carnage and ran at a full sprint down the rocky path, fleeing the village. He became aware of a weeping sound and realized it was coming from him, but the sobbing quickly morphed into hyper-ventilation. Gasping for breath, he dropped to his knees on the rocky mountain path. Tears streaming down his face, he looked to heaven and asked the only question his mind could formulate . . . the only question that mattered.

Why, Lord? Why?

PART I

Then you will be handed over to be persecuted and put

to death, and you will be hated by all nations because

of me. At that time, many will turn away from the

faith and will betray and hate each other. . . .

MATTHEW 24:9-10

CHAPTER ONE

Faith and firepower . . . those were the two things Jedidiah Johnson thought about from when he woke in the morning until his head hit the pillow each night. While some people might find the pairing troubling, as a combat team leader for Shepherds North America, worrying about faith and firepower was literally in Jed's job description. Because without an abundance of both, the enemy his team faced would prevail.

Battling evil, it turns out, is complicated.

Before Jed enlisted in the military at age eighteen, he'd aspired to become a pastor. In those naive, carefree days he'd only contemplated faith. Later, while serving as a Navy SEAL at the pointy tip of the spear, he'd measured his worth by the skillful and judicious application of firepower. But over the past several months, those two versions of himself—men he'd always viewed as distinct and separate people—had reunited to become one. The reunification process had not been easy, with both the operator and the man of God not fully trusting each other. Thankfully, he'd had plenty of help along the way, from his Joshua Bravo teammates, from the Shepherd commander Ben Morvant, and from an unlikely teacher—his "adopted niece" Sarah Beth Yarnell.

As he climbed into the driver's seat of his Silverado High Country pickup truck, he made a conscious decision to jettison the emotional baggage he made a habit of carrying around. This afternoon was about living in the moment and having fun. Today would be the first time he'd visited Sarah Beth at St. George's Academy, the special boarding school for children with the gift of second sight. The Watchers, as the children were known, functioned as the Shepherds' eyes and ears in the invisible war raging around the globe for the hearts, minds, and souls of humanity. Where the Dark Ones spread chaos, hate, and death, the Shepherds and the Watchers battled tirelessly to stop them.

Jed piloted his pickup through Trinity Loop campus to the main entrance, where he nodded to the guard at the main gate on his way out. The sunglasses-wearing, no-nonsense security officer had grown on Jed over the past few months, and he couldn't help but wonder if Sanderson might have what it took to be a Shepherd.

I'll have to talk to Ben about that, he thought and made a mental note to bring it up the next time he saw Morvant.

After leaving the complex, he made his way to Sams Creek Road, where he headed south for eight miles to pick up State Route 70. As the crow flies, St. George's Academy was just ten miles southwest of Trinity Loop, their proximity not accidental. In a spun-up helo, a quick-response security team from Trinity could probably get to the school in under five minutes. But for Jed in his pickup truck, the rural roads of Tennessee turned that ten-mile distance into twenty plus, all on roads with forty-five miles per hour speed limits. It would take him every bit of thirty-five minutes to make the trek— assuming he didn't get stuck behind a combine en route.

With the radio blasting Big & Rich, Jed carved up the winding country roads. Smiling and singing along, he even rolled the windows down and let in some fresh Tennessee air. A handful of hit songs later, he arrived at the access road to St. George's. The school itself was set back on a large and sprawling campus with sports fields, a swimming pool, and even an equestrian center. But as he pulled up to the security checkpoint, he couldn't help but notice that the academy's perimeter defenses paled in comparison to what was installed at Trinity Loop. The only countermeasures he could see were what looked like retractable security balusters in front of the guard shack, an iron gate on a swing arm, and a fenced berm that ran the length of the southern property line.

Hmm, he thought. *I'm surprised they don't have a bigger security presence.*

Jed fished out his Trinity Loop CAC card, the ID for the nonofficial cover for Shepherds North America, and presented it to the guard at the gate. Even though he couldn't see them, Jed assured himself that a heavily armed, rapid-response force waited hidden and at the ready, twenty-four hours a day, to protect the very gifted and vulnerable young people living on this campus. The gate guard scanned the card and, after getting a green flash on his tablet, waved Jed through.

He limited his speed to twenty-five as he meandered to visitor parking. As he took in the scenery and activity around him, he felt like he'd driven onto the set of a movie. To his right girls' lacrosse teams were playing on green manicured playing fields. To his left some kids were playing Frisbee next to a man-made lake replete with a wooden dock, a family of ducks, walking trails, and park benches. A two-story redbrick cathedral-style building dominated the landscape with a spire-topped clock tower that drew the eye up to heaven.

Quite a place to get an education, he thought, remembering his dumpy old middle school in Murfreesboro.

He parked in the front row of visitor parking, slipped on his Trinity ball cap, and followed the sidewalk to the main entrance. An armed security officer wearing a charcoal-colored uniform and black kit gave him a quick once-over, then the bro nod of approval as Jed approached the set of double doors leading into the main building. Through the glass he could see Sarah Beth smoothing the pleats on her plaid uniform skirt while she chewed gently on her lower lip, a habit he knew she was trying to break. He sensed both her excitement and her nervousness. They'd not seen each other since the barbecue at the Yarnells' house—one that had been cut abruptly short by the sudden deployment of Joshua Bravo team to Rome to stop the fallen Shepherd Nicholas Woland as he led a team of Dark Ones trying to kidnap the pope from the Vatican.

She looked up a heartbeat later and flashed him a beaming smile.

"Uncle Jed!" she said, running to him as he pulled the door open and stepped across the threshold.

Before he could even respond, she'd jumped up and wrapped her arms around his neck. He chuckled as he hoisted her up in a bear hug. "How are you, kid?"

A sudden tsunami of memories and emotions washed over him—fear and dread when she was trapped at the Dark Ones' compound, relief and strength when Jed found her hiding in the tree hollow in the woods, panic when black-clad assaulters broke into her old house trying to take her a second time, guilt and self-loathing when her parents argued about whether to move away or send her to St. George's, shame and embarrassment on her first day of school when a girl named Darilyn made fun of her Target brand shoes, repugnance watching Rector Senai executed by a glowing-eyed Nick Woland in the Vatican, worry and shock seeing Detective Maria Perez show up on Jed's arm at the team barbecue . . .

With each flashbulb memory he felt the accompanying emotions as strong and powerful as if they were his own. Lump in his throat, he lowered her to the floor and took a knee in front of her.

"Wow, you've got, um . . . a lot on your mind, kiddo," he said, reaching up to wipe a tear from her cheek.

"I don't know why that happened," she said, powering a smile onto her face. "When I hugged you, it was like a floodgate opened and all the stuff I'd been bottling up came to the surface. I'm sorry I pushed in on you. Apparently that's what you get for being friends with a weirdo."

"You're not a weirdo, Sarah Beth."

She bobbed her head from side to side theatrically. "Give it time—you'll come around."

This candid comment got him laughing. "I missed you, kid. Sorry I couldn't get here sooner for a visit."

"I missed you too, Uncle Jed," she said with a self-conscious smile.

Jed stood up and made an exaggerated show of looking around the vestibule. "Wow, this is quite a place."

"Come on," she said with a jolt of buoyancy. "I want to show you everything!"

She grabbed his hand and took off, dragging him behind her.

Are you really okay, Sarah Beth? he asked and felt himself probing to make sure.

"I'm really fine, Uncle Jed," she assured him, out loud. "But let's either talk or Watcher snapchat. It's confusing to go back and forth." She gave him a stern look. "I didn't mean to push all that stuff on you, but it's also rude to mine my thoughts without my permission. I mean, thoughts deserve to be private, right?"

"Yeah, of course they do," he said, grinning. "But I told you I can't really control it very well. Sometimes I just reach out. I'm sorry."

"Actually, you know what," she said, glancing at him with a sly smile. "Try again. See if you can get what I'm thinking."

"But you just told me not to."

"I know, but now I'm telling you to try. I want to show you something."

"Okay," he said and reached out for her with his mind, but this time instead of reading her thoughts and emotions, he hit the equivalent of an invisible brick wall. Screwing up his face, he tried again and bumped into it again.

"Boom, that just happened," she said and snapped her fingers at him with a smackdown attitude.

"What was that?" he said, his curiosity seriously piqued.

"I blocked you, dude. With my invisible wall."

"Oooooh . . . teach me to do that you must, Jedi Master Yarnell," he said, doing his best Yoda impression.

She smirked. "We'll see . . ."

As she dragged him around, she explained that the main building—which housed the dormitories, classrooms, dining hall, chapel, and administrative offices—was designed in the shape of a cross. It clicked firmly into place in his mind, but on a subconscious level the SEAL in him had already been constructing a mental map of the floor plan. For the operator, situational awareness was a life-or-death proposition.

". . . originally, this was the only building," she explained, "but they expanded when they ran out of room. So now there's the pool house, the equestrian center, and they're building a new student center because the commons here are super lame. The new one is going to have a movie theater, a food court, and even a bowling alley. How cool is that?"

"Sounds pretty cool."

"Supposedly they were going to build a skateboard park, but I think that's on hold now," she said, leading him outside to show him the grounds. "Olivia says that there would be, like, tons of liability if someone got hurt."

"Probably true," he said with a nod as he took a seat on a bench along the path that led down to the lake. "Who's Olivia?"

"Oh, she's my best friend I've made since I've been here." She sat down beside him. "I wish I could be roommates with Olivia. But no, my roommates are . . . never mind."

"Darilyn and Elizabeth?" he said, their names coming to him like a breath.

"Yeah," she said.

Her wall was down again, and her raw teenage angst hit him like a sledge.

They don't like me because I'm different. They're jealous, especially Darilyn. They all have their stupid little cliques, and nobody wants to hang out with me. Mandatory one-on-one meetings twice a week with Pastor Dee don't help either. It just draws more attention to me instead of less. Grown-ups are so clueless . . .

Jed leaned forward and rested his forearms on his thighs. "I know it's easy for me to say, as a grown-up, but the things that make you feel left out now—those things that make some kids a little distant from you—are the same things that will someday draw those very kids to you. Right now they want to be like everyone else, but with time they'll admire you for being yourself. They'll follow you because you are a natural-born leader."

Sarah Beth chuckled. "Yeah, right. I'm a leader that nobody wants to listen to, follow, or even hang out with. . . . Darilyn, she's the natural-born leader. Not me."

Someday you'll see, he thought. *When it matters, you'll be the one they look to for strength, not her.*

They sat in silence, watching the sun paint the sky fire red as it dropped below the western horizon. As the night crept in, so did a hint of melancholy . . . in both of them. He thought he sensed her poking around inside his mind for a second, but then the feeling was gone.

"Does he come to you at night?" she asked softly.

"Yes," he said, knowing exactly which *he* Sarah Beth referred to.

"In your dreams?"

"Yes." He looked up at her. "You too?"

She nodded. "He's the reason I learned how to build the wall. To keep *him* out. It works when I'm awake, and I think being here at St. George's helps too. It's weird, but I feel stronger here, with all the other Watchers around, than I did before I came. But at night, when I'm asleep and relaxed . . . he sneaks in and he tortures me in my dreams."

"Me too."

"Sometimes I wake up screaming."

"Me too."

"I think Victor really hates me. I think he wants me dead, Uncle Jed."

He took her little hand into his bear paw and gave it a gentle squeeze. "He's afraid of you," Jed said softly. "He's afraid of your gifts, and that fear makes him lash out and it also makes him very dangerous."

"Do you think he's going to come for me again? I mean, he's already tried twice. What's to stop him from trying a third time?"

Jed took a moment to decide how to answer before simply saying, "It's good that you're here, Sarah Beth, at St. George's. You're safe here."

"Are you sure?"

"Are you kidding me? A school with hundreds of Watchers and Trinity Loop ten miles away? It will be a cold day in hell before he can step foot inside these gates," he said with all the SEAL bravado he could muster.

She seemed to like that answer because she smiled and popped to her feet. "C'mon," she said, grabbing his wrist and giving it a tug.

"Where are we going now?"

"To dinner so I can show off my Navy SEAL uncle. It's pizza night and the pizza here is, like, legit better than even DeSano's. No joke."

"Well," Jed said, following her back toward the main building, "I've never had DeSano's, believe it or not, but everyone says it's incredible, so if you say this is better, then count me in."

"And so long as it doesn't rain, we're having outdoor movie night with the high school kids tonight, too," she said, looking over and chewing on her lower lip. "I mean, unless you have a date with Detective Perez or something . . ."

Jed sensed a flash of something dark regarding Maria, but when he tried to suss out what it was, he bumped into her invisible wall.

"Nope, I'm all yours," he said quickly, wondering if she could feel when someone bumped up against the wall. "I can stay for the movie . . . I mean, if guests are allowed to stay that late."

"Visitors can definitely stay for the movie," she said. "Mom and Dad stayed for one once, and you're on my guardian list, so there ya go."

"There ya go," Jed said with a laugh, but he was surprised by the revelation that Rachel and David would afford him guardian status. Maybe it was more like protector status since he was a Shepherd.

I'll have to look into that one.

A few paces later, his mobile phone rang, interrupting Sarah Beth as she yammered on about the time she'd tried paddle boarding in the lake.

"Sorry, Sarah Beth, I gotta take this," he said, retrieving his mobile phone and glancing at the caller ID.

"Sure," she said, visibly deflating.

"Johnson," he said, taking a step away from her.

"Jed, it's Ben," the Shepherd commander said, his voice all business. "There's been an incident."

"What? Where?" he said, his stomach going sour in anticipation of what could only be bad news.

"Peru."

"Huh?" Jed said, genuinely confused.

"I'll read you in on what we know—which isn't much—when you get back. Wheels up at 2200. You're taking a red-eye to Lima. Think about who from Joshua Bravo you want to take with you," Morvant said and the line went dead.

Jed lowered the phone from his ear and looked at it in disbelief.

"You're going to *Peru?*" Sarah Beth said, crossing her arms and giving him the stink eye. "Tonight? Really?"

He shook his head and winced, deciding not to point out she'd broken her own rule—taking things from his head without permission. "I'm sorry, kiddo . . . I don't like it either, but duty calls. If the boss says I gotta go, then I gotta go."

"Typical," she said, turning her back on him, but before he could step close enough to give her shoulder a squeeze and apologize, she turned around with a resigned smile. "It's okay. I'll be okay. I get it. Somebody down there needs your help, and I—of all people—know what that feels like."

Her strength and mature response assuaged the guilt he was feeling. "Thanks, Sarah Beth. That means a lot to hear you say that."

She nodded.

"We'll do pizza and a movie when I get back, even if it has to be on the TV in the common room. Cool?"

"Cool," she said.

They stared at each other for an awkward moment, but she broke first and ran in to give him a goodbye hug. "Be careful, Uncle Jed, and come home safe."

Hugging her back, he said, "Always."

CHAPTER TWO

Jed turned sideways on the bench seat as the cramped minibus rumbled through the heart of Cuzco. He'd only managed to sleep a couple of hours during the multiple flights necessary to get from Nashville to this narrow, poorly maintained road in Cuzco. He just didn't fit on planes very well, and even if he'd had a comfy bed, curiosity about this assignment had his mind spinning and would have kept him up anyway. The curved facade of a massive structure with white-painted concrete pillars and red accents drew his gaze out the left-side windows.

"That's Estadio Inca Garcilaso de la Vega," Bex said, butchering the Spanish as she looked up from her DK Eyewitness guidebook. The former combat medic and 18 Delta was one of two female members of Joshua

Bravo, and she was borderline giddy today. "It seats forty-two thousand and is the home to the Sportivo Cienciano football club. . . . Whoa, it says here that the Cienciano team was founded in 1901."

"Seriously, Bex, how did you have time to buy that guidebook?" Jed said, looking at her.

"Oh, I didn't. I already had it. I love to travel. I absolutely love it. Visiting Peru, and Machu Picchu specifically, has been on my bucket list for a loooong time," she said, drawing out the word for extra emphasis.

Jed glanced at Nisha, who sat behind Bex and was grinning at her teammate. There was something magical about seeing kidlike excitement in adults, and they both felt it.

"Me too," Nisha said as she gathered her shoulder-length onyx hair into a stubby ponytail. "I want to step foot on every continent and meet as many different kinds of people on this earth as possible before my ticket gets punched."

Jed nodded at the sentiment and turned to Eli, the final member of their ISR team. "What about you, Eli? Do you like traveling?"

The veteran Shepherd and Florida native shrugged. "Not really. It's kinda a hassle. Edgewater's got everything I need—good fishing, Dustin's Bar-B-Q, and Daytona Beach. Other than Nashville, that's the only place I really care to be."

"That's a very Eli thing to say," Bex said.

"Just being honest," Eli said. "But hey, Bex, knock yourself out, keep reading. I'm happy to hear anything you wanna tell me about this place."

"Well," Bex said happily, having been given free rein to geek out, "according to this, Cuzco was founded in 1100 AD by Manco Capac, the first Incan ruler. It became the capital city of the empire, and they believed spiritual lines of power, or *ceques*, radiated out from here. Oh, and here's a fun fact: it says that the Incans considered Cuzco to be 'the navel of the world.'"

"Hold on," Eli said with a chuckle. "You're telling me this place is the Earth's belly button?"

"Apparently," Bex said.

"So if we're inside it, what does that make us?" Nisha said.

"Belly button lint?" Jed offered.

Eli's laughter at the joke was so contagious it got them all going.

"I think the high altitude is making us all slaphappy," Nisha said.

"I think you're right—that and lack of sleep," Bex said, wiping tears from her cheeks as they all settled down.

Jed smiled and shook his head. He'd been blessed with an incredible team. Ben had let him decide who from Joshua Bravo would travel on this mission, and it had been a tough decision.

Leaving Johnny behind, however—that part had been easy. Jed had dropped the exasperating Shepherd from his short list first, unwilling to suffer Johnny's incessant second-guessing and snide comments. After Rome, Jed knew he had to figure out a long-term solution for managing the talented operator who was letting his resentment of Jed's promotion to team leader affect his work. Ignoring the problem and leaving Johnny behind would only make things worse. He'd have to do something soon—but what?

He pushed the thoughts aside for another time.

With fits and spurts, the bus navigated midday traffic along Cuzco's main thoroughfare, traffic which Jed noticed was barely regulated. When they finally arrived at their hotel, Palacio del Inka, Jed couldn't get out fast enough. He stepped off the cramped minibus into the cool mountain air and immediately stretched his back. While he twisted at the waist to work out the kinks, a young woman—mid- to late twenties—marched straight up to him and stuck out her hand.

"Gayle James, Global Gospel Missions," she said with a worried smile. Jed wondered if the eyeglasses she wore were part of her NOC or had a real prescription. "Sorry I couldn't meet you guys at the airport, but I was concerned it might . . . Never mind, it doesn't matter. Anyway, I couldn't meet you. Sorry about the bus." She was dressed casually in blue jeans and a gray fleece top with the letters *GGM* and a Roman cross embroidered on the left chest in bright-red needlework. She held a compact umbrella in her left hand, carried no purse, and he noted a mobile phone–shaped bulge in her right front pocket. Her mousy-brown hair was styled in an asymmetrical pixie cut with bangs that swept from left to right. To Jed, she looked like a woman who valued functionality over flair.

"It's fine," Jed said, shaking her hand and towering over her. He towered over most people, but he had at least a foot on Gayle, maybe more. "Jedidiah Johnson with Trinity. Nice to meet you."

"I know it's a long trip from CONUS. I figured we'd meet here to give you a chance to unpack and freshen up before asking you to take a miserable helo ride up the mountain," she said and then greeted each of the other members in turn. "I'll be driving you to the private hangar where the helicopter is waiting."

"We appreciate that," Jed said. "Give us fifteen and we'll meet you out front."

"Excellent, I'll be waiting for you over there." She pointed to a white van parked in the hotel circle drive.

True to his word, fifteen minutes later Jed and the team piled into the van. He took the front passenger seat and, after clicking his seat belt, looked over at their chaperone in the driver's seat. Gayle James certainly didn't look CIA, as he'd been briefed by the Trinity head shed. During his time as a SEAL, he had worked with plenty of spooks. Over the years, he'd noticed a trend—the CIA was getting better and better at recruiting officers and agents that didn't look or act like spies. Gayle James was yet another data point reinforcing that evolution.

"I just want to let you guys know," Gayle said, checking her rearview mirror, "that a Señor Alejandro Campos will probably be joining us for the, um . . . *tour*. On paper, Campos is the Peruvian representative of the state's Agencia Peruana de Cooperación Internacional—the government organization tasked with supervising and regulating NGOs like GGM. APCI closely monitors the activity of the NGOs to prevent them being utilized by criminals or foreign enterprises. But in reality, Campos is a counterintelligence officer for Dirección Nacional de Inteligencia, which is like Peru's version of Homeland Security."

Jed nodded, not surprised that the Peruvian government would be watching them.

"Do you know Campos well?" Nisha asked.

"We've interacted a couple of times. He seems like a decent enough fellow," Gayle said with a little shrug. "And he's not corrupt, if that's what you're worried about."

"Actually no, since you said he's Peruvian intelligence, I was more interested if your NOC is intact?" Nisha said.

"Yeah, I think so . . . no indications to the contrary. And to preserve the trust, I notified him of your visit this morning, which is why I'm letting you know in case he's waiting for us at the hangar."

"Well, we appreciate that, Gayle. Thank you," Jed said with an easy smile and a quick glance back at Nisha.

"Have you been to the scene yet?" Nisha said, asking the question they were all dying to know the answer to.

"No, but one of my missionaries, Dagan Meier, was in the village when it happened. He's there now and you'll be able to interview him," Gayle said. "And the answer to your next question is no, Dagan is not an asset—he's an actual GGM missionary. So please question him accordingly."

"Roger that," Jed said, loving her efficiency and no-nonsense approach. "Thanks for the heads-up."

He'd only known her twenty minutes, and he decided he already liked this spook.

The drive from the hotel to the hangar was the minibus ride all over again, with Gayle fighting traffic and narrowly avoiding a half-dozen close calls with crazy local drivers. When they finally arrived at the airfield, Jed spied a handsome thirtysomething Peruvian dude standing beside the helicopter.

"I assume that's Campos?" he said, looking sideways at Gayle.

"Yep," she said.

The helo, which Jed recognized as a UH-1H Super Huey, was rated for crew plus eight, so unfortunately there was plenty of capacity in the passenger compartment for Señor Campos to tag along.

Lucky us . . .

Gayle drove straight up to the helo and parked on the tarmac. Jed and his teammates climbed out and let their CIA escort take the lead with introductions, which she did with perfectly executed awkwardness.

Campos greeted each of them in turn with a smile and a firm handshake, settling his attention on Jed. "No offense, but you do not look like missionaries," the counterintelligence agent said with a wry and knowing grin.

Jed smiled back while trying to read the man's thoughts, which, to his dismay, were in Spanish. "That's because we're not," Jed said, handing Campos a business card. "We specialize in security and private investigation services. We've been hired by GGM because of the potential liability and PR fallout from this situation."

Campos stuffed the business card in his pocket without looking at it, communicating exactly what he thought of the validity of the information it held. "Yes, yes, I completely understand," he said. "How many missionaries are we bringing back? This helo is rated to carry eight and we'll be flying very close to the service ceiling. There are six of us standing here right now."

"Just one, Dagan Meier," Gayle said.

"Very good, let's go," Campos said. Then, turning to Jed, he added, "I am no expert in such matters, so I'm very much looking forward to hearing what the *professionals* think caused this despicable tragedy in my country."

With great effort, Jed resisted taking the bait and simply replied, "As are we."

CHAPTER THREE

Gayle James clutched the cold aluminum rail of the canvas bench seat beneath her legs and closed her eyes. She had never been a big fan of flying, but during her final exam at the Farm in Virginia—a full-week live-fire exercise before graduating from the CIA's basic training for officers in the clandestine services—they'd included a simulated helicopter crash so realistic it had scared the crap out of her. Flying in fixed-wing aircraft was stressful enough, but flying in a helicopter, especially one whining in protest as it pushed up against its service ceiling, was simply terrifying.

She had much more important things to worry about—like this strange team of contractors her boss had told her to babysit and Alejandro Campos watching her every move—but in this moment she didn't care. All she cared about was not dying. With great effort, she forced herself to run through two cycles of four-count tactical breathing—just like they'd taught her at the Farm—and felt her pulse slow, the pounding in her temple quieting, but her death grip on the cold aluminum remained.

"Are you okay, Gayle?" Campos asked, his distinct voice instantly recognizable in her David Clark headphones.

Unlike her, Campos seemed unfazed by the bobbling helicopter. He looked completely relaxed, his legs crossed at the knee, white teeth gleaming against his bronze skin.

"I'm fine," she said, forcing a smile onto her face.

"You certainly have chosen a peculiar line of work, for having such a fear, *querida*." His dark eyes stared through her, as they always did when he said things meant to probe her relationship with the United States intelligence community.

"Well, I'm not a field-worker, Alex. I'm the program administrator," she said, refusing to play his games. "This was not in the job description when I agreed to this post. Right now, I should be at a desk in Lima and off work by four to sun myself on the Playa Makaha—not riding in this death trap."

As if adding an exclamation mark to her comment, the Huey dropped jarringly in a pocket of unstable air before resuming the climb.

In addition to Campos, she felt the big contractor, Jedidiah Johnson, watching her. And one of the women, Nisha.

"Hutan Q'ero village is at very high elevation—just over four thousand meters—where the air is thin. The ceiling for this helicopter is just over fifty-eight hundred meters, so we are safe. Not to worry, Gayle. It is bumpy because of the windy mountain passes but safe. I promise you."

"I know," she said, suddenly wondering why exactly she had joined the CIA in the first place.

I'm a better missionary than spy, she thought and chuckled to herself. In the corner of her eye, she noticed Jedidiah chuckling along with her. *I hope I didn't say that out loud.*

The big man looked away, but the smile lingered on his face.

"You know, Gayle, this initial report from your missionary is not making sense," Campos said, relentless in trying to get her talking. "Fire from the sky . . . Sodom and Gomorrah . . . piles of ashes. I don't know what he's getting at, but I am pretty sure God does not rain fire down anymore, yes?

I believe these are Old Testament ideas, but God's new covenant through Jesus' sacrifice on the cross put a stop to this."

She raised her eyebrows in surprise at this last comment.

Campos waved a hand. "Ten years of Catholic school, you learn some things."

Gayle felt the helicopter slow rapidly and tilt, and for a moment she stopped breathing, afraid the Huey had stalled.

"There's no stall speed in a rotary-wing aircraft," Jedidiah said as if reading her mind, his voice calm and confident. "The pilots are flaring into a hover in preparation to land."

She nodded at him but looked out the square window beside her anyway to confirm she wasn't about to die. Seeing the side of the mountain coming up beneath them, she shut her eyes and clutched the aluminum rail even tighter as the helo—buffeted in the mountain winds—rocked and rolled before finally settling to the ground.

"It's over now, Gayle," Campos said. "You can open your eyes."

She let out a long whistling sigh and opened her eyes to find the Peruvian intelligence agent grinning at her.

So glad I could entertain you . . .

"I hate helicopters too," Nisha said, but she hadn't been clutching the seat rail for dear life during the flight like Gayle had.

"Me too," the contractor named Eli said with a friendly nod, but she'd noticed him sleeping during the ride.

Unlike Campos, at least they're making an effort to let me save face, she decided.

As the turbine engine driving the rotors wound down, Jedidiah slid open the cargo door in the starboard side of the helo and he and his team stepped out, followed by Campos. Gayle undid her lap belt with trembling hands and disembarked last. As soon as she stepped out, a blast of cold mountain air greeted her, sending a chill up her spine. She immediately zipped her jacket up to her chin and joined the others, who were standing in a frozen huddle but not from the cold. Even the cocky, jovial Campos now stood slack-jawed as he looked out at the scene before them.

A single hut remained of the once-thriving village—the rest burned to the ground. And scattered between the ruins, she saw conical piles of charred . . .

Dear Lord, are those bodies?

The piles of ash looked like blackened versions of the towering anthills she'd seen in the outback of Australia while traveling one summer during college, only these were a bit wider at the base. As she shuffled in a trance toward the closest one, the sound of crying children reached her. In her peripheral vision, she noticed Campos cross himself.

"There's no impact craters," Eli said as he walked toward the closest of the smoldering structures.

"And no blast pattern," Jedidiah added as he surveyed the scene. "No scattered debris . . . no signs of flying shrapnel."

"I think these huts burned to the ground in place," Eli said. "Like somebody lit them on fire from inside. This looks like arson, not an attack."

"Are those piles of ash . . . people?" Nisha said, her voice seeming to catch in her throat.

"No way," Eli said. "Not possible."

"I wouldn't be so sure," the contractor called Bex said, kneeling next to one of the conical piles.

Gayle listened as her "guests" took the lead, doing exactly what they had been sent to do, which was good because she was far from an expert in such things. Her job involved intelligence collection and asset management, not battle damage assessment or crime scene investigations. Nonetheless, so far, she agreed with what she was hearing. She saw no impact craters—no twisted metal or even small fragments suggesting this had been done by a bomb or missile.

Movement caught her eye as a woman—with both fear and anger on her face—strode toward her, a crying infant on the hip. The woman wore gray baggy slacks and Nike tennis shoes beneath a brightly colored woven poncho wrap. Strands of black unwashed hair jutted out from under a similarly brightly colored woven cap. She marched straight up to Gayle and berated her unintelligibly.

"I don't understand," Gayle said and looked to Campos for help.

"It's Quechua," he said and then told the woman, *"Por favor, hable en español."*

The woman turned to Campos. *"Tu Dios hizo esto?"* she demanded in Spanish this time. *"Fue tu Jesús?"*

Gayle felt the blood drain from her face. Although not yet fluent in speaking, her comprehension in Spanish was 95 percent.

"No," she said. "Tell her that God did not do this, that this was not Jesus."

Campos translated, touching the woman's arm gently, but the woman recoiled. She rattled something off in quick, broken Spanish, her eyes fixed on Gayle instead of Campos, then strode angrily toward the remaining hut, the baby looking back from around her arm.

"She said that you—she means Global Gospel Missions, not you personally, I'm sure—that you brought your God here and now He has killed her family and most of her people." He looked around the smoldering remains of the village. "What really happened here?"

"I don't know . . . A meteor shower, maybe?"

"Oh, come now, Gayle," Campos said, his expression going stern for the first time. "We are both professionals and Christians. You know who I work for. I know who you work for. Maybe it is time to stop playing games, yes?"

She met his gaze but didn't answer.

"These were my countrymen. I *need* to know what happened here."

"I honestly don't know, Alex," she said, pressing her lips together in a hard line. "This is not my area of expertise."

"And that's why they are here? Your new friends," he said, nodding at the four contractors who were scouring the village and taking photographs.

She nodded.

"Pillars of salt . . . ," a male voice said from behind her.

Gayle spun around to see Dagan Meier walking up the path. He looked much older than the twenty-one-year-old she'd met when he arrived in Lima for his assignment with GGM just three weeks ago. Dagan's now-old eyes were bloodshot from tears and had the faraway look of a man returned from a bloody battlefield. His hair flapped in windblown disarray while his fingers picked at the spine of a worn leather Bible he carried.

"What did you say?" she said.

"Pillars of salt," Dagan said, his attention fixed on a pile of ash a few feet away. "Remember what happened to Lot's wife when she tried to flee Sodom and Gomorrah? In Genesis . . . she turned to look and she was punished. Remember?"

Dagan stopped next to her and began to weep. Reflexively she wrapped an arm around him. While she tried to comfort the young missionary, she noticed Jedidiah's eyes on them from where he knelt beside a pillar of ash. Instead of looking away, she held his gaze and felt an eerie, palpable strength of purpose from the stranger.

She felt his . . . certitude. Certitude about *what*, she could not say, but certitude nonetheless.

The moment passed and Dagan shrugged off her arm. He walked to one of the smoldering huts, head hung in defeat. She watched him in silence, and her chest tightened as he tossed his well-worn Bible into the ashes where she imagined a family had once been gathered around a hearth.

"I told the survivors that God couldn't have done this because God is not here," Dagan said, turning back to her and then looking up into the bright-blue sky. "Evil, yes . . . but not God."

With that, the young missionary shuffled past her and down the gentle slope to where the helicopter sat parked beside the drop-off, a sheer cliff on the side of the mountain. For a moment, the horrible thought that the devastated young man would walk past the helicopter and fling himself off the cliff gripped her. She even took a first step to sprint after him but stopped when he vectored toward the Huey. After climbing in, Dagan took a seat on the canvas bench and began to weep.

Gayle turned to say something to Campos, but he'd already wandered off in the direction of the others. She started after him but then stopped, taking advantage of the fact she was alone to check in with her boss. Pulling out her compact, encrypted satphone, she dialed the number from memory.

"Go," said a male voice, all business.

"Steve, it's Gayle," she said, aware of the tremor in her voice.

"I know," the voice on the other end replied, annoyed perhaps.

Of course he knows. He doesn't need me to use my name, either.

"Are you okay?" he asked, a simple question but one crammed with subtext.

She closed her eyes and gave a soft snort. "I don't know," she said. "I mean, yes—operationally, I'm fine. But it's just . . ."

Just what?

When she failed to complete the thought, he said, "Is the Sierra Seven team there with you?"

"Yes," she said, glancing at the task force investigators the Sierra Seven code referred to.

"And what do they have to say?"

"They're still investigating, but it's obvious that whatever did this was not a conventional weapon. Not a missile or an IED, that's for sure."

"So the initial reporting was accurate?"

"Yes."

"Okay, take lots of pictures, grab a sample, and keep a close eye on the Sierra Seven folks," he said. "And, Gayle . . ."

"Yes?"

"When they leave Cuzco, I want you to book a flight back to CONUS. Out of an abundance of caution, I'm pulling you out of there temporarily until we know what we're dealing with."

"Understood," she said, and the line went dead.

She pocketed the satphone.

Her feet felt leaden, like they were cast in concrete. She looked over her shoulder, back at the helicopter where the young missionary still wept, his hunched shoulders bobbing with each breath. Flush with emotion, she surprised herself by saying a short prayer—one of the very few she'd said in a while—making sure to add a petition for Dagan at the end. Then with a heavy heart, she retrieved the digital camera from the zipper pocket of her fleece and began the solemn task of documenting the mysterious violence that had been dealt upon these poor, innocent people.

The machinations of men and war are clever and cruel, she thought as she zoomed in on one of the piles of ash, *but this is a power no mortal should have the authority to wield.*

CHAPTER FOUR

Jed forced his mind away from the horrors of what he'd seen on the mountain and tried, instead, to think through the images more technically. Tactically, even. The sights were terrible enough—charred buildings; piles of ash presumably once men, women, and children; the anguish and fear in the faces of the survivors—but when you added the smell of burnt flesh and sulfur, well, it was hard not to invoke Old Testament images of God's wrath as the young missionary had rambled incessantly about. For Jed, passages of fire and brimstone from the book of Revelation had also come to mind. Because what earthly power could possibly mete out such destruction?

Which is precisely the question the Dark Ones would want people to ask after an attack like this. They want to make people believe in a vengeful God, a God of judgment and retribution, a God who doesn't care . . . or better yet, a God who doesn't exist at all.

The very fact these thoughts and doubts came to him was the evidence he needed that this was the work of Victor and the Dark Ones. It was right out of their playbook—violence and horror, not for its own sake, not to conquer territory or change geopolitics, but to shake faith and wrestle people away from a loving God.

The trip up the mountain had been sobering and had left Jed and his team with more questions than answers. They'd gathered no proof that the Dark Ones were behind the attack, and yet it felt like the only plausible explanation. The Q'ero were not a threat to any state actor. They were not terrorists or extremists bent on undermining the Peruvian government or any government for that matter. It simply made no sense for these people to be targeted.

Unless this was just a test and there is more yet to come.

The waiter stepped up to the table, shaking Jed from the chilling thought. Scanning the faces of his teammates, he realized that everyone at the table had also been lost in their own silent thoughts about the horrors they'd witnessed. There had been little banter on the helo flight back or the drive into town for dinner.

"Señor, have you decided on an entrée?" the waiter said, pen and notepad held at the ready as he addressed Jed.

Jed tried to place his order, but before he could finish, Eli cut him off, injecting some much-needed normalcy into the group with a little smack talk.

"Bro, I'm sorry, but I'm not going to let you do it. We traveled over three thousand miles to an ancient city in the heart of the Andes—no way can you order a cheeseburger." Eli turned to their host. "Gayle, didn't you say this is the best restaurant in Cuzco?"

She nodded and smiled, jerked back from her own thoughts. "Yes, it's quite famous for its Peruvian fusion cuisine. Incredible flavors. If you want beef, Jed, I recommend you try the lomo saltado."

Jed looked down at the menu and scanned her recommendation: *Beef fillet stir-fried with vegetables, yellow chili, soy sauce, served over quinoa with huancaína sauce.* He pursed his lips and looked back at the burger entry and then at Eli. "But it's printed right here—*La Bestia Burger*," he said, tapping the menu with his index finger. "Now I'm not fluent, but I'm pretty sure that translates to the world's best burger. And see, here's the thing, Eli: when I'm not working, my life is basically a quest to find the world's best burger . . . so it would be sacrilege for me *not* to order something called La Bestia Burger in the best restaurant in Peru."

Eli shook his head in exaggerated disapproval.

"Dude, it's not like you're some gourmet food critic. You put pickles on everything. What are *you* ordering?" Jed said.

"The ceviche," Eli said.

"Of course you are, because that's like slimy, raw fish soaked in pickle juice, right?"

"*Lime* juice, bro, not pickle juice," Eli said, the banter starting to break the group out of their funk. "Lime juice."

Jed grinned and, feeling better, turned back to the waiter. "La Bestia Burger, *por favor*."

"*Sí, señor.*" The server jotted a note in his pad and moved on.

The rest of the party ordered, the waiter departed, and the conversation drifted to some much-needed small talk.

"So this plaza we're looking at," Nisha said, gesturing out from their second-story open balcony seating to the expansive town square below. "Is it the center of old town?"

Gayle nodded. "It's called Plaza de Armas, and it's the cultural and tourism epicenter of Cuzco. Tons of great eateries and shops, the Janes & Kirtland fountain, of course, and two very famous cathedrals. Maybe the churches are something you would be interesting in seeing before you leave?"

"If we have time, that would be nice," Nisha said politely.

Jed squirmed, the vulnerability of the location making it difficult to relax. There was simply no "safe" seat at a table on a balcony. Their party was in clear view to everyone in the courtyard outside as well as everyone dining inside. He had no wall to position his back against. Eli had it even worse, having taken a seat on the opposite side of the table with his back to the courtyard. When the hostess had seated them, the two lifelong operators had locked eyes and reached a meeting of the minds—taking opposite sides and opposite corners of the table: *I'll watch your six and you watch mine.*

Paranoia . . . this was the operator's strength and also their curse.

Jed felt Nisha's gaze.

She'd sat directly across the table from him, and he'd already twice accidently bumped her legs trying to find a comfortable position in the cramped quarters on the balcony with its pushed-together tables and too-small chairs.

"Hi," he said, greeting her as if they'd not spent the entire day together. She'd been practically catatonic on the flight back, so totally immersed in her own thoughts after what they'd seen. Frankly, he was a little worried about her, but her warm, familiar smile suggested she'd found her way back.

She chuckled. "Hi."

Maybe I should order wine so Jed can have a glass, relax, and stop fidgeting.

"Sorry, I'm having trouble fitting comfortably," he said, realizing too late he'd read her thoughts without permission. "Big-guy problem."

"I know," she said, and the corner of her mouth curled up in that little Nisha smile thing she did whenever she busted him on anything. "You don't fit on planes, you don't fit on minibuses, you don't fit on tiny chairs on tiny balconies . . . It must be an eternal aggravation to live in a world standardized for bodies three-quarters the size of yours."

"Yeah, and I'm sorry for kicking your shins, like, five times. They really should put me at my own table," he said. "I'm basically Wreck-It Ralph in real life."

This comment garnered a laugh from everyone at the table. After several more minutes of small talk, the conversation at the table comfortably turned to what they'd seen on the mountain. Thankfully, Gayle had not invited Campos to join them for dinner, so they could speak openly.

"So let me ask the hard and obvious question first—have any of you ever seen anything like what we witnessed at that village before?" Gayle asked, her voice falling low to mask the conversation below the din of diners around them.

All four Shepherds shook their heads in unison, but Eli spoke for the group. "We've seen our fair share of carnage, but no, we've never encountered *anything* like that before."

"That was some for-real Sodom and Gomorrah stuff of nightmares back there," Bex chimed in, putting into words exactly what Jed had been thinking.

"Medically speaking," Nisha said, turning to Bex, "what were we looking at there? I mean, what sort of weapon can do that to a person?"

Bex blew a little snort of air out her nose and said, "During my time on active duty as a combat medic, I saw the human body after being shot up, blown up, and burned up, but I've never seen it reduced to a pile of char like that. Even a Hellfire missile doesn't do that to a human being."

"So nothing in our arsenal or the enemy's arsenal that you're aware of can do that sort of damage?" Nisha pressed.

Bex nodded. "I mean, you guys know how incendiary devices work. There's always a blast radius. Even thermobaric weapons, which would be exothermically capable of doing that to a human body, are accompanied by a tremendous pressure wave. That can't leave the remains in a tidy little pile, you know what I mean? And we saw no other evidence of a pressure wave on the mountain—no disembodied limbs, no structural damage, no impact craters . . . It was almost as if those people were instantaneously cooked from the inside out while standing in place."

An uncomfortable silence hung over the table as they all processed the implications. Had they just witnessed a real fire-and-brimstone wrath-of-God event?

"So you think it was *supernatural* in origin?" Gayle said, her voice low and quiet. "That's your conclusion?"

"No," Jed said quickly, before anyone else could answer. He wondered if Gayle had concluded that they were some sort of real-life X-Files task force and resisted a smile. "We're not saying that. I think what Bex is saying, what we're all saying, is that we've never seen anything like that and we don't know. That doesn't mean what happened on the mountain was supernatural. As Arthur C. Clarke once famously said, 'Any sufficiently advanced technology is indistinguishable from magic.' What we saw in that village is most likely technology we've not seen before."

Is that what you really think, Jed? Nisha's question came to him unbidden and he wondered if she'd pushed it or if he was still tuned to her, like an unchanged television channel playing in the background.

It's what I hope the truth to be.

"What if this is some kind of new energy weapon?" Nisha said. "We suspect that both the Chinese and Russians have been using pulsed microwave, nonlethal weapons on diplomats and intelligence service employees for years. Could this be the next incarnation of that program?"

Jed turned to Eli. "I think she might be on to something. Do we have any contacts at DARPA or ONR we could reach out to about this?"

"If that's the recommendation, I think my home office can take that ball and run with it," Gayle said. "We have connections and relationships in place, and of course there's DS&T in-house who can look at this. My logic in bringing you here first was to rule out a more supernaturally based origin because, well, I don't need to tell you why . . ."

Feeling suddenly and inexplicably melancholy, Jed looked out onto the Plaza de Armas and the scores of tourists meandering around for late-evening sightseeing in Cuzco's most famous square. His mind went to a terrible place . . . and he imagined one of the nearby couples, lovingly walking hand in hand one second and then being vaporized the next by a tongue of fire, leaving only two tiny pillars of char on the cobblestones. If the massacre here in the Andes was God's handiwork, why would He punish the Q'ero tribe? What sins had they committed to warrant such a fate?

This is no act of divine justice, Jed reassured himself. *The Dark Ones are behind this . . . I know they are.*

His eyes, pulled by a warrior's instinct or perhaps something else, ticked right. Down in the square below, he noticed a figure twenty-five yards away standing unmoving as tourists and evening diners walked past in both directions. The person, who based on body proportions Jed judged to be male, was wearing a hooded sweatshirt and dark pants. Despite the face being bathed in shadow, Jed was certain the man was staring at their table.

"Jed, dude—something got your antennae up?" Eli said.

"Not sure," he murmured, not taking his eyes off the shadowy observer. In his peripheral vision, Jed noted that their server had returned carrying plated entrées.

"La Bestia Burger," the waiter said with pride, reaching to set Jed's burger and fries in front of him.

Despite the aroma of prime sirloin grilled to perfection wafting up to his nostrils, Jed did not look down . . . because the hooded figure in the square was still brazenly looking at them. Then the man's eyes flashed the color of flame.

In an instant, Jed was out of his chair, reflexively swinging over the balcony railing, his body not giving his brain the opportunity to veto the decision. He dropped ten feet to the courtyard below, rolled out of the fall, and popped up to his feet. The hooded figure froze in surprise, then waited for Jed to start running before turning to flee. Behind him, Jed heard his teammates calling for him to stop, but their voices seemed so very small and far away. This was all the confirmation he needed. The Dark Ones had burned those innocent villagers to ash and for what? Because they could? Or was it some sort of statement . . . or worse, a field test of a new horrific weapon?

Time to find out.

The hooded Dark One turned left and fled the plaza just before Catedral del Cuzco. Jed pursued the man onto Córdoba del Tucumán road, then bolted after him up a narrow cobblestone alley that ran uphill between two rows of two-story buildings. The northern side of Cuzco was built onto the slope of Pukamuqu mountain. And thanks to the combination of high altitude and slope, he felt himself quickly growing winded. The dark, narrow passage the Dark One had chosen for his escape had been built ages ago when foot traffic, not automobile traffic, dominated the old town. Jed imagined his Silverado's side mirrors would probably scrape the stucco-covered stone walls. Like other Dark Ones Jed had faced off against, his quarry moved with almost-superhuman speed and endurance, and it took everything Jed had not to lose the man.

So what are you going to do if you catch him? the SEAL inside asked as Jed's wits returned.

We're disappearing this guy. Time to play twenty questions, Shepherds style.

The SEAL laughed. *Since when has a Dark One ever gone quietly?*

All of the capture/kill engagements Jed had participated in as a Shepherd had ended with kills. They'd not managed to take a single Dark One alive. In fact, fighting to the death—with every tooth, nail, and muscle fiber in the body—seemed to be the Dark Ones' modus operandi. And why not? The demons abandoned their human hosts at the moment of death, so why not use the vessel up completely first?

A hundred yards up the alley, his quarry sprinted past an intersecting alley on the left. Jed was surprised he didn't turn the corner to escape line of sight, but the man just kept on running straight. Anticipating a possible blindside, Jed pulled his Sig P365XL from the small-of-the-back holster he wore and stopped short of the junction. He dropped into a crouch and readied himself at the corner. Across the alley, a white-and-blue street sign bathed in a shaft of moonlight caught his eye.

Calle Purgatorio.

Purgatorio—Dante's purgatory.

It had been a decade since he'd read *The Divine Comedy*, and even then, he'd only skimmed it for the sake of morbid curiosity. He was an operator, not a scholar, after all, but this word came to him like a taunt as he climbed his own mountain, chasing the devil's wrath. He shook off the weirdly prophetic and distracting thought and whipped his weapon around the bend to scan for threats. A middle-aged woman dropped her shopping bag and screamed as she came nose to muzzle with Jed's gun.

He met her terrified, wide-eyed gaze and, finding no glowing irises, sidestepped to scan behind her.

Clear, the SEAL announced in his head.

He turned up the alley just in time to see the Dark One disappear into what looked like an open courtyard one block away. With a growl of frustration, Jed took off in pursuit yet again, having fallen farther behind. He dug deep, pushing himself to the edge of hypoxia as his lungs heaved to satisfy his body's desperate call for oxygen from the thin, highland air. As he closed in on the entrance to the courtyard, the fleeing Dark One abruptly stopped and turned around to face him. The demon soldier's eyes flashed once— beckoning Jed to battle—from where he stood in the middle of a green space marked by a handful of trees and park benches.

This time, instead of pausing to clear his corners, Jed abandoned caution for expediency and charged into the courtyard at full tilt. As he emerged from the alley, he noted a white delivery van idling on his left with the headlights off. He cleared the van's front bumper in a flash, but in his peripheral vision he saw it pull forward and block access to the alley behind him. Two other vans, one at his ten o'clock and another at his two o'clock, executed similar maneuvers, blocking what he realized were all exits from the courtyard. The rabbit he thought he'd been chasing had turned out to be a fox instead, and now he was the one who'd gotten caught in a snare.

Stupid, stupid, stupid, he thought as he surveyed the courtyard. *They baited me and I fell for it hook, line, and sinker.*

Doors opened and multiple hooded figures stepped out of the three vans and began to converge on him from right, left, and behind. Jed's already-elevated pulse rate ticked up a notch as the direness of his situation sank in. He wasn't kitted up—which meant no body armor, no rifle, no comms—and he'd run away from his backup without telling them where he was going. Performing a slow, methodical 360-degree scan over his weapon, he took a head count:

Three . . . four, five . . . three more makes eight . . . plus the ringleader.

Nine versus one.

Wonderful.

The figure standing in the courtyard pulled back his hood, revealing his face.

"Welcome to Cuzco, Jedidiah Johnson," the Dark One said in heavily accented English. "We can do this the hard way or the easy way, but the end result will be the same. Intact or broken in pieces, you're coming with me."

CHAPTER FIVE

Jed spun and fired first, putting a 9mm round into the forehead of the closest of the attackers behind him. He shifted his Romeo Zero red dot onto the second assaulter and dropped him with a double tap to the head. Jed hadn't been a Shepherd long, but he'd already learned that head shots were critical when battling Dark Ones, because they just kept coming unless their human host was killed completely. His six cleared, he whirled back to the front, where the lead Dark One still stood brazenly in the center of the courtyard while two trios of attackers charged him from the right and left on converging vectors. This gang of attackers was armed but not like operators. Instead of wielding pistols or rifles, they looked like a street gang—running at him with bats, clubs, and pipes. Apparently the ringleader had been deadly serious on his threat to take Jed broken in pieces.

Given the speed of the assault, the number of attackers, and the fact he was firing a subcompact pistol and not a rifle, Jed had no choice but to target center mass in this onslaught. He emptied the ten remaining rounds in his magazine with methodical precision, managing to put at least one round into the chest of every single attacker before the horde converged on him. But despite his dialed-in marksmanship, only three of the six assaulters fell—leaving two on the left and one on the right charging him. With no time to change magazines, he juked right just in time to avoid a downward swing of a metal pipe from the right attacker. The pipe came down with a metallic clang as it crashed into a cobblestone. Jed kicked the man in the side of the knee, hyperextending the joint.

The fighter howled and dropped his weapon.

Jed picked up the pipe and spun to engage the other two assaulters, one of whom had a cricket bat and the other a police baton. He blocked the cricket bat midswing before it could connect with his head. The impact sent a reverberating tremor down both Jed's forearms and into his elbows. He backpedaled, trying to get separation, but the dude with the baton circled around behind him to create a 180-degree offset from his friend. Fighting multiples was a horrible proposition, even for a former SEAL as big and skilled as Jed. In a choreographed fight scene in the movies, the bad guys politely took turns, giving the hero time to dispatch them sequentially.

Not in real life.

They came at him simultaneously, faces twisted with rage and murder in their glowing eyes.

Jed heard the whistle of the cricket bat and parried the strike with the pipe while taking a blow from the police baton in the back. With a grunt, he whirled and managed to land a retaliatory strike, hitting the rear attacker in the upper arm. Anticipating the bat swinging for his head, he ducked, but the blow connected with his right shoulder, sending a spike of pain up into his neck. Enraged, he turned and charged the fighter wielding the cricket bat. With a primal bellow, he rained down a rapid and relentless series of strikes on the man—breaking the attacker's forearms and finishing him off with a skull-crushing strike.

A blow to the side of his head set Jed's ear on fire and lit up stars in his vision. He spun, his equilibrium shaken, and stumbled to a knee. In his peripheral vision, he saw the baton go up and raised his pipe to block the incoming blow. His adversary adjusted midswing and whacked Jed on the back of the hand, causing him to drop his weapon. Understanding he'd be punished with pain but knowing that getting inside was the best tactical option, Jed rushed his opponent. The baton came down hard on his upper back, but he tackled the club-wielding attacker like a linebacker anyway, driving the man to the cobblestones, and slamming his body weight down on top of him with a sickening crunch. He'd drawn back his right fist to pound the man's face when he felt himself suddenly struck with a powerful blow sending him inexplicably flying through the air. He hit the ground with an agonizing thud a few feet away. An involuntary groan of pain escaped his lips as he looked up to find the Dark One in the hooded sweatshirt glaring down, eyes glowing like embers. Several of the thugs Jed thought he'd dispatched were now back on their feet, weapons in hand, walking to stand beside the leader.

"Like I said, Jedidiah Johnson, intact or in pieces, you're coming with me," the Dark One said with a victorious sneer and then bent at the waist to pick up the metal pipe.

Jed scanned the ground around him for something, anything, to defend himself against the reassembled horde, but there was nothing.

"Take him," the leader said, and the attackers charged.

A deafening crash reverberated in the square.

Jed turned in the direction of the sound to see the white van that had been blocking the alley entrance now being plowed sideways into the courtyard by a delivery truck. The truck doors opened and three operators, moving in fluid, coordinated precision, stepped out and engaged the enemy fighters. Muzzle flashes lit up the courtyard like lightning as Jed's Shepherd teammates unleashed a firestorm on the dark fighters, dropping every last one of them except for the leader, who turned to flee.

"Oh no you don't," Jed growled and set off after him.

Only this time, instead of chasing the demon soldier alone, Nisha, Eli, and Bex were at his side. The Dark One moved with preternatural speed and made for the northeast corner.

"Don't kill him. I want to take him alive," Jed yelled as he saw Eli bringing his weapon up.

"*What?*" the veteran Shepherd said.

"We need to know what happened here."

With an angry grimace, Eli lowered his aim and unloaded a four-round volley at the Dark One's legs. One or more rounds connected because the fleeing demon warrior stumbled and fell. He quickly scrambled to his feet, but not before the Shepherds were on top of him. It took all four of them to subdue the man and none of his teammates emerged unscathed from the melee—Bex earned a bloody nose, Nisha had deep fingernail gouges dripping blood down her neck, and Eli and Jed received multiple fresh contusions for their efforts.

They carried the Dark One, flex-cuffed and gagged, writhing and bucking, back to the delivery truck that had been used as a battering ram to break into the courtyard moments earlier. When Jed climbed into the front passenger seat, he was surprised to see Gayle behind the wheel.

"You're bleeding from your ear, Jed," Gayle said, concern in her eyes. "Are you okay?"

"I've felt better," he said, shutting the passenger door. "Thanks for coming to get me."

"Anytime." She whipped the truck around in a circle to exfil down the alley.

"Took you long enough," Jed said, wincing in pain as he turned in his seat to look at Eli in the back.

"Well, we had to finish dinner first," Eli said, pulling a black hood over the Dark One's head.

"Did you at least bring me my burger in a to-go container?"

Eli kicked the Dark One in the stomach and then turned to Jed. "Sorry, bro. I didn't want it to get cold, so I went ahead and ate it. And let me tell you, it was the La Bestia-est burger I've ever had."

Jed shook his head. "Thanks for that."

"Easy day," Eli said, grinning and using the Navy SEAL catchphrase just to rub it in.

"So what's the plan?" Gayle said. "We just drew a whole lot of attention to ourselves. No way I'm taking this guy back to the hotel, and I don't have anywhere to hide him here in Cuzco. Campos is already watching me . . . I'm sorry, but I can't afford to get dragged into whatever it is you're planning."

"I understand, but we're going to have to keep him in this truck until a company plane arrives," Eli said. "We flew commercial on the way down, but the head shed is bringing in a bizjet from Brazil for our exfil."

"You already talked to Morvant?" Jed said, surprised.

"Made the call while we were en route to rescue your crazy ass."

"So Ben doesn't know about our special friend back there?"

Eli smiled. "Not yet . . ."

"Are you taking him with you?" Gayle asked.

"Of course," Jed said.

"We don't know who this guy is," Gayle said. "What if he's a Peruvian citizen?"

"Then Peru is going to have one less citizen to worry about," Eli said. "But don't worry; we're not going to involve you."

Gayle nodded in reply, but Jed could see the gears turning in her head.

"Would you like us to keep you in the loop?" he asked. "Let you know what we find out?"

"Yes," she said, glancing at him with a humble smile. "Because if my life implodes because of this, it sure would be nice if you guys didn't turn into vapor on me . . . if you know what I mean."

Jed glanced over his shoulder at Eli, who shrugged his opinion on the matter. Gayle had done them a solid tonight and it wasn't in Jed's DNA to not return the favor.

"If it comes to that, we won't leave you out to dry," he said, gently probing his swollen and throbbing left ear. "You have my word."

CHAPTER SIX

Jed winced as he stepped out of the Ford Expedition inside the covered garage at their partner "white site" in Santa Ana Poniente. He'd taken a significant beating during the ambush in Cuzco yesterday, and pain throbbed in numerous locations. During the flight from Peru to Mexico City, Bex had used a superslick portable ultrasound device to rule out broken bones and organ damage. She'd been most worried about a skull fracture or potential intercranial hemorrhage and consequently had scanned his head three times during the six-hour flight. He'd tried to reassure her that there wasn't anything between his ears worth worrying about, but she'd kept a close eye on him until she was certain he was fine.

"You sure you don't want Toradol?" Bex asked, stepping up beside him. "You look like you're really hurting."

"I'll manage," he said and suppressed a chuckle at her swollen nose and double black eyes from the punch she'd taken.

"I know—I look like a raccoon," Bex said. "He popped me good."

"That's the concussion laughing, not me," he said, crossing his heart. "I swear."

The industrial, chain-driven garage door they'd entered through came down behind them, making a terrible racket. They'd disembarked inside a hangar at the airport with the hangar doors shut and loaded their "guest" directly into the Expedition for the drive to the white site. They wouldn't unload him until this door closed fully, to minimize the risk of prying eyes observing the personnel transfer if they were being surveilled. This facility— an actual working paint manufacturing plant—was owned and operated by an American expat and former Army officer named José Baldan. Tall, lean, and tanned, Baldan stepped through a door and walked up to greet them. He wore an easygoing smile, kept a regulation high-and-tight haircut, and looked a decade younger than the early fifties Eli had described.

"Elias!" José said, walking up to give Eli a bear hug. "How are you, my friend?"

"I'm good, brother; how are you?" Eli said, returning the backslapping hug.

"Busy—very, very busy."

"They say busy is the new fine." Eli chuckled.

"So true, so very true." José turned with a smile to Jed, Nisha, and Bex, his gaze settling on Bex. "Welcome to Mexico City. It looks like you paid a toll to bring me your new friend."

"You could say that," Bex said, sticking out her hand to greet the man. "I'm Bex."

"Nice to meet you," José said and clasped her hand. He then shook hands with Nisha and Jed. "You know, it's rare to capture a Dark One. Congratu- lations, you guys—very impressive."

"Thanks," Bex said, answering for the group.

"Interrogation of the Dark One inside is unlikely to yield much, but if we can reach the man inside—well, that is another matter. Unfortunately, in my experience, the demon or demons inside will drive the host to fight to the death, leaving us nothing but a depleted husk with no pulse."

Jed raised an eyebrow, the clinical description sounding reasonable but the idea chilling.

"Okay, I read your report, looked at the pictures, and I'm ready to meet your friend. Let's do this," José said, nodding at their SUV.

Jed followed Eli around to the back of the Expedition, where they opened the tailgate and dragged out their hooded captive, whose wrists were still bound in plasticuffs. Bex had given the dark warrior three separate sedative injections over the past nine hours, as the drug's potency and longevity seemed to be greatly diminished compared to in a regular person. Each taking an arm, Jed and Eli followed José into the facility, herding their uncooperative captive this way and that to a windowless room that smelled of bleach and paint. The room looked like a typical sterile interrogation suite, with a table and two chairs—all bolted to the floor—and nothing else. A video camera was mounted in each of the room's four corners and a single duct blew stale air down from overhead. Jed noticed that a piece of orange string had been tied to the duct grate cover and was oscillating in the airstream like a wriggling worm on a fishhook.

"Put him in that seat," José said, gesturing to the far chair. "I'll be right back."

Jed and Eli forced their captive into the seat and held him down while they waited for José, who returned a moment later with handcuffs and leg irons that they used to chain him securely to eye hooks bolted into the floor.

"Hood off?" Jed asked.

Their host nodded. "And the gag can come off."

Jed removed the hood and Eli undid the gag, taking obvious care so as not to get bitten in the process. Squinting and red-faced, their guest worked his jaw side to side, then lambasted them with insults and curses in Spanish.

"Do you need anything else?" Eli asked José.

"No thank you, my friends," the former Army officer said, exuding a palpable calm and confidence as he took a seat across from the Dark One.

Jed followed Eli out of the interrogation room, shut the door behind him, and then joined Bex and Nisha in the monitoring suite, where the video and audio feeds from the four cameras were streaming on four large flat-screen televisions. A young woman, black hair pulled up and back on her head, sat at a workstation overseeing the session. She didn't turn to greet Eli and Jed, nor did they interrupt her from her work. He noticed on her computer monitor that she'd already used facial rec to find the man's identity and begin to populate data on him.

"Welcome. You can call me Mr. J. While you're here, I'll be your sole point of contact," José said in English to the Dark One. "Can I offer you some water?"

The man glared at him for a long moment, then nodded.

The woman at the workstation popped out of her chair and ran a bottled water and a plastic straw to the room. On-screen, Jed watched as José uncapped the water, stuck the straw into the bottle, and walked over to give the Dark One a drink. After letting the man drink half the bottle, José set the water down on the table and returned to his chair.

"What is your name?" José asked.

"His name is Rodrigo Valencia," the girl at the workstation said into a microphone. "He is thirty-two years old, Chilean native born in Santiago. He's employed by PMC Egality, Latin American division."

"Our name is Chaos," the man said, staring unblinking at José.

"Not a false statement," José said, shifting his chair to cross his legs.

"I'm going to take my thumbs and press them through your eyes and into your brain while you scream," the Dark One said.

"Mmm-hmm . . . You have a lot of rage inside . . ."

"What's José doing?" Jed whispered in Eli's ear.

"Talking," Eli said without a trace of sarcasm.

"But this guy ain't going to talk. We need to get him in some stress positions and start enhanced or we're going to be here forever."

Eli shook his head. "Enhanced doesn't work with Dark Ones. José is the best I've ever seen. Just watch."

"It's hot inside—the rage, hmm? Always burning, burning . . . burning . . . ," José continued.

The Dark One cursed his interrogator with a long stream of obscenities and then writhed against his restraints.

"Does that make you feel better, Rodrigo, when you let the anger out? Does it lessen the pain when you let the beast have its way?"

The Dark One laughed and Jed saw its eyes flash with flame. "You know nothing, Shepherd. I'm going to gouge—"

"My eyes out—with your thumbs. Yes, I know," José said, cutting the other man off. "Tell me, Rodrigo. What happened on the mountain? How did you do it?"

"That was God's work—punishment from heaven for sins committed."

"Is it a new weapon your master developed? How does it work?"

On the monitor, Jed watched the Dark One narrow his gaze at José. "We're going to find your family, your daughter, and we're going to ravage her and your wife while you watch."

Jed shifted his gaze from a monitor fixed on the Dark One to a feed focused on José's face, but the Shepherd's expression of confident empathy did not waver or wane in the face of the threat.

"How many wives and daughters have you ravaged, Rodrigo?" José asked.

"Dozens," the Dark One growled.

José nodded. "Do you hear their screams at night? Do you relive their tears?"

The Dark One's eyes flashed red and a vulpine smile curled his lips. "I savor those memories—their suffering, their fear."

"Do you, or is that the beast inside talking, Rodrigo?"

"Stop calling me that!"

"Why does it bother you? It's your name, after all."

"Our name is Chaos!"

The demon soldier tried to lunge across the table toward José, but the chains held fast and snapped him back into his seat. "I'm going to kill you. I'm going to rip you to pieces."

"The demon will never let you go, Rodrigo . . . but *you* can let go of *it*. I know it doesn't feel that way. I know it feels like fishhooks pulling at your flesh, but I promise you it is in your power to release the beast. Only you can do this."

"Lies," the Dark One seethed and Jed saw a snarling twisted double visage appear for the first time, superimposed over the Chilean man's face. "It is too late for him. I am all he has left after your God abandoned him. Together we are Chaos and only through me can he find strength."

"Does it frighten you, Chaos—the thought of Rodrigo letting you go?"

"I fear nothing. I will kill all of you, and your God will do nothing to stop me."

"Ah, but that is a lie, Chaos," José said, crossing his legs like a professor having an academic debate with his graduate student, "because we both know you can't hurt me. I belong to Yeshua. I am protected from you."

"Do not speak that name," the man screamed, his voice shrill and his eyes flaring deep red. "And I don't need to hurt you—I can have the mortal do it. He is free to choose."

"Yes," José said, leaning in now and nodding. "He is free to choose. And you're right, he can choose the path of violence, and nothing protects me from that . . . except for my years of military training and my friends here. But you, Chaos—I reject you. You have no power over me."

The man's head tilted back, chin toward the ceiling, and he let out a bloodcurdling scream that, to Jed, sounded like an animal in pain.

"But he can also choose the other path. The path of redemption. The path of love. And that is what I offer him now—a choice. A choice that has always been there, but one that you have kept from him, because you, Chaos, are afraid of us because of the power of Yeshua." José leaned in, putting his elbows on the table. "I know you can hear me, Rodrigo. Do not let Chaos rob you of your voice. If you want to speak with me, then you can do so . . ."

"You will not have him!" Chaos screamed, but José was unfazed.

"It's never too late to repent. It's never too late for forgiveness, Rodrigo. It's never too late for God's love."

"It's too late for me," the man said, the timbre of his voice changing for the first time and a shuddering sigh following.

"No," José said, shaking his head. "It is never too late for Christ."

Jed watched as the man's face contorted, the eyes again flaring deep red.

"It *is* too late!" Rodrigo shouted, the voice once again that of the Dark One. "You have done too much. You have sinned too greatly. God can never love you now after all you have done. Even the sins of before pale compared to all you have done with me! You have served the enemy and now you are ours. We are your only hope."

José leaned back, folding his hands in his lap.

Rodrigo's eyes closed tightly, his head shaking as if from a bad headache. "How can it still be true for me?" the softer voice asked, and tears streamed down the man's cheeks. "I ran from God so long ago. I have fought Him so hard. I have hurt so many."

José reached out a hand, squeezing the man's arm in solidarity. Rodrigo looked up at him, brief hope in his eyes, but then winced in pain. José jerked his hand away just before the demon regained control and grabbed for him.

"I'm going to break these chains and then I'm going to kill you, Shepherd. And all your friends. And your family," the man snarled.

Unmoved by the threat, José narrowed his eyes at the sweaty, snarling, thrashing mess across the table. "Have you heard the parable of the workers in the vineyard?"

"Matthew 20," the Dark One said, suddenly settling down despite the rancor in his voice. "More proof of your God's inequity and ineptitude—"

"The kingdom of heaven is like the landowner who went out early in the morning to hire laborers for his vineyard," José said, talking over the other. "He rounded up all the available workers he could find, offered to pay them a full day's wages, and sent them off to harvest grapes. At nine in the morning, while visiting the market, he saw additional workers standing idly and offered to pay them a full day's wage for working in the vineyard, and so they went. Seeing that there was still plenty of work yet, he went back to the market at noon, at three, and finally at five o'clock in the afternoon, recruiting more workers with idle hands, making them the same offer. When the workday was over, he paid all the laborers the same wage, regardless of the total number of hours each man worked. Many of the workers who'd been hired on early in the day grumbled and complained about the unfairness of the situation, feeling the latecomers did not deserve the same wages as those who'd put in many more hours in the field, but the landowner was undaunted and made good on his promise paying the last the same as the first."

The Dark One laughed. "The same reward for different effort—only a fool would follow such an unjust God. Where is the fairness?"

"It is not surprising that you miss the point, Chaos, but I suspect Rodrigo is beginning to see it, aren't you, brother? In my paradigm, it is the latecomers who missed out in this story. The promise of salvation is not only about eternity—it is about being in relationship with God here, now, on earth. It is about the comfort and the overwhelming joy of being in His presence. It is about the joy of doing His work. So in the parable, there is a cost to those who miss the joy of working for the Lord, being called according to His purpose, even if the gift of eternal salvation is the same. I wish I had been one of the workers who found God first thing in the morning," José said with a wistful smile. "In my case, I found my way to Him—after all of His years of calling—at noon, but I have known His love ever since. It's five o'clock for you, Rodrigo, but not too late to join us. God's offer of salvation is still open to you, and I and the others welcome you into our brotherhood with open arms and without resentment. For all of us it is only through God's grace that we are welcome. It is true for you today, if you want it."

The handcuffed man said nothing for a long moment.

"Jesus, forgive me my sins," he sobbed.

Then suddenly he began to convulse.

"No!" a voice screamed, terrified, using Rodrigo's mouth one last time. Jed watched the double visage appear again, a ghostly, grotesque, and snarling face atop the human one, as a battle for control raged inside Rodrigo.

Rodrigo tilted his head back and screamed in anguish. "I am sorry, Father God, for my weakness . . . for everything. Please forgive me. Forgive me, Lord. Let me serve You . . ."

Jed saw the demon separate from the man's body, shoot across the room, and vanish, leaving a faint amber glowing imprint on the wall. The man in the chair slumped, forehead bowed, chin limp on his chest.

"Whoa," Jed said under his breath.

"Did you see it leave his body?" Bex said, her black-and-blue–framed eyes as wide as dinner plates.

He nodded.

"Man, I wish I could see that. Just once," she said.

No one else said anything, but their collective gaze locked on the monitor with the liberated soul who sat slumped in his chair.

"Rodrigo?" José asked. "Can you hear me?"

The man groaned and his head lolled for a moment before he slowly began to raise his chin. He looked ten years older to Jed than he had only moments ago. He smiled wanly at José and then began to sob uncontrollably, in torso-shaking lurches.

"I'm so sorry," he cried. "I'm just so sorry."

"It's over, my brother," José said, his voice that of a father talking to an injured child. "It's finally over."

"What have I done?" the man muttered. "Dear God, what have I done?"

"You lost your way, but now you are found. All you need to do now is embrace the light."

"There are things, important things I must tell you," the man said, getting control of himself with sudden urgency in his voice.

José shifted his gaze to one of the cameras in the corner for the first time since the interrogation began, a not-so-subtle cue to pay attention. "I'm listening," he said and returned his attention to Rodrigo.

"What happened on the mountain was just a test, and a successful one at that."

"A test of what?"

"A new weapon."

"What kind of weapon?"

"A directed energy weapon—capable of vaporizing a human being in milliseconds."

"And the Dark Ones possess this technology?"

"Yes," Rodrigo said, nodding vigorously.

"How and where did they obtain this weapon?" José asked.

"I don't know," Rodrigo said, now seemingly in control of all his faculties. "I don't know much. My job was to go to the village, confirm in person what imagery had recorded, and keep an eye out for Shepherds."

José glanced at the camera but this time gestured with his hand. The girl at the workstation, who'd yet to introduce herself, swiveled in her chair and addressed Jed's team collectively. "He wants to know if you have any questions. If you ask me, I in turn will relay them to his earpiece."

"What is the next target?" Nisha said without a moment's hesitation.

The woman nodded, turned back to her computer monitor, and spoke into her boom mic. "What is the next target?"

José returned his gaze to his charge and asked the question.

"I don't know. They didn't tell me this," the former demon warrior said. "I know only that the test was successful."

"How is the weapon deployed?" Jed asked. "Is it ground-based, is it airborne, or is it fired from space?"

"I was not told this information, but it must be airborne. I don't know what platform they're using," Rodrigo answered after the question was relayed.

José questioned Rodrigo for fifteen more minutes, but precious little else was learned about the weapon. With the demon departed, the ex–Dark One was repentant and eager to share, but the information he possessed pertained almost exclusively to Peruvian operations. When asked about leading Jedidiah to the courtyard and into an ambush, he confessed that this had been entirely his idea—believing that if he could catch a Shepherd and deliver one alive, he would win favor with his superiors. After collectively exhausting their questions, José left the interrogation suite and returned to caucus with Jed and the team in the control room.

"So what do you guys think?" José said, leaning against the wall and scanning their faces.

"First of all, wow. I'm standing here awestruck at what I just witnessed," Jed said. "That was simply remarkable, José."

"Sometimes freeing a Dark One from the devil's grasp is a simple matter. Other times it is not. In the case of Rodrigo, I could feel that he wanted to be free. I unlocked and opened the door to God's love, and then he made the choice to walk through it. Most of the time exorcism happens from within."

Gooseflesh stood up as Jed thought back to the night of Rachel's attack and would-be rape in the basement seventeen years ago at the hands of a possessed classmate. All this time, Jed had believed he'd beaten the demon out of Kenny Bailey, but if what José said was true, then it had never been Jed's doing. Somewhere inside, Kenny had recognized the monster he'd become and cast out the demon himself. Kenny had, through his free will, chosen the light. It made perfect sense and it felt right, except the realization was upsetting to the operator inside. As a man of action, he'd taken great solace in the fact that despite running away later, he'd always believed that *he* had saved Rachel. Was that not the case?

Feeling suddenly unsettled, he asked, "You said *most* of the time. What happens when the afflicted does not want to let go? What happens if they refuse God's love and have chosen the path of darkness?"

José gave Jed a tight-lipped smile. "That, my friend, is a situation above my pay grade, and such an exorcism would require gifts that I do not possess."

Jed nodded and decided this was a "Ben question" he'd need to follow up on later.

"So now what?" Nisha said. "Where does this leave our investigation? Do we continue to question Rodrigo and squeeze him for more?"

"No, this is not like a CIA black site interrogation. Rodrigo is liberated. As you can see, he's a willing and cooperative witness now. I will continue to talk with him and learn more about his Peruvian operation, but rest assured, he was telling the truth. If he knew more about the weapon, he would have shared," José said.

"Thank you," Jed said, sticking out his hand to José. "This was incredibly enlightening."

"You're welcome here anytime, my brother," José said, clasping Jed's hand and forearm with a two-handed grip. "And safe travels back to Tennessee."

CHAPTER SEVEN

Jed watched Ben pace, unsure what, if anything, he should say to interrupt the brooding—or to just remind his boss he was still in the room. He could not recall seeing the Shepherd commander this unsettled, not even when they'd learned of Victor's plan to attack the Vatican and kidnap the pope. Jed understood Ben's angst. It didn't take a thought reader to know what ran through the man's head—terrifying scenarios in which this new weapon the Dark Ones possessed could be used. Jed shifted his gaze to scan the faces of the personnel gathered at the table, which included every team leader and their respective spiritual advisers, known as tactical spiritual leaders, among them David Yarnell, Jed's own TSL. In addition, Trinity's senior staff were assembled—key director-level personnel he'd not had the privilege to meet, including Intelligence Director Julia Nesbitt, Chief of Security Kip Wenger,

Med Ops Director Todd Wilkins, Air Logistics Commander Jack Stewart, and the headmaster of St. George's, Jean-Baptiste Allard.

"My greatest fear, people," Ben said, addressing the group without turning to face them, his pacing continuing, "is getting the call from Jean that a dozen of our kids have been vaporized at recess or during a soccer match. If there's one thing I've always taken stock in, one thing that's allowed me to sleep soundly at night, it's the knowledge that our young Watchers are safe on their campus. Not only is the security robust, but trying to launch an assault on that school without telegraphing it in advance is virtually impossible. Collectively, the students at St. George's would identify any planned attack before the Dark Ones had a chance to deploy a team and assault the campus. But this weapon changes everything. There's the potential for zero latency between intent and action, no time necessary to mobilize. It's a point-and-shoot weapon, and if it's controlled via satellite, we'll never see it coming."

"And Trinity Loop is no more protected than St. George's," Security Chief Wenger said. "We don't live and work under a dome. They could pick you off, Ben, the second you step outside. They could pick off any of us, walking from the parking lot to our office or in between buildings."

A somber, heavy melancholy settled over the room. They'd logged a major victory over the Dark Ones in Rome not so long ago, and the Shepherds had been running on a winner's high. Now that win felt like a lifetime ago. In Naval Special Warfare, the "umbrella strategy" governing all their operations had been to deploy technologies and tactics that provided the teams with an asymmetric advantage in the battle space. With satellites looking down from space, drones armed with Hellfire missiles turning donuts at thirty thousand feet, the Army's 160th SOAR helicopters, and a rock-solid OTH communications network, Jed had always felt safe and empowered. For him, the umbrella metaphor felt real, because he really had an umbrella of technology overhead and surrounding him whenever he was on the ground.

As a Shepherd, most of those same umbrella components were present—as Trinity seemed closely modeled after the Joint Special Operations Command. And in addition to the traditional tactical and logistical support elements, the Watcher corps added another dimension of protection—much like Naval Special Warfare's Group Ten. It had taken him a while to trust and embrace the "spiritual umbrella," but now he was all in. Which was why this new weapon was such a gut punch. Its existence shattered his paradigm of security. The Dark Ones had obtained technology that gave *them* an asymmetric advantage—a weapon that redefined the battle space and had the ability to blast holes in the protective umbrella the Shepherds and Watchers depended on.

"How could this have happened without us knowing about it?" one of the platoon leaders asked. "I mean, the US military doesn't even have a weapon like this . . . at least, not that I've heard about."

"I know," Ben said. "Not even Lockheed Martin's ATHENA or HELIOS lasers have this capability. This is something new. Something different—and perfect for Victor and his mission to separate people from their faith. This Old Testament fire and brimstone stuff or end of times images from Revelation are exactly the message Victor wants to send with this weapon, what he wants the world to think. But we know better—we know that the new covenant in Christ changes the rules and our relationship with God." The room hushed and heads nodded all around, including that of Mike Moore, Ben's personal TSL. "Remember that to the human eye, lightning looks like it strikes from the clouds, but that is not the case. The upward streamer from the ground happens first, and what we see is the return stroke. In the case of lightning strikes, our own eyes deceive us. We don't know what this weapon is or how it works. That's why we sent a team to the site, and that team brought back important intelligence."

Ben looked directly at Jed and Jed took the cue.

"That's right," he said. "We captured a Dark One we encountered at the target site, surveilling my team in Cuzco. Without getting into all the details, the long and short of it is he confirmed this attack to be from the Dark Ones and, just as important, that this is a technology-based weapon. What we don't know is who supplied the weapon and what platform it is being deployed from."

"Or even how it works," Intelligence Director Julia Nesbitt pointed out. "We need to answer those questions and we need to do it ASAP."

"And we need to take immediate precautions at St. George's and here on the Trinity campus until we understand what we're dealing with," the security chief added before anyone else could comment. "That means no kids outside, period. And it also means the suspension of outdoor gatherings, outdoor PT, and rethinking the way we commute and move around. I'm going to order the construction of temporary covered walkways between buildings and to the main parking lot. In addition, I intend to implement door-to-door pickup and drop-off protocols for all senior staff and platoon commanders. No more walking, running, or biking to work."

The proclamation earned groans, grimaces, and nods as the reality of their situation sank in. Sidebar conversations once again erupted as people felt compelled to express their personal opinions on the efficacy and viability of the security chief's plan.

"Quiet," Ben barked. "This is not productive. Everyone in this room is competent and creative, and I encourage you to provide input and constructive criticism so we can optimize Chief Wenger's plan. But Kip is right. The status quo will not suffice. To address this threat, we are going to have to make procedural changes. Many of these changes will be aggravating and cut into your personal liberty and productivity, but that's the life we've chosen. Instead of being sand in the gears, we're all going to help Chief Wenger, however he needs it."

The ruckus settled down and Jed noticed most everyone in the room nodding. The meeting went another fifteen minutes before Ben dismissed them. Jed hadn't even scooted back his chair from the table before Julia Nesbitt summoned him and David for a sidebar conversation with Ben and Mike Moore and another man he didn't know.

"We've not officially met, but Ben and I dialogue regularly about you and your team," the intelligence director said as she shook hands with Jed. "I'd also like you to meet Damien Gough. Damien is my CISA, or conventional intelligence and signals analyst, and handles the traditional collection streams as well as serving as our liaison with the Pentagon and the IC at large. He's one of the brightest, most committed and hardworking people I've ever had the privilege to work with, and I'm confident you guys will get on swimmingly."

"Nice to meet you," Jed said, shaking Damien's hand.

"Jed," Ben said, taking the lead back, "Julia and I have decided that Joshua Bravo is going to round out the task force for prosecuting the directed energy weapon threat. Damien recruited Nisha, and he's well aware of her intellect and capabilities. You and the rest of your team have proven yourselves as out-of-the-box thinkers and adaptive problem solvers in the field. You'll be working hand in glove with Damien and we're giving basically unlimited resources to go where you need to go and do what you need to do. This weapon is an existential threat to our program and our people just as much as to our mission. I cannot emphasize enough how important it is that you succeed."

"I understand," Jed said, feeling the weight of Ben's words as well as the entire organization on his shoulders. "I won't let you down."

While he meant the words with all his heart, he had never felt more like a fish out of water. He was an operator—a door kicker and direct-action asset. He had precious little experience investigating, analyzing intelligence, or coordinating intelligence assets. He was the nail such people generally hammered.

"I know you won't, Jed," Ben said, clapping him on the shoulder and most likely reading his mind and mood. "Now go collect your team and work with the intelligence shop to put together an action plan. The clock is ticking."

CHAPTER EIGHT

SCIF

CIA HEADQUARTERS

LANGLEY, VIRGINIA

1443 HOURS LOCAL

Gayle shifted uncomfortably in her seat, wondering when Steve would say something. He'd been staring at her for a long time, and she wasn't sure what she'd said or done to deserve it. From what she knew of him, Steve Schmidt was somewhat of a pariah in the agency—a Langley institution in his own right who was revered, envied, and disliked all at the same time. The old-school operations officer—now the department chief—had reached the point in his tenure where he was both unpromotable and unfireable. His unapologetic demeanor and political repugnance ensured he would never become director or even assistant director, but no director could imagine running the CIA without Schmidt as a member of their inner circle. He was an important man to have in your corner, and she'd worked hard to ingratiate herself to him, despite limited opportunities to interact since she'd been stationed in Lima.

She'd not held anything back during this debrief of the events in Peru, even sharing her candid opinions on the very odd but likable group of contract task force operators she'd spent the day with. She'd been worried that Steve would be upset about her not attempting to intervene in their disappearing of a Peruvian national, but he hadn't blinked an eye. *Weird.* What she'd witnessed in that courtyard in Cuzco had really messed with her headspace. There was something not normal about that man. It had taken all four of the Trinity operators to subdue him, and Jedidiah and Eli were not small dudes. Combine the courtyard incident with what she'd witnessed in the mountain village and her perception of the world was forever altered from what it had been forty-eight hours ago . . .

"Why are you staring at me like that?" she finally said, unable to stand it anymore.

"I'm trying to decide," Schmidt said, unblinking.

"Trying to decide what?"

"Trying to decide what to do with you, Gayle," he replied, the words perfectly audible despite his mouth barely moving. Steve was one of *those* kind of talkers, and she wondered if it was an acquired skill from years of fieldwork where talking without moving your lips was a highly advantageous skill. Regardless, she suspected he would make a heck of a ventriloquist, and she had to suppress a grin at a mental image of "Grandpa Steve" performing for his grandchildren with a Snoopy sock puppet with button eyes and floppy ears.

"How much longer do you think it will take? Because I've really gotta pee," she said, just keeping it real.

He pursed his lips at her, the expression framed and amplified by the well-kept silver goatee he wore. "I've decided. I'm pulling you out of Peru."

"What?"

"Yeah," he said, rubbing a hand over his shaved and mostly bald pate. "I think it's the right call."

"So you're firing me?" she said, her voice sounding far less indignant than she'd meant it to.

"Quite the opposite. Some might consider the position I'm about to offer you as a promotion."

"Oh," she said, feeling her cheeks flush while her heart rate went along on this emotional roller coaster. "Does that mean you want me here, on your team?"

"Yes, I want you here, but not on my team," he said, still messing with her.

"Okay, um, so what exactly are we talking about?" she said, hating that he was forcing her to pull the punch line out of him instead of just hitting her with it.

"I want you to take over Sierra Seven liaison duties from Mark. He's going to be retiring in October and until three minutes ago, I hadn't picked his replacement. I think it should be you."

"But I'm not—"

"Great, then it's settled," he said, cutting her off and giving her his trademark "Steve Schmidt smile," which was composed of equal parts judgment and joy. "I'll let Mark know so you two can get to know each other, he can read you in on everything he's working on and his contacts inside the Shepherds organization, and then you can start transitioning."

"Shepherds? I'm not familiar with that term," she said, screwing up her face at him.

"Yeah, that's what they call themselves. Trinity is the official cover for their North American operation. Mark will read you in. What you think you know is just tip-of-the-iceberg stuff."

"Oh, okay . . . ," she said, feeling even more unsettled than before.

"In the meantime, I want you to take point on getting to the bottom of whatever this *thing* is you witnessed in Peru. From photographs and everything you told me, it looks like it was a field test of a breakthrough technology in the directed energy weapon arena, and it scares the hell out of me. We're already investigating four dozen pulsed RF attacks on intelligence officers that took place over the past twelve months. Obviously headaches, disorientation, and nausea are nothing compared to being vaporized, so we need to know if a thread connects both the technology and the potential players. The threat is off the charts."

"Don't take this the wrong way, Steve, but am I really the best person to be leading a directed energy weapon investigation? I mean, I'm not an engineer or one of those STEM brainiacs," Gayle said, resuming her squirming in her chair. "I don't see how I bring the right skill set to this task."

"You misunderstand—I didn't mean take point on the *entire* investigation. I mean take point with the Shepherds as they run theirs. We need to funnel whatever findings they dig up into our wheelhouse. To do that, you'll need to get with DS&T and the actual STEM brainiacs leading the directed energy weapon team aggregating and evaluating all the reports and data from incidents around the world. But they're not read into Sierra Seven, so you're going to have to be careful and very intentional what you report and how you report it."

"Okay," she said, still trying to wrap her brain around this whole thing. "What about sharing in the other direction?"

"You mean sharing our findings with the Shepherds?" he said.

"Exactly. This is a give-and-take business we're in, after all."

He grinned at her. "It is . . . and as long as you follow the golden rule of intelligence collection, you'll be fine."

"And what is the golden rule?"

"It's quite simple, really—so long as you take more than you give, you're golden."

This made her laugh. "I should have seen that coming."

"Any questions for me before you go pee?" he said, apparently tickled with himself for the rhyme.

"Yeah, a big one, actually," she said.

"Hit me."

"Is it the agency's intention or desire that I infiltrate the Shepherds? I mean, how do we categorize them? Are they a partner, an ally, an asset . . . an adversary?"

"Like everything in our world, the answer to your question is a gray area. I would call what we have with them a strategic partnership. They are an ally far more than an adversary, to be sure, but their goals are their own and may not always match well with ours. Does that make sense?"

She nodded.

"As far as infiltrating their ranks, from what I understand from Mark, that's not really possible. In fact, if they catch even the slightest hint that your intentions are less than honorable, you'll be blackballed and I'll have to find someone else. It's a delicate dance I'm asking you to perform . . . But I wouldn't worry too much. My gut tells me you're the right girl for the job. From the debrief, sounds like they already trust you. So just keep doing what you're doing."

He scooted his chair back from the table and stuck out his hand to her. She stood and shook it.

"Congratulations, Gayle," he said and gave her a closed-lip smile. "And good luck."

"Thank you, sir."

"Don't ever call me sir." He walked out of the SCIF.

Her bladder full to bursting, Gayle quick-stepped down the hall in search of the nearest ladies' room. After that biological exigency was dealt with, she would begin the intriguing work of learning everything she could about this mysterious task force she had just inherited.

CHAPTER NINE

Jed's head bobbed with microsleep.

Here they were, working on the greatest threat the Shepherds had ever faced, and he was having trouble keeping his eyes open. How messed up was that? It just showed how completely conditioned his body had become to operating on adrenaline. Operators like him sat at the apex of the flight-or-fight hierarchy, and because the energy weapon threat was not immediate and tangible, his brain had given it the neurological shrug.

"Is this boring you, Jed?" Damien Gough, the Shepherd CISA, said with thinly veiled irritation.

"I'm sorry, dude. I'm spent." Jed pressed to his feet to walk and get his blood flowing. "I didn't get any sleep last night."

Damien nodded, but Jed wasn't sure if it was with understanding or judgment. The dude was clearly wicked smart, but he did not present as a former operator. Sometimes guys who didn't spend much time in the field had trouble relating to the physical toll it took on a body. *He's probably a former intel or crypto weenie,* Jed thought. He looked over at Eli, whose chin happened to also be bouncing off his chest. Bex and Nisha weren't doing much better.

"The four of you look dead to the world," Julia Nesbitt said, glancing sideways at Damien as she did. "Why don't you get some rest and we'll start fresh at 0800 tomorrow."

"Are you sure?" Jed said, praying her offer wasn't lip service.

She nodded. "I'm sure. We'll be much more productive if your minds are rested and alert. Damien and I have plenty to do that doesn't involve your input."

Damien nodded his agreement at this last statement.

"All right, we appreciate that," Jed said and gave Eli's shoulder a squeeze to wake up the veteran. "C'mon, guys, we're making it an early night."

No one argued with him.

"Remember the new protocol," Damien said. "Door-to-door covered transit only. We have a vehicle assigned to this detail now. The driver's name is Sam."

"Roger that," Jed said and led his weary crew out of what he'd come to think of as the Shepherds' N2 shack.

A silver Chevy Tahoe waited outside the building, idling along the curb. In the hours since the leadership meeting this morning, Trinity Loop's facilities team had been busy. A covered walkway from the front entrance of the building all the way to the curb had been constructed out of scaffolding and sheets of corrugated metal roofing. It wasn't pretty and it certainly was no magic shield, but it complicated targeting if the Dark Ones were gearing up to assassinate Shepherds from the sky. Unless they were using thermal imaging and targeting personnel indiscriminately, this simple mechanical obstruction and protocol change would make picking off specific personnel difficult.

Jed's phone rang in his pocket.

"You guys go ahead and load up. I'll be there in a second," he said to Eli, and then pressing the phone to his ear, he took the call. "Jedidiah Johnson."

"Hi, Jed, it's Gayle James," a woman's voice said on the line.

"Hi, Gayle, how are you?" he said.

"I'm great. How are you holding up?"

"Fine," he said. "FYI, this is my mobile, so we're talking on an unsecure line."

"Roger that, and I'm sorry for calling after hours, but, um, I was hoping to arrange a face-to-face with you and Nisha."

"Gayle, we're back in CONUS and have no plans to return to Peru in the foreseeable future."

"I know. I'm back in CONUS too," she said. "In fact, I'm going to be in Nashville tomorrow, if you're not too busy."

He hesitated, his mind running through a half-dozen nefarious scenarios before settling on an impromptu challenge-response authentication he could use to validate he was talking to the real Gayle. "You know, that sounds great, but before I commit, I was wondering if you remember the name of the entrée that I ordered for dinner the other night in Cuzco?"

"You mean the entrée you didn't get a chance to eat?" she said with a chuckle.

"Yeah, that's the one."

"Such a shame, because it was the La Bestia–looking burger I've ever seen."

He smiled. "Why don't you give me a call when you get into town. You looking to do a hotwash?"

"Yes. I think this event has management pretty spooked."

"Ditto here. Let me know when you're in town and we'll decide on a time and place to meet."

"Sounds good. Thanks, Jed."

"Travel safe," he said. "Oh, and, Gayle . . ."

"Yeah?"

"You might think about wearing a hat."

"Will do," she said with a chuckle and the line went dead.

Before pocketing his phone, Jed scrolled through the half-dozen text messages from Detective Maria Perez he'd left unanswered over the past few days. He'd also missed several calls and had two voice mails waiting from her. Guilt flared in his chest. This was no way to start a relationship with a woman, especially one he really liked. But he'd explicitly told Maria what to expect from him on the communication front. He'd tried to prepare her for the reality of dating someone like him. He'd assumed that as a detective, she understood that his delayed responses—or total lack thereof—was not an indicator of how he felt about her. But he also knew that it was one thing to be on the giving side of indifference and another thing entirely to be on the receiving end.

He imagined what Eli would have to say on the matter. Probably something like, *"Dude, girls aren't wired like us. . . . For them, radio silence means 'He hates me.'"*

Jed started thumb-typing a quick explanation text but then erased it.

Too clinical . . . it's gotta be thoughtful and sweet.

He tried again but stopped midsentence and erased this attempt too, for a different reason.

If she knows I'm back, she's gonna want to meet up . . .

"I don't have time for this right now," he grumbled and shoved his phone in his pocket. "I'll call her when I get home."

Feeling guilty and annoyed at the same time, he walked the path under the makeshift canopy to the big SUV, dragging tail the whole way. The driver delivered Bex and Nisha to Trinity Tower first, dropping them under the covered entry portico. Next, he took Eli to his neighborhood home—pulling into the garage to do it—and then finally stopped curbside in front of Jed's town house in the Galilee complex.

"Looks like you've got a visitor waiting," the driver said, waking Jed. "You might wanna explain the new protocol to her."

Jed, who hadn't even realized he'd nodded off during the short drive from Eli's neighborhood, followed the driver's gaze. Sure enough, someone stood on the tiny landing of the front stoop. When he saw who it was, his heart skipped a beat.

"Roger that," Jed said, pulling on the door handle. "Thanks for the lift."

"Do you want me to wait? I can take her wherever she needs to go," the driver said.

"That's her car parked along the curb. Thanks, brother, but I think we got this."

"Easy day, be safe."

"You too," Jed said and sprinted from the SUV to the front porch.

"Rachel, what in the world are you doing here?" he said, quickly unlocking the door and shepherding her inside. "Don't you know about the new protocol? It's not safe to be outside."

"I was standing under the overhang," she said with a defensive tinge to her voice. "I'm not a kid, Jed. I am capable of risk calculation decisions."

He knew her well enough to know that nothing good would come from debating the topic with her, so he simply nodded and flipped on the wall switch to light up the foyer in his darkened brownstone.

"Please excuse the boxes everywhere. I haven't had a chance to unpack yet," he said.

"I know how that goes," she said, crossing her arms over her chest.

"So, um . . . ," he began, facing her.

"Why am I here?" she said, finishing his sentence for him.

"Yeah."

"We need to talk, Jed."

"Oooookay," he said, drawing out the *O* and gesturing to the living room. "Can I get you something to drink? Iced tea, water, beer . . . ?"

"No thank you," she said, moving into the living room and taking a seat in one of two club chairs.

He nodded and took a seat on the love seat opposite her on the other side of the coffee table. This was the first time he'd been alone with Rachel—his once and only true love—in over fifteen years. It felt . . . weird.

"So . . . does David know you're here?" he began, regretting the question instantly when he saw her expression sour.

"I'm not even going to justify that question with a response," she said, her eyes drilling into him. "No matter how I unpack it, the subtext is offensive."

"I don't know why I said that," he said, feeling his cheeks getting hot.

She nodded, but the look in her eyes signaled *apology not accepted*. After an awkward beat, she said, "You know what? I can't let it drop. Do you think I would come here behind my husband's back? David and I don't keep things from each other. Or maybe you thought I would need his permission and he wouldn't give it?"

"No, I swear, Rachel, it was just a stupid icebreaker. That's all."

"Heckuva way to break the ice, Jed," she said.

"I'm sorry. I guess I'm just surprised and a little caught off guard finding you on my doorstep, unannounced and alone. We've not been alone together, since . . . you know."

"Since you ran away," she said, sending a barb flying his way.

But it didn't hurt as much as he thought it would, because it was true. "Yeah, since I ran away," he echoed.

"Why *did* you run away, Jed?" she said, her lips pressed into a thin, hard line.

"Wow, okay, we're going to start there—danger close with the first salvo, huh?" he said, shifting uncomfortably in his seat.

"It wasn't my intention, but since we've already gotten off on the wrong foot, why not?" she said, still glaring at him. "I mean, after all, it is the question I've been asking myself practically every day for over fifteen years. So why beat around the bush any longer? Why did you abandon us?"

"Us?"

"Yes, Jed, *us*. I'm not the only person you walked away from. You left David behind too."

He sighed and shifted his gaze to the middle distance, unable to meet her eyes as he spoke. "For me, running away was the solution. Leaving you was the . . ."

"Was the *what*?" she said when he didn't finish his sentence.

"Leaving you was the problem."

"What is that supposed to mean?" she snapped, her voice hot with anger. "Was it because I was damaged goods—too tainted for you to touch after that night? Is that what you're saying?"

"Is that what you've thought all these years?" he said, mustering the courage to look her in the eyes, which were suddenly rimmed with tears.

She didn't answer, just glared at him over her quivering lower lip.

"Maybe it doesn't matter anymore," she choked. "David loves me for who I am just as much as for who I was. We've built a life together. I just . . . I just wish I could understand. You left me, but you left him, too. And your family—your home. Everything. Even your faith and your dreams."

He felt tears of his own pressing as he unpacked the emotional and pitiful truth from the grave where he'd buried it all these years. It didn't help that he was just so dead tired.

"I . . . I came within milliseconds of taking Kenny Bailey's life that night,

Rachel. I was going to kill him. I *wanted* to kill him . . . for what he tried to do to you. I promised myself that if anyone ever touched you like that again, I *would* kill them. And when I saw Kenny at the trial, the compulsion was overpowering; I wanted to pound his face into a pulp and watch him die. Something happened to me that night. Whatever was inside Kenny, it felt like . . . like maybe it had gotten inside of me too. How could I love you after that? And how could I trust God after seeing what I saw?"

She swallowed hard but didn't wipe the tears that were running down both her cheeks. "And what *did* you see that night, Jed? I asked you, remember? I asked you several times, but you wouldn't tell me. You shut me out. I needed you then more than ever, but you wouldn't talk to me. You wouldn't even look at me. You shunned me like I was . . . like I was a leper."

He wiped his now-running nose with the back of his hand. "I know, and it's the single biggest regret of my life. But I had questions—questions I needed answers to."

"And don't you think I had questions too?" she shouted.

He nodded.

"What did you see that night? I need to know the truth, Jed," she said. "For my sanity I need to know what you saw."

He exhaled slowly through his teeth. "I saw pure evil. I saw the twisted face of the demon that was inside Kenny. When he looked at me, I saw two faces—one superimposed on the other. And then I saw it leave his body, and only then did I recognize what I had done to Kenny. I was mortified and ashamed and . . . I was afraid."

He watched Rachel try desperately to regain her composure by taking several deep breaths before she spoke again.

"His eyes were glowing, Jed—the whole time he was trying to rape me, I saw hellfire burning in his eyes. And his grip, his voice, even his breath—they were inhuman. I knew when it was happening that the thing on top of me wasn't Kenny. In my heart, I knew what he was, but how could I tell that to the police? How could I tell that to the lawyers? I was a seventeen-year-old girl at a party where kids had been drinking. If I started spouting Bible verses about demons and talking about glowing red eyes, what do you think would have happened? I couldn't even find the courage to tell my parents. But if *you* had stood beside me, vouched for me, told me what you had seen and that I wasn't crazy . . ." She shook her head. "I can't tell you how different my life would have been."

"I know," he said, his voice barely more than a whisper.

"For months I tried to convince myself that it was a hallucination. That it was all in my head. That the trauma and the violence and fear had made me see things and that my continued fixation on the idea that Kenny had been possessed by a demon was the manifestation of post-traumatic stress. But do you want to know who did stand by me when you ran away? David . . . David was there for me when nobody else was. It was David who gave me the confidence to finally speak the truth about what I saw, and it was David who believed me."

Jed looked down at his hands in his lap, feeling sick to his stomach. He'd always suspected this was how it had played out, that in his absence David had slithered into the void and replaced him. But now, listening to her, he understood that from her perspective it wasn't like that. David hadn't taken *his* place. David already had a place of his own. They'd been the three musketeers and when Jed ran away, David had manned up and done what Jed couldn't. Ironically, while Jed sought refuge in the Teams, David had embodied the Navy's core values of honor, commitment, and courage at home and in Rachel's eyes.

"I'm sorry, Rachel," he said at last, looking up to meet her tearstained face. "I'm sorry I abandoned you. I know I can never make it up to you. All I can do is promise you that I'm not the same man now as I was then."

"That's actually the reason I'm here," she said and blew air through pursed lips. "Because now that you're back in our lives, I'm feeling very . . . very nervous."

"Nervous? What do you mean?"

"You rescued my little girl. Without you, Sarah Beth would probably be dead, and for that, I'm eternally grateful. But now it really feels like you're dragging her back into harm's way."

He bristled at the comment. "I would never put Sarah Beth in danger. What exactly are you insinuating?"

"A couple of days ago, Pastor Dee asked me and David to a meeting at St. George's to talk about putting Sarah Beth into an accelerated Watcher program."

"That's great news," he said.

"No, it's not."

"I don't understand."

"Oh, Pastor Dee said all the right things, dressed it up with a bow on top, about how special Sarah Beth is, how gifted she is, how they see great things in her future. But when you cut through all the propaganda, what they're really saying is they need her power. They want her to do what Corbin Worth does for them. They want her in the field, on missions augmenting the Shepherd units," she said and then narrowed her eyes at him. "And then it clicked—that's the real reason you went to campus for pizza and movie night with Sarah Beth. It should have occurred to me when you asked us about visiting, but I see it all clearly now."

"What in the world are you talking about?"

"I think it's pretty obvious. We told the school no to the accelerated program, so what do they do? They send you in. And like the covert operator you are, you go behind our backs to take advantage of your relationship with her and fill her head with visions of glorious service. You know how much she looks up to you. In Sarah Beth's mind, you walk on water. All it would take is one word from you and she'd defy us and go into the training program."

He tamped down his reflexive anger at the accusation. Getting angry would only further inflame the situation. "First of all, I want to reassure you that's not what's going on here. The only person who asked me to visit Sarah Beth at St. George's was Sarah Beth. I didn't even know about your meeting with Pastor Dee or the accelerated program, and nobody in the Shepherds asked me to conduct an influence campaign on your daughter. And quite frankly, I'm a little disturbed that you think this organization—an organization dedicated to biblical principles—would do something so conniving and that you think *I* would go behind your back like that."

She didn't answer immediately, just held his gaze looking for any hints of insincerity. Apparently finding none, she sighed and said, "Okay, I believe you. I don't know why but I do . . . but that doesn't make everything okay. This whole situation is so stressful. Which is why David and I are meeting with Pastor Dee tomorrow morning to put this issue to bed once and for all."

"Rachel, that's your business. And as Sarah Beth's parents, which Watcher programs she participates in are your decision, but I want you to know that I would *never* do anything to put that kid in harm's way. I know I ran away from my problems and my commitment to you before, but I won't abandon Sarah Beth. And I would never, through action or inaction, put her in danger."

"I believe you mean that, and I believe that's your intention. But I also believe that come hell or high water, you will, seemingly by no fault of your own, drag my daughter into your world, because, Jed, that's what you do. You are in the profession of diving headfirst into harm's way."

"Mmm-hmm," he said, nodding. "From the outside, I can see how you might feel that way, but the Shepherds are protectors, not hunters. The evil in this world is here, working, conniving, and prowling around looking for vulnerable souls to devour. Someone has to be the line of defense. If not us, who?"

Neither of them said anything for a long while, and Jed wondered if she was done baring her soul.

The answer was no.

"After the Dark Ones' second attempt to kidnap Sarah Beth, David and I knew we were in deep trouble. We knew they would come for Sarah Beth again, and the third time they wouldn't fail. The status quo was never going to cut it, and so we boiled it down to two choices: either run far, far away or enroll Sarah Beth into St. George's. Given the amount of security at the school and the proximity to the Shepherds, St. George's made the most sense. On top of that, she begged us to go, so the decision felt right. But now . . . now I'm beginning to think we might have made a mistake. I'm just as worried about her safety as I was before. Maybe more so, now that I know how they want to use my daughter for their spec ops program. And then tonight David tells me about some sort of new weapon that can incinerate a person from space and that I'm not allowed to go outside anymore . . ." She let out a hard exhale and shook her head. "I just don't see how my family can be a part of this anymore."

Jed tugged at his chin, not really sure what to say. All the points she made were valid, but he also knew that her judgment was colored by stress and emotion.

"I get it. I really do. But there's no question in my mind that St. George's is the safest place on earth for Sarah Beth. This new threat is global. The first target was the Q'ero tribe in the mountains of Peru! You can't get any more remote than that. Don't you get it? There is no running from this threat. Victor is not like some wandering bear. You can't just hide and hope he'll go away. The only way to stop him, to stop all the fear and uncertainty, is to end him. That's what we're trying to do. All of us—the Shepherds and the Watchers—we work together to guide and protect each other. Without the Watchers, the Shepherds are blind and impotent. Without the Shepherds, the Watchers are vulnerable and powerless. Everyone has a role to play. How and what that contribution looks like is different for each person, but it's part of the deal. I think it's important that you don't create a false equivalency in your mind."

"False equivalency . . . what's that supposed to mean?"

"It means if after the second attack, instead of joining, you guys had run away—had tried to go it alone and fly under the radar—you wouldn't feel any more secure and confident about Sarah Beth's safety than you do now. In fact, I'd argue that you'd all be basket cases by now—or more likely, you'd all be dead. This isn't something where you just get a new name and move to a new town. You're fleeing from dark, evil forces in a spiritual war, Rachel. How do you hide from demons who can invade your thoughts? And even if you could, that's no way to live—always looking over your shoulder wondering when and how they were coming for Sarah Beth and how you would stop them when they did. There are over two hundred kids in that school with the gift of second sight, and their little antennae are always piqued. Ain't no way nohow the Dark Ones are going to waltz onto that campus and take Sarah Beth in the night. It's just not going to happen. As for your concern about the accelerated program and Sarah Beth being pressured into field-work, this is not the military and it's not a dictatorship. She's your daughter, your dependent. If you and David say no to fieldwork, then as far as the Shepherds are concerned, the answer is *no*."

She nodded but he could tell she wasn't convinced.

"You've given me a lot to think about, Jed," she said, abruptly getting to her feet. "Thanks for the talk."

"Yeah, sure, anytime," he said awkwardly. As he stood to escort her out, he felt cheated of the catharsis that usually comes after a hard, soul-baring conversation like this. She'd not given him even a hint of absolution, and he found himself quietly resenting her for that.

But you didn't ask for it either, did you?

Without waiting for him, Rachel walked out of the living room into the foyer.

"Rachel," he said, trotting after her. "Hold up. Let me at least walk you out."

"Why, so we can both get vaporized?" she murmured with a fatalistic laugh. "No thanks, I'll see myself out."

He tried to think of something to say but couldn't find the words.

She paused at the threshold. "You know, it's funny . . . sometimes I can't help but be a little jealous of her."

"Jealous of who?" he said, totally confused.

"Sarah Beth, of course." She gave a tight-lipped smile. "I wish somebody had found me when I was her age and asked me to attend St. George's . . . because if they had, maybe none of this would have ever happened."

The comment hit him like a jab to the nose, rendering him mute.

"Good night, Jed," she said with a wan smile and stepped out into the night.

"Be safe, Rachel," he called after her but too late.

He didn't shut the front door until she was inside her car and driving away. He walked to the kitchen, his brain still parsing the words of her parting comment as he poured himself a glass of water.

"I wish somebody had found me when I was her age and asked me to attend St. George's . . ."

"Why would Rachel have been recruited for St. George's?" he murmured.

He felt his heart skip a beat at the possibility.

Unless . . . all along she's had the gift of second sight just like Sarah Beth.

Feeling suddenly light-headed, he had to brace himself against the counter.

If it's true, how could I have been so blind?

If it's true, it changes everything.

CHAPTER TEN

Nashville police detective Maria Perez paced back and forth in the small break room, staring at her mobile. Not only was Jed not answering his phone—she'd called him three times today—but he hadn't answered any of her flirtatious texts either. Did she dare try again? She was already treading into controlling girlfriend territory *way* too early in their budding relationship.

And now he was ghosting her.

She wanted to scream.

Frown on her face, she absently massaged the scar on her abdomen, left behind from the bullet she had taken for the team, as she replayed the timeline of events in her mind. The last time she'd seen Jed, he'd explained over coffee that he was about to begin a training evolution that would put him "out of pocket" for three weeks. It was unclear to her whether he was giving the training or receiving it, but regardless the module should have ended by now. They'd agreed to touch base and reconnect after, but that hadn't happened. She could see he'd read her texts, but he'd still not responded to any of them or returned her calls, all of which had gone straight to voice mail.

Her thoughts went to Nisha—the attractive woman she'd met at the Yarnells' cookout. Yes, the woman was Jed's teammate, but Maria recognized that look—the one she'd seen when Nisha looked at Jed, but also the one Nisha had shot Maria when she'd arrived as Jed's plus-one. Not disapproving . . . more threatened. Jealous. If Jed had lost interest over the past three weeks because of Nisha courting him, it could represent a big problem.

I've got to get his attention fixed back on me. Whatever it takes.

She strode to the coffee maker, but the thought of a cup nauseated her, so she resumed pacing instead.

The break room door swung open, giving her a start.

"What are you still doing here, Perez?" Lieutenant Marcum Reiss said from the doorway, an eyebrow up as if questioning her judgment.

"I'm heading home in a second, boss," she said.

"It's eight o'clock, Perez," Reiss grumbled. "Which part of 'take it slow and ease back into things' didn't resonate with you?"

"I am taking it easy, boss," she said. "I promise. I didn't even leave the precinct today. Catching up on paperwork the whole day. I'm up next to catch a case, and I guess I hoped . . ."

Reiss's face softened. "I get it, Maria," he said, nodding. "You love your job and you're eager to get back, but the gunshot injury protocols are well studied and exist for a reason . . . that reason is your mental health. You're no good to anyone if you have an emotional or physical breakdown. You need balance in your life."

"You say that, but *you're* here, sir," she pointed out with a smile.

"Don't be a smart-ass." He chuckled. "Look, before I promoted, this job almost cost me my marriage. But no more. My balance is my family—Susan and the kids. And I've also taken up running. Now I know you don't have a family yet, but you need something outside of here, okay? Not because you got shot in the line of duty, but because you're a good detective and also a good person. Don't let this job steal your joy."

"I won't, sir," she said. "I'm heading out now, I promise. And I'll take it slow and easy."

"Do that," he called after her as she left the break room.

She sighed and looked at her phone again.

Nothing.

She chewed the inside of her cheek, thinking what to do next. So long as Jed was uncooperative, she couldn't execute her mission. And Victor was anything but a patient man—or whatever he really was.

Maybe it's time to shift to the backup plan.

She tapped a message into her phone.

Hey, Rachel. With Jed tied up, I'm feeling lonely. Wanna grab coffee or lunch tomorrow? Would love to catch up with you and hear how Sarah Beth is doing.

Maria smiled. If Jed was tied up with work—or that tramp Nisha—then she'd have to get to Sarah Beth another way. And once the little brat was taken care of, Victor would finally be happy and she could focus her full attention on infiltrating the Shepherds.

Her phone chimed.

Love to but busy early tomorrow. David and I have a meeting with SB's school. David working after. How about lunch? You pick the place.

Perfect . . .

She sent a reply, picking a place that was nice but out of the way from prying eyes and ears. Feeling better, she slipped her phone in her suit pant pocket and smiled. Originally Jed had seemed the easier conduit, but Rachel was lonely—a woman in need of a friend. Someone she could laugh with but also ventilate to. That's exactly who Maria had modeled herself to be. But there was something about Rachel that was hard to crack. Also, she had an unnaturally strong connection with her daughter, which could be a problem. Maria worried that Sarah Beth could get inside her head, like Victor. Once she'd thought she'd even felt the little brat rooting around in her memories, but she'd had a couple of glasses of wine that night and dismissed it.

Probably just my paranoia at work.

She pulled her Glock service pistol from the lockbox in her top desk drawer and slipped the weapon into the holster on her hip. Then she grabbed her shoulder bag from the bottom drawer and headed out of the precinct to her Nashville MPD car and fired the beast up. She'd work out, drink some wine, and revise her strategy.

Maybe I've been going about this the wrong way, she thought. *Maybe instead of pushing so hard, I need to let Jed come to me. Play a little hard to get . . .*

And on that cue, her phone chimed with a text message notification. She pulled it from her bag and looked at the screen.

Hi, Maria, so sorry for the radio silence, but I just got back in town. Meet for coffee tomorrow? Can't wait to reconnect!

Flush with possibility, she thumb-typed her reply: **How about getting together for drinks tonight? I'm available . . .**

His reply took over a minute:

Would love to, but I'm completely wiped. I'd be terrible company. Going to bed. Tomorrow, okay?

Irritation blossomed in her chest, but she tamped it down and decided to take his word at face value. He'd responded and wanted to see her. That was a win.

Sounds good. Can't wait to see you!

She added the kiss emoji at the end and waited.

And waited . . .

Finally her phone dinged and she saw that he'd responded in kind.

A victorious smile curled her lips. It had taken time and persistence, but her plan was working. She was worming her way into both Jed's and Rachel's hearts. When the opportunity to complete her mission presented itself, they'd never see it coming.

CHAPTER ELEVEN

Identifying a coffee shop he could access without going outside was a challenge, but eventually Jed found a solution—a Starbucks built into the lobby of the Margaritaville hotel downtown. Grumbling to himself, he stomped through the covered parking lot toward the garage entrance to the hotel. An existence where he couldn't go outside for fear of being vaporized at any given moment was no way to live.

If this is the future of warfare, then we're all doomed, he realized with creeping dread. *Which is why we've got to find this weapon and destroy it.*

Suddenly feeling the crush of time, he glanced at his watch. He wasn't late, but that was irrelevant, because he didn't have time for this. He'd offered to meet Maria, driven by a sense of guilt and obligation, but that had been last night . . . when he'd been exhausted and still reeling from his soul-baring, emotionally charged conversation with Rachel. Now, rested and clearheaded, he regretted that decision. Everyone else on his team was working like dogs at Trinity on the case, while he ducked out to have coffee with his girlfriend.

Hold on—is that what she is now . . . my girlfriend?

This was the first time he'd privately referred to Maria as his girlfriend, and it left him shocked and more than a little unsettled. They'd been on a handful of outings together, and only one qualified as a *real* date. The other times they'd gotten together had been like this—forcing a meetup into their mutually busy schedules to see each other face-to-face. But that's the way new relationships started, and that was okay. He wasn't a one-night stand kind of person and he suspected neither was she. Obviously she was interested in him—she'd blown his phone up with texts and voice mails the last couple of days. And he couldn't deny the feelings he was starting to have for her.

But the timing was terrible.

I don't know how the married guys do it, he thought. *Add kids and a dog or two and how is a guy supposed to do his job and make time to meet everyone's needs?*

He passed through the hotel lobby and doglegged left toward the Starbucks. He spied Maria through the glass doors, standing inside and seemingly lost in thought. In the split second before she noticed him, he saw a facet of her he'd not seen before. She looked . . . vulnerable. Not physically but like an elementary schooler looks waiting alone on the sidewalk for the bus to arrive—brave with duty and expectation yet anxious because, well, what if the bus fails to come? The epiphany moved him, and he felt a strong pull of attraction for her.

"Jed!" she called and trotted over to give him a hug the instant he crossed the threshold into the coffee shop.

"Hi," he said, grinning, and wrapped his arms around her as she threw herself against him.

"I missed you," she said, her head turned to the side, cheek settled in the little crook between his shoulder and pectoral muscle.

"I missed you too," he said with a little laugh.

"What's so funny?" she said, chuckling but pulling back to look up at him.

"Well, it's not like I've been off to war or something. It was just a three-week training evolution."

"So . . . I'm not allowed to miss you unless it's a month or longer?" she said, her tone defensive but her smile playful.

"That's not what I meant," he said and quickly redirected. "You look really good by the way."

And she did, dressed in black leggings and a fuzzy rose-colored fleece. She had her hair pulled back into a sporty ponytail and was wearing Nike trainers.

She demurred. "*Really?* These are just my workout clothes."

"Yeah, well, you look hot."

"Thanks," she said, her cheeks instantly flushing with color.

"Should we order?" he said, turning toward the counter. "What do you want? My treat."

"That's sweet, thank you," she said, gave him her request, and set off to grab them a table.

He ordered, paid, and carried their coffees to the two-person bistro table a few minutes later.

"Why did you pick this place?" she asked, accepting her coffee from his outstretched hand. "I mean, it's fine, but I prefer the little coffee shop we met at last time."

"I know, but I had something to pick up in the neighborhood, so this was convenient," he lied.

"What were you picking up?" she asked, smiling over her cup.

"It doesn't matter," he said, not wanting to get into a discussion about the existence of space assassination lasers. Even if she believed him—which he deemed unlikely—he didn't want to talk about it. "Let's talk about you. How's the recovery going? You back at work and feeling good?"

"Yeah, and very happy about that. Without work and you out of town, um, let's just say I was going stir-crazy."

He nodded and took a sip of his nitro coldbrew. "I hear ya . . ."

"Do you like that?" she said, her gaze ticking to his drink.

"First time I've tried it, but it's good," he said. "I could see this becoming my go-to. Tastes kinda like Guinness but as a coffee."

"Hmm, interesting. I'll have to try it sometime," she said. After an awkward beat she flashed him a coy smile. "Now that you're back, should we plan another night out? There's a new restaurant I'd like to try."

"Yes, buuuut . . . ," he said, dragging out the word. "It looks like I'm going on another training op soon, possibly in the next forty-eight hours."

"Is that so?" she said, her expression falling.

"Yep, something's come up."

"Don't you think maybe we're past the lying-to-each-other stage of this relationship?" she said, her gaze going frosty. "I was at the Cathedral of the Incarnation that day, Jed, remember? I know what you do for a living."

"Well, I really have been training for the past three weeks," he said, strangely not offended or upset by her comment. He'd not read her in on the Shepherds' actual charter, but she'd pieced together plenty. "But that's not the point. I thought we had an understanding, Maria. You're no stranger to compartmentalization. I can't share what I'm working on with you. Just like you can't share case details with me. Why do you insist on testing me?"

"I'm not testing you, Jed. And I'm not asking to be read in, but I do think I deserve the professional and personal courtesy of straight talk. You know what I'm sayin'?"

He nodded. "I do, but you could also just trust me and know that I'll share what I can when I can and won't share what I can't when I can't. The reason why I'm traveling doesn't change the obligation."

"A fair point," she said and reached out and clasped his left hand, which was resting on the table. "I'm sorry. I was just looking forward to spending time with you now that you're back, and to hear you say you're leaving again is disappointing."

He squeezed her hand. "I'm disappointed too. Believe me, this thing I'm working on now, I wish I wasn't . . . I really wish I wasn't."

The temptation to sneak in and read her thoughts was overpowering, but he fought off the compulsion. Like Sarah Beth was fond of pointing out, *It's rude to snoop.*

"What's that look for?" she asked with a cautious smile.

"Just wondering what you're thinking . . ."

"Ah, that's easy. I'm wondering about us."

"And what *exactly* are you wondering?"

"Whether we have a future together or if we're both destined to be perpetually single."

Feeling strangely unburdened after the conversation with Rachel, he said, "I've never been one for making guarantees about the future, but I'm interested in exploring how a future with you in my life might play out. . . . What about you?"

She answered by leaning in and staring into his eyes.

Much to his own surprise, he found himself leaning across the table to kiss her. The instant their lips made contact, her gravity sucked him into her headspace. Inside, he felt a confusing symphony of emotions from her—yearning and desperation, victory and shame. She wanted this kiss so very badly and yet he sensed she was at war with herself for liking it.

He finished the kiss and as their lips parted, so did his connection.

If that's what it's like to be a woman in love, then I'm glad I'm a dude.

"What?" she said, a coy smile on her face.

"What, what?" he said, grinning back.

"Do I have coffee breath? Sorry if I do."

"No," he said with a chuckle. "I liked it . . . I mean kissing you, not your coffee breath."

She gave his hand a squeeze, then let go. "This was nice, Jed, but I've got a spin class in a few minutes I need to get to."

"Sure, no problem. And I should probably be heading back myself."

"How about when you're ready for our next date, you let me know. In the meantime, I'll be thinking about that kiss," she said, radiating more confidence and certainty than he'd seen from her before.

"I'll call you as soon as I'm free," he said, rising from his chair, "but until then, I'll be thinking about it too."

CHAPTER
TWELVE

Sarah Beth twisted the hem of her plaid skirt as she sat on the worn wooden bench outside Pastor Dee's office. She couldn't think of a single thing she could possibly be in trouble for, but there were many kinds of trouble in life—something she'd been learning all about this past year.

Are you already at the office, baby girl? her mom asked in her mind.

She smiled.

Communicating this way with her mom had been frustratingly random for years, but recently it had become a regular thing. She didn't know if it was because her own abilities were growing or her mom was just becoming more receptive to the idea, but she liked that the last few weeks they'd been sharing thoughts several times a day. She knew part of it was Mom's jealousy that Uncle Jed talked to her that way, a jealousy she didn't really understand but tried to be respectful of.

And she knew that Jed wasn't really her uncle. She'd pieced together Jed's old relationship with her mom and fractured friendship with her dad—gleaning more details than any of them realized. She wasn't six years old anymore, and she also had the benefit of her gifts, which she'd fully taken advantage of. She knew that her dad had once been Jed's best friend, but that had ended long ago and Jed was still angry at Dad, though the reason remained elusive.

She also knew that Jed had once been in love with Mom.

And maybe he was still in love with her, a little.

It was emotionally complicated.

Like everything in life . . .

Yep, just sitting here waiting to see what I'm in trouble for, she answered, hoping she sounded like she was joking in her mom's head.

You're not in trouble, silly girl, came the reply, quick and honest.

Then does this have anything to do with the "no going outside" rule the headmaster announced last night?

Not directly, but we can talk more about that later. We're here.

The double shadow of her parents appeared in the frosted glass panel of the admin office door. As the door swung open, she popped to her feet and ran to wrap them both in a hug. She breathed them in—her mom's hair, the smell of her dad's skin, the "home" smell of their clothes. Then she let go, wiping away an embarrassed tear with the back of her hand.

"Hey, are you okay?" Dad asked, real concern in his voice and face.

"Yeah," she said, screwing a smile onto her face. "I always realize how much I miss you as soon as I see you, and I'm, um, really sorry the school called you in for whatever this is."

Her mom's face twisted with that *oh, my little girl* look and she took her hands. "It's nothing like that, Sarah Beth. *We* asked for this meeting with Pastor Dee. You're doing great here, and we just want to involve you in big decisions about your future."

"Big decisions?" she asked, now feeling more confused and worried than ever.

"I've been doing some thinking," her mom said, then glanced at her dad and quickly corrected herself. "Your dad and I have *both* been doing some thinking. We had a long talk last night and as a result, we've had a change of heart about your education and training here."

A wave of panic hit Sarah Beth. Despite whatever middle school drama she had with her roommates, she would literally *die* if they pulled her out of St. George's. How could she possibly live with all the gifts and voices and visions and bad things, without the security and community of this place? She might not fit in perfectly here, but out there she was just a freak.

"You're not pulling me out of school, are you?" she stammered. "Please don't say you're putting me back in public school."

"No, no, sweetheart," her mom said and pulled her in for a hug. "Quite the opposite . . ."

"Oh, good," she said with a shaky sigh of relief. "Because I like it here."

"Pastor Dee says y'all can go on in," the receptionist said with a smile, ending their conversation.

She followed her parents into Pastor Dee's office, noticing they seemed different this morning. Her dad seemed taller or something. More confident. And he looked stronger than she remembered. And her mom seemed less angry and stressed out than usual. Like somebody had lifted a thousand-pound weight off her back. Her smiles were like they used be—not the fake, forced ones she'd been wearing all the time recently.

"Hello, Yarnell family," Pastor Dee said from behind her large and somewhat-cluttered desk. Her voice felt warm to Sarah Beth, as it always did. Sarah Beth reflexively took her usual seat—the left corner of the gray leather sofa across the coffee table from the oversize chair Pastor Dee preferred. Her mother squeezed in beside her close, taking her hand, a move that would have horrified her in public but felt soothing here. She let out a sigh and reached out into the mind place, looking for Pastor Dee's thread. She found it, but then Pastor Dee frowned and shook her head slightly, so she pulled back in.

Don't do that, Sarah Beth. It's impolite . . .

The rebuke, her mom's voice in her head, surprised Sarah Beth since she'd not opened herself up to her. She shot her mom a quizzical look, but her mom just shook her head and put a finger to her lips.

"I know why you called this meeting, and I want you to know that the staff and I always value and respect parents' wishes and decisions when it comes to the education and safety of their children," Pastor Dee said, kicking things off.

"We know, Pastor Dee," her mom said. "And we also want you to know that we've had a change of heart since our last conversation."

"You have?" Pastor Dee said, looking both delighted and confused.

"We have," her dad said and reached out to give her mom's hand a squeeze.

"Oh, well, that's blessed news," Pastor Dee said, a big smile spreading across her face.

"Um, I'm confused. What are we talking about? Am I in trouble?" Sarah Beth said, looking back and forth between all their faces.

"No, Sarah Beth, you've done nothing wrong. This is not a disciplinary meeting. In fact, you're doing everything right. Also, you should know that this is our second meeting with Pastor Dee—we met with her a few days ago," her dad said, uncharacteristically taking the reins.

"You met without me?" she asked, hating the very idea of that.

"Yep," Dad said, unfazed by her tone. "Parents do that sometimes." He chuckled and his soft gaze made her feel a bit better. "Because of all that's happened, most recently with your involvement in the operation at the Vatican—"

"I'm so sorry about that," she interrupted, feeling a little panic growing inside her again. "It's just it all happened so fast. I didn't see how I could do nothing. The team was in danger, and I'd seen things, important things." She glanced at her mom, not really sure how much she knew—or was supposed to know—about details of the last mission. "I went straight to Pastor Dee after and told her and I promise . . . I *promise* . . . it'll never happen again."

Her mom wrapped an arm around her. "You're not in trouble for that, Sarah Beth. You're not being disciplined or suspended or anything like that. Quite the opposite."

She met her mom's empathetic stare and picked up something else from her—a feeling that was difficult to put into words. Her mom had always been conflicted about St. George's. She'd snooped on her parents' arguments about whether the Watcher program was a good thing or a bad thing.

Whether being at St. George's made her safer or made her a target. From the beginning, her dad had been all in on her going here, but not her mom. Today, however, she felt something different, like her mom had flipped the switch and finally come around to her dad's point of view.

"The truth is, Sarah Beth, after you told me what you did at the Vatican with helping the Shepherds, I reached out to your parents," Pastor Dee said. "You and I have spoken many times about how special your gifts are, haven't we?"

She nodded, feeling much more like a child than she liked.

"I explained to your parents how very unique some of your gifts are and how advanced you are compared to the other students. And so during the last meeting, I asked your mom and dad what they thought about accelerating your training."

"And?" Sarah Beth said, excited and nervous, glancing from Pastor Dee to her parents and back again.

We said no, her mother said in her head.

"What? Why?"

"Why what, dear?" Pastor Dee said, confused for a moment, but then glanced at her mother and nodded with recognition. "Oh, I see."

"But I want to do it," she stammered. "I want to have better control. I want to be able to do something with these, these—" she gritted her teeth—"these things that make me different. I want them to matter. Why would you say no? Do you have any idea what it's like to have all this inside you and to want to control it but not be able to?"

"Actually I do, Sarah Beth," her mom said, her voice a lullaby, "which is why your dad and I reevaluated our previous decision and decided to include *you* in the conversation."

Why? she asked her mom in their secret, parallel conversation. *What changed?*

I was scared, Sarah Beth, her mom answered. *I was scared they'd take advantage of you—use you like a sacrificial pawn in some cosmic chess match.*

"But I want to do God's work and use my gifts," she said aloud. "I want all this craziness to have a purpose. To have meaning . . ."

"That's right, and so do we," Pastor Dee said. She paused and let silence ebb away the charged emotion in the room, something she excelled at, before continuing. "In our first meeting, I never got a chance to explain exactly what we're talking about here. As a result, your parents may have been left with a false impression of the program I'm proposing."

"How so?" Mom asked.

Pastor Dee shifted her gaze to Mom. "Well, for starters, officially there's no such thing as an accelerated Watcher program. When we have students with special gifts or needs, we give them individual attention—as I've been doing with Sarah Beth since she arrived. But beyond that, there's no formal program to accelerate the curriculum. Quite honestly, there's never really been a need, because even our most advanced students, like Corbin Worth, step into their roles as upperclassmen when their gifts and maturity levels are peaking at the same time. What I'm proposing for Sarah Beth is more like individual tutoring than an AP track at a traditional school. We will be learning as we go how best to serve her."

"That makes sense," her dad said.

"It does," her mom agreed, "but still does little to quell my real concern."

"That Sarah Beth will be thrust into more adult situations, into potentially *dangerous* situations, long before she is ready?" Pastor Dee said.

"Exactly. I've seen how you use Corbin Worth. As a mother, I'm not ready to put my child in such danger. And I'm not sure I would be regardless of her age," her mom said, but her tone was different than usual. More curious than condemning.

"I understand. Every mother of every Green Beret and Navy SEAL no doubt feels similarly—"

"But their children are adults," her mom interrupted.

"Yes, but they are still their mothers' children summoned to service. If God has called Sarah Beth by giving her these gifts of the Holy Spirit, then He has summoned her to service as well. He's summoned all of us. He's called us to help, love, and support her on the path she must walk."

"Mom," Sarah Beth said, suddenly feeling very grown-up, "I know you don't completely understand what it feels like for me, but I want you to. I want you to see that having all of this and not understanding it or being able to control it is so much harder . . ."

"And more dangerous," Pastor Dee added softly.

Sarah Beth felt the weight of the words and agreed but didn't want to scare her mother back into her old state of mind. She held her mom's eyes, and they exchanged teary smiles.

I understand far better than you know, Daughter, her mom said.

For the second time, she wanted to ask what her mom meant by that, but Dad interrupted.

"Pastor Dee, Rachel and I have prayed about this a lot. As hard as it is, as parents, we believe that properly preparing Sarah Beth—helping her learn how to manage and utilize the gifts God gave her—as quickly as possible is the best way to keep her safe. However, operationally speaking . . ."

"Sarah Beth will not ever deploy outside this compound without your permission, David. No child here does, and I promise you the few who travel are exceptions. Decisions to allow our students outside the walls of St. George's requires a tremendous amount of prayer, discussion, and consultation with families. But we do feel strongly we owe it to Sarah Beth to provide additional instruction and training."

"We agree," her mom said with decisive finality. "We trust you, Sarah Beth, and we trust in what God has planned for you. But you must promise me that you won't keep things from us like you did with the Vatican."

"I promise, Mom. I'll never hide things from you again," she said, wrapping her arms around her mother and feeling the shaking breath as her mom hugged her back. She pulled away and looked at both her parents. "Thank you."

You've earned this, Mom said in her head. Then she turned to Pastor Dee. "We're trusting you, Pastor Dee, and expect you to keep us informed every step of the way."

"And I appreciate and thank you for your trust," Pastor Dee said, folding her hands in her lap. "I take that responsibility very, very seriously."

"So . . . ," Sarah Beth said, playfully narrowing her eyes. "Since it's decided, does that mean I get to learn what's behind the white door?"

Pastor Dee rolled her eyes and smiled. "All in good time, child. All in good time."

Sarah Beth felt a wave of excitement and a paradoxical sense of dread at this new and unexpected turn of events. She was thrilled at the prospect of what she'd learn but also uneasy. Because if God needed her now, it must mean something terrible was coming.

CHAPTER THIRTEEN

After jumping through the requisite security hoops at the front gate, Gayle James followed Trinity Loop Road to visitor parking. A quarter of the outdoor lot had been "functionally" converted to covered parking with a series of carport structures placed end to end. After parking in an open slip in the front row, she climbed out of the car to greet Jed, who was standing at the curb under a scaffold-supported awning that ran from the parking lot to the building. It had been only a few days since she'd seen him, but already she'd forgotten just how massive the guy was. When she clasped his outstretched hand, her own looked like a child's hand inside.

"How was your trip?" he said, shaking her hand firmly without squeezing.

"Easy. I caught a nonstop from Dulles." Looking around, she added, "Wow, you guys rolled out threat protocols quickly. Looks like you're taking this threat pretty seriously."

"Yeah, well, we can't have our staff getting vaporized on the way to and from work," he said with a crooked smile. "Or our guests."

"I appreciate that," she said, returning his smile.

"C'mon," he said, gesturing to a stately three-story brick building ahead that looked like it belonged on the Vanderbilt campus. "We've got the team assembled."

She followed him along the path and inside. A few minutes later, he ushered her into a slick "nerve center" style tactical operations center where she immediately spied Nisha, Eli, and Bex along with some new faces.

"Hi, Gayle, I'm Damien Gough," an early middle-aged man with glasses and wavy dark hair said, shaking her hand. "I'm CISA here at Trinity, or head of conventional intelligence and signals analysis. I've worked with Mark for several years now. I understand he's retiring and you're his replacement."

"That's right," she said. "Mark apologizes for not being able to make this trip, but his wife is in the hospital and . . ."

"We spoke," Damien said with a knowing and empathetic smile.

Next she shook hands with Julia Nesbitt, the intelligence director for Trinity. With the meet and greet out of the way, the assembled gathered around a large oval-shaped conference table made of polished white marble with the unmistakable shape of a shepherd's crook in the middle, created by what looked like naturally occurring gray veining.

"Before we get started, I just gotta ask . . . this is something you had made, right?" Gayle said, pointing to the ghost-gray image in the marble.

"Actually, no," Julia said. "It was quarried that way. When the slab was cut, the fabricator in Italy reached out to the church and eventually it made its way here."

"That's pretty cool," Gayle said.

"Indeed," the director said and then after a momentary pause got down to business. "As you can see, Ms. James, we're taking this threat quite seriously. It is our number one intelligence collection priority and our number one threat prosecution priority. The only problem is . . . since Peru, we find ourselves with precious little to prosecute. I hope and pray that your prompt visit here today is because the Agency has something of consequence to share with us so we can get to work trying to neutralize the threat."

Gayle felt her cheeks get hot and hated herself for it. She usually had a pretty good poker face, but around these people she suddenly felt like red-cheeked Pinocchio. She did have one lead, but her conversation with Steve in the SCIF at Langley weighed heavy on her conscience. *"So long as you take more than you give, you're golden."* How was she supposed to horse-trade information with these people if she had to show them all her cards the instant she sat down at the table?

She forced a smile on her face and said, "I wish that were the case. Actually, I'm here because we were hoping you'd found something new. I understand from Mark that you guys, um, have some collection tools that aren't exactly at our disposal. For the record, he didn't specify what those tools were, only that they defy and sometimes supersede even the best SIGINT collection technologies in our arsenal."

This comment was met with nods around the table.

"That's true," Julia said. "And while we're certainly going to task our Watcher program to start looking, we have nothing fresh and actionable now."

Something in her face suggested there was more to that story, but Gayle shook the feeling off. If so, she'd never know. That was the game, right?

Gayle exhaled, trying not to look too deflated. She was about to say something vague when Jed spoke up.

"Gayle, what you need to know is that we've stood up a dedicated special task force for prosecuting this threat. My team—including Eli, Nisha, and Bex—will be the field component, while Julia and Damien spearhead things from here. The problem is, we're a heat-seeking missile without a heat signature to home in on," he said.

"What about that guy from Cuzco that you black-bagged? Were you able to extract any actionable intelligence from him?" she asked.

"Not really," Julia said, answering for Jed. "All we did was confirm our suspicions that we're dealing with a directed energy weapon of unknown technology, that it was fired from altitude and not line of sight from the ground, and that it was acquired by a well-financed terrorist organization we monitor closely. But like Jed said, that still doesn't give us the next bread crumb to follow."

Gayle nodded and sat, lips pressed tightly together, in the uncomfortable silence that followed. Before leaving for Nashville, she'd met with DS&T

and they'd discussed the incident in the mountains. The guru from the CIA's Directorate of Science and Technology had been visibly shaken by Gayle's retelling of the event. As the lead investigator researching the growing number of reports of Havana Syndrome at State, inside the IC, and at active-duty military stations overseas, the team was an expert in directed energy weapon attacks. The microwave emitters believed responsible for the crippling neurological symptoms suffered by those targeted were portable and difficult to detect. This weapon, however, was a completely different beast altogether. When pressed, the team had reluctantly read Gayle in on a recent development concerning a Chinese scientist working at the Scientific Research Steering Committee—the PLA's version of DARPA—who had recently been in contact with a CIA asset inside China with concerns about lethal high energy weapons research and had asked to defect, but he hadn't been taken seriously.

But now . . .

"There is one potential lead, but I'm not sure it will pan out," she offered, unsure exactly how to get more than she gave here—as ordered.

"So what's that?" Jed asked bluntly.

"Well," she said, deciding just to trust her gut and go for it, "the CIA received information from a Chinese scientist working with SRSC who claimed he had information on an emerging weapons system that could do something that sounds an awful lot like what we saw in Peru . . ."

"And you're just mentioning this now?" Jed asked.

"I was just made aware of it myself," she snapped, more defensively than she'd intended. "We get dozens of leads every day. Many are so far-fetched as to be dismissed out of hand, as this one was, and the agency has to be highly selective about facilitating defectors in the current political environment." She watched Jed roll his eyes at that and felt her cheeks flush. "Look, I get it, but that's the world we work in. I don't make the rules. We can't just snatch a dozen Chinese nationals a month and not expect escalation with the CCP. But now, with what happened in Peru, we need to revisit the claims made by this guy . . ."

"What's his status?" Julia asked coolly. Gayle felt the entire tone shifting and realized she needed to salvage her role on this combined task force if she was to have a seat at the table at all.

"I'm waiting to hear," she fibbed. Before she could answer, she needed to consult with Langley. "I was hoping to get word before I got to this meeting, but nothing yet."

"So what's your ask?"

She looked over at Nisha, who now eyed her suspiciously. Time to take control of the narrative before the Shepherds penned their own.

"Look, guys," Gayle said, folding her hands on the table in front of her. "I know there is a lot of rice bowl mentality in our line of work—people not wanting to share information on things they view as their private purview. And I know that some of you may have been burned by some OGA task force or organic CIA assets in the past, but that's not how I work. I'm here because I want to be here. I don't care about credit or cost sharing or intelligence crossover. I saw what happened up there on the mountain—what happened to those people. I want to find out where this came from and stop the people involved before more innocent people are hurt—especially if the United States is a target. That is why I joined CIA—to safeguard and save lives, just like you guys. Whatever the issues the various head sheds involved might have, I trust you." She turned to Jed and held his eyes until his face softened and he gave her a nod. Then she turned back to Nisha. "My ask is that we work this together, and that should include working up a plan to get close to this Chinese weapons scientist. I'll be looking for a green light for a cooperative joint task force to do just that."

"I don't know if getting close is enough. I think we need to get him out of China," Jed said, but he was looking at Julia now. "I doubt he'll cooperate unless he's safe and away from Chinese eyes. Over the past decade, China's become an oppressive security state."

She nodded. "Agreed. If we can get him here, we have a chance to learn the truth."

"Now when you say here . . ." Gayle looked around nervously. They didn't really expect that the CIA would disappear a Chinese national and then just turn him over to a small outfit in the hills of Tennessee, did they?

"Here means Trinity," Jed assured her, "with all principals involved present, of course, but this snatch and grab should be done by my team."

She watched Jed fold his thick arms over his broad chest, a statement she took to mean that in his mind the matter was settled. Despite her own rice bowl misgivings, she had a feeling that Jed was right, that they were the best positioned to act on any intelligence gained from the operation. Selling that to management was another matter altogether.

"How about I check in with my bosses at Langley right now and see if there's any update?" she offered. She needed guidance but also a break from a conversation that was spiraling rapidly out of her control.

"Of course," Julia said and rose, gesturing toward the door. "If you'd like, you can use my office, which is secured within the SCIF and protected from prying eyes and ears. You can use my secure line or just have privacy with your own device if you prefer."

"That would be great, thanks," Gayle said. If they intended to listen in on her, they would do it whether she was on her phone or theirs, she supposed. Might as well show a little trust and comradery. And anyway, she knew that Steve would be able to scramble the signal on his end if he wanted. She followed Julia out of the SCIF conference room and around the corner to a small but tidy office.

The Shepherds intelligence director gestured for Gayle to have a seat at her desk, which she did. "You needn't worry about us listening in, I promise," she said. "We don't spy on our friends and allies."

Gayle nodded but suspected the conversation would be recorded nonetheless. She thanked Julia, and a moment later, she was alone to make her call.

Schmidt answered on the first ring.

"Schmidt," he barked into the phone.

"It's me, Gayle James," she said, then glancing around the empty room, added, "on an unsecure line."

"I show your signal scrambled, but I assume that means you're in Nashville," he said dismissively. "What's up?"

Gayle gave him a quick overview of the short meeting so far and her desire to follow up on the Chinese scientist.

"The only problem," she said softly, "is the Shepherds want to exfil this guy. They even offered to take on the operation themselves so they can bring the asset to their HQ."

The laugh on the other end of the line made her raise her eyebrows.

"How is that a problem?" her boss asked but then answered before she could begin to think. "Disappearing Chinese nationals is complicated these days, Gayle. It requires multiple cutouts and backstories. They just offered to become all the needed cutouts at once. We have complete deniability because they don't really exist, not in any official way. Even in their contractor role, they are not avowed. If they jack it up, they're just a bunch of cowboy contractors—like those floaters down in Venezuela. No blowback for us."

Gayle swallowed hard. No wonder no one wanted to work with the CIA. What her boss was proposing was cold as ice.

"So I tell them what?"

"Tell them you got the green light for *them* to take point on the op. We'll start sending any and all intelligence we have and even arrange the pickup point with the shopper who's working the Chinese guy now. He's already asked to defect. There's an upcoming science conference in Hong Kong we were whiteboarding an operation for. The timing couldn't be more perfect. We've laid the groundwork; now all we do is step back and let the Shepherds take the risk."

"And if they want to bring him back here?"

"Let 'em," Schmidt said, laughing again. "We'll take custody when they're done, and you'll be there for the initial debrief as part of the subordinate task force arrangement you're going to propose when we hang up."

"So I'm on the team and they report to me, but I let them take lead?"

There was a long pause that made her more uncomfortable.

"Yes, but I don't want you traveling with them. If they get picked up by Chinese intelligence at the airport, I don't want you anywhere near them," he said.

"I travel alone?"

"Yeah, you fly commercial in a benign OC. I'll see if we can get you into the Four Seasons. You'll love it there. You run the TOC but keep distance to maintain our deniability. If the whole thing gets rolled up, we claim you were there to try and stop some rogue American contractors from kidnapping a Chinese scientist." Another laugh. "Man, this is gonna be great. Awesome work, James. I'll get everything rolling. Expect data on your high side within the hour."

The line went dead and she replaced the receiver and sighed.

She decided she hated her new job. Using people, sometimes even burning assets, that was part of the job. But not your friends. Steve was old-school, but the joint operations world that had grown out of the twenty-year war on terror had become more collegial and cooperative than ever. Sure, the CIA didn't exactly lead the charge when it came to teamwork, but even the Agency had embraced the new paradigm.

Until the times when it didn't suit them . . .

She thought of Jed, Bex, Nisha, and Eli. Thought of letting them twist and flap in the wind if this op went south.

I'll just have to say a prayer that nothing goes sideways.

Because if it did, she certainly wasn't going to sit on her hands while the Shepherds took the fall, regardless of Steve's orders. The day she was comfortable walking away from a trusted partner was the day she needed to find a new job. Resigned to her decision, she stepped out of the office and headed back to the conference room to give the Shepherds the "good" news. She'd never been part of an operation to defect an asset from a Communist country, and the prospect both excited and terrified her.

As she pulled the door open to the SCIF, she couldn't help but think, *So this is what it feels like to be a spy.*

PART II

What if God, although choosing to show his wrath and
make his power known, bore with great patience the
objects of his wrath—prepared for destruction?

ROMANS 9:22

CHAPTER FOURTEEN

"Where do you want me to start?" Jed said, pacing back and forth in front of the picture window with the breathtaking view of Hong Kong's Victoria Harbour outside. "I mean, there are literally a dozen things I hate about this op."

"Well, how about we start with what has you the most concerned," Eli said from an oversize chair beside the window, coffee in hand, ankle propped up on his knee.

"About our safety or mission success?"

"You pick," the former CAG operator said, sipping the frothy beverage he'd gotten, along with a plate full of fruit and cheese, from the concierge lounge they had access to.

Jed sighed and dropped into the other chair beside the small round table between him and Eli.

"Mostly I don't like that we're dependent on nameless, faceless bureaucrats at OGA who we were forced to partner with on this op," he admitted.

"Ah," Eli said and sipped his coffee again. Then as if he'd made some psychoanalytical breakthrough on a patient, he added, "But, bro, that's just the life of an operator. How many times were you at the pointy tip of the spear on some half-baked scheme with poorly shared intelligence to satisfy some unknown OGA agenda?"

"Plenty," Jed said, finally able to chuckle at the absurd sight of his friend snacking on cheese and crackers in the luxury hotel room. "And I hated it then, too. But this—I don't know—this is worse because we're not in Iraq or Afghanistan or North Africa with some QRF contingency. If this goes sideways, I'm worried that CIA will walk away like we don't exist and leave us to rot in some Chinese prison."

"Oh, that's exactly what they'll do, Jed. That's why they didn't let Gayle travel with us and why she's at the Four Seasons instead of here with us. They've already set up plausible deniability to disavow us entirely. If this goes bad, the cover story will be that we're rogue contractors gone off the rails. That's what CIA does. It's the job." The former Delta member leaned in toward him. "So we best not let things go sideways, huh?"

Jed snorted a laugh. "Yeah, I guess. I wish it was some straight-up direct-action mission—something more in our wheelhouse. I've done plenty of snatch and grabs, but they were all in third world cities or some desert compound off the grid. Never a city like Hong Kong. This is so, so . . ."

"Urban?"

"Yeah, urban." He sighed and leaned forward, elbows on thighs, mirroring Eli's posture. "But it needs to be us obviously. Since the Dark Ones are involved, we can't afford to let this guy disappear into some black site program never to be heard from again."

A knock on the door connecting their room to the adjoining one grabbed their attention.

"It's open," Jed called, having unlocked the connector already.

The door pushed open and Nisha and Bex walked in, Nisha's face unreadable and Bex looking a little uncertain.

"'Sup, guys?" Bex called.

"Just gearing up to do some planning." Eli smiled and drained the last of his coffee.

Jed rose and met them as they crossed the room, directing them with a hand toward the round table with four chairs.

"Where are the other guys?" Nisha asked, referring to the remaining four Shepherds of Joshua Bravo. Carl and Hyeon were sharing an identical room across the hall from Jed and Eli, with a connector to Johnny and Grayson's room across from Bex and Nisha.

"They'll be here in a few minutes," Jed said, holding Nisha's eyes. "I wanted to talk with you first, if that's okay."

"Yeah," she said, her voice curious, as she took a seat. "Everything okay?"

He shrugged. "Do you trust Gayle?"

Nisha laughed. "As much as I ever trust organic CIA. By that I mean I have a good feeling about Gayle. I think she's a straight shooter and wants to help. But in the end, her allegiance is to an organization that's burned me before. Don't get me wrong," she said, raising a hand. "I have tremendous respect for the work that CS and ground guys do at CIA. Tremendous respect. But CIA has moved slowly and with greater reluctance into the joint ops world we all know and thrive in. In the end, theirs is a CIA agenda and if it matches ours, great, but if not . . ."

It occurred to Jed that while he knew the nature of the work Nisha had done before joining the Shepherds, he didn't know her backstory. He'd always assumed she was CIA, but that assumption appeared to be wrong. He wondered, for the hundredth time, what spooky organization she'd worked for previously and how she had ended up at Trinity.

"The point is, I trust Gayle personally, but she traveled separately for a reason," she said, finishing her thought. "My guess is they turn and leave us in a second if they feel the need. So . . . I trust her *judgment* while she's on task, but we should assume we are running this on our own if things go bad."

"That's what Eli thought too, which brings me to this: Nisha, I need you to run point on this operation." She opened her mouth to object, but he held up a hand. "This is not me passing off operational authority. I'm team lead. I take responsibility for decisions and outcomes. But I'm a door kicker. Your specialty is small-footprint covert operations and spy craft . . . or am I mistaken?"

"You are not," she said and folded her arms across her chest.

"So as team leader, it's my job to make sure that each member of the team is tasked properly based on their strengths and weaknesses. You've run these kinds of ops before—me not so much—especially in a setting like this. So my question is, are you comfortable taking lead on this?"

She thought a moment, then looked up. "I am, but if we get into a gunfight, the team lead shifts to you. Fair enough?"

"Yep," he said with a nod.

"Good with me too, if anyone is asking," Eli said and slapped Jed on the shoulder. "The Lord knows if there's a balcony that needs jumping off of, we all know who to call."

"Exactly," Jed said with a self-deprecating grin. He turned back to Nisha. "You've looked over all the intel?"

"I have," Nisha said. "As well as the conference schedules and the layout of the city on this side of the bay. We know that Zhao Xiang will be at the convention center across the street for most of the time. We also know that the CCP are highly protective of this scientist and might suspect Zhao is becoming dissatisfied. He will be under heavy surveillance and likely will have both overt and covert minders watching his every move. We also learned he's attending an unpublicized meeting, not at the convention center."

"Where is that meeting?" Eli asked, all business now.

"Here, at the Renaissance. Gayle believes that meeting will be in boardroom six on the mezzanine level."

"Why does she think that?" Jed asked.

"She didn't say, but she seemed pretty confident, which tells me she's leveraging a separate collection activity. That meeting is the day after tomorrow at 1100, right before a big luncheon scheduled over at the convention center."

"Is Zhao staying here at the hotel?" Jed asked hopefully.

Nisha shook her head and frowned. "No. We think his handlers have him squirreled away in a government facility on the mainland side."

"So they fight the traffic back and forth every day for the convention?" Eli said.

"We think so, but they're making it difficult to track his movements. Regardless, even if we figure out where he's staying—and we likely won't—the odds of snatching him from whatever secure location they're holding him in are low," Nisha said.

"That means we're forced to take him here in Hong Kong at the convention center," Eli said.

Nisha nodded and opened a satellite view of the surrounding area on a tablet computer. Jed noted the Grand Hyatt Hong Kong just to their west. The Hong Kong Convention and Exhibition Centre, which to Jed looked like an enormous spaceship, was located across the green space overpass spanning the Central–Wan Chai Bypass tunnel. Two large helipads sat just beyond the northeast corner of the ultramodern structure, beyond Golden Bauhinia Square along Victoria Harbour.

"We have a few options," she said, "all of them with their own unique challenges and potential advantages. One benefit of an operation to snatch him at the convention center is they expect thousands of people from all over the world at the convention, so there's the advantage of chaos we can create and the confusion that could help us get away. The flip side, of course, is that we would expect him to be in a large group, which will include plenty of armed Chinese agents from Second Bureau—the short name for the Joint Staff Department of the Central Military Commission Intelligence Bureau, which is their DIA equivalent."

Eli let a breath whistle out through his teeth. "On the other hand, the meeting here is small and probably a bit easier to breach. Getting him covertly out of the building, however, that's a different matter . . ."

"What are the other choices?" Jed asked, feeling the likelihood of success dwindling the longer they talked.

"Well, one choice would be to get him en route, between sites, on his way to the convention. The problem is, we don't know his schedule. I mean, we know when he's speaking, but we have no idea where he'll be coming from. He might helo in and we could take him between the helipads and the convention center, or he could come by car, but they're not going to tell us that."

"But we know he's here, day after tomorrow at 1100," Eli pointed out.

Nisha nodded.

"And that he'll then go to the convention center for his 1330 meeting from here. My guess is he would make that journey by foot. It's only a distance of about a hundred and fifty yards."

"Yes, but heavy security and surveillance at every point in between."

Jed sighed, leaned back in his chair, and scrubbed his face. It would seem he'd volunteered them for a job that was a true mission impossible. "This sucks," he said simply.

Nisha shot a glance at Bex, who smiled and nodded. "We did have one other idea that might be an option, thanks to Bex's combat medic brain."

"Which is?" Jed sat up, his hope renewed.

"Before I tell you, I need to lead with a disclaimer that this idea would require some for-real James Bond level orchestration, Jed."

"So something totally out of my wheelhouse, you're saying?"

"Not totally," she said with a laugh.

"I'm listening," Jed said, realizing she'd piqued his curiosity.

As Nisha pitched the plan, a smile spread across his face. Joshua Bravo was truly the most innovative team he'd ever operated with. Despite the obstacles, he felt confident they were going to pull this off . . . but first, a call to Ben was in order. For all its audaciousness, Nisha's operation came with one big caveat—she was going to need to call in a favor from her past and pull in resources from outside both the CIA and Trinity.

CHAPTER FIFTEEN

Butterflies in her stomach, Sarah Beth raised her fist to knock on the white door at the end of the hallway. This door stood in stark contrast to all others with their dark-stained, lacquered finish. The White Room, as everyone called it, was a closely guarded mystery in a school full of mysteries. Despite pressing her fellow classmates for details, Sarah Beth had yet to find anyone who knew what was inside.

But now she was standing at the threshold, about to have one of the school's most tantalizing secrets revealed to her.

The door clicked and swung open a split second before her knuckles could make contact, and she whiffed in the air.

"Hi," Corbin Worth said, grinning in the doorway.

"Hi," Sarah Beth said, fangirling a little despite herself. She idolized the upperclassman who was the undisputed rock star Watcher at St. George's Academy.

"It's good to see you, Sarah Beth," Corbin said, moving to the side to make room for her to enter.

"You too," she said, hating the giddiness in her voice. She stepped through a cased opening into a windowless room with a white marble tile floor, stark white walls, and a small white sofa along the opposite wall.

Corbin shut the door behind her. "Are you doing okay? Do you like your roommates and classes so far?"

"Yeah, they're nice; it's all good," she said, distracted by the overwhelming disappointment she was feeling. "So . . . this is it? *This* is the White Room?"

"Yes and no," Corbin said with a chuckle. "You'll see . . ."

Sarah Beth scanned the spartan space for another door but there wasn't one. *Strange.* It was as if Corbin had been waiting for her inside what was basically a glorified closet. Then suddenly she felt her insides get heavy. A wave of vertigo washed over her as she tried to make sense of the pronounced gravity she was experiencing.

"What in the world?" she said through a breath. "Are we in some kind of elevator?"

"Yep. Weird, isn't it?" Corbin said. "We're going up by the way."

"Freaky," she said, getting her bearings just as the *elevator* came to a halt. "Hold on a minute—what's below us now?"

Corbin grinned. "An identical waiting room attached to the lift below this one."

"So any students that try to sneak a peek will just see the same little white room as this one and be none the wiser?"

"Exactly."

"Very cool."

"If you think that's cool, then wait till you see this," Corbin said, stepping past her to push open a white door identical to the one Sarah Beth had walked through on the ground level.

Sarah Beth's eyes went wide as she scanned the magnificent space beyond—a large and beautifully appointed rotunda with the most impressive stained-glass dome ceiling she'd ever seen. As she stepped into the circular room, her gaze automatically went up to where a white dove—with wings a dozen feet wide—soared against a background of blue.

"The symbol of the Watchers," Corbin said. "Our symbol . . ."

Gooseflesh stood up on Sarah Beth's forearms and she felt a profound sense of peace and tranquility wash over her.

"What do you think?" a familiar adult voice said, drawing Sarah Beth's gaze back down. Pastor Dee was approaching from the opposite side of the room.

"It's incredible," she said, sweeping her gaze over an outer ring of ornate columns and biblical paintings before finally settling on the ten-foot-tall fountain gurgling in the middle of the room.

"I thought you'd like it here," Pastor Dee said with her trademark easy smile.

"What is this place?" Sarah Beth asked.

"It's our Sanctuary—not like the sanctuary in the campus chapel, but in the practical sense, if you know what I mean," Corbin said.

Pastor Dee laid her hand on Sarah Beth's shoulder. "The school's founder was very intentional about wanting a safe and tranquil place for students to train, pray, and connect with other Watchers around the world."

"Then why are we the only ones here?" she asked.

"The Sanctuary is not a break room or common space, Sarah Beth," Pastor Dee said. "This is a special place intended for intense meditation, prayer, and learning. Only a select group of students, like Corbin and yourself, are given access privileges."

Sarah Beth nodded. "How many students are allowed?"

"At present, less than a dozen," Pastor Dee said. "That surprises you?"

"Yeah," she said, feeling suddenly light-headed. "I know I'm advanced for my grade, but I assumed everyone else could do what I'm doing by the time they were in high school. I mean, that's how it works, right?"

Corbin and Pastor Dee shared a look.

"I wish that were true, sweetie," Pastor Dee said, "but that's not the case. Ninety-five percent of the students in this school will never develop the skills you and Corbin have."

"Then why even have a school in the first place?" Sarah Beth said, feeling as if the ground beneath her feet were swaying. "Are you saying St. George's

Academy is nothing more than a screening tool—like, to find diamonds in the rough?"

"The fact that you'd even think such a thing is upsetting," Pastor Dee said. "We are one of the top private Christian schools in the entire world. Our charter is to protect, educate, and develop our students—*in that order*."

"I'm sorry," Sarah Beth said. "I didn't mean to offend you. I know it's a great school. I was just . . . I don't know, surprised. I thought when I came here, I would finally fit in. I thought all the kids here would be like me. But instead, I still feel like a freak."

Pastor Dee's eyes softened, and she gave Sarah Beth a hug before saying, "First of all, you're not a freak, and I never want to hear you say that again. But also, every student here *is* like you. They all have gifts, and even though you are more capable than the average student, that does not diminish their contribution or their worth. Remember Paul describing the body of Christ and how every single part is important for the whole body to work? The same is true here. Alone, one young Watcher with limited mastery of his or her individual skills is vulnerable and weak against the Dark Ones. But together, the student body is very powerful, as promised by Jesus in Matthew 18. Remember the metaphor of the bundle of sticks—it's easy to snap a single twig, but put a dozen twigs into a bundle and together they are unbreakable. This is the power and purpose of St. George's. Every student, whether they realize it or not, amplifies and augments every other student's gifts."

"There is a force multiplier effect when we're all together," Corbin said.

"Makes sense," Sarah Beth said, her gaze suddenly drawn to the fountain in the middle of the room, where a sculpture of St. George slaying a slithering dragon—marble and bronze, wet and glistening—rose from a pool of gurgling water jets. Water sounds echoed off the dome, creating a soothing and natural cadence . . . like a babbling brook in a forest. Encircling the fountain, a ring of comfortable-looking sofas and recliner chairs faced inward, each with a dedicated side table.

Oh yeah, I'm definitely going to be spending lots of time here.

Pastor Dee glanced at her watch. "We have about forty-five minutes before dinner, so if you're up for it, we can start your first lesson."

"Okay, sounds good."

Corbin smiled and gestured for Sarah Beth to join her on one of the sofas. Pastor Dee sat opposite them on an ottoman, leaning in, elbows on knees.

"You've already demonstrated a gift for locating. You and I have done it together, but you've also done it alone," Corbin said.

She nodded again.

"So far, and correct me if I'm wrong, you've only been able to locate those people with whom you have a strong connection. Like Jedidiah and your mom. Is that correct?"

She pursed her lips and bobbed her head from side to side. "Yes and no. During the Vatican attack, I had a lucid dream . . . I felt like I was there with the Dark Ones in the Ethiopian College on the Vatican grounds."

"Okay, that's sort of a different skill—more advanced but related," Corbin said. "If you can master locating, then we'll work on projecting next."

"Oh, so that's what it's called," Sarah Beth said, excited to hear that what she'd experienced was more than just being trapped halfway between being asleep and awake, which was sort of what it had felt like.

"Yep, projecting is very cool. But we're getting ahead of ourselves. First, we need you to master locating. It's, like, the foundation of what we do."

"Got it."

"So why don't you lean back, close your eyes, and relax. I'm going to be talking to you the whole time, but I'm *not* going to pop into your headspace because I don't want the amplification effect. It's important that you can find the threads yourself and follow them without my help. There are going to be times when you're alone and under pressure and you need to be able to use your skills without it."

"I understand." Sarah Beth thought a moment about telling Corbin she had followed threads several times on her own already. She glanced over at Pastor Dee, who was smiling patiently at them, and decided that she would wait.

"I want you to try to find your roommates," Corbin said. "Remind me of their names."

"Darilyn and Elizabeth."

"Okay, I want you to try to find Darilyn first. Reach out and look for her thread."

Sarah Beth closed her eyes, inhaled through her nose, held the breath, and then exhaled to relax and center herself. In the background, she heard the gurgling of the fountain and let herself float in her mind and . . . nothing. No threads.

Irritated, she sighed.

"What's wrong?" Corbin said.

"I can't find her. In fact, I don't find any threads."

"Just try to relax."

"I am relaxed," she said and opened her eyes. "I think that might be the problem, actually."

"What do you mean?"

"Well, it seems like the times when I need to find someone are when it's an emergency. Like if Uncle Jed's in danger, or my parents are in trouble, or something bad is about to happen. I think I'm only good at this when there's stress and urgency."

"Yeah, given your background . . . that totally makes sense." Corbin rubbed her temples and then looked at Pastor Dee. "Maybe with her, the Sanctuary is the wrong environment?"

"No, no, no," Sarah Beth said before Pastor Dee could answer. "I like it here. I was just, you know, talking. I can do it—I know I can." She shut her eyes. "Let's keep trying."

"All right," Corbin said. "Why don't you try picturing Darilyn's face. Sometimes that helps me."

"Okay," she said, imagining her roommate flashing one of her superior smiles.

"Any luck?"

"No . . . But she's on the soccer team, which means she's probably on her way from practice to our dorm room . . ."

She shuddered, felt an acceleration, and snapped into the main dormitory hallway for the middle school girls. A trio of familiar faces were heading her way, Darilyn walking in the middle of two other seventh graders, all dressed in their practice uniforms. Sarah Beth tried to move out of the way, but before she could, Darilyn walked right through her. She whirled, noting the wispy, iridescent thread trailing behind her roommate.

"I found her," she announced, victory in her voice.

That's cheating, Corbin said, suddenly standing beside her in the hall. *You projected, but the exercise was to find Darilyn's thread.*

Her thread's right there. How is it cheating? she fired back.

Projecting and locating are not the same thing, Corbin said. *You deduced she was going to be here because you're familiar with her schedule and you knew this was the route she'd take.*

So what? I call that problem-solving.

And I call that knowing the answer and working backward to prove it, Corbin said. *But in the real world, 99 percent of the time you're not going to know the schedule and location of the person you've been tasked to locate. That's the whole point of the exercise.*

But that's like trying to find a needle in a haystack, Sarah Beth said, deflating.

Exactly! Corbin said. *Now you're catching on.*

By the way, I thought you said you weren't going to pop into my headspace, she quipped.

This isn't your *headspace. This is the hallway.*

Ah, she said with a laugh and opened her eyes to snap back into the Sanctuary. "I'll keep that in mind."

"You're going to need to master this skill, Sarah Beth. Locating is one of the most important things we do," Corbin said, meeting her eyes. "So let's go again?"

Sarah Beth nodded.

"Now, I want you to find your other roommate, Elizabeth, but this time no cheating . . ."

CHAPTER SIXTEEN

Maria pulled into the abandoned parking lot outside the dilapidated warehouse and wondered if she'd driven to the correct address. She left the engine running, transmission in drive and foot on the brake, while she scanned the property for signs of life. The building itself was windowless, save for a small, dark porthole in the metal door next to the loading bays. Knee-high weeds chased the perimeter chain-link fence, and a pile of discarded wooden shipping pallets formed a haphazard and unsightly rubbish heap off to the side of the entrance. The gate had been hanging open upon her arrival, a rusty chain and unclasped padlock dangling from the crossbar.

"Hmm," she murmured, fetching the hand-scrawled address on the slip of paper in her armrest cup holder and checking against the one she'd entered in the navigation app on her phone. "Looks like this is the right place."

With an annoyed exhale, she shifted the transmission into park, turned off the engine, and climbed out of her car. Her right wrist brushed against the Glock 23 she wore holstered on her hip. *There's nothing to be afraid of,* she told herself, but fear gripped her regardless. Despite its abandoned appearance, this place felt intrusive and ominous. She steeled herself with a deep breath, put on her *I'm a cop, so don't mess with me* face, and marched to the half flight of concrete stairs that led up to the building's only door.

A low-slung shadow darted across the loading dock right in front of her.

She gasped and belatedly pulled her weapon. Heart racing, she scanned over her pistol until her gaze met a pair of neon-yellow cat eyes staring back at her from a safe distance at the corner by the third bay.

"Nasty little thing," she said to it.

It hissed at her, then disappeared around the corner.

She hated black cats . . .

Feeling like an idiot, she holstered her weapon, took the stairs, and walked up to the door. If Victor had asked her here, it wasn't to kill her, right? He could do that anywhere, using his legion of Dark Ones.

Or kill me from inside my head or make me crash my car, even shoot myself.

The thought was not particularly reassuring. She peered in the little square window at head height but saw nothing except darkness. Either the facility was pitch-black inside or the window had been painted over. She quickly looked for a call box and, not finding anything of the sort, tried the handle, which was locked. Exasperation mounting, she scanned the eaves for under-mounted security cameras. Finding one overhead just a few feet to her left, she swiveled and stared directly into the dark iris looking down at her. After several long seconds, she heard a click. She gave the camera a two-finger salute and tried the door and this time found it compliant. The stout-looking door swung open more easily than she expected, and she lost her grip on the handle but caught it before it slammed into the metal stair railing.

Closing the door behind her, she entered an empty front office lit by a single lamp on the corner of a worn metal desk. With a backward glance, she confirmed her initial hunch that the window was painted over. The spartan office looked like it had once served as the reception area for an auto parts business, as time-yellowed posters for Callahan brake pads, spark plugs, and other products hung on the wall.

She pursed her lips.

Enough of your games, Victor. Why did you summon me here?

The lone door on the far wall of the office opened and a very large man dressed in cargo pants and a tight black T-shirt stood in the doorway.

"Detective Perez?" he asked, his voice low and husky.

"Yes," she said, meeting his intimidating gaze.

"This way." He turned to lead her inside.

To her utter surprise, the inside of the facility was both brightly lit and buzzing with activity. Every square inch of the walls and ceiling was covered by what looked like a thick layer of foil-backed insulation. The effect was dizzying, as the reflective amplification of the overhead halogen lights made her feel like she was trapped inside a mirror ball. She blinked twice, letting her eyes adjust to the light, and then took in the rest of the hive-like scene as a small army of operator types milled about. A half-dozen black APVs—ominous-looking armored vehicles that looked like something from metro PD's SWAT unit—sat parked in pairs in three columns. With their faceted, geometric armor panels and sharp angular features, the assault vehicles looked like the unlikely offspring of a stealth fighter and a Humvee.

"Detective Perez," a familiar, oily voice said behind her. "Welcome. We've been waiting for you."

She turned to find Victor walking silently up behind her. In the stark and bright illumination, she saw him more clearly than she ever had before, and it made her shudder inside. His skin had an unnatural green-gray pallor—as if she saw him in night vision. Like a sheet of wax paper, the skin of his face shone smooth, wrinkle-free, and barely hid the network of veins snaking every which way beneath the surface. His taut lips were the color of a two-day-old bruise and the teeth behind were gray and cracked like aged driftwood. His long, greasy black hair hung in strands, more like jellyfish tendrils than hair, and she could see his scalp in between them. He was, without a doubt, the most repugnant and grotesque human being she'd ever had the misfortune to gaze upon. And yet his eyes . . .

His eyes were beautiful.

Hypnotic.

Twin rings of fire, dancing around obsidian disks as black as the depths of space.

"What is this place?" she said, breaking eye contact and shaking herself from his trance.

The big operator who'd escorted her, who now stood at Victor's side, chuckled at her question.

"Leave us," Victor said with a sideways glance at the man, his voice a serpent's hiss. The operator nodded and walked away without a word. "This is Dark Horizon's Nashville staging facility."

"If I didn't know better, I'd say it looks like you're preparing for war," she said, sweeping her gaze across the cavernous space.

"It appears you don't . . . ," Victor said, curling his thin bloodless lips, ". . . know better. But then, aren't we always at war, my dear?"

She kept her expression neutral, but the comment made her heart skip a beat. Rather than explain, he motioned for her to follow him. He led her past the row of armored assault vehicles, which she saw were parked in line with the loading bay doors, ready to roll at a moment's notice. Beyond the APVs, she saw a strange-looking device, about the size of a refrigerator, sitting on a shipping pallet. Beside the odd machine sat a half-dozen shipping crates about the same size—additional devices? she wondered. Four support legs held the body of the contraption off the ground. On the underbelly, a satellite-looking dish pointed downward, and above it, exposed wires, stainless steel tubing, and heat-radiating fins protruded from all sorts of places. It reminded her of the death ray from the movie *Megamind* and she was about to joke as much when he read her thoughts.

"That's exactly what it is," he said, turning to her.

She chuckled uncomfortably, but when he didn't react, she said, "You're serious?"

He nodded. "It is a directed energy weapon that incinerates the target from the inside out. We call it the Wrath of God."

"Who are you planning to use this on?" she asked, shaken to the core that such a thing existed.

"Whomever we choose," he said with a disturbing closed-lip smile.

Like Sarah Beth Yarnell, she thought and imagined the girl outside playing on a playground and then erupting into flames.

"She is certainly very high on the list," he said. "Since our other efforts to reach her have so far failed." Her blood ran cold at the words, but there was no more malice than ususal in Victor's gaze. "We have multiple operations underway, but then we are more than capable of keeping more than one ball in the air. The girl is a nuisance but also a threat to the damage we plan to do to the faithful with our new weapon. She must be dealt with, and if your ongoing efforts continue to bear no fruit, alternatives must be found. The use of our weapon on the girl would easily bring success where you failed, but it might also limit our ability to use it for our primary objective. Our attack with this weapon will shake the faith of many, will show God as having turned His back on America and its people. Those who believe will question; those who don't will scoff at the notion of a loving God. Souls will belong to our master. The girl puts that important operation at risk, but using our weapon on her may jeopardize it as much or more. So you see my dilemma?"

Maria felt her mouth go dry. Perhaps she was here to meet her end after all?

"Is it a satellite?" she asked, trying to appear calm, then trotting to catch up with him as he turned and continued to stroll.

"No," he said, offering no other insights.

He led her to what looked like an Army command field tent pitched inside the warehouse. Black electrical wiring and colored data cables snaked across the floor and disappeared underneath the fabric panels, presumably powering workstations and lights. She followed him inside through the pinned-back door flap and found it configured like a tactical operations center with multiple computer workstations, flat-screen monitors mounted to vertical racks made from bolted-together aluminum poles. A large rectangular table sat in the middle of the tent, its surface covered with a half-dozen enlarged satellite pictures. Even from a distance, she could see that the imagery had been annotated in red and black pen, with names, perhaps, or times—she couldn't tell. The locations were all cities, but the only one she recognized with certainty was Chicago.

"Leave us," Victor said, dismissing the handful of people in the tent like she imagined one might shoo away noisy children disrupting the grown-up table at a family dinner.

Not that I'd know anything about family dinners . . .

Before leaving, they hid their work with thin plastic tarps. Victor walked to the opposite side of the now-covered war-gaming table, steepled his fingers, and looked at her expectantly.

"So you're planning an attack?" she said.

He nodded.

She could feel the pulse pounding in her temple and hear it in her ears—*shush . . . shush . . . shush.* They'd hidden the plans from her, and he'd not stopped them, which begged the question . . . *Why am I here?*

"Are you not one of my most trusted lieutenants?" he said, his voice tinged with judgment, although good or bad she could not tell.

"I . . . I hope so," she stammered.

"You hope so, or you know so?"

"I wouldn't want to be presumptuous . . . I'm just one of many, serving our Dark Prince."

He was at her side in a heartbeat, moving with supernatural speed. He grabbed her by the chin and tilted her face up to look at his, the long nails on his bony fingers digging into her cheeks.

"Look at us," he said, his voice a chorus.

She met his gaze of fire and ice and wondered if this was it for her. So far, she'd failed to deliver on her secret assignment to ensure the young Watcher's demise. Maybe he'd finally had enough. But what was she supposed to do? The Yarnell girl had stubbornly not left campus since he'd given her the tasking. Besides, these things took time, especially trying to seduce marks as capable and noble as Jedidiah Johnson.

"I sense a waning of your commitment to the cause," he hissed.

When he didn't release his grip, she said, "No, I assure you I'm fully committed. I believe I've had some breakthroughs. I'm making progress. Earning their trust."

"But you're hoping the burden of eliminating the child will be lifted from you?" he said. She could feel him inside her, his presence nauseating. "You find it distasteful. You want someone else to do it . . ."

"A part of me, yes," she said, knowing that lying to him was pointless. "I was never comfortable with the assignment. She's only a child, after all."

"Pffft—ignore the vessel. She's a warrior, not a child." His eyes narrowing to slits, he added, "Empathy is the weapon of the enemy. Promise us you'll never forget that, Maria."

"I promise," she said and felt her legs trembling beneath her.

He released his grip on her face. "The time has come to escalate. Plans are already underway, as you can see. You still have a role to play in the girl's demise, and your service will be rewarded."

She felt a tear chasing down her cheek and slip over her jawline . . . Strange, because she hadn't felt herself tearing up.

She touched her cheek with her fingertips, and they came away with a crimson smear.

"Oh, look what we've done," Victor said, smiling without apology.

She cast her eyes down and said nothing.

"Now," he said, turning and pacing away. "Let's talk about your role in the upcoming operation . . ."

"Okay," she said, wondering if he was planning an attack against Trinity Loop. Or maybe St. George's was the target? Or something larger, like the White House? She glanced at the crates, wondering how many weapons Victor possessed. How many targets could he strike simultaneously? She shook the thoughts off. He would tell her what she needed to know and nothing more.

"I sense a new threat rising—one I thought we had cast aside years ago," he said. "You must deal with her. Keep her distracted so that we might complete the task you've failed to accomplish."

It was not lost on her that he had not answered her question.

"Rachel?" she asked, her detective's mind putting the pieces together.

"Very good," he hissed. "Unless, of course, this small task is also beyond your capability. We would hate to make you *uncomfortable*."

"No, I can do it. She trusts me," she said, hoping beyond hope that was true. "But as you know, she lives on the Trinity campus now. She's surrounded by Shepherds."

"Don't worry, we have a plan for them."

"And the children?" she pressed, desperately needing to understand his endgame. "They're always watching."

"Yes," Victor said, his voice the sound of many. "Which is why we have been gathering . . . gathering . . . gathering . . . until we are ready to challenge them all. When we are done, the remaining faithful in America will believe themselves abandoned by God, and in the wake of our victory, we will deal with the girl and her friends."

CHAPTER SEVENTEEN

Jed moved about the room with a stern and suspicious look on his face and tried desperately not to make eye contact with the two Chinese men dressed in suits who were standing by the window. Nisha had told him that if he had to speak, he should speak English and use a thick Russian or German accent—whichever he thought he could pull off best. He'd decided on German, leaving the fake Russian accent for Grayson. As a door-kicking SEAL, he'd perfected neither, nor any other spooky, NOC-related acting skills. But on one deployment to Iraq he'd worked closely with German special forces operators from KSK Rapid Forces Division and thought he could reproduce the accent he'd heard every day for four months. He'd never had to act like anything other than an operator when he'd come through a door. Scaling down to civilian clothes on a few operations in the Baltics was as close to James Bond as he'd ever come.

"*Nì zài shéi de bâohu duì?*" one of the Chinese men said.

Jed looked up from where he was inspecting the back side of a credenza beneath a large flat-screen TV monitor on the wall and frowned at the man. His cover was that he was acting as private security for one of the German scientists who been a late addition to the conference roster. In reality, Jed knew next to nothing about his charge—or even if he was a member of the spooky team that arrived early this morning compliments of Nisha. The Chinese were notorious for bugging hotel and conference rooms, which made it within his rights as a supposed contract security specialist to insist on sweeping the room in advance of the meeting. The Chinese security contingent had agreed—provided they were allowed to supervise his inspection.

"I don't speak Chinese," Jed said in English flavored with what he felt like was the worst German accent ever.

"I asked whose protection detail you are on," the Chinese man replied in flawless, virtually unaccented English.

"I am German, so obviously I protect Dr. Weider and the rest of the German contingent," he growled. "Now let me do my job, *danke.*"

The Chinese agent glared at him, then turned to his smaller but equally menacing partner and said, *"Yúchûn de wàiguó rén,"* with a chuckle.

"They think you're stupid," Nisha said in his earpiece and Jed could practically hear the smile in her voice. "We have facial recognition on the bigger guy from the database. He's PLA Unit 61486. They're tasked with stealing military trade secrets from the West, so his presence is not related to Zhao's security. The other guy didn't return a hit. If you find any of their bugs, leave them in play. We wouldn't want to dissuade them of your stupidity."

Jed resisted the urge to reply. The irony of the situation was not lost on him—pretending to sweep for devices while he was in fact planting bugs of his own. Feeling very much like James Bond, he delicately placed the tiny camera—no bigger than a sesame seed—onto the right top corner of the room's wall-mounted flat-panel TV, just as Nisha had instructed.

After that, he made a show of running a hand along the under edge of the beautiful dark-wood table, then squatted down to inspect the underside. When he returned to his feet, the two men were whispering and smiling again, no doubt at his expense. Instead of retreating at the discomfort he felt, he headed directly toward the men standing beside the large window overlooking the bay. The smaller man crossed his arms on his chest and refused to let Jed pass.

Jed sighed.

"We are three men doing our jobs, *ja?*" he said, feeling his accent improving as he spoke. "My job is to keep my client safe. I know you have hidden cameras and microphones in this room. I will never find them all. That is okay, because my job is safety and security, not counterintelligence. I search for bombs and poisons. Move so I am doing my job, *bitte.*"

The larger man nodded to his colleague, who uncrossed his arms and moved from the window. Jed made a show of checking behind the curtains and along the windows. Then he pulled compact binoculars from his coat and scanned the area north of the Renaissance hotel, toward the convention center, searching for spotters and possible sniper hides.

"These curtains will be closed, *ja?*"

"Yes," the Chinese man in charge answered. "It is very secure. You have my word."

"*Tài gànxièle,*" Jed said with a deep nod, butchering the Chinese words of thanks intentionally—though it wasn't a huge stretch. He left the conference room, shutting the door behind him. In the hall, he nodded to two uniformed Chinese soldiers who were flanking the door before striding off.

"Great job," said an unfamiliar voice in his ear. Jed assumed it belonged to "John," the team leader for the spooky contractors assisting them for the snatch and grab. With Ben's authorization, Nisha had pulled the team together using contacts from her past life. She'd been weirdly secretive about the whole thing, communicating with Ben directly. Jed had asked John, the only team member he'd actually met, which group in the IC they were with. The man had simply laughed at the question and winked at Nisha.

"That's a story for another time, Jed," she'd said.

Jed took the stairs up the three flights to the fourth floor and resisted, again with great difficulty, the urge to look in both directions before unlocking the room with his pass card. He'd been assured that the Chinese were watching with cameras everywhere they went, so there was no point in acting suspicious. Outside of their hotel room, his every move was being watched, so the key, Nisha had said, was to behave in ways most authentic to their NOC. Jed entered his hotel room and passed through the connecting door into Nisha and Bex's room—which was serving as a miniature TOC with multiple laptop computers set up as workstations.

"You're sure we're good to talk?" he asked, looking at Nisha instead of John.

John answered regardless. "Yes, it's all good. The Chinese have capable technology, but ours is better, Senior Chief," the sandy-haired man—who looked more like a surfer than a spy—said with a grin.

"Please call me Jed," he grumbled, not sure why the spook was calling him by his Navy rank.

"Cool," John said.

Nisha took over. "What John meant to say is that we have jamming tech in service scrambling the Chinese microphones and cameras in our rooms. You can talk in the clear."

"Won't that look suspicious?" he asked, still unsure.

"It would almost look more suspicious if we *didn't* use it," Nisha said. "This physics conference is really about weapons technology and everyone knows it. There are numerous countries represented—both allies and adversaries of China—and they fully expect us to conduct countersurveillance. It would be a red flag if we didn't."

"That's it, bro," John said and hiked a thumb at Nisha. "Like Lime Seltzer said."

"You know I hate when you call me that," Nisha said but laughed good-naturedly at the inside joke. Jed felt confused by what seemed almost like jealousy flashing inside him. He shook the feeling off and leaned in over Nisha's shoulder at the console. There were video feeds from both directions in the hallway leading to the conference rooms on the mezzanine level, one from a camera facing outward from the lobby level north door out onto the park separating the Renaissance hotel from the Hong Kong Convention and Exhibition Centre, and another in the upper left corner. That image was a fish-eye lens view of the conference room he'd just left. The two Chinese agents appeared to be having a collegial conversation with none other than Grayson, his Shepherds teammate and former Army SF operator.

"Audio?" John asked and Nisha typed a command into the computer in front of her.

"How come they don't jam our signals?" Jed asked.

"They don't need to," Nisha said. "Not in there. It's assumed everyone is listening, and anyway there are principals in the room who will report back everything discussed, so what would be the point? They have plenty of signal jamming going on, most of it we detected on the seventh and eighth floors, and the entire St. Regis hotel is a SIGINT black hole."

"Here's something you probably didn't know about Nisha, Senior," John said. "There's no one in the business better at snatching people out of foreign countries—whether defectors or those who are, let's say, less excited about their travel plans."

One surprise after another here in the Shepherds.

Whoever Nisha had been before, he was grateful she was running the show now.

"What's he saying?" Jed asked, satisfied, nodding at the computer where the audio continued to stream.

"They're just chatting. Grayson's supposed to be the Russian security head protecting Dr. Vinchenko. The Chinese and Russians are buds, for the most part. It would be like us in a room with guys from MI6. Plenty more trust than they had with the German security detail."

Jed nodded, happy he'd chosen the German NOC.

He watched Grayson laugh, then wave and leave.

The Chinese agents remained, pacing casually back and forth by the window. Jed glanced at his watch—ten more minutes and the principals for the meeting would begin to arrive. The door on the left of the screen opened again and two new Chinese men, both clad in black pants and vests, with bow ties at the necks of their starched white shirts, came in pushing a large silver cart.

"Those waiters are our boys," John said, rubbing his hands in satisfaction.

Jed watched as the two men went to work, spreading out a buffet of fruit as well as meats and cheeses on the credenza, which looked weirdly bowed in the fish-eye image at the bottom of his screen, their heads getting impossibly big and their legs tiny as they came close to the camera. Then one peeled off and began to set up a station of coffee, tea, and sodas beside the door while the other set water glasses and several pitchers of water on the long table surrounded by high-back black leather chairs.

Despite not being in the room, Jed's nerves were on edge. The plan was to drug the Chinese scientist and create a medical emergency and pretext for getting him out of the conference. Snatching him from his handlers and exfiltrating him in the aftermath was going to be the *Mission: Impossible* part of the job.

"Why not just put the compound in a prefilled water glass ahead of time?" Jed asked.

"Can't be sure where our guy will sit," John said. "Don't want some dude from France dropping unconscious instead. Besides, it's much harder to see or taste the compound in tea or coffee."

"What if he doesn't have tea coffee or tea?" Jed pressed.

"Then we'll adapt and overcome," Nisha said, her face a bit exasperated. "Jed, just relax. This is what we do—what I *used* to do. Our job is to make sure he drops. Your job is to catch him."

"And that's all set up?"

"Yes," Nisha reassured him, smiling now. "Hyeon is standing by with two of John's contractors and we have the ambulances ready to go, including Bex. Johnny and Carl are in position in the escort vehicles and we'll fall in on them. It's all good, Jed."

He nodded.

In his experience, it was never "all good," and surprises and failures were the rule, not the exception.

No good plan survives first contact with the enemy.

It seemed like absolute precision and predictability would be required to pull this off, but this was no movie and he was no Ethan Hunt.

"What if he doesn't drop on the walk over? What if the drug works too fast or too slow and jacks up the timing?"

"We can move the medical team in from their position to the hotel or into the convention center if needed. There's a legit medical team at the convention center that we have infiltrated, and we have a girl in the nurse's office here in the hotel. It will complicate the exfil, but we can still make it work."

"Nisha's the best in the business, Jed." John squeezed his shoulder. "Relax, bro."

Jed nodded, but the overstepping gesture from the smiling spook in chinos and a sport shirt made him feel even more the third wheel. Being told to relax by this dude he didn't know, who would be safe and secure in the hotel suite while Jed was in the field, was starting to irritate him. He tapped his left ear, the pressure wave activating the micro earbud into VOX mode.

"Joshua Six, One—sitrep?"

"In position with Five. All good here. Angel Three and Four are with us, by the way," Hyeon replied, referring to the two Chinese operatives from John's med team in the ambulance with him and Bex.

Jed had no idea if those dudes were managed local assets, double agents working for the CIA, or simply contractors of Chinese American descent working for whatever deep, dark task force John came from. The cocky spook hadn't seen fit to read him in on the details, and neither had Nisha.

"Roger that," Jed said. "Just keep doing what you're doing and try to blend in."

"For the record, you guys do know that I'm Korean, not Chinese, right?" Hyeon came back.

Jed chuckled and shook his head. Hyeon had brought that up more than once since landing in Hong Kong. "No one's asking you to speak Mandarin, bro," Jed replied before John could steal his thunder.

"In that case, we're all set," Hyeon said. "You get the target to the park and we'll do the rest."

"Check."

Easier said than done.

Jed looked at his watch.

He was supposed to meet his principal, Dr. Weider, down in the lobby and escort him to the meeting in five minutes. Despite repeated asks, John had refused to confirm for Jed whether the man was the actual physicist drafted as an unwitting pawn in their little spy game or a spook disguised as the man. The ambiguity of this op was driving Jed crazy.

So many moving parts.

So much to go wrong.

That's why I became an operator, he thought and realized he'd give anything to be fast-roping in on a Taliban stronghold in the Hindu Kush instead of this.

"All right, it's showtime," he said with a nod to Nisha as he headed for the door. "See you soon."

"You'll do great," she said and flashed him that little lip-curl thing she did. "And I'll be watching you the whole time."

CHAPTER EIGHTEEN

Gayle pursed her lips, hating the role she was being forced to play. She felt frustrated, alone, and her nerves were making her neurotic.

Congratulations—you're a spy, her inner comedian chimed in.

She shifted the phone from her left ear to her right.

"There's *nothing* else you can share?" Nisha asked on the heavily encrypted line.

"Not at present," Gayle said into the receiver. "But we have eyes up. Are you streaming?"

"Yeah," Nisha said. "We're monitoring what you're sharing—satellite feed from the looks of it—but we can't reposition, zoom in or out, or toggle between optical and thermal. You have us limited to about a square mile around the op site."

"I know and I'm sorry about that, but I can't transfer control," Gayle said and meant it. "I'll start mixing things up, but tell me what you need to see, and I'll make it happen on the exfil."

"Yep," Nisha said, not happy with the answer from the tone of her voice. "Our team is moving in now to the meeting, so we're looking at an hour at least—probably more—before they move."

Gayle knew Trinity had staffed the op through one of the IC's myriad of special task force units, but even Steve hadn't been able to determine which one. She had a sketch from Nisha and Jed on how they intended to move the "package" but no idea how they planned to secure it.

"I'm going to hang up now unless you're offering something," Nisha said, ready to shut down this sidebar conversation, which was taking place off the party line from the rest of the team.

"Nothing at the moment."

"Roger that," Nisha said and the line went dead.

Gayle didn't know which of the supersecret task forces Nisha used to work for, but the way the woman was managing the op so far definitely made a statement: *We have no expectation of getting help from the CIA, nor do we need it.* Perhaps, in Nisha's previous life, she'd been burned by the rice bowl politics, a practice still prevalent in the intelligence community—especially the CIA.

And if it's not that, then maybe it's because I'm over here asking for updates with a nice safe offset and plausible deniability while she takes all the risk.

Gayle left her micro earpiece in its case and put on the headset instead, plugging it into the USB port of her laptop. Then she tapped on the comms icon at the bottom of the screen, opening the program, and clicked on the frequency bar she'd labeled Team 1—which was the augmented Shepherds team. The bar labeled Team 2 was a separate circuit—comms with the CIA team hiding in the shadows to whisk her out of Hong Kong if things went bad. Steve had been explicit that the Shepherds would be left to fend for themselves if the Chinese got involved, but Gayle wasn't sure if she would be able to go along with that . . .

It was an order she'd struggled with since arriving last night.

"Joshua Actual, Mother—how copy?" Gayle said, making her presence known on the comms circuit for the first time. For this operation her call sign was Mother, but it didn't carry the weight it usually did. She wasn't running the show, and she wasn't authorized to intervene and save the day if things went south. Today she was "Mother" in name only.

"Five by, Mother," Nisha said. "One is in position and mute but can hear you."

"Mother, check." She zoomed the satellite feed onto the park between the Renaissance hotel and the convention center. Nothing jumped out at her as unusual. People milled about between the two. Cars passed beneath the park through the Central–Wan Chai Bypass tunnel. A helicopter sat static on the helipad at the northeast edge of the center, two additional pads empty beside it. There were the expected EMS and police vehicles in and around the center, but nothing out of the ordinary to her eye.

And I'm looking. So if I don't see what they have set up, hopefully that means neither do the Chinese.

"Good hunting, Joshua One."

She leaned back in the comfortable chair at the desk in her decadent corner suite. She couldn't see the convention center from here, but she could look across Victoria Harbour and the Kowloon business district across from them. Her corner room was all glass, and she let her gaze drift west, past Victoria Peak and across the north edge of the Lung Fu Shan Park. She stared pensively at Little Green Island and Green Island beyond, both easily visible from her high and luxurious perch.

It's like a mirage, she thought. *It all looks so normal . . . this city and harbor with its boats and buildings and busy people running about.*

"Except some of those people are demons," she murmured and shook her head.

Everything had happened so quickly after the trip up the mountain in Peru. It was like one day she was living one life, and then *bam*, she became someone else. The things she'd seen in that courtyard in Cuzco defied logic— like the man with glowing eyes who moved with supernatural speed and had the strength of three men. And instead of trying to convince her what she'd seen was a trick of the light or a hypoxic hallucination, her boss had put her in charge of it. The fact that the Shepherds organization existed at all was proof that what she'd seen was *reality.*

Good and evil were waging a war of souls, and she'd been drafted and sent to the front lines. And yet they still expected her to behave and function like a regular case officer. How was that supposed to work? Quite possibly the weirdest thing of all was that the CIA already knew about the Dark Ones and the Shepherds . . . just one more compartmentalized program.

What's next? she thought. *Aliens, vampires . . . magic?*

Her inner comedian instantly imagined her at lunch with Steve and him casually telling her over a ham sandwich that her next assignment would be to liaise with the monster hunters.

"And if you do well at that, Gayle," she said, imitating his voice, "you can expect a promotion to the magic department."

She chuckled, but the humor turned stale—like telling jokes at a funeral.

Because it's not a joke. The Dark Ones are real and so is this mission.

She looked back at her computer screen, and the nagging feeling of being powerless but in charge instantly returned. Her hands had been tied by the Agency, but she had a strong feeling that before this was over, the Shepherds were going to need her help. How and when she'd execute to deliver that help was still foggy in her mind, but she felt confident that when the time came, she'd know what to do.

Until then, she did the only other thing she could think of and said a prayer for her new friends' success and safety.

CHAPTER NINETEEN

Jed paced, his hands clasped in front of him and in position for a quick draw of the H&K pistol in his waistband. He felt almost no concern that he would need to use it—much less in any kind of quick-draw scenario—but it certainly completed the look of a burly bodyguard operator on mission. Unlike movies and TV, where the protection specialist stood at attention beside the door behind which his protectee worked, in real life it was far more effective to be on the move, blending in with crowds and making it hard to determine who was being protected. Once the package was on the move, then of course Jed became a show of force, but for now he paced the hallway and lobby of the mezzanine level, scanning groups of people, checking behind doors, placing himself between the conference room and people of concern.

Moving helped, he realized. Giving his body purpose seemed to acclimate his mind to the role.

"Okay, it's showtime," Nisha said in his ear. "The waitstaff are offering snacks and beverages."

He forced himself to resist the urge to mumble something in reply, instead peering out from the arched entrance to the mezzanine and lobby below.

"Our guy is taking orders now . . . coming to Zhao in just a second . . . Okay, he's asking him what he wants . . ."

Jed smiled, on the inside at least, while maintaining the grim and stern face of the character he portrayed. *God bless Nisha.* Her running commentary was no doubt for his benefit, not spooky standard operating procedure. He wandered slowly down the hall toward conference room number six.

"Looks like Zhao has asked for coffee or tea—hard to hear him, but I think he said tea," she said.

Jed paced past the door, stealing a glance and then making a disappointed *tsk* sound. Whatever did or didn't happen on the other side of the door, he couldn't do anything about it. Two shorter but thick-looking bodyguards dressed in tan linen suits passed him walking the other way, scanning him up and down before giving the slight nod as they passed. The Venezuelan security team, he knew. Beyond them Grayson, posing as the Russian guard, stared at him and then gave a dismissive snort before looking away.

Perfect impersonation of a Russian operator, he thought. He stopped by the door and checked his watch, trying to look like someone trying not to look bored.

"Okay, the drug is in the tea with no flags up," Nisha continued. "Waitstaff are delivering it to him now."

Jed pictured the scene unfolding in his mind's eye, based on her play-by-play.

"Waiter put the cup in front of him, but Zhao is talking to the guy beside him . . ."

"He's making a joke," John added, irritating Jed for some reason.

"They're both laughing," Nisha said. In Jed's mind, Zhao was in the center of the screen across from the camera, his face distorted by the fish-eye lens, but he supposed he didn't really know where the man sat. "Zhao is at the head of the table, to the far left of my screen," Nisha said as if reading his mind. Possible, he supposed. If Nisha had any gifts, she'd not seen fit to share that with him.

He resumed pacing, deciding it was better not to look like someone receiving information via an earpiece and staring at the floor. But this time he walked slowly, away from the lobby and toward the two other conference rooms beyond number six. He stole a glance at Grayson, whose eyes flashed sympathy before scowling at him and setting off on his own stroll back toward the mezzanine lobby. Jed made a show of looking into the open door of another conference room, scanning for any threats—or so it would appear to anyone watching him.

"The target took a sip," Nisha said in his ear. "He's not making a funny face or anything, so I'm guessing he doesn't taste anything odd. . . . The Chinese security guys are by the window and seem unconcerned. Just took another sip . . . and he put the cup down. He's talking now. C'mon, buddy, drink up . . ."

"It's teatime, not a game of beer pong. He's not going to chug it," John said back with a chuckle. "Let's be patient. This is working out the way we intended."

"Our waiters are leaving the room . . ."

Jed turned and saw the doors to conference room six open and their two Chinese "waiters" exit, pushing an empty cart ahead of them. They passed Grayson and the Venezuelan bodyguards and disappeared around a corner.

"Zhao is reaching for the cup . . . took another sip . . ."

The wait was agonizing, made more so by his need to look completely unaware of what might be going on behind the door. He paced, listening to Nisha's diligent play-by-play while imagining it on the screen in his mind.

Check the lobby.

Another sip.

Back past the door, ignoring Grayson, who now scrolled on his cell phone as if receiving a message.

A sip. The cup pushed forward and away.

Check the stairs up from the lobby floor.

Another sip—no, it was aborted by the need to reply to something the Russian scientist asked. Okay, there's the sip.

Fifteen minutes went by in what felt like an hour.

The waiters returned.

Zhao's tea was refreshed—tea poured from a new carafe.

Sip.

Stare past the door.

Sip.

"They're packing up to leave," Nisha said in Jed's ear.

He barely cut himself off from asking the question, but she answered it in any case.

"He drank about half the cup, it looks like, but maybe got most of the drug, because they refilled it?"

"It'll be enough," John declared, but how could he know that?

The door opened and the shorter of the two Chinese security men stuck his head out. He called to Grayson, then gave Jed a curt nod. He waved his hand to the two Venezuelan goons, who laughed together, far more casual in their duties, from the dead end of the wall past the door.

All four of them arrived at the door, just as their various principals filed through, briefcases over shoulders, assistants shuffling behind them, and the heavily armed Chinese corralling them like goats from behind. Down the hall toward the mezzanine lobby, four green-uniformed soldiers stood with their arms crossed, waiting to escort Zhao.

This was it. Showtime.

The plan would either work or it wouldn't.

They would whisk Zhao away and he would tell the Shepherds everything they needed to know about the energy weapon.

Or the Chinese state police would intervene, and they'd be arrested and sent to a Chinese gulag for the rest of their lives.

Or perhaps they'd be shot dead in the park between the Renaissance hotel and the Hong Kong convention center.

The possibilities were endless.

CHAPTER TWENTY

Jed scanned the park for unexpected threats as the entire contingent of scientists, staff, and security from the morning meeting walked as a group over to the convention center. He kept his hands clasped in front of him within easy reach of the German Heckler & Koch VP9 pistol in an appendix holster along his waistband. To the east, across the green space, he saw two narrow high-top ambulances—*John's* ambulances. Evac via ambulance was the exfil plan, but looking at them now, he wondered if two EMS vehicles pulled right up to the park might look suspicious to the Chinese security detail. *Must not look too suspicious,* he thought, *because the police haven't interrogated the drivers yet.* And the police were here. He spied multiple police cars, parked in the east and west corners of the park. He also noted a multipurpose truck parked nearby—not exactly a SWAT vehicle, but close enough that he assumed it held a squad of paramilitary police inside.

Wonderful.

"Got eyes on you, One," said Hyeon, who was stationed inside ambulance one. "I hold Dr. Zhao toward the front of your group, flanked by four Chinese guards. He's walking pretty normal, Joshua Actual; you sure this drug is gonna work?"

Jed had been thinking the same thing. They'd succeeded in slipping the drug into Zhao's tea, but the man had not *finished* the cup. How could they be certain to what extent, and more importantly when, the drug would take effect? In just a couple of minutes, they would be at the stairs, descending to the convention center, and then it would be too late. Jed stepped in tighter next to his charge, the German scientist—or fake German scientist—Dr. Weider.

"Any second now," John said with his trademark, gratingly calm tone.

But Jed decided they couldn't take that chance. He needed to do something to buy them more time. Zhao had to drop during the walk over or the plan would fail. Thinking quickly, he stumbled into Grayson, who was walking with his charge just ahead. Grayson for his part stumbled and created a bigger commotion, causing the entire party to halt—looking every bit like the Keystone Cops, bumping into one another.

"What is this?" Jed called out tersely, aware he'd dropped the German accent. *Crap!* "Why are we stopping?" he asked, this time with an impressively authentic accent in place.

He put a hand on the arm of Dr. Weider and pulled him left, out of the crowd, as Grayson did the same with his own principal.

"All right, all right, guys, that's not necessary," John said in his ear, and he could picture him rubbing his hands together. "Zhao's going down."

"Someone is ill," a voice called from the crowd ahead.

The contingent fractured into smaller groups of two and three as security professionals pulled their principals clear. The uniformed Chinese soldiers were clustered around Zhao, who lay on his back in the grass, clutching his chest and moaning.

"He's having a heart attack," someone called out in heavily accented English. "We need an ambulance."

There was a burst of chatter and shouting in Chinese, which Jed couldn't understand.

Jed grabbed Dr. Weider by the arm, tugging him away from the group toward the west, but Weider jerked his arm free.

"*Was ist los?*" Weider shrieked, panic in his voice. "*Was machen sie?* They've poisoned him—they've killed Dr. Zhao!"

"*Kommen Sie mit uns,*" Jed demanded, telling Weider to come with him using the German phrase he'd memorized. "*Wir gehen. Jetzt!*" He tried again to reposition Weider, but the German scientist resisted him in a panic.

"I'm having heart attack," Weider screamed in broken English, pale-faced and clutching his chest. "They've poisoned us all."

And with that, Weider collapsed at Jed's feet.

"Emergency!" Jed shouted and waved at the two ambulances, noting that one of the Chinese soldiers had already started a fast jog toward the two stationary rigs. The blue lights came to life, and both ambulances accelerated in their direction. Grayson was already jogging west, headed for the edge of the park, his hand firm on the arm of his charge, free hand inside his jacket. Jed watched the pair intently, Grayson's head on a swivel, as the two ambulances tore across the grass in their direction.

Separated from the group of agents and soldiers crowded around Dr. Zhao, Jed took a knee beside Weider, who lay sprawled on the ground. The German's eyes were glazed beneath half-closed lids. His breaths came in punctuated, raspy gasps and beads of sweat speckled the man's forehead. Wondering if Weider might have been given the drug too, Jed checked for a pulse at the neck and found it strong and regular.

Someone behind him shouted in Chinese. "*Fashêngle shênme? Ta shòushangle ma?*"

Jed looked up, surprised to see that the sharp, crisp Chinese came from none other than Hyeon, who was decked out as a Hong Kong EMS first responder.

"No Chinese," Jed said, shaking his head. "English?"

"What happened to him?" Hyeon said, his accent thick and believable as he knelt beside the German and pulled a stethoscope from his bag.

"He collapsed," Jed said in English, reminding himself to keep the German accent thick but believable. He glanced over at the other group, relieved that none of the Chinese security were paying any attention to him, their full attention on Dr. Zhao, who was being treated by two other medics. "Food poisoning?"

He watched as Hyeon listened to the German's lungs and then took his blood pressure.

"He having a heart attack," Hyeon said, feigning broken English and motioning to a second man, who brought a stretcher over, jogging beside the wheeled device that bumped along the grass. "We treat him in ambulance. Must go to hospital fast."

Jed helped lift Weider onto the stretcher, taking his feet as Hyeon and the other "medic" lifted at the shoulders and head. Hyeon and his partner ran the stretcher toward the ambulance, which sat idling with the rear doors open. Jed glanced at Grayson, who still escorted his Russian scientist by the arm to the underpass below.

"Four is descending to the car. We'll have him off the X before the ambulances depart," Nisha said in his ear. "Stand by."

As he helped lift the stretcher into the ambulance, Jed glanced over his shoulder to see the two medics pushing Zhao's stretcher toward the second ambulance. Unfortunately, the two Chinese agents from the conference room and one uniformed soldier were running beside them, and he could already hear a heated argument between the medics and agents about accompanying Zhao. The larger agent, who towered over the two paramedics, pulled back the edge of his coat to show them his pistol.

The two paramedics froze, and to Jed's dismay, the Chinese agent climbed into the back of the ambulance as they loaded Zhao inside.

"You ride with us, please," Hyeon said to Jed. "In case man wakes, we need speaking with him. No German."

"*Ja*," Jed said.

He glanced again at the other ambulance, where the doors were already closed. The others—two uniformed soldiers and the smaller man in the dark suit—took off at a sprint back toward the Renaissance hotel, no doubt to retrieve their own vehicle and trail the ambulance. Jed jerked the doors closed behind him and slid onto the bench seat beside Hyeon. The Shepherd gave him a big, familiar grin as the ambulance accelerated.

"Now we get to the *Mission: Impossible* stuff," Hyeon said and raised his eyebrows twice.

Jed nodded but knew this was the most dangerous part of the entire evolution. "Still not sure how this works," he said, holding on to the bottom of his seat to keep from being tossed to the floor as the driver navigated at high speed toward the edge of the park.

"Just like David Copperfield, bro. It's all smoke and mirrors and the power of suggestion."

A moment later, the ambulance came to an abrupt stop. Jed imagined the other ambulance pulling in tight beside them. He heard a click as Hyeon activated a hidden side panel door which shifted inward and dropped out of the way, just as a small, mirrored panel flipped out between the two ambulances, filling the gap at the front of the new opening. Feeling a hand on his shoulder, Jed turned to see the smiling face of the German scientist now sitting up and in perfect health.

"Fun and games," Weider said in American English, confirming his true pedigree.

"Four is clear," Grayson announced in his ear, but Jed ignored the call, focused on the task at hand as the side of the second ambulance, just ten inches away, opened a mirror-image hidden panel.

In the rectangular window, Bex's face popped into view.

"You ready?" she asked.

"Pass him through," Jed answered.

Three sets of arms appeared, cradling the unconscious Dr. Zhao, and passed the scientist through the gap to Jed, Hyeon, and "Dr. Weider." They quickly loaded him onto the stretcher, with Hyeon cradling the man's head to make sure it didn't smack on anything during the transfer.

"How are the Chinese not seeing this?" Jed asked, looking at the confederate playing Dr. Weider.

"Same way the magician saws a woman in half or elevates someone onstage. The mirrors in place on the open panels give the illusion that they are looking at the space between ambulances. Trust me—we've done this before." The man's thick Texas accent now replaced his German accent. The man looked fifteen years younger in the blink of an eye. Jed chuckled and shook his head.

Spooks . . .

"What do you want us to do with the Chinese security agent?" Bex asked, pulling his attention back to the narrow passage where she looked through the rectangular hole expectantly.

"What's his status?" Jed asked.

"Alive, but unconscious," she replied. "I was able to dose him with ketamine and then etomidate. He'll be out for an hour or more."

"Leave him," Jed said.

Moments later, the Chinese medic who had been driving their ambulance traded places with Bex, who rolled smoothly through the opening and into Jed's ambulance. Hyeon closed the secret panel, gave Bex a high five, then crawled through the cab opening to assume the driver's seat. With the personnel transfer complete, the ambulances could now diverge.

Jed watched Bex place oxygen tubing and a nasal cannula around Zhao's nose and attach EKG leads to his chest.

"Is he okay?" he asked, trying to stay out of her way.

"Completely stable," she said with a nod.

"How long will he be out?"

She pursed her lips and shrugged. "A good while, I think. They said to expect hours for the drug to metabolize and his condition to resolve."

The acceleration picked up and Jed held on to the bench as Bex shifted to the swivel chair mounted at the head of the stretcher. His stomach rose as they descended the steep, right-hand spiral down from the park to the main road. Moments later, they sped west and Jed glanced up front to see the heavy traffic parting like the Red Sea as Hyeon sped down the center lane, lights and sirens running full blast.

"How's our six, Actual?"

"You're clear for now," Nisha said, her voice tense. This was the key part of the exfil. Somehow they needed to lose themselves in the dense traffic of Hong Kong before the Chinese security team picked them up. In theory, the Chinese agents and police would follow the other ambulance, which they believed had departed the scene carrying Dr. Zhao and his Chinese minder. Hopefully they assigned low priority to the ambulance carrying the German scientist and his bodyguard.

"Kill the lights and sirens when you can," Jed said through the open cabin door.

"I think it plays better if we run them all the way to the hospital, Jed," Hyeon called from the front. "There's an overhang at the ambulance entrance to the ER blocking any eyes from above. We sit a minute under that, kill the lights, and then drift back out having supposedly dropped off our patient."

Jed nodded. It made sense, but the SEAL inside hated the lights and "look at me" scream of the sirens. How these spooks did ops like this day after day was beyond him . . .

"Joshua One, Mother," said Gayle, joining the party line.

"One," Jed replied, his heart skipping a beat at the tension in her voice.

"Joshua, we may have a problem."

"What's up?" he asked, leaning forward to look out the front windshield, where Hyeon continued to weave expertly through the thick traffic.

"Nightingale Two may be in trouble," Gayle announced in his ear, using the call sign for the other ambulance. Jed and his team were riding in Nightingale One. "The Chinese security team is catching up to them. If they stop them, we're screwed."

"Crap," Bex said, looking up at him.

An understatement. Once they found the ambulance contained only a drugged Chinese agent and that Zhao was missing, it wouldn't take them long to connect the dots.

"Anything headed our way?" he asked.

"Not yet," Gayle said.

He grabbed the bench seat as Hyeon made the turn onto what he remembered would be the exit off the flyway for Garden Road. Another moment and they would be merging onto Queensway Road. In two minutes, perhaps less, they would arrive at Canossa Hospital, across the street from the Hong Kong Zoological and Botanical Gardens. Hyeon had made great time.

"What's the plan for Nightingale Two?" he asked. "We need more time."

"I'm directing them to divert from St. Paul's Hospital and abandon Nightingale Two in a parking garage. They'll leave the Chinese agent inside and exfil from there. My guess is you have at least ten minutes—fifteen at the most—before we're blown."

Jed gritted his teeth. That got them safely to the hospital, but then what?

Hong Kong had surveillance everywhere now that the Chinese had taken control. He closed his eyes, imagining the satellite map he'd burned into his mind.

"There's another parking garage in the north building of Garden Towers, near Canossa Hospital," he said, talking to everyone now, not just Gayle.

"Check," Hyeon said, glancing over his shoulder.

"Joshua Actual, unless you have one more trick up your sleeves, we're going to need Four to pick us up there," he said, hoping that Nisha and John had a contingency in place he didn't know about.

"I think I can do you one better," Gayle said quickly, stepping on any response from Nisha. "Four, resume your scheduled exfil via the ferry. One, proceed to ground floor of the parking garage and stand by for instructions."

"Roger that, Mother," Jed said, unable to suppress a tight grin.

Maybe he'd misjudged the CIA.

Apparently Gayle wasn't going to leave them high and dry after all.

CHAPTER TWENTY-ONE

Gayle stared in horror at the satellite feed on her laptop. A convoy of police vehicles, lights flashing, was screaming down the highway in the direction of St. Paul's Hospital—exactly where Nightingale Two had been headed before she had diverted them to the parking garage.

Coincidence? I think not.

"Joshua, Mother—you have incoming," she said into her boom mic, her voice a tight cord. "They'll be at the hospital in five minutes. When they discover the package was not admitted, it won't take long for them to pull CCTV footage and trace your route to the parking garage. It's time to ditch the ambulance."

"The package is not *ambulatory*," came Jed's immediate and tense reply. "Until we have replacement wheels, we ain't ditching anything."

"Understood," she said through gritted teeth.

"Mother, Actual—tell me the truth," Nisha said, her tone hot and clipped. "Do you have an exfil in progress or do *I* need to make it happen?"

"In progress. I got this," she said and prayed she could deliver on that promise, regardless of what happened to her career. She clicked the icon labeled Team 2 on her computer to open the comms channel to her standby CIA team, which consisted of a driver, a pilot, and a shooter. These men were tasked with managing her exfil in the event of an emergency.

Well, I think this constitutes an emergency.

"Dragon," a stern voice greeted her on the line. "Execute Alpha?"

Alpha was the code word to activate the protocol.

"Negative, Dragon," she said, packing everything but her computer into the bag. "Stand by for new tasking. You have alternate passengers."

"I was told to prepare for your emergency exfil only—"

"The situation has changed," she said, summoning her most commanding voice and a little disappointed at the result. "Proceed to the ground floor parking garage for Garden Towers north. Picking up five—four shooters and the package. Package is not ambulatory. Expedite."

"Is there incoming pressure?"

"Yes. Hurry," she said.

After a flurry of curses, her exfil team leader acknowledged the order and then said, "What about you? We need to get you first."

"There's no time. Don't worry about me. I'm a big girl . . . I'll get to the airfield."

"Roger, Dragon diverting to alternate pickup," the team leader said.

Gayle transferred comms from her notebook to her smartphone, shoved the computer in her backpack, and marched out of her hotel room.

"Hey, little sis, I sent an Uber to pick up your friends," she said, calling Nisha and abandoning call signs now that she was in the hotel hallway where people could hear her.

"Understood, big sis," Nisha came back. "Do you have an Uber for yourself?"

"Unfortunately, that was my Uber. Looks like I'm going to have to hail a taxi," she said, opting to take the stairs instead of the elevator.

"Hey, we have a rental car," Nisha said, her voice calmer and softer than

Gayle had heard it the entire op. "Happy to swing by and pick you up, especially since it looks like we're all going to the same party now."

A smile curled Gayle's lips. "I'd appreciate that very much."

"See you in five at the corner outside the hotel."

"Thanks, sis," she said, taking the stairs at an athletic pace now.

"It's the least I can do," Nisha replied, "for a sister."

Despite the danger and the risk, for the first time since she'd arrived in Hong Kong, Gayle felt good about the op and herself. She and the Shepherds were in this thing together, to the end . . . and regardless of whatever end that might be, she'd be able to sleep with a clean conscience.

CHAPTER TWENTY-TWO

Jed watched Bex take Zhao's vitals from where they all huddled in the back of the ambulance. Her face looked tense and a bead of sweat ran from her hairline down her temple.

"How's he doing?" he asked.

"I mean, he's alive but completely out," she said. "I don't know what this drug they dosed him with is, but it's hard-core."

"So any chance of him being able to walk in the next five minutes?"

She looked at him like he'd just asked the stupidest question in the history of questions. "No, Jed, zero chance."

"Dude, we gotta get outta here," Hyeon said. "The police are on their way."

"I know," Jed said, tapping his foot to dissipate the nervous energy in his leg.

"We're in a parking garage, bro. All they have to do is block the entrance and exit and we're toast."

"*I know!*" Jed fired back and looked at his watch.

In covert operations, waiting was like an operator's kryptonite. The inability to act, to move, to change the tactical picture . . . it was like being paralyzed.

"Waiting is the worst," his fellow former frogman hissed, confirming Jed's feeling to be universal. "I'd rather be in a straight-up firefight than just sitting here."

"Not in the middle of Hong Kong, you wouldn't," Bex said. "We're outgunned a gazillion to one, boys. Our *only* chance is to slip away."

Jed nodded. *I know . . .*

Hyeon said nothing.

On the stretcher, Dr. Zhao made a long, rattling snore.

Jed looked at his watch again; only twelve seconds had passed.

A shadow passed, dimming the natural light in the back of the ambulance. Jed glanced through the cab cutout and through the windshield as he reached for the pistol in his waistband. Two women walked past the front of the ambulance, loaded down with plastic shopping bags, and glanced at the ambulance as they did.

Jed looked again at his watch.

Thirteen more seconds burned.

"There are long guns under the bench seat," Hyeon said, his voice more serious now, "should it come to that."

"It won't," Jed said, hoping that was true.

"Joshua, this is Dragon," a new and unfamiliar male voice said on the comms channel. "Entering the garage. Sitrep?"

He exhaled a sigh of relief. "We're in an ambulance on the ground level. You can't miss us. Four to ride plus one piece of luggage."

"Check, I see you."

"Any tails on?"

"None observed," Gayle said in his ear. Her voice was tense, and he wondered if this little rescue had been authorized by her head shed or if she'd gone off script. "Police have reached St. Paul's Hospital, but nobody heading your way yet."

"Thirty seconds, Joshua," Dragon said. "We'll give you ten seconds, so be ready to move."

"I've got all of the surveillance cameras in your garage and four other random garages down for the next two minutes," John chimed in, taking Jed by surprise. He'd not heard from the spook for so long he'd assumed they'd already secured.

"How is that even possible?" Bex murmured.

"He's just that good," the spook who'd posed as Dr. Weider said.

"Maybe this *Mission: Impossible*, Jason Bourne stuff ain't so bad after all," Hyeon said.

"It's Ethan Hunt, dude," Bex said, standing bent over in the small ambulance and running her arms under Dr. Zhao's armpits from behind, joining her hands on his chest. Jed moved to the feet, ready to pop open the door, complete the fireman's carry of the Chinese scientist, and hustle to their rescue vehicle.

"What?" Hyeon asked, confused.

"You're mixing stuff up. Ethan Hunt is from *Mission: Impossible*. Jason Bourne is a whole different thing."

"Whatever," Hyeon said, rolling his eyes.

"Ready for you," Dragon announced in Jed's ear, just as he heard a squeal of rubber tires on polished floor echo through the parking deck.

He popped open the rear ambulance doors just as the side door of a Mercedes Sprinter van slid open beside them. Jed lifted the Chinese scientist by the legs and watched his head loll to one side as Bex lifted him as well, awkwardly maneuvering him off the stretcher, the unattached nasal cannula and wires to his EKG leads dangling from his chest and face. In three great strides, they crossed to the van and Jed all but jumped inside, laying Zhao on the rear bench seat, where Bex slid to cradle the unconscious man's head in her lap.

Jed took a seat beside the driver while Hyeon and "Dr. Weider" jumped in and slammed the slider closed. Without a word, the driver made a two-point backing turn, and seconds later they were out of the garage, keeping a slow and relaxed speed.

"Where's Gayle?" Jed said, having assumed she was in the van.

"She caught another ride," the driver said, all business.

"She's with us," Nisha said in his ear, and Jed could hear the smile in her voice.

He nodded, connecting the dots. *She gave up her ride for us.*

"Dragon has the package and is heading to the Ark," the driver reported.

"Roger, Dragon," Gayle said. "Stay frosty. A call went out through the police channels just now to stop all ambulances. It won't be long before they find your abandoned ambulance."

The driver grumbled his displeasure at the news.

"Mother?" Jed said, picturing Gayle sitting with her notebook computer on her lap in the back of a different panel van with John and Nisha.

"Yes?" she said.

"Thanks."

"You're welcome," she said. "But we're not out of the woods yet. We've got to get everyone to the airport before they shut things down. Doing that will be a miracle."

"We're used to miracles," Hyeon said with a laugh, reaching up to give Jed a squeeze on the shoulder. "Right, boss?"

"Yeah," he said. "I suppose we are."

As they headed west, Jed closed his eyes a moment in silent prayer for a minimum of thirty more minutes of divine intervention on their behalf.

CHAPTER
TWENTY-THREE

Jed added a touch of cream to the large cup of coffee he prepared for himself in the forward galley of the luxury corporate jet and thought about answered prayers. They were airborne and over international waters, with Dr. Zhao on board, their entire team unscathed . . . Now he could finally relax.

He took a celebratory sip and silently thanked God with what had become his go-to prayer lately: *Thanks for keeping us safe, Father. And thank You for the opportunity to do Your work.*

Feeling hopeful for the first time in days, he walked aft, hunched despite the decent headroom of the Bombardier jet. He squeezed Eli's shoulder as he passed, and the operator looked up and smiled.

"No coffee for me?" the former Army CAG operator called after him.

"You know where it is," he said without looking back. "No flight attendant on this bus, bro."

David looked up at him from beside Eli, legs crossed and a Bible open in his lap.

"You good, Jed?" his TSL asked. David had stayed behind on the jet for the op, but he'd insisted on making the trip and Jed knew he'd been listening in on the comms the entire time.

"Yeah," he said, then added, "You were silent on this one. Everything okay for you?"

"Yep," David said, closing his Bible and smiling. "On this one it seemed like less was more in your ear. No point in me talking to hear myself speak. And anyway, with no Dark Ones in the mix, I figured it best to let the pros do their thing."

Jed nodded. He wanted to ask about Sarah Beth but decided that was best a private conversation.

At the rear of the jet, just forward of the lavatory, the last row of seats had been removed and a bed had been secured to the floor in their place. Dr. Zhao lay still on his back, eyes half-open and looking very much dead.

"Is he okay?" Jed asked, knowing he'd asked that question four times already today.

"Yeah, he's stable," Bex said, and Jed could tell she was barely holding back from ribbing him. "Oxygen sats are 99 percent. Good vitals. Normal EKG. That John dude said it could be a few more hours till Zhao comes to."

"All righty then," he said.

On a lark, he tried reaching out with his mind looking for Zhao's thread but found nothing. Maybe it didn't work like that. And anyway, if the dude was literally comatose, what would he see or hear? Would Zhao's mind be a void or broadcasting static?

I wonder, he thought and decided to ask Ben when they got back.

"Got a sec, Jed?" Nisha said from nearby.

"Sure." He folded himself into a vacant seat across from her and beside Gayle.

"We've been talking about the, um, disposition of Dr. Zhao."

"*They've* been talking about it," John interrupted from the row behind.

"I have no horse in this race. I'm the extract guy, and extract is complete. It's customary to reward mission complete with a cocktail. So who's buying?"

"Next time." Jed smiled. Despite not wanting to, he was starting to like the guy. Not the spooky cowboy image John seemed so bent on personifying, but the pro on the inside. The dude had delivered in spades, and Jed understood why Nisha trusted him. John was competent, cool under pressure, and didn't blink in the face of danger.

John made some quip about cash bars and cheap dates, then made a show of looking out the window as if he was no longer part of the conversation.

Jed turned back to Nisha. "I'm sorry. You were saying?"

"Speaking frankly, Jed, I'm concerned that CIA is going to try and take control of the interrogation and custody of Dr. Zhao," Nisha said.

"Is that the plan, Gayle?" he asked pointedly, turning to look at her.

"No," Gayle said. "I have agreement from my boss that initial interviews will be handled by Trinity. I need to be present so CIA is in the loop on any actionable intelligence, but you guys are lead on this. The hard part is over. We got him out. My job now is to assist you however I can."

"Sounds good," Jed said and looked at Nisha. He wasn't seeing the problem here.

"And then what?" Nisha pressed.

"What do you mean?" Jed asked.

"Jed, stop thinking like an operator. After we get what we need, then what? Do we hand Zhao over to CIA, where he's pressured to build the same type of doomsday weapon for them that he built for the Chinese? That's the endgame I see coming."

"They wouldn't do that . . . would they?" He'd not contemplated that scenario, but now that she'd put the bug in his brain . . .

He watched Nisha's chestnut-colored eyes flash with something almost like rage—a memory of something in her past, perhaps, and part of what chased her out of whatever John's spooky task force was and over to the Shepherds. He knew her well enough to know that she'd left her old life because she wanted to do the right thing. One thing was suddenly clear to him—Nisha was done operating according to an "end justifies the means" moral code.

"Jed, do you actually trust the CIA?" she asked, holding his gaze. "Because I don't."

"Can you promise us that CIA won't drop this guy in some dark hole and make him build the weapon again?" Jed said, turning to Gayle.

"I can tell you he won't be dropped in a dark hole, yes," Gayle said, clearly offended by the picture he'd painted. "We're not the bad guys here. We don't disappear good people to black sites and order about minions like some Dr. Evil character."

"Then you're saying CIA will hold no stake in Zhao's future?" he said. "After the debriefs, he's free to go and live his life as he pleases?"

She shook her head but then curled her lower lip. "Honestly, I can't promise that. There's always a quid pro quo with these things and he certainly will be expected to share anything he knows with us in exchange for a new life in America. And, guys, don't we want to know about the weapon? To defend against it, we need to understand it, right?"

"But will CIA's Skunk Works try to build such a weapon?" Jed pressed.

"I . . . I don't know what DS&T will do. I don't know what the big bosses will say. Last week I was a field officer in Peru. If I'm being honest, I'm way out of my league here. I don't even know if I'm going to have a job when we get back. Look, I want to say no, to believe that we wouldn't, but I can't look you straight in the eyes and make that promise . . ." She let her voice trail off.

Jed nodded. Nisha was right about this. They needed to be sure such a horrifying weapon wasn't replicated. That felt above his pay grade, but Nisha had challenged him with a leadership question that he'd failed to think of. Ben wouldn't have missed it. A leader's job was to think about future outcomes and repercussions two and three steps down the road. To consider unintended consequences and what-if scenarios.

I didn't think about any of those things . . .

He sighed.

"I'm glad you brought this up, Nisha," he said as he rose. "I'll run this matter up our internal chain of command."

"And your organization will be different?" Gayle challenged defensively.

"Without a doubt," Jed said with a smile meant to disarm. "We serve a different Higher Authority." She nodded, but her face still looked confused.

"Gayle, I really appreciate your honesty here. And I really appreciate you saving our bacon in Hong Kong. I know you put it all on the line for us. I really hope it doesn't come back and bite you."

She nodded, her smile now genuine but her eyes heavy with worry.

"Is he awake yet, Bex?" he asked over his shoulder before heading forward again.

"Jed, I swear . . ."

He chuckled and waved a hand.

Nisha's worry about the long-term disposition of Dr. Zhao was a concern, but first things first. They needed to learn about the weapon, locate it, and destroy it.

That wasn't being shortsighted or mission-centric.

That was triage.

CHAPTER TWENTY-FOUR

Jed looked at the lucid Chinese scientist and saw that the man was a mess of conflicting emotions. Yes, Dr. Zhao had been "liberated" from a life of scientific servitude to the CCP. But in the Chinese defense industrial complex, he'd been a highly respected researcher and man of influence. Now he was a defector. In China, he'd had a security detail 24-7 to protect him for the Chinese state. In the US, he'd need a security detail 24-7 to protect him *from* the Chinese state. The Chinese government did not operate with a "turn the other cheek" philosophy when it came to things like defection. Zhao's extraction would have consequences for all parties involved. Retribution was almost guaranteed, and the scientist would be looking over his shoulder for the rest of his life.

"I'm sorry this happened to you. Are you okay?" Nisha said, sitting down next to the man at the round four-person table where he sat, staring into a steaming cup of black coffee. A half-eaten granola bar, in a peeled-back wrapper, sat on the white Formica top with a little pile of crumbs beside it.

Zhao nodded. "My wife died two years ago. I wanted to leave China for long time . . . but now that it happen, I feel like bad person. Like traitor."

Instead of coddling the man, she said, "Why do you feel that way?"

He looked up at her. "Because instead of trying to fix problem, I run away. A good Chinese man stay and fight more bravely."

"Then why didn't you, when you had the chance?"

He hesitated, seemingly taken aback by her direct manner. "Because I was afraid . . ."

Jed watched Nisha nod and say, "And for good reason. If you had tried to sabotage the project, you would have been punished—sent to a facility for *reeducation* and then put back to work. Stopping the work was never a realistic option for you. Besides ending your own life, there was nothing you could have done to fight the machine. Exerting control over its people, this is what the Chinese government does. They are very good at it."

Zhao's gaze went to the middle distance and he mumbled something in Mandarin.

"You are a brave man, Dr. Zhao," she said, leaning in to try to catch his eye. "Defecting was the hardest decision you could make. The most difficult choice. A good Chinese man is one who puts the lives of his countrymen ahead of his own and makes such hard choices. This weapon is evil. This weapon should not exist."

Zhao turned abruptly to face her. "I will not help your government build a copy of the weapon. That is not why I agree to come here. I come here to warn, to educate about the risks, and to help America stop this Chinese program by telling the world. This weapon must be banned by United Nations, just like biological weapons are banned."

Nisha nodded. "We understand and we agree."

"I believe you, but what about bosses? Do they understand and agree?"

"Yes," Jed said abruptly, interjecting for the first time and not sure why. "You have our word."

Silence hung in the air a moment as they each contemplated the veracity of the promise, a promise that Jed wondered if he was even in a position to make. Movement in his peripheral vision caught Jed's eye and he turned to find Eli standing in the open doorway to the hall.

"All the principals are assembled," the veteran Shepherd said with an easy smile. "They're ready for you."

"That's your cue, Dr. Zhao," Nisha said, sliding her chair back from the table and rising. "Why don't you go with my friend Eli, and we'll join you in a moment."

The Chinese scientist nodded, got up from the table, and did as instructed, pausing at the threshold for a curious backward glance before disappearing.

"What's up?" Jed said, curious about the holdback.

"Why do you do that?" she said, narrowing her eyes at him.

"Do what?"

"Butt into conversations I'm managing, usually at inopportune times. I had it under control. I didn't need you to step in with your command assurance. And it's not the first time you've done it, either, Jed," Nisha said.

He exhaled through his nose and mulled the question. *Why* do *I do it?*

"I guess because I didn't want you to feel compelled to make a promise that might compromise your integrity. If somebody had to make a promise on behalf of the organization that might be broken, I'd rather it be me."

Her expression softened and she did her lip-curl thing. "That's very noble of you, Jed, but it's not your job to manage my integrity. I'm a professional, just like you, and for that matter given my background, I've navigated many more dicey asset management situations than you have."

"Yep . . . I reckon you have," he said. "Sorry I stepped on your toes."

"Apology accepted."

"So are we good?"

"Yeah, we're good," she said with a chuckle. "C'mon, they'll be waiting on us."

Together, they left the break room and walked quickly to the executive conference room where the Shepherds' senior leadership was assembled. Their CIA liaison, Gayle, had a place at the table as well. Jed and Nisha took seats in two open chairs and the debrief got quickly underway.

After getting the introductions and formalities out of the way, Ben didn't pull any punches.

"Dr. Zhao, I'm just going to go straight for what we in this country call *the meat and potatoes,"* the Shepherd commander said. "Will you please tell us everything we need to know about this weapon and how we can stop it?"

"First let me apologize for poor English. I understand almost all, but not fluent in speaking," Zhao said.

"Well, none of us here speak Mandarin, so you have absolutely nothing to apologize for. We are incredibly grateful to you."

Zhao nodded and then knit his fingers together. "Now I answer questions. Only way to stop weapon is destroy weapon first. After you targeted, it is too late. The speed is light, so you cannot avoid."

"Okay, that's what I thought," Ben said, "but we all needed to hear you say it. Please continue."

"The weapon compact for amount of energy it produce. Prototype is 1.5 meters by 1.5 meters by 2.25 meters."

"That's much smaller than I thought," Ben said, his expression grave. "That gives plenty of flexibility for selecting a platform to deploy it."

"Yes and no," Zhao said. "Weapon demands large energy reservoir. To vaporize human requires three gigajoules of energy—approximately 800 kilowatt-hours."

"Whoa," Eli said. "That's a lot of juice."

"How many kilowatt-hours does, say, a Tesla car battery have?" Nisha asked.

"Top Tesla has 100 kilowatt-hour battery," Zhao answered.

"Hold on, discharging this weapon one time is like draining the power of eight Teslas?" Jed said, dumbfounded.

Zhao nodded.

"That's a lot of weight in batteries to have to haul around," Nisha said.

"Yes," Zhao said, "but we develop new battery using vapor catalyst that so much reduce weight compared to Tesla lithium-ion battery. One-hundred-kilowatt-hour battery weigh only four hundred kilos."

"Times eight that makes thirty-two hundred kilos of battery per shot," Jed said, doing the math in his head.

"This correct."

"Seems like a terribly inefficient way to kill a person," Eli said and set his service weapon on the table for effect. "I've got a whole magazine of death right here and each shot weighs less than fifteen grams."

"Yes, but efficiency not purpose of directed energy weapon. Weapon made with one purpose—make people afraid." Zhao paused to let the power of his words sink in.

"Well, it sure as hell works," Bex said. "After what we saw in Peru, I have nightmares about being vaporized."

"There no defense for energy weapon like this. You think safe in building, right? Wrong. If building not enough shielding, then can work through walls. Can work from long range and not affected by wind like bullet."

Jed's guts suddenly felt heavy, like they were filled with liquid lead. Since Peru, he'd been operating under the assumption that so long as they were covered, they were safe, at least from being individually targeted. But if that was not the case, then the risk profile had shifted dramatically. A half-dozen side conversations started up in the room as people reacted to the news.

"All right, settle down, everyone," Ben said. "This is bad news but it's not surprising. We've suspected for a while that the low-energy directed energy weapons causing Havana Syndrome could penetrate hotel room walls. This is the same situation apparently."

"Not exactly," Bex chimed in. "Getting vertigo and vomiting are not the same thing at all as being vaporized."

"Agreed, but targeting is still a constraint and when we find out the operational spectrum the weapon operates in, we can install shielding. Every microwave oven on the planet has a Faraday screen over the viewing window. We can install similar tech here, isn't that right, Dr. Zhao?" Ben said, trying to calm them down.

"Yes, is true, shielding can be made, but weapon is multimodal. Has twelve emitters . . . modulate across the 300 MHz to 300 GHz frequency band to optimize damage and give weapon ability to destroy biological and electronic targets. If you target fighter jet, you choose whether to vaporize pilot or plane computer or both."

"Awesome," Eli said under his breath. "This just keeps getting better and better."

"What type of platform did your laboratory design the weapon to be carried by?" Ben asked. "Given the weight constraints, it would have to be something large."

"All testing ground-based, but prototype unit going to install on AG600."

"I'm not familiar with the AG600," Ben said.

"It's an amphibious turboprop the size of a 737," Pastor Mike said, apparently up to speed on his Chinese aviation platforms.

"Ah, so that's a pretty big footprint."

"Yes, but not happen because prototype disappear," Zhao said.

"What do you mean it disappeared?" Ben said.

"One day weapon in testing warehouse, next day gone."

Ben glanced at Pastor Mike, who pursed his lips. Jed knew what question he'd ask the Chinese scientist next, and it turned out to be the exact question Ben had on his mind as well.

"Was the weapon stolen?" the Shepherd commander asked.

Zhao laughed. "Warehouse very, very secure on military base. This not possible."

"Then that means the Chinese must have knowingly sold the weapon to—" Bex wisely stopped herself midsentence.

Jed felt pretty confident that Dr. Zhao was not read in on, or probably even aware of, the existence of the Dark Ones. Supernatural warfare and demon-possessed terrorists hiding in plain sight were not exactly the type of conversation one just waded into casually with the uninitiated. To broach the topic now jeopardized both Zhao's opinion of them and his willingness to continue to be open and forthcoming.

"Dr. Zhao, in the days or weeks leading up to the weapon's disappearance, did you happen to notice visitors to the facility, visitors whom you did not recognize? Foreign nationals perhaps?" the Shepherd intelligence chief, Julia Nesbitt, asked, pivoting brilliantly.

"Yes, I see them," Zhao said. "Foreign men, look at weapon."

Ben pulled out his phone, tapped it a few times, then held up the screen to show a photograph of Victor to Zhao. "Do you recognize this man?"

Zhao squinted at the pic, then shook his head. "No."

"What about this man?" Ben asked, swiping to another image. "Or this man?"

"Last one," Zhao said, perking up. "Yes, this man visit warehouse."

Ben exchanged looks with Pastor Mike. Jed recognized Victor, of course, but he'd never seen the other two dudes. They were obviously Dark Ones, probably Victor's lieutenants, and he realized in that moment how much he still had to learn about the Dark Ones' global hierarchy and various HVTs operating in the shadows around the world.

The Q and A with Dr. Zhao continued for another thirty minutes as the team tried to extract as much knowledge from the Chinese weapon creator as possible. Peru had obviously been a proof-of-concept test of the weapon on whatever aviation platform the Dark Ones were using. Now the Shepherds had to hurry up and find the plane and the weapon before they hit whatever their real mission objective was. To Jed that seemed obvious: the Trinity complex broadly and the man across from him—the man who led Trinity—specifically. Jed hazarded a guess he might also have made that short list, with his link to Victor and his having rescued Sarah Beth from the demon's clutches.

Ben assigned a security detail to Dr. Zhao and offered to let him stay on campus until a permanent WITSEC-type solution could be arranged with the CIA. Zhao was working under the mistaken assumption he was in CIA custody presently, and nobody, including Gayle, had taken any active steps to dissuade him of this belief.

All in good time . . .

Once the Chinese scientist was safely whisked away, the debrief continued in a much more freewheeling and emotionally charged manner than it had before. Like the good leader he was, Ben let everyone vent and express their concerns until the process was no longer productive. At that point, he cut it off and gave everyone their marching orders . . . everyone except Jed.

"Jed, hang back a second," Ben said after ending the meeting.

"Sure thing, boss." Once they were alone, Jed asked, "What's up?"

"Pastor Mike is having a similar discussion with David as we speak about putting Sarah Beth onto this case," Ben said. "The Yarnells have expressed concerns and misgivings about accelerating their daughter too quickly, but this particular threat is too dangerous not to leverage all our best talent, and that girl is exceptionally gifted."

Jed nodded. "Yes, she is . . . but why are you talking to me about it?"

"Two reasons. First, because David might need a sounding board, someone to talk to about it. Second, because from what I've seen, the girl has bonded with you. If she has a vision, I wouldn't be surprised if you're the person she reaches out to first."

"Understood," Jed said. "I'll make sure I'm available for both of them. But, Ben . . ." He paused, not sure how to express the fear he had.

"We will not allow Sarah Beth to be any more involved than her parents agree to," Ben said, holding his eyes. "We will be asking David and Rachel to pray for guidance from the Holy Spirit on this one, and I have been praying in earnest as well. We will do the right thing, Jed. And she's not leaving the Watcher compound, I can assure you."

Jed nodded, feeling better and then guilty for worrying anything else could be true—especially from Ben Morvant.

Ben clasped Jed on the shoulder. "How are things with Johnny?"

Jed snapped back from ruminating about Sarah Beth and the Shepherds' plans for her and shifted uncomfortably. "What do you mean?"

"Pretty obvious there's still some tension there and not just because you didn't want him with you in Peru. Are you handling it okay? Do we need to make a change?"

Jed sighed. "Honestly, Ben, he's our weak link. Not as an operator, obviously. He's top-notch in the field. I mean team cohesion. He's pretty clearly not happy with my being in the lead at Bravo, for whatever reason. It manifested in ways that proved . . . problematic. Especially in Rome."

Ben nodded. "He's a great operator, Jed, that's true. But we need Joshua Bravo to be tight. We're thinking about making your team into our special missions unit, something we've not done before, and based in no small part on the fact that you, like me, have some unique gifts of value. But we can't exploit that if your team isn't dialed in. I can transfer him out if you need me to."

Jed thought about that a moment. He knew that Edwin Epperson might yet be recruited, and he'd love to have him on his team if that happened. But Johnny was a great operator with tons of experience in the unit. He should be of great value, but he needed to fall in line. And that was on Jed, as a leader, to fix.

"No," he said. "We'll get it all smoothed out. I'd like to keep him."

"Very well. Make sure you do. And be ready for what comes next, because whatever the Dark Ones' target is, Joshua Bravo is going to be my 0300 alert team. As of now, you guys are locked and loaded and ready to roll out in thirty minutes or less. Have everyone prep gear and stand by."

CHAPTER TWENTY-FIVE

YARNELL RESIDENCE

BETHLEHEM BOULEVARD

TRINITY LOOP HOUSING COMPLEX

0712 HOURS LOCAL

Rachel paced the kitchen, a lukewarm cup of coffee in her right hand and her left arm wrapped around her waist in an unconscious hug—not against the cold, but to contain the emotions inside her. The team had gotten back to Trinity late last night, but David hadn't come home yet. Like an idiot she'd stayed up waiting for him and her nerves were fraying from lack of sleep. He'd called to tell her he was popping in for a change of clothes and that he had something to talk to her about. Something important.

She knew it had to do with Sarah Beth.

Maybe it was just the tone of his voice—one he used whenever he was thinking about their daughter. Maybe it was years of marriage to a good man—a man who broke the stereotypes and was an honest communicator. Maybe it was a mother's intuition.

Or maybe it was the *other* thing.

It still reared its head now and again, outside of her control and seemingly never when she needed it. Like a voice in another room, speaking just too softly to be clearly understood. It was *so* frustrating.

The security alarm chirped as David came through the front door—meaning he had left his car in the driveway and wouldn't be here long. That he wasn't following the new rule about pulling all the way into the garage before getting out of the car also seemed telling. The details David had shared with her about the weapon were vague, probably on purpose, but one thing felt certain: the Shepherds and Watchers were in grave danger.

Again.

"Rachel?" he called out.

She set her cup on the island, let out a long sigh, and put her best loving smile on her face as she headed toward the family room. She hurried to him, wrapping her arms around his neck and pressing her face against his chest as he hugged her. She liked the warmth of him but also the rediscovered confidence and swagger that had risen to the surface these last few weeks.

"Everything okay?" he said, kissing the top of her head and smoothing her hair.

"You tell me, David," she said, suddenly stiffening, his worries coming to her like a breath.

"Things are escalating. This weapon is the stuff of nightmares, and it's out there right now, in the Dark Ones' possession. We know Victor is planning to use it, but we don't know when or who he's targeting," he said, stopping short of the punch line.

"Go on, spit it out. They want to use Sarah Beth to find it, don't they?"

"Baby, it's just that she has an ability that they haven't seen in a long time, an ability to locate—"

"I knew it. I knew it!" she snapped, jerking away from him. She paced away, back to the couch in the living room and collapsed there, emotionally drained. "This is how it works. They sweet-talk you into giving an inch; then they take a mile. We say yes to the advanced training and suddenly now they need her in the field. Well, screw that. Screw them! Sarah Beth is not going in the field. No way, nohow."

David sat beside her, a tight smile on his face meant to reassure.

"I wasn't going to suggest that," he said, leaving his hands in his lap, respecting her apparent need for distance. "You and I are on the same page here, baby—the same team. She will never go out in the field unless we both agree. But there are things she can do from the safety of the school."

"Uh-uh, no," she said, shaking her head emphatically.

He exhaled loud enough to make his exasperation known. "And what happens if spiritual intelligence comes to her unbidden? Is she just supposed to ignore it? Look, Rachel, she possesses gifts with capabilities still beyond her control. Remember what happened with the Vatican attack? If not for our daughter, the pope would be dead right now."

He made a good point. Maybe Watcher skills were by their very nature beyond human control. Maybe the gifted only had one decision to make— either accept and embrace the gift or deny and ignore it. Sarah Beth had chosen the former, while Rachel had made the mistake of doing the latter.

Only God has real control.

She shuddered and hugged herself. "I don't know . . . I'm not sure about this anymore."

"What's going on with you?" David said, worry lines creasing his forehead. "After our conversation the other night . . . I thought we had all this sorted."

"I did too, but I feel so powerless. So . . . useless," she stammered. "She's at that school, by herself, where I can't help her. Where I can't protect her. And if I can't do that, what good am I to her?"

"Rachel, what in the world are you talking about? First off, her safety is the reason we sent her there, because we're not equipped to protect her on our own. Second, she's not alone; she's surrounded by hundreds of people. And third, you're her *mother*. She trusts you more than anyone else in the world. She loves and adores you. What more do you need?"

"What more do I need?" she echoed and started to laugh. "How about purpose?"

"I don't understand," he said, his puppy-dog gaze telling her he still didn't get it.

"You were recruited into the Shepherds, David. You're involved in all the planning, all the missions, all the decision making—you and Jed both. You both have a role. A purpose. A mission. Even our little girl has a mission.

But what about me, hmm? What's my mission? What's my purpose? To clean this house? To be Sarah Beth's mom? To fret and worry and wring my hands like a lunatic, pacing this living room alone while my husband and daughter battle the devil's army on the front lines? It's not fair. I'm capable of more than that. I want to serve . . . like the rest of you."

"Whoa, okay. I didn't know you felt that way," he said, and she sensed that he wanted to reach for her hand but restrained himself.

"It's not your fault," she said, waving a hand at him and feeling herself soften. "Look, I know the middle of a life-threatening crisis is the worst time to voice any of this, but with our baby girl in the mix, it's hard to think clearly without purpose myself." She sighed. "Sorry, I know that's redundant. But look—before we got sucked into this nightmare, we already had plans for me to go back to work. Maybe not back to grad school like we discussed, but something. It was already hard to just wait for our girl to get home from school and now . . . well, now she's not coming home every day. And that time, all of that empty time, it magnifies my worry about her." She turned to him and took his hands in hers, trying to summon a smile. "And about you, David. I'm the wife left behind when the soldier deploys, and I have to fill the time with something. But it's different than that, even, because I *know*—I know the things going on, the evil you guys confront. How do I just go take classes knowing everyone I care about is in that fight?"

David squeezed her hands back, pain on his face. "I'm so sorry, Rachel. I've been selfish, I think. I found my purpose and I feel . . . well, disappointed in myself for not recognizing that you were on your own on the home front—for not putting myself in your shoes. I don't know what role is open for you, but I can ask Mike Moore. Okay? I'll talk to him and together we'll find a mission for you."

She nodded and neither of them said anything for a long moment.

"I know what the Dark Ones are capable of, David," she said, refusing to look away or even blink, despite the little-girl voice inside, a voice from her past self, screaming at her to shut up. "And I know that Victor isn't going to stop, ever, until Sarah Beth is dead. He's going to try again. He's going to come for her."

"How can you know that?" he said.

"I can feel it. Just like I felt it before they came for me."

"Before *who* came for you?" he said, his mouth open and eyes wide. "What are you talking about, Rachel?"

"That night . . . he sent one of them for me," she said, and now she did turn away again. Guilt, pain, fear, regret, bitterness—a cacophony of emotions enveloped her at once, each vying for attention.

"You mean *that* night? The night of the bonfire?"

"Yes," she said, tears suddenly rimming her eyes.

"Rachel, what are you telling me?"

"I'm telling you that I used to be like Sarah Beth. I was never as gifted as she is, but I had visions. I could hear voices . . . people's thoughts. At the time, I was terrified—felt I might be going crazy. When I finally couldn't take it anymore, I worked up the courage to tell Pastor Tobias from youth group, but I never got a chance because, you know, *it* happened."

"Did Jed know?"

"No," she said. "I never told anyone. Over time, it faded, and I began to convince myself it had just been my crazy imagination. It couldn't be real, right? But when it started with Sarah Beth, I knew . . ."

He came to her and held her tight as she collapsed onto him, sobbing. "Why didn't you tell me?"

"I don't know," she said and realized that was the truth. "But I'm telling you now so you'll understand."

"Understand what exactly?" he asked gently.

"Why I've been bitter. Why I've been so angry . . ."

"Because you had to face it alone?"

"Yes," she said, her tears now usurped by angst. "Where were the Shepherds when I needed them? Why didn't the Watchers recruit me and explain that I wasn't losing my mind? Teach me how to use and harness the gift—how to use it for something good? Where was my knight in shining armor to whisk me away before that thing tried to rape me in the basement?"

"I don't know, baby," he said, kissing her cheek. "But God was there. And He did send someone to rescue you."

"Who?"

"Jed," he whispered softly. "The same knight he sent to rescue our baby girl all these years later. God saved you, Rachel, and He used Jed to do it back then just like He's using Jed and all the other Shepherds to save people today."

"And you," she said, thinking maybe he needed to hear it. "You saved me. You never left me."

"God used me to do my part, I guess," he said and sat back down on the couch, pulling her down and letting her fall against him.

She could feel inside him that he needed to go. But he held her anyway.

"Okay," she said after a long while.

"Okay what?"

"Sarah Beth can help the Shepherds look for the weapon but only from the safety of the school."

"Understood," he said. "And besides, the school is on lockdown. She's not going anywhere, even if she wanted to."

"Is there anything else I need to know about?"

"Ben's put Joshua Bravo on alert. If anything pops, we're getting mobilized."

"Of course you are," she said, shaking her head.

"I figured you'd love that," he said with a half-hearted chuckle. Then, his tone once again serious, he asked, "Rachel, are you going to be okay?"

"Me? I'll be fine . . . The dishes and the laundry certainly aren't going to wash themselves," she said, laying on the sarcasm.

"I meant, are you going to be okay here all alone?"

She shrugged. "Maybe I'll invite Maria over for a lockdown wine party. We're *literally* in the same boat on this since our men keep running off and leaving us."

"The two of you have been spending quite a bit of time together."

"Can you blame us?"

"It's not an accusation. Just an observation."

"Well, we have a lot in common. And she just got her unescorted visitor clearance approved, so she can come and go, which is nice."

He smiled at her and then leaned in and kissed her lips. "I need to get back."

"I know," she said with a brave smile. "Be careful."

"I will."

"I love you."

"I love you, too," he said, and she kissed him one more time for luck.

CHAPTER TWENTY-SIX

Sarah Beth had trouble sleeping and woke well before dawn. Not because of nightmares like usual, but because she couldn't stop thinking about the White Room and the hidden Sanctuary beyond. At twelve, she seemed too old for *giddy*, but secretly she felt a little giddy. She couldn't wait to get back there. Suddenly, being different came with a perk—one that she intended to utilize at every opportunity. She could practically feel the room calling to her.

Instead of joining her roommates for a sit-down breakfast in the dining hall, she'd grabbed a banana en route to the White Room. First period started at 0825, so that gave her almost an hour to practice locating before heading to class.

She reached the white door and looked for the camera she knew was looking down at her from somewhere. But before she found the hidden lens, she heard a magnetic lock click. Grinning, she pulled the white door open and stepped inside the tiny white room.

"Up, please," she said after closing the door behind her.

The oversize elevator began to move and expeditiously delivered her one floor up to the Sanctuary. Stepping across the threshold, the miasma of fresh-cut flowers, and that humid lake water smell that all running fountains seem to have, greeted her warmly.

Corbin looked up from one of the lounge chairs and grinned. "I had a feeling I'd see you here this morning."

"Back at you," she said.

"Do you want to practice locating some more with me?"

"Definitely," she said and walked over to take a seat in a lounge chair beside Corbin.

"Any questions before we get started?"

"Yeah," Sarah Beth said. "Are you able to locate somebody you've never met before?"

Corbin nodded. "Yes, but it's much more difficult. One of the hardest things a Watcher is asked to do."

"But how? I mean, it seems impossible."

"It's not impossible. Let's just go back to the basics—finding and using threads," Corbin said. "In the beginning, they're so dim they're practically invisible. In fact, most Watchers don't notice them until after they learn that threads exist."

"That's how it was for me. I was able to find my mom and Uncle Jed before I knew about threads."

"But now you see their threads, right?"

Sarah Beth nodded. "The more I practice searching, the more threads I see. Or feel, maybe. It's hard to tell the difference, you know, in *there*."

"Yeah, I get it. The words can't explain it. But okay, good, that's how it was for me too. Now, I don't know how every Watcher does it, but my old Keeper, Father Maclin, who used to be a Watcher, liked to say that threads are like spiderweb strands. They're sticky. When one person encounters another, their threads stick together. And the connections are strong—they don't break or anything; they just persist in time and space."

"Oh, I see, so every person is sorta like dragging their own spiderweb behind them wherever they go, and when they bump into somebody, their webs stick together."

"Pretty much. It's a lot like worldly relationships, right? Once you connect with someone, you *know* them. Part of them, like a memory of them—or maybe more like a Polaroid photo of them, is just part of you. The stronger the relationship, the stronger that is—and the same is true here. But remember, it's just as true for a bad connection as a good one."

"Like Victor," Sarah Beth said softly, the image of him at the table in the mountains—his pale, transparent skin and those long, skeleton-like hands— flashed in her head and gave her a chill. For a moment, she could almost see—or feel—that black thread calling to her.

"Yes," Corbin said, calling her back. "Like Victor. And other Dark Ones as well, so remember these things can be two-way streets, and keep yourself safe like Pastor Dee taught you. Not many Dark Ones can get inside you. But powerful ones—like Victor—can."

Sarah Beth nodded and forced thoughts of Victor out of her head. "So every new person I meet is like a hub, connecting me to all of their threads . . . which means I can follow other people's threads to someone I've never met?"

"Yes, exactly," Corbin said, smiling broadly—a tutor proud of her pupil. "And it keeps going on and on from there. When you get to the next person, it's like a new hub, and you can follow all those threads."

A mental image came to Sarah Beth of an ever-expanding, infinite spider-web connecting all the people on earth. "Dude . . . that's insane. We're talking, like, billions of connections."

"Trillions," Corbin said with a wry grin.

"Then how am I ever supposed to find anybody? I mean, I don't have time to trace trillions of connections. Is that really what you do all day, just wander around following random threads hoping to get lucky and find the right one?"

"No, I'd totally quit if that's how it worked. But two things—first, remember, this is a gift from God, a gift of the Holy Spirit. So always pray for God to guide you, and He will, I promise. But second, there are a couple of cool tricks you can use as well, to keep you focused and on task. Have you ever heard of something called six degrees of separation?"

"Yeah," she said, scrunching up her nose. "It's like something to do with Kevin Bacon?"

Corbin laughed. "Well, yes and no. The Kevin Bacon thing is related, sorta like a joke, but the basic premise of the six degrees of separation theory is that, on average, all people are separated by six social connections or less. In other words, with only six nodes, you can theoretically connect with anyone on earth. For example, you know me. But what you might not know is that I have an older sister—not a Watcher by the way—who lives in New York and goes to Juilliard. She has a roommate and her roommate's sister happens to be friends with Suri Cruise. And Suri Cruise is Tom Cruise's daughter. So if you do the math, that means you're less than six degrees of separation from Tom Cruise."

"Seriously?" Sarah Beth asked, her eyes going wide.

"Actually, I made that one up, but you could totally see how it might be true, right?"

Sarah Beth laughed but nodded.

"And the weird thing is, lots of times those stories are actually true," Corbin said, "and it turns out that the six degrees phenomenon works for Watchers too. In fact, it works even better for us because the people don't even have to know each other for us to track them. All we need is for them to have crossed paths."

"But there are a gazillion intersecting threads. How do you know which ones to follow?"

"That, sister, is the key to everything," Corbin said. "Close your eyes and I'll show you how."

Sarah Beth leaned back in her lounge chair and shut her eyes. A heartbeat later, Corbin popped into a shared headspace.

Hi, she said.

Hi. Ready to do this? Corbin said.

Yeah.

All right, I want you to name somebody famous that you've never met. It should be somebody that—as far as you know—your friends, family, and acquaintances don't know either.

Okay, Sarah Beth said. *How about Taylor Swift?*

Sure, Taylor Swift, Corbin echoed. *I'm sure we can get to her in six threads or less.*

What do I do? Sarah Beth said.

I want you to—hang on, my phone's ringing, Corbin said. *Let's pop out.*

Sarah Beth felt a rapid acceleration back to her body. She blinked twice and turned her head to see Corbin sitting up, mobile phone pressed to her ear, expression serious.

"Roger that, I'll be right down," Corbin said and then after a pause added, "Yes, she's here with me in the Sanctuary. . . . Are you sure? Okay, I'll bring her . . . Yep, yep, we're on our way."

"What's going on?" Sarah Beth said, butterflies taking flight in her stomach.

"Something's happened," Corbin said, stuffing her phone into her pocket and grabbing her backpack from the floor. "They need us."

"Who needs us?" Sarah Beth said, wriggling her way out of the comfortable recliner.

"The Shepherds. C'mon, let's go."

"Where are we going?" she said, scrambling after Corbin, who was already striding toward the elevator.

"Down," Corbin said without bothering to turn to look at her. "To the Watcher TOC."

Sarah Beth followed Corbin into the elevator and shut the white door behind her. Her stomach lifted, the same feeling she got riding a roller coaster downhill, as the room began to quickly descend. Moments later, she felt her legs get heavy as they slowed to a stop. Unlike the white wooden doors on the ground floor and Sanctuary levels, the door on this basement level was solid stainless steel and didn't have a handle.

Corbin stepped up toward the door and waited. A bell chimed and the imposing steel door slid open. They stepped together into a tiny antechamber beside a heavy metal door, a small window filled with thick glass, but even this was darkened. She imagined one could see through from the other side, however.

"Leave your mobile phone and anything else electronic—even earbuds—outside," Corbin said, reaching to her left, where Sarah Beth now saw the wall was a tall collection of metal drawers, four vertical rows and ten to a row. Corbin dropped her phone inside and gestured with her head for Sarah Beth to do the same, which she did, fishing out her earbud case and dropping that in as well. Corbin slid the drawer in and then pressed her palm on a glass panel beside the door, resulting in a metallic click, and the door swung open. Sarah Beth followed the older girl through the door and found herself in a darkened room, but one almost alive with the buzz of activity.

"C'mon," Corbin said.

Sarah Beth folded her arms over her chest and followed Corbin inside. The contrast between this place and the Sanctuary felt jarring. Teachers and students she didn't recognize turned to look at her as she trailed after Corbin along the back of the room. A half flight of stairs led down into a circular floor space filled with computer workstations and standing desks. A gigantic, curved screen covered the semicircular back wall and displayed dozens of small windows streaming different video feeds.

"The official name is the Center, but most people just call it the Bullpen," Corbin said over her shoulder. "It's kinda nuts down there sometimes."

"Yeah, seriously," Sarah Beth said, looking sideways as she walked. A few steps later, she bumped into Corbin's back. "Oh, sorry."

She sensed Corbin's irritation at her klutziness, but the older girl didn't say anything.

"Hard to concentrate with all the commotion going on?" Pastor Dee said with a warm smile.

"Yes, ma'am," Sarah Beth said, blushing in the low-level light.

"Headmaster Allard is waiting for us in the SCIF," Pastor Dee said, her gaze ticking back and forth between them.

"What's a SCIF?" Sarah Beth asked.

"It's an acronym," Corbin said. "It stands for sensitive compartmented information facility."

"A very secure room where we can have discussions and video calls with the Shepherds without having to worry about people eavesdropping who are aren't supposed to be listening," Pastor Dee explained.

Sarah Beth nodded. "Makes sense."

Pastor Dee led the way to a nearby conference room with a long rectangular table surrounded by black leather chairs. The walls were covered with hundreds of gray protruding pyramids, which Sarah Beth decided, despite their ominous look, were made of cut foam. Corbin closed the door behind them, and Sarah Beth heard a hiss as it sealed shut.

Seated at the head of the table was Headmaster Jean-Baptiste Allard, a man she'd seen many times but only met once, on her first visit to the school with her parents. Seated to the headmaster's left was Corbin's Keeper, Pastor Margaret, a middle-aged woman with long, flowing auburn hair whom Sarah Beth recognized but had never spoken with. Two other upperclassmen Watchers, both boys she didn't know, and their respective Keepers were already seated at the table.

"Hello, Sarah Beth," Headmaster Allard said, flashing her a dad smile.

"Hi," she said, shifting her weight back and forth between her feet. Her heart was pounding in her chest, and she hoped she didn't look as nervous as she felt.

"I'm Pastor Margaret," Corbin's Keeper said. "I've heard such wonderful things about you, Sarah Beth. Welcome to the Bullpen."

"Nice to meet you."

The other two Keepers introduced themselves and their Watchers, Brayden and Josh.

She nodded to each, then, suddenly feeling uncertain, turned to Pastor Dee and half whispered, "Um, Pastor Dee, my parents said they don't want me doing stuff with the Shepherds yet. They don't think I'm old enough."

"That's true, Sarah Beth, but Headmaster Allard talked with them and they gave their blessing for you participate in this discussion. You will *not* be leaving campus or working in the field in any capacity. You have my solemn promise on that."

She nodded and had to suppress the excited smile threatening just below the surface. She'd respected her parents' wishes by speaking up, and now she could be part of whatever *this* was without having to worry.

"Have a seat, ladies." Headmaster Allard gestured to the remaining open chairs.

The trio settled in around the table with Corbin dropping in beside her Keeper and Sarah Beth and Pastor Dee sitting opposite them. Only after she was seated did Sarah Beth notice the large-screen monitor on the far wall. The video feed was already on and displayed what she guessed was another SCIF. Seated around the conference table in that room were both familiar and unfamiliar faces—including her dad; Uncle Jed; the Shepherd commander, Ben Morvant; the pretty Indian woman she'd met at the team barbecue; and three people she recognized but didn't know by name.

Her dad smiled at her, which instantly buoyed her spirits. He believed in her and she knew that if it weren't for her mom, she'd probably be starting fieldwork by her next birthday. Next, she looked at Jed—who also smiled—and he gave her an encouraging nod. She nodded back just as the Shepherd commander began to speak.

"Thank you for assembling on such short notice . . ." The commander proceeded to walk them through a new and urgent threat concerning some sort of energy weapon that the Dark Ones had acquired. The Shepherds didn't know when or where the weapon was going to be deployed or the target. All they knew was the weapon was real, had been used on people in Peru, and now was going to be used here in the US, they thought. Her mind immediately conjured images of the Death Star from *Return of the Jedi* with its bright-green annihilation laser.

Do the Dark Ones really have their own Death Star? This is not good, not good at all.

The thought made her cringe and her mind immediately went to Victor, which sent a shiver down her spine. Victor seemed like a Star Wars villain in real life—with the intimidating presence of Darth Vader and the disgusting creepiness of Emperor Palpatine rolled into one.

I hate him . . .

I hate him, I hate him, I hate him.

"What was that, Sarah Beth?" someone's voice said. It was Ben Morvant . . . Oh no, she'd just interrupted the Shepherd commander.

"I'm sorry. I . . . I . . . didn't mean to say anything," she said, shrinking in her chair.

"This is an open forum," the commander said with an easy smile. "We couldn't do this without you kids. I know the heavy burden we're putting on you with this request. So please feel free to speak your mind."

She nodded but couldn't bring herself to make eye contact with him.

"I think what Sarah Beth might have been starting to say is that our search will go much faster if we have a lead—a person of interest for example—to give us a starting point," Corbin said, jumping in and saving her.

"With such a big threat, I'm surprised our students aren't already keyed into this. It's very strange," Headmaster Allard said before Morvant could reply.

"Me too. This is highly unusual for this student body to be collectively in the dark," Pastor Dee said. "Have any reports come in from Watchers off campus? Have our European and Asian counterparts discovered anything on the matter?"

"No. We've been prosecuting this threat for about a week and we know the Dark Ones have been plotting the operation for much longer than that. We've not seen this kind of spiritual OPSEC from them in a very long time," the Shepherd commander said. "As for your requested starting point, Miss Worth, I believe we can help you there. Jed, why don't I turn the mic over to you."

"We've just returned from an overseas op and exfiltrated one of the lead scientists building the weapon. He has not had any direct dealings with the Dark Ones to his knowledge, but he did see this man at the test facility." Jed pressed a button on the notebook computer in front of him. A window popped up on the screen with a black-and-white photograph of a middle-aged man with a square jaw and buzz-cut military-style hair. The man in the photo was attractive for an old guy but very intense and severe-looking. "Have any of you had any dealings with him before?"

"I have," Corbin said. "He's a tricky Dark One . . . very good at scrubbing his threads."

"What does that mean?" Sarah Beth whispered to Pastor Dee.

"Later," Pastor Dee whispered back.

"Do you think you can find him?" Jed asked, worry lines creasing his normally smooth forehead.

"Did you cross paths with him on your last operation?" Corbin asked.

"No," Jed said, "but Dr. Zhao, the scientist who helped develop the weapon overseas, saw him at the testing facility where the weapon was being held."

"Did they interact?" Corbin asked.

"I don't think so."

"Hopefully it's enough," Corbin said, more to herself than to the room.

"Don't worry. My kids will find him," Headmaster Allard said, and Sarah Beth wondered how he could make that statement with such confidence.

I mean, it's not like he's doing any of the work.

Sarah Beth felt herself blush at the thought. She needed to remember that her gift was just that—a gift from God that came with incredible responsibility. It wasn't about her; it was about doing God's work. He had gifted her for a reason, and she imagined Headmaster Allard knew better than anyone how powerful the gifts could be, right? She said a short prayer, first for clarity to use her gifts, and then sheepishly she added a prayer for humility. She opened her eyes and saw Pastor Dee smiling at her.

The video conference wrapped up and the headmaster and Keepers all took turns contributing to a group "pep talk" to encourage the Watchers. Sarah Beth appreciated the effort, but Corbin, Brayden, and Josh all had *get me outta here* looks on their faces. Sarah Beth sensed, at least from Corbin, that they just wanted to stop talking and get to work.

Headmaster Allard led the group in prayer, then dismissed them to work on the task at hand. "I'll inform all of your instructors that you'll be missing classes today and as long as the tasking requires."

"Thanks, Headmaster," Josh said with a *too cool for school* attitude. He pushed back from the table and, turning to Brayden, said, "You wanna tag team this, bro?"

Brayden responded wordlessly with a right-handed shaka, and the two boys strolled out of the SCIF without even bothering to consult their Keepers.

"Sarah Beth, why don't you work with Corbin on this," Paster Dee said, stating the obvious but in a way that came across like she cared, which Sarah Beth knew she did.

"Yeah, of course," Sarah Beth said. "That would be great."

"C'mon, Sarah Beth. Let's head back to the Sanctuary." Corbin smiled at her own Keeper and started for the door.

Sarah Beth trotted after her and realized something about Watchers and Keepers that hadn't really occurred to her until she saw how the upperclassmen handled themselves. So long as they were on campus, the experienced Watchers didn't really need their Keepers—or at least they acted like they didn't. Inside the safety of these walls, the adults were pretty much like glorified hall monitors. They couldn't do the work that needed to be done. The kids were the stars of the show, and the upperclassmen knew it.

"Aren't we going to work here, in the Center?" Sarah Beth asked as they walked behind the dimly lit but frenetic Bullpen.

"No way," Corbin said, shooting an incredulous look over her shoulder. "Do you want to?"

"I don't know," she said, looking at the giant monitor wall. "It's kind of exciting down here."

"I hate TOCs. If I can work from the Sanctuary, that's always my first choice," Corbin said.

"I trust you," Sarah Beth said, watching the two boys slip into a pair of cool-looking recliners with TV screens on movable mounts attached to the armrests.

They took the White Room elevator back up to the Sanctuary and once again, as soon as Sarah Beth stepped out, she felt her anxiousness begin to fade and her heart rate slow. The calming effect of the space was undeniable.

"You're right; this is better," she said, following Corbin back to the same two chairs they'd been using before they got summoned to the Center.

"Sooo much better," Corbin said, settling into her chair.

"It's so weird—like, a few minutes ago we were going to try to locate Taylor Swift for fun and now we have to find a Dark One who wants to use the Death Star on us," Sarah Beth said, plopping down into her chair, the seat cushion deflating loudly beneath her butt as she did.

"Hold on a second. The Shepherds didn't say the Dark Ones were targeting Watchers with the weapon," Corbin said, turning to Sarah Beth.

"Who else are they going to use it on? I mean, they hate us. Victor is always trying to kidnap or kill us, so it's just logical. Which makes me wonder something."

"What?"

"Well, if the Shepherds have known about this weapon for a while, why haven't any Watchers picked something up on this?" Sarah Beth said. "Do you think they're trying to block us?"

"It's certainly possible," Corbin said.

"How?"

"Certain Dark Ones are very good at actively masking their thoughts, locations, and memories. Victor takes it up a level from there, maintaining a psychic wall around himself at all times. That's very hard to do and takes a lot of energy. Most people can't keep it up for more than a few hours, but Victor is different," Corbin explained. "He might be doing that with this weapon, shielding all the people involved from us. I don't think he's ever done that before, because the amount of concentration that would take would be insane, but he is the devil's right-hand man, so who knows what he's capable of."

"Is that the same thing as scrubbing? You mentioned that word earlier."

"No . . . ," Corbin said, letting a pause hang on the air as if she really didn't want to answer the question.

"What?"

The older girl blew air through her lips. "Remember what I just taught you about locating people by tracing their threads from contact to contact?"

"Yeah," she said, not liking the look on Corbin's face.

"Well, this guy—he scrubs those connections so Watchers can't locate him by tracing threads."

"By *scrub* do you mean *kill*?"

Corbin pursed her lips and nodded.

"He kills people simply because they crossed paths with him?" Sarah Beth stammered, aghast. "Random people, he just kills them?"

"Yeah . . . but he's strategic about it; otherwise he'd be killing nonstop."

"Has he—you know—*scrubbed* anyone we know? Anyone from here or from Trinity?"

"No one from here, Sarah Beth. We're safe here because we have each other," Corbin said, her voice solemn. "Enough about that. Let's get to work. We need to find this guy." She extended her hand to Sarah Beth. "We'll do it together. The power of two."

"Okay," Sarah Beth said, clasping her fingers around Corbin's. Corbin squeezed back.

"Father God, guide us," Corbin said softly. "Help us find our way to what we need to see. Help us do Your will and always light the path You have for us."

Amen, Sarah Beth added in her head. Then she took a deep breath, closed her eyes, and slipped into the Watcher world.

CHAPTER TWENTY-SEVEN

USAF C-17 ASSIGNED TO 305TH AIR MOBILITY WING

ON APPROACH TO RUNWAY 31

ATLANTIC CITY INTERNATIONAL AIRPORT

EGG HARBOR TOWNSHIP, NEW JERSEY

1104 HOURS LOCAL

Jed pondered the tremendous reach of the Shepherds organization as the huge but nearly empty cargo jet banked left on its turn from base leg to final. With a call, Ben had mobilized support for the Hong Kong op from whatever spooky task force Nisha apparently served in before joining Trinity. They'd fallen in on operators from the JSOC unit known commonly in the community as CAG, and in the public as Delta Force, just a few months ago in Iraq. They'd worked inside the Vatican, where Shepherds had a secret presence. And now he was on final approach in an active-duty Air Force C-17, made available to them in less than an hour after Corbin and Sarah Beth had found a potential lead, as vague as that lead seemed. They were arriving, with all of these expensive assets in play, with basically a sketch and a "feeling" that the target was in the northeast.

Ben was like the Wizard of Oz, and Jed couldn't help but wonder how much more was hidden behind this curtain.

The instant the jet touched down, his teammates rose and began collecting gear, unfazed by the swaying of the still-taxiing jet. Jed rose out of the comfortable airline-style seat—one of only a dozen and a half or so secured in the forward area of the cargo hold of the enormous plane—and walked aft. He stopped at the door just aft of the wing and peered out through the small, porthole-style window, one of the few windows this plane had. As the plane turned left, he gazed at the airport's main civilian terminal, crowded with commercial airliners and full of passengers going about their day completely unaware of the imminent danger.

Story of my life—chasing the evil in the shadows while the rest of the world goes on oblivious.

"Any chance we might hit the casinos—maybe take in a show?" Grayson joked, a big smile on his face.

"Yeah, right," Johnny said, rolling his eyes.

"Maybe when it's done," Jed said, ignoring Johnny and slapping Grayson on the arm. "Hit one of those buffets, maybe."

"Oh, I'm in," Eli said with a chuckle, slinging his bag over his shoulder and dragging a large Pelican case behind him as he headed toward the aft cargo ramp, which already began its slow descent down. Johnny spun on a heel and followed him, avoiding looking at Jed, or at least that's how it felt. Maybe the Shepherd felt frustrated to have been left behind on the trip to South America. Or maybe he just still resented that Jed, the nugget, was promoted to team leader. Whatever it was, Ben was right—Jed was going to have to address it soon, or the rift with Johnny would begin to erode the team's ability to function at the highest level.

He squinted at the bright sun as he walked down the ramp, spotting the bright-blue Air Force bus meant to take them off the flight line. Beyond, he saw the two rows of ghost-gray F-16 Falcons on the ramp, their red tail flash atop the vertical stabilizer matching the red devil's head squadron emblem painted beneath it. Jed smiled at the irony and heard the whine of the two additional jets taxiing onto the taxiway beyond, both with their canopies still up as they looped around behind the C-17 in preparation for takeoff. He wondered if they were part of the combat air patrols he imagined would be standing up all along the eastern seaboard, ready if needed to splash the plane containing the Dark Ones' new, insidious weapon.

Moments later they were on the bus, Jed dropping into the worn bench at the front, his large frame needing the extra legroom, and across the aisle from where Gayle and Nisha sat. Johnny slipped past him, again without a glance much less the customary bro nod, and headed to the back. Eli and Grayson dropped into the seat behind him, and Hyeon and Bex took the seat across from them, behind Nisha. Carl, like most snipers he knew, took a seat by himself, the long case containing his sniper rifle occupying the seat beside him.

Jed resisted the urge to engage in small talk, instead letting the team banter among themselves. The bus swung in a slow arc, showing him the row of hangars beyond the C-17—already being refueled by a team of Air Force personnel—and the small base beyond it. Other than the hangars, and the alert hangar past the taxiway where the two F-16s, canopies now down, were completing their preflight, the small base contained only a dozen or fewer buildings making up the south end of the commercial airport. Across the runways to the north sat the larger, civilian side of the airfield—housing the Atlantic City International Airport terminals. But the south side was home to the 177th Fighter Wing and the 119th Fighter Squadron, the "Jersey Devils," making up the New Jersey Air National Guard. The bus bumped and shook on questionable shocks as it lumbered over the ground runners for the open gate; then the driver accelerated down the road, grinding the gears as he did, between nondescript industrial-looking buildings. They traveled only a block before the bus creaked to a halt in a half-empty parking lot beside a short sidewalk leading to a white building, a small awning over a wall of dark glass and doors.

"Now that's door-to-door service," the junior airman driving the bus said, opening the door with a push bar right out of the seventies.

"Take everything?" Bex asked, flinging a large medical bag onto her shoulder.

"Yeah," Jed said. "We'll see where we can stage our gear inside."

Jed followed Nisha and Gayle down the steps of the bus.

"You guys need help with your gear?" asked one of the two Air Force BDU-clad airmen, no more than nineteen, Jed guessed, clean-cut and thin.

"Nah, we got it," Carl answered from behind him and Jed smiled. Operators weren't giving up control of their gear, and for sure no sniper would relinquish control of his weapons and kit.

Between the airmen stood a fit, flight suit–clad aviator, a blue flight cap on his head and dark aviator glasses on his face. The gold oak leaves on his shoulders made him a major and the black patch holding his star-topped silver wings on his left chest identified him as a command pilot, but instead of a name on his tag, he wore his call sign—Rhino.

The major extended a hand to Jed, sensing perhaps that he was in charge.

"I'm Major Reynolds," he said, his smile confident and his shake firm. "I'm the deputy commander of the fighter squadron. Colonel Mitchell asked me to meet you and bring you to the conference room."

"I'm Jed."

"Okay, Jed," the major said, still smiling but his tone serious. "We don't get a lot of spooky visitors here at the Guard, so I'm looking forward to hearing what's up."

Jed nodded.

We'll see, he thought.

Major Reynolds and the airmen led them inside, where they were greeted by the kiss of cool, industrial air. They walked past the wall of pictures of the command staff surrounding the devil's head unit patch engraved in wood. To the right, beside a picture labeled *Lieutenant Colonel David Sharpe*, listed as the commander of the 119th Fighter Squadron, hung the photo of a serious-looking Major Craig Reynolds, deputy commander, in dress blues.

Jed scanned the other pictures—including Colonel Derrick Mitchell at the top center above the plaque, the 177th wing commander—as they passed by and headed down the hallway to the left. Just a short distance down, one of the airmen opened a large wooden door, then stood aside as Major Reynolds led them into a generously sized conference room, with a large dark wood table surrounded by a dozen tall-back black-leather chairs. At the far end, a door opened and an older but equally fit man walked in, clad in a green-bag flight suit, graying temples framing a tanned face.

"Gentlemen and ladies, welcome," he said, and Jed liked him immediately.

"Craig, you stay if you would. Airmen, thanks for your help. Give us the room, will you?"

"Yes, sir," one of the young men said, his shoulders back and his spine straight; then the two attendants left, closing the door behind them.

"Take a seat," the colonel said and dropped into the chair at the head of the table beside his office door. "My deputy will be along in a moment with some spooks who arrived a little while ago . . ." He looked Jed up and down as the team took their seats. "Not as spooky as you guys, I'll say, but you know what I mean. You guys JSOC?" The colonel leaned back in his chair and for a moment Jed thought he might clunk his desert boots up on the table.

"No, sir," Jed answered. "We're with a special task force . . ."

"Yeah, yeah," the colonel said with a good-natured grin, waving a hand. "You can spare me the company line. I did a tour as a JTAC with AFSOC and deployed with JSOC teams on multiple occasions, so I know operators when I see them. It doesn't matter in any case. What can we do for you folks?" he asked as the door behind him opened and a woman officer—also in a flight suit and also sporting command pilot wings—led in two other people, a man and woman, both clad in Army cammies. "Denise, these guys are with a 'special task force,'" he said as if sharing an inside joke.

"Is that so? Great to meet you," the officer said, all business. "Your friends beat you here, but they haven't had much to say."

"I told you what we know, which is basically nothing," the man beside her said, the older of the two, an officer with twin bars of a captain on the flap on the front of his cammies.

"Lieutenant Colonel Summers is the deputy wing commander and you've met Rhino, the deputy squadron commander. The CO of the 119th is David Sharpe, but he's TAD at present, so Rhino is acting. So should we chat or just give you the room?"

Jed smiled at the man. He'd dropped his time at the JSOC unit very strategically, and it did in fact make Jed feel better about the man.

"Sir, perhaps we can bring our Army intel colleagues up to speed with you here and then let you decide what is appropriate to share and with whom." It was a very diplomatic way to say that he needed everyone else out of the room. If not for the special ops pedigree, Jed guessed he might have asked the colonel to leave as well.

"You heard him, guys," Colonel Mitchell said. "We'll catch up shortly."

The squadron commander and Mitchell's deputy nodded and left, clearly not delighted, but they were senior officers who got it.

The two Army intel specialists took seats beside the colonel.

"I'm Captain Bill Nolte and this is Specialist Wanda Young," the man said, again looking toward Jed instinctively.

"It's great to meet you, Bill," Jed said, avoiding rank and title to further the "task force" narrative. "This is my team." He made quick, first-name-only introductions of everyone, including Gayle, whom he did not differentiate from the rest of the team, for which she gave him a grateful nod.

"Specialist Young here is one of the best 35 Foxtrots in the unit," Bill said with a nod to his colleague. "Since no one told us anything other than to haul ass up here, I figured I'd bring the best."

"Thank you, sir," the woman said, apparently genuinely flattered. Jed guessed there wasn't a lot of hollow flattery thrown around in whatever group they worked for.

"We're from the 706th Military Intelligence Group," Bill said, his tone suggesting that would explain everything, but it didn't—not for Jed, at least, who had never heard of them.

Too many units, with too many people, sharing too little information and somehow I'm supposed to remember all their names, discern the pecking order, and figure how to get them cooperating with each other without busting my NOC. Yeah, right.

"Are you up from Georgia or Virginia?" Nisha asked, giving the man a knowing smile.

"Virginia," Bill said. "We're Det Bravo."

"Perfect," Nisha said. "We'll need some help from the folks you augment."

"Not a problem," Bill said. "Our orders came from the ODNI and had no limitations."

"Great," Jed said, not fully understanding the insider banter but thankful he had Nisha. What he did gather was this was a highly plugged-in intelligence unit, probably working side by side with the NSA or more, and they were tasked by Washington to give Jed's team unlimited support.

ODNI again. Just how high up is Ben connected?

"So here's what we've got." Jed pulled out a stiff folder from the backpack at his feet. "There is, we believe, an imminent terror attack in the works. Highly, highly reliable intelligence suggests that it will originate in the northeast, possibly New Jersey or Pennsylvania. It's a group you are unlikely to be familiar with, but one we specialize in, and while you may not know them, they have been involved directly, both operationally and in a supporting role, with many if not all of the organizations you *are* familiar with."

Bill and Specialist Wanda Young exchanged glances, and Bill frowned.

"Who did you say you were with?" Bill asked. Then he waved a hand. "Not specifically, of course, because I know you won't tell me. But are you IC or military? I ask because it would help us out to know what playground you're playing in."

"You've not worked in our playground before," Eli said.

"But," Jed added, giving Eli a wry grin, "if it helps, we work in the space *between* the IC and DoD."

He pulled out a printed photo of a sketch Corbin had made, marveling at the detail and quality of her art. He slid it across to them.

"What's this?" Wanda asked.

"This is where we believe the target is located."

"Where is it?" Bill asked.

"Well, that's what we need help determining," Jed said. He was aware of Colonel Mitchell's head turning slightly left and right, like a man watching a tennis match, listening carefully and quietly to the exchange.

"Obviously," the female intelligence specialist said. "But I mean, where *generally* do you think it is? I mean, where was the artist located when this was sketched?"

"Hard to say," Jed said, trying his best to dodge the question. "Like I said, we believe it's in this area somewhere—New Jersey or Pennsylvania, maybe southern New York."

"I think what Wanda is asking is where was the operative positioned at the time that sketch was made?" Bill said, frustration in his voice.

"Hard to say," Jed said. Bill let out a snort and handed the sketch back to Wanda. "Look, I'm not being cagey or trying to protect an asset. Nothing like that. We just, literally, don't know."

"Hard to say, huh?" Bill sighed. He bent over and looked at the sketch again. "Look, guys, we'll help however we can, but I gotta be honest, this picture is about as helpful as a picture of a needle and a guess that it might be in a haystack somewhere. You have no markings on this sketch at all—no names or building numbers, no geography in the background. This looks like about a hundred thousand other hangars or warehouses all around the country . . ."

"Hangar, probably," Wanda said. "There's a wind sock . . ."

"A warehouse could have a wind sock for helicopters to land," Bill argued.

"Yeah, but see these circles in front, on the concrete outside—spaced evenly. They look like airplane tie-downs. The details are remarkable for a hand-drawn sketch. This is likely at an FBO or on the executive side of a larger airport."

Bill gave a grudging nod. "Like I said, she's the best 35 Foxtrot we have. But still, this is not much to go on."

"We can run it through the image stock pretty quick with the computers over at—" Wanda stopped and glanced at her boss. "Over at the parent command."

"Yeah, we can start there," Bill agreed. "But still . . ."

"I know," Wanda said. "It's not much. Any chance you can get us more? Any other landmarks at all? Anything?"

Jed nodded. "We can ask. Our intel people never cease to amaze us," he said, a memory of Corbin and Sarah Beth playing the card game Speed at a blur in the eastern Tennessee safe house coming to him. "Do you have a TOC we can stream intel to as we get it?"

"We can set up here," Bill said and glanced over at the colonel, who nodded.

"Of course," Colonel Mitchell said. "What kind of space do you need?"

"Not much," Specialist Wanda Young said. "Enough to set up a few computers and run a line to our own satellite antenna."

"Perhaps we can commandeer one of the hangars, and my team and these guys can all set up in one place," Bill added.

"Works for me," Mitchell said. He pressed a button on the small box beside him and then spoke into it. "Hey, Rhino, come back in here."

Major Reynolds emerged through the connecting door in seconds.

"Rhino, free up a hangar right away for these guys to use as a TOC.

They'll need to set up satellite comms and I imagine they'll need access to the high side for all their computers."

"I'll make it happen immediately," Rhino said. "You need to run line to your antenna up high—like the roof of the hangar?"

"We don't have to, sir, but it would be great if we could," Wanda answered.

"Done," Rhino said. "You've got everything you need in the Pelicans you brought?"

"Yes, sir," Wanda said.

"I'll get some of our ground specialists to help you get up and running."

"Thank you, sir."

"And, Craig, have security posted around the hangar you give them and add security to the gate. Let's go to condition Alpha while they're here," the colonel added.

"I agree, sir," Rhino said.

"So," Colonel Mitchell said, crossing his arms and staring at Jed. "I'm gonna read between the lines a little here, son. You have a sketch of what looks like a hangar, an imminent threat, and you're staging from a fighter base. We also have been tasked with additional CAP—that's combat air patrols—and we're aware that's true for the entire East Coast. Can I assume this is an airborne threat?"

"Yes, sir, you can," Jed answered.

"And if this is some 9/11 kind of thing, is there a chance we'll be shooting something down, Jed?"

"We hope not, sir," Jed said. "We hope our intel assets can help us find the target before they can get it airborne."

"Let's hope so, son," the colonel said, rising from his seat now. "Splashing a civil aircraft over densely populated areas is almost certain to end with some collateral damage. We need to avoid that, okay?"

"Yes, sir. That's the goal," Jed said, rising and shaking the colonel's outstretched hand.

"Rhino, get them settled and then meet back with me in the ops center," the colonel said as he headed through the door into his office. "We need to update the flight board and overlap our CAP for now. I'll be flying some of these, and Summers will fly lead on some as well. Let's keep senior pilots coupled with our less experienced guys on every hop. If this hits the fan, I want cool heads in control of the triggers."

"You got it, Colonel."

And with that, the wing commander was gone, shutting the door behind him.

"Let's get you set up," the squadron commander said. "Sounds like we all have a lot of work to do."

"Listen, I need more," Bill said, sidling up beside Jed. "This sounds like the real deal, and if you want to find this threat in time, you need to give me more to work with."

"We're working on it, I promise," Jed said. "Nisha and Gayle represent our N2 shop here; they'll be sharing everything we have with you in real time."

The man nodded, but his face suggested he had his doubts. As if to allay both their fears, Jed felt the vibration of his secure phone and fished it out of his cargo pocket.

"Yeah? This is Jed."

"It's Corbin," an excited voice said on the other end. "I've got something!"

Jed snapped his fingers to get the attention of the team and waved Nisha over, grinning at Bill as he did.

"What've ya got, Corbin?" he said, using her name more to convey to Nisha what was going on.

"I'm sending another sketch," she said excitedly. "It's like a skyline, but kind of a small town—looks like a beach town. I saw it through the eyes of the same dude as the hangar. It's a partial view, like out a window or something, but it's pretty detailed."

"Corbin, you rock," Jed exclaimed.

"The whole team is working hard on this," she said, and he could almost see her modest blush, the same one she wore every time he complimented her. "It should be on your tablet now."

"Keep up the good work and send us anything you see. Nothing is too small or insignificant," he said, and after she promised to do so, he ended the call.

Jed fished the small tablet out of his pocket and pressed his fingerprint onto the reader. The device opened and he tapped the icon for the incoming image. As always, he marveled at not just the detail but the beauty, scale, and depth of the sketch he knew Corbin had done almost effortlessly. The drawing depicted a beach town, the sketch cut off at the edges as if the scene was being viewed through a small window. Jed had the sense the viewer Corbin had channeled must have been looking through an airplane window—either flying very low or perhaps on approach to a nearby airport because the image was an aerial view of the surf-side homes, condos, and shops.

"Will this help?" he said, showing the image to Bill.

"Oh, hell yeah," Bill said. "This is something I can work with. Combined with the other image, I should be able to get you a location."

"How soon?" Jed asked. "Because the clock is really ticking here."

"Quickly," Bill said, not committing to a time, Jed noticed.

Jed handed the tablet to Nisha, who jogged out of the room behind the two Army intel specialists. Jed knew they were connected to NSA as well as the other spooky intel organization in northern Virginia. They'd also have instant support from NCTC in DC.

They'd have the answer fast, he felt certain.

"Take everything, check gear, and be ready to roll," he said to Eli. "We're now on alert five."

He needed everyone ready to mobilize on a moment's notice. The enemy was close now . . . he could feel it.

CHAPTER TWENTY-EIGHT

Jed's hands flew over his gear as he checked extra magazines, blow-out kit, radio frequencies, blades, and grenades—two M84 flash-bangs on the left and two M67 frags on the right—and the myriad of little things he kept handy. He watched the team as each blazed quickly through their own ritual, the exception being Nisha, who moved more methodically. She had proven she could handle herself in a firefight, both in Rome and Iraq, and she'd even outperformed half the team in the kill house, but he knew that operating was not her preferred element.

"You wanna stay back and run TOC comms for us here?" he asked, leaning close and speaking in a hushed voice.

"Why?" she asked with a wry grin. "Worried you can't keep up?"

"No," he said awkwardly, "I just . . ."

"Relax, Jed," she said, tightening the cummerbund of her plate-carrying vest and then slipping a Sig Sauer P229 pistol into the holster on the front. "I'm just messing with you. I get that I'm no SEAL or Green Beret, but I'll carry my weight. If I'm to make any sense of the intelligence we uncover on the X, I need to be there. I need to . . ." She hesitated and looked over at him.

"Feel it?" he asked, fascinated by all he was learning about his teammate this week.

"Yeah," she said, chuckling. "Sort of. It's almost more like, I don't know, like a residue left behind, you know?"

He did and nodded.

Outside the hangar, a pair of UH-60L Black Hawk helicopters from First Battalion, 150th Aviation regiment were spinning up. He slipped on his helmet and the Peltor noise-canceling headset and instantly the whine of their engines became background hum. He checked the frequency on his encrypted radio.

"Comms check," he said into his boom mic, then slipped his assault rifle over his head and onto his chest. "Joshua Bravo is now Sword. This is Sword One, how copy Sword Variable?"

"Sword One, you're five by," came the cool voice of the watch coordinator in the TOC back in Nashville.

"One, Zero—I've got your back," David's voice added, and Jed smiled, picturing his TSL in a headset in the TOC. They'd come a long way when David's voice brought him comfort instead of grating his nerves.

"Watcher One is with you," came another voice, a teenage male voice, and he felt disappointed to not hear Corbin in his ear—or his head.

"Copy, Watcher One," Jed said, nodding to Eli, then tilting his head toward the open hangar door and the helicopters spun up on the ramp just outside. Eli spun a fist over his head and chopped toward the helos, and Joshua Bravo headed out in two lines of four. "You got anything for us, Watcher?"

"No, sir," said the young but steady voice. "It's quiet for all of us back here—weirdly so, in fact. We're working hard and I'll chime in when we get something."

"Roger." Jed hustled to the lead of the stick of operators forming a line to the left. He did a quick comms check, listening as his team of operators checked in, then switched over to check the dedicated air channel.

"Vandal Flight, Sword One—radio check," he said.

"Vandal One," the first helo pilot replied.

"Vandal Two, five by. Let's do this," came the enthusiastic reply of the middle-aged warrant he had met earlier, a blooded veteran of both Iraq and Afghanistan who was at the controls for bird two.

Jed took his place in the rear corner of the open port side door of the helo and watched the others pile in. A moment later, the bird nosed forward, the rotors thrummed, and his stomach dropped as they popped into the air. As soon as they were airborne, the pilot banked left, heading south away from the active runways at less than five hundred feet off the ground. They completed the half circle, headed east over the Atlantic City boardwalk, and once over the ocean, turned north to follow the coast. Moments later, Vandal Two sidled in beside them to the left, and Jed could see Grayson and Johnny through the starboard side door.

Point Pleasant, the New Jersey beach town in Corbin's second drawing, sat on the Atlantic Ocean just sixty miles north of them—less than a twenty-minute flight in the Black Hawks. Seven miles northwest of the town was the Monmouth Executive Airport, where the intel magicians had determined that a large corporate hangar, owned by a farm equipment manufacturer, was the hangar in Corbin's first drawing. This hangar was the target, the site where Victor's minions—and dare he hope Victor himself?—had set up shop to deploy the directed energy weapon. The hangar sat off by itself, on the south side of runway 14/32—a baseball field to the west abutting a football field and two matching soccer fields adjacent to the south, all surrounded by trees. It was a perfect location for the Dark Ones—away from peering eyes at the outskirts of suburbia. Tactically speaking, however, Jed could use this to his advantage. Off by itself, the hangar was hard to defend, with a wooded field south from which to make an initial approach.

"Sword One, Variable," Ben's voice said on the comms channel.

Jed smiled. He was glad to know his boss was in the TOC. "One," he said, acknowledging the query.

"We just received the feed from a drone pass over the target. Two vehicles in the lot with a single tango by the parking side entrance, midhangar, apparently having a smoke. Four tangos inside—two in the north corner close to one another and stationary, perhaps seated. Two other midhangar are moving about. Will give you final pass when you're on approach but sent the last image to your tablet."

"Sword One, roger," Jed said, but he didn't pull the tablet out. He could see in his mind what Ben reported, and the layout of the hangar was already burned into his brain from the brief.

What he really needed was confirmation that the tangos at the hangar were bad guys—part of the threat—and not just innocent people in the wrong place at the wrong time.

"Watcher, you have anything on the tangos?" Jed asked.

"Negative, Sword," came a young man's frustrated voice. "I don't get it. We can get to them but just can't get in. It's like they're inside some crazy cone of silence or something."

Jed frowned. He wondered a moment if Corbin could get inside but assumed she was already working on it. There wasn't anything bigger than this going on INCONUS for the Shepherds, and he knew both Ben and Pastor Dee would not have their best Watcher on the bench.

"Seven minutes," came the call from the pilot in his headset, his encrypted radio set to both the tactical and air channels.

"Seven minutes," Jed announced in the voice-activated mic, holding up seven fingers and showing them to the other three Shepherds. He got nods back.

The helo dropped in altitude and screamed low across what Jed remembered was the Bel-Aire Golf club. He chuckled as he saw a golfer throw his arms up in frustration at the noise, the man's Pro-Am winning putt interrupted. After conducting a touch-and-go simulated landing at the airfield for the appearance of a training evolution, the pilots banked southeast and executed a downwind leg, outside the airport boundary along the edge of the woods and empty sports fields.

The helo slowed upon reaching the drop zone, hovering at treetop level and out of sight of the target hangar. Carl kicked the rope bags out and Jed shifted into position for the slide. He twisted his hands together, locking them on the thick rope, and grabbed the free end dangling out the door with his feet, his right boot locking in tightly against the arch of his left. He descended quickly, no longer worried about the pain on landing from his healed hip. He glanced at Nisha, descending beside him on the second rope with perfect form. Above, he felt the jerk of Carl coming on the rope as he hit the halfway mark of the barely thirty-foot slide. A heartbeat later, he was on the ground at the edge of the football field, part of the small sports park just outside the airport perimeter, separated from the fence line by woods. He quick-stepped clear of the rope and took a knee, scanning his sector over his rifle as Nisha did the same to his right. He heard and felt the thud of the ropes hitting the ground behind him, released from Vandal One, which confirmed that Carl and Hyeon were on the ground and clear. Above, the Black Hawk zoomed away just as Vandal Two passed overhead.

Flawless.

The whole thing had taken barely five seconds.

He scanned the tree line just beyond the football field. Seeing nothing, he motioned his team to follow and moved into the woods. They fanned out, Jed and Nisha moving left and Hyeon trailing just behind and right of Carl. Like a single organism, they moved with near-silent precision through the trees.

"Sword, Variable—sitrep," Ben said in his ear. "You have one tango still by the rear door, suggesting he may be a sentry. There are three tangos at the north end, the thermal silhouettes suggesting they may be sitting at a table. Fourth is midhangar moving about. No approaching vehicles on the access road that we can see."

Jed answered with a double click.

They reached the first break in the trees and Jed peered across an open field at two derelict trailers, seemingly unoccupied on a trash-covered lot. He chopped a hand and the team sprinted across the lot to the next patch of cover. He moved the team through the thinning grove of trees between the trash field and the edge of the airport perimeter road until the target hangar was in sight. Jed raised a closed fist over his left shoulder and took a knee, feeling the rest of the team spreading out and doing the same.

He watched the rear sentry pacing back and forth by the door, a cigarette in between the fingers of his right hand. Not nervous—just bored.

And completely unprepared for what was about to come.

Jed watched their two Black Hawks conduct another touch-and-go on the field to his right, flaring and dropping onto the pavement, then rolling out down the runway and lifting off again. He could see Eli's and Bex's legs dangling out the port side door of Vandal Two, which was all part of the ruse.

The plan was to commence the assault when the helicopters came back on the final "training" landing. Jed had briefed the pilot on how much time they needed before they diverted over to the hangar, so Vandal flight would make the call. Vandal Two would drop the other four Shepherds on the ramp side of the hangar and both teams would converge and breach simultaneously.

It was a good plan, except for the fact they'd yet to confirm the people in the hangar were actual bad guys. The thought had been nagging him for a while, and with just minutes before bullets started flying, it would be really nice to get a positive Dark One confirmation from back home.

"Watcher, Sword One—anything at all on the tangos in the hangar?" Jed asked on the radio.

"No," came a dejected reply. "I'm soooo sorry, Sword. I am really trying. We all are."

"All good, Watcher," he whispered.

But it wasn't, was it? Why were they having such trouble?

"One minute," the pilot of Vandal One announced in Jed's Peltor headset.

Jed closed his eyes, trying desperately to remember how to follow a thread to another mind. He'd not done it *on purpose* before and only successfully with Corbin helping to guide him. He reached out—trying to feel his way into any of the minds in the hangar—but instead of finding threads, he hit a wall. No wonder the Watchers couldn't get in. It was as if someone had set up a spiritual version of a communications jammer around the target.

"Thirty seconds," the pilot said in his ear, snapping him out of the mind place.

Jed opened his eyes and popped into a combat crouch.

"Ten seconds, Sword," came the pilot's cool, low voice.

Jed locked his gaze on the door sentry, who'd turned his back to their position. He raised a closed fist, holding and readying his team tight behind him—Carl to his right, Hyeon and Nisha spread out to his left.

An instant later, the pilot called, "Sword, Vandal—go, go, go . . ."

Jed chopped a hand forward and surged out of the tree line, leaning forward into his rifle, still in a combat crouch, aware of Carl matching pace just to his left. Hyeon and Nisha would angle slightly right, clearing the near corner of the building as Jed and Carl made for the door and the single sentry. They moved swiftly, eager to cover the distance before the sentry turned and they lost the element of surprise.

Reaching the perimeter fence, Carl took a knee to cover while Jed went up and over. Fingers locked into the chain link, Jed took the eight-foot fence with only two big kicks of his legs, rolling over the top with his back protected from the barbed wire topper by his plate carrier vest. Midroll he gained control of his rifle before dropping the eight feet back to the ground and landing in a crouch. Rifle up, he placed the red dot of his holographic sight, magnified through the Vortex magnifier, onto the back of the sentry's head while Carl cleared the fence. Hyeon and Nisha would be doing the same at an offset. At the moment, their only real threat was the sentry walking toward the far corner of the hangar. Carl tapped Jed's shoulder and they were off, sprinting through the grass toward the hangar, angling to stay out of the tango's peripheral vision.

As they closed range, Jed could make out the sentry's weapon, a short, fully automatic machine pistol under his right armpit. He hoped to reach the man for a silent kill and not be forced to fire, but it felt more unlikely with every passing second. Jed hovered his red targeting dot nearly motionless on the side of the man's head, a learned and practiced skill of keeping his torso floating above his churning legs.

The sentry abruptly froze.

Jed surged forward.

The man whirled.

Jed took a knee, steadied his aim, and when the man's eyes flashed red—confirming he was indeed a Dark One—he squeezed the trigger. The sentry's head jerked backward as Jed's suppressed round tore through his skull. The body pitched over and dropped into the gravel beside the hangar. Jed had angled his shot carefully, minimizing the likelihood that the round would exit the man's head and impact the hangar wall, alerting the tangos inside to their presence.

"Variable, One—" Jed said, but Ben talked over him with the info he wanted.

"No movement inside on thermal, One," came Ben's cool voice.

Ben had not mentioned the status and position of the four-man team still riding in Vandal Two, but Jed was out of time and had to assume they were on schedule to drop and breach on the opposite side of the hangar. He moved to the door, Carl crossing behind him and taking position on the far side.

Jed scanned the parking lot and surrounding area behind for threats as his teammate prepared to set a breacher charge on the hangar door. He felt a squeeze on his right shoulder announcing Nisha and Hyeon had joined them.

"Vandal Two—five seconds," came the report Jed had been waiting for.

"Check the door," Nisha said. "Feels open."

Jed nodded to Carl, who reached a hand onto the knob, turned it, and a big grin spread across the operator's face.

First lucky break . . .

The door was unlocked; no need for a breacher. Carl rocked his head up and down, establishing a three-nod cadence as Jed pulled a flash-bang grenade from his kit. On three, Carl jerked the door open. Jed pulled the pin, tossed the banger inside, and Carl shut the door quickly behind his toss.

"Sword Two on the slide," Eli announced in his ear, just as the sound of the second helicopter arriving into a hover on the ramp side of the hangar reached him.

The whump of the flash-bang rocked the corrugated metal of the hangar wall.

"Go," Jed barked and Carl jerked the hangar door open.

Low in his crouch, Jed slipped inside and cleared left. He felt Carl enter and clear right, with Hyeon and Nisha on their heels. His corner clear, Jed vectored left, exiting the lane of potential defensive fire, which came a heartbeat later. A barrage of gunfire tore through the hangar door now ten feet behind him, tracers screaming through the smoke from the grenade like laser beams. The shots went wild, the bad guy shooters still blind from the flash-bang.

He moved left, Carl trailing with him to his right, reading the play, as Nisha and Hyeon continued to push to the center. Movement in the smoke to center got his eye, but the pair of Shepherds unloaded a volley.

Jed heard a scream and a body drop followed by a rifle clattering to the floor.

"Sword One, keep your stick clear of the center hangar door. Blowing it in three . . . two . . . one . . ."

Jed squeezed his eyes shut a moment to protect his vision from the blast, but the charge was perfect, with precious little visible explosion inside the hangar. Then the door pulled open, daylight streaming in and backlighting the silhouettes of Eli and his stick spreading out as they entered and cleared corners.

A double tap echoed from the north corner, where Eli's team had just breached.

Two tangos appeared though the hazy smoke ahead, both with rifles. Jed spun left, trusting Carl with the tango to the right. Carl fired first, two thumps of suppressed fire. Jed was about to squeeze his own trigger when the fighter in his sights dropped his weapon, threw his hands up, and dropped to his knees in surrender.

Jed circled, his red dot still floating on the man's head. He'd never seen a Dark One surrender, and his pulse pounded in his temples, fully expecting the flash of a suicide vest detonation any moment. Dark Ones weren't conventional jihadists, but they were fanatics with demons inside coercing their every move.

"Clear," Eli hollered, loud enough for Jed to hear a beat before the voice reached him in his Peltors.

"Six is clear," Grayson echoed.

"Three is clear," Carl confirmed.

"One is clear, but I have a crow," Jed announced, advancing slowly toward the man kneeling in front of him. "Show me inside your jacket."

The man did, his face and eyes showing more fear than evil. He pulled open his jacket in both directions, then shot his hands back up into the air.

"On the ground, legs spread, and arms out at your sides," Jed commanded next.

While Jed held his targeting dot on the man's head, Carl surged forward, placing a knee in the center of the man's back, flex-cuffing the tango's hands in the small of his back, and then patting him down with the back of a gloved hand. When he was satisfied, Carl gave Jed a nod.

"Three deceased tangos confirmed inside the hangar," Eli announced.

"One down outside at the rear," Hyeon added, since Eli had not been on that side for the breach.

"And one crow secured," Carl said.

"Any other signatures, Variable?" Jed asked into his boom mic.

"Negative, Sword One," Ben answered. "Show just you and the tangos you've accounted for. What've you got?"

Jed turned in a slow circle, chest tightening as the smoke thinned to reveal his worst fear. "No plane," he said. "We've got an empty hangar."

"One, we have a large crate at the south end of the hangar," Nisha called from across the room. "It appears to be the right dimensions."

"Is that a jackpot call?" Jed said, hope rising as he watched her move to peek inside the open crate.

"Negative," Nisha said, dashing his hope before it could really take hold. "It's empty."

That meant the weapon probably had been here, Jed realized, and now it could be anywhere.

"Dry hole, Variable," Jed said, unable to mask his disappointment and worry. "We'll be off the X in two minutes with whatever intel we can take and one crow to interrogate."

His words might have filled the team in the TOC with hope, but they did nothing for him.

Because the weapon could easily be airborne right now, and they still didn't know the target. Victor, maddeningly, remained a step ahead.

"Variable, we need to interrogate any satellite overflight imagery and any other local security camera footage that might have recorded any and all aircraft coming and going from this hangar in the last twenty-four hours."

"Copy, Sword," Ben answered. "Retrieve what you can from the hangar and clear out. We estimate a police presence in less than four minutes, so be gone before then."

"Where do you want us?" Jed asked, jogging toward the north end of the hangar to help Eli and the rest of Joshua Bravo collect any electronics that might be in the hangar and to photograph anything that might be useful.

"Back to your point of origin," Ben said, referring to the Air National

Guard base in Atlantic City where they'd briefed. "We'll have more direction by the time you land. Secure the crow. I'm on my way to you."

Ben's coming to us. Does that mean he has fresh intel—something he doesn't want to put out on the air?

"Roger that, Variable," Jed said.

"Vandal is on the X and ready for dust off," the lead pilot reported.

"Sixty seconds," Jed replied as he watched his teammates dumping a couple of cell phones and a laptop into a canvas bag that Johnny had pulled from his kit. Behind him, Carl and Hyeon were dragging their prisoner toward the north hangar door as Nisha and Bex photographed and inspected the empty wooden crate.

There was precious little else to take.

Jed scanned the dead bodies littering the floor of the hangar and prayed their prisoner would have something to say.

CHAPTER
TWENTY-NINE

The conversation with Johnny was one Jed wasn't looking forward to having but one that needed to be had. The two of them needed to sort out all the emotional baggage they'd both been carrying before they next found themselves in combat. The stress had been weighing on Jed for weeks, but there simply hadn't been time before now to have a one-on-one.

Jed motioned for Johnny to join him, and the Shepherd's sour expression signaled what he thought of that.

"You summoned me?" Johnny said with an edge to his voice.

"Yeah," Jed said. "I think we need to talk about the dynamic here—about the friction we're having, you and me—before it degrades the team."

Johnny looked at him with bemused defiance, arms crossed, as he took a seat in the makeshift ready area they had created in the hangar. "So you're gonna give me some sort of reprimand, I suppose?"

Jed sighed and took a seat opposite him. "Nope. I want to talk to you as a teammate—brother to brother."

"Not as team leader?" Johnny asked, cocking his head to the side.

"As *teammates*," he said, leaning in. "Look, man, it's pretty clear you have a problem with my leadership of Joshua Bravo, but we need to sort it out or it's going to affect our readiness—affect the entire team. No holds barred, brother. What is it?"

Johnny looked surprised, disarmed even.

"It's not you personally," Johnny said, clearly softening. "It's just, I came up the hard way in this organization. After my time in SOF, I felt the calling—you know what I mean? It's like, you don't exactly choose the Shepherds, right? It calls to you. It's a God thing . . ."

Jed nodded and smiled. That he definitely got.

"When I came here, I was put on the security detail with Sanderson and the other guys. I don't know why. Morvant said he felt that was God's plan in the short term. That *short term* turned into two years—*two years* before I got called up to a team. I've been with Joshua Bravo since, serving and doing everything asked of me without complaint. Then you come along . . ."

"And I cut to the front of the line and take the leadership job?" Jed said. "A job you hoped to grow into?"

Johnny laughed. He seemed to be as genuine right now as Jed could remember ever seeing him. All the bravado and snark were gone.

"You know, the thing is, I don't even want to lead a team. At least I don't think I do. But Eli—he was being groomed and next in line. CAG operator, born leader, amazing fighter, humble. Then you roll in and now he's serving under you. Since when does that make sense?"

Jed nodded again. "Johnny, I don't have a good answer for you. I was as surprised as you when they assigned me to a leadership position. But here's the thing, bro. We're both SOF operators and we understand big-boy rules. We don't pick the team; the team picks us, just like back in the military. What I've learned from Ben's leadership and David's spiritual counsel is that our Higher Authority is calling the shots. We need to yield to His purpose to succeed at our mission. He decides our maximum and our minimum contributions. Remember the Scripture David shared about the first being last and needing to serve others before the journey can begin? That resonated with me, because in the SEAL Teams, the leaders I most respected were just like that—servant leaders. They put Team and mission before themselves. Servant leaders never ask anything of their teammates they aren't already giving themselves. That's what I'll always try to do at the helm of Joshua Bravo, Johnny. Mission before self, team before self—always."

Johnny's eyes softened further, but he looked down, perhaps not sure what to say.

Man, I really screwed this up. I treated Jed like he was no better than my jackass father, who left us.

Jed shut the words out, not wanting to invade his teammate's thoughts.

"Johnny, here's what I can offer you," he said, leaning in now. "There's a place for you on this team as long as you want it. I will stand shoulder to shoulder and serve at your side. But if you believe that you'd be more productive and fulfilled somewhere else, I can get you transferred to another team. I'll take the heat for it—say it was my idea and my inability to provide the leadership you deserve."

Johnny looked up at him now. "You'd take the hit? Make it look like your fault?"

Jed shrugged. "Team before self."

The sound of footsteps to their right drew both their attention.

"Hey, Jed, sorry to interrupt, but Ben's here," Eli said, jogging up.

"Thanks for the heads-up."

Eli turned to Johnny, sensing he'd interrupted something, perhaps. "'Sup, Johnny?"

"Eli," Johnny said with a nod.

Jed pressed to his feet. "Think about it and let me know."

The younger operator nodded slowly—in understanding, not in answer—and Jed felt something pass between them. He followed Eli out of the hangar and watched the inbound Gulfstream G700 corporate jet taxi around the bend at the north corner of the military side of the Atlantic City airport and then head their way.

A hand on his shoulder while he waited made Jed jump, and he laughed at himself. *Big deal Navy SEAL, letting an Army intel pogue sneak up on him.*

"This your guys?" Captain Bill Nolte asked, jerking a thumb to where the jet sat on the taxiway, the airstair allowing four soldiers inside to inspect the interior before letting it onto the ramp with hundreds of millions of dollars' worth of F-16s and other equipment.

"Yeah," Jed said. "My boss, actually. You got any good news for me?"

Nolte shook his head. "No, sorry. We're still wading through and have NSA and the Activity at Fort Belvoir working with us—a dedicated team, actually, so whoever you guys are, ODNI is clearing hurdles left and right for you. So far, we got a big zero. We've decrypted a bunch of stuff on the phones and the one laptop, but there is just nothing actionable. Not yet at least. These things take time."

"Unfortunately, time is something we don't have," Jed said.

"If you could get your supersecret sketch artist to send us another picture, we'd gladly run down any new threads he can offer."

Jed nodded. The jet taxied over, stopping less than fifty yards away. The whine of the turbines slowed and got quiet, the door opened, and the airstair lowered slowly and smoothly. Ben appeared in the doorway, a duffel with his kit and weapons over one shoulder and a coyote-tan backpack over the other. His khaki cargo pants, boots, and 5.11 shirt announced that another operator had arrived. He nodded at Jed and descended. Jed stepped away from Nolte's side and walked ahead to meet Ben.

"How's it going, brother?" Ben said, his familiar warm smile still present despite what felt to Jed to be a rather hopeless situation.

"Been better, Ben," Jed said, releasing the firm handshake and reaching out to grab Ben's backpack. "I hope you're bringing good news."

Ben shook his head, but his confident smile did not waver. "God will provide, Jed."

"I know," Jed said.

Ben's eyes flicked to the Army intel officer waiting nearby and in a quiet voice he said, "The kids are working hard. Bet we get something any minute."

Movement caught Jed's eye as David emerged from the jet, a black backpack on his shoulder. He gave Jed a wave, and Jed waved back.

"And Sarah Beth?" Jed asked, his tone loading more than he intended.

"She's working with Corbin, but we are trying to respect her parents' concerns about her advancement and workload . . ."

"Understood," he said, relieved she was involved but also satisfied that Ben would not exceed the already-long leash given by David and Rachel.

David arrived and, to Jed's surprise, gave him a big hug.

"You good, man?" David asked, confidence brimming in his eyes.

"All good, brother. The team will be glad you're here. Y'all got here quick."

"Yep, this is literally the fastest corporate jet available," Ben said. "It routinely flies at 0.93 Mach, but in testing they took it all the way to 0.99. That's seven hundred and fifty miles an hour. Once we get a location, we'll want the speed."

Jed nodded, pursing his lips at that thought. "How many jets do the Shepherds own exactly?" he asked, imagining the price tag of the super-modern Bombardier on the ramp to be well over $50 million.

"None," Ben said with a chuckle, "but we have lots of friends and bene-factors."

Jed had plenty of questions about the details of *that*, but it was a discussion for another time and the Army spook was walking up.

"You must be Captain Bill Nolte," Ben said, greeting the man.

"I am," Bill said, apparently surprised to be called by name.

They shook hands.

"I'm David Yarnell," David said and shook the man's hand as well.

"I've worked some with Lieutenant Colonel Wyatt Page," Ben said, a hand on the man's back as they strode now toward hangar four. "He says great things about you and also about Specialist Young. He promised we're in good hands."

"Well, that's nice to hear," Bill said with a laugh. "It's an honor working for a legend like the colonel." The Army captain looked over at Ben now as if checking to see if he looked familiar. "Did you work over at the Activity?"

"Me? No, no," Ben said, waving the idea off. "But Wyatt and I did some other joint task force–type projects together."

The foursome entered the hangar through the small door built into the enormous sliding ones that met in the middle. The interior of the hangar had been converted into a TOC—all set up and ready to support the next op.

"You got a call coming in, Jed," Ben said with a sideways glance as he set down his bags.

"I do?" Jed murmured as the satphone in his pocket vibrated.

I hate it when he does that . . .

"Jedidiah," he said, putting the phone to his ear.

"It's Corbin. We found it, Jed. The plane."

He snapped a finger loudly, waving Eli over. "They found the plane," he said to Ben and Eli, then to Corbin said, "Great job. Where is it?"

"What I meant was we found *which* plane it is, but we don't know where it is. We used the thread for the guy you captured—who, I can tell you, has no idea what's going on, by the way—but his thread led us to the pilot. Then we, and by *we*, I mostly mean Sarah Beth—who is awesome—located the pilots. There's actually two of them. I'm sending you a sketch . . ." There was some fumbling and she spoke to someone off the phone, but it sounded muffled; then the tablet dinged in his other pocket. "I saw this through the eyes of the pilot."

Jed held the phone against his shoulder with a head tilt and fished out his tablet and opened it with his thumbprint, then tapped the incoming message icon. He was looking at the control panel of an airplane. Ben joined him and Bill walked up to look from the other side.

"What am I looking at here?" he asked, holding the tablet and switching the phone to speaker.

"Well, there's a couple of things," Corbin said, her voice a teenager telling a story of being asked to the prom. "Hopefully, from the layout of the dials and stuff you can figure out what kind of plane it is."

Jed glanced over at Bill, who nodded with a *definitely doable* expression.

"And that," the Army intel officer said, tapping a finger on the screen to a small rectangular plaque with some numbers and letters on it, "is the aircraft's tail number. N6677L. That's a US-registered plane."

"That's what we thought," Corbin said excitedly. "And look at the radio panel between the seats—can you see it?"

"Yeah," Jed said. The bottom of the two was larger and had the numbers 135.2 glowing in pale blue. The top one seemed more narrow compared to the one beneath. The numbers 0427 glowed red in the panel.

"So he set that code into the one on top. Josh—he's another Watcher—he's like a total airplane geek. He wants to fly fighters for the military or something. Anyway, he knows about that stuff and he said that code is how the air traffic controllers can identify a specific plane . . ."

"It's a transponder," Bill agreed. "The code is called a squawk code. And your friend Josh is exactly right."

"Yes! That's what Josh said. Jed, he was so excited. So you can find them, right?"

"Yes," Bill said confidently. "If it's all turned on and pinging, we can find them."

"But what if they're using a different squawk code now?" Eli chimed in. "They might have changed it."

"I don't think so," Corbin said. "I watched him set this code just a minute ago. They're, like, literally taking off right now."

"They're in the air?" Jed asked, his chest getting tight.

"Yes, but you can find them, right?"

"We can find them," Bill said and dashed over to help Specialist Young, who was already throwing laptops into a bag.

"We'll find them, Corbin," Jed said. "Good work."

"Everyone," Ben called, addressing the hangar, "grab your gear and get to the jet. We're taking off right now."

Joshua Bravo ran as a group to their gear staged by the door, Eli squeezing Jed's shoulder and heading off to join them.

"And then what?" Jed asked.

"What do you mean?" Ben said, jogging to grab his gear.

"They're in the air, Ben. Are we supposed to shoot them down? What I mean is, what's the plan here, boss?" He grabbed his own weapons and kit and jogged to catch up to Ben.

"We'll do what we need to do, Jed. We adapt and overcome. We find a way," Ben said, heading out the hangar door. "But, Jed . . ."

"Yeah?"

"Probably a good idea to make sure we have a couple of those F-16s riding shotgun with us." Ben nodded at a pair of fighters on the tarmac. "Just in case."

CHAPTER THIRTY

"We found 'em!" Nisha announced.

Jed looked across the aisle at where Captain Bill Nolte, Nisha, and Specialist Wanda Young were crowded around four laptops on the table between them in the oversize, leather club-style airplane seats.

"Already?" Jed said, looking over at Ben and David. Ben gave a calm, knowing nod, and David pumped a fist in the air. They'd only been airborne for two minutes and were still in the steep climb out. "Where?"

"You've got 'em?" one of pilots said, walking aft out of the cockpit. The flier had gray close-cropped hair, a rugged face, and wore cargo pants and a black sports shirt with an embroidered symbol on the breast Jed had never seen. "I'm Terry and I'm flying left seat up front."

"Um, shouldn't you be flying the plane?" Jed asked, unstrapping and moving across the aisle rapidly.

"There's two of us," the man said with a shrug. "No big challenge getting us up to altitude, especially in this high-tech beast. More important to know where we're going. We filed a flight plan to Philadelphia, so we'll need to update that pretty soon."

Jed slid a knee onto the rearward-facing seat behind Bill. The screen Bill and Nisha were crowded in on was a moving display—an aeronautical map—with a red triangle in the middle of the screen, surrounded by dozens of other blips and green squares.

"This is him," Bill said. "November-six-six-seven-seven-Lima is a Boeing 717. It's owned by TransAmerica freight. Operating under Part 91, so lots less scrutiny than if they were, say, an air carrier under Part 121. They departed out of Fayetteville and are now coming up on intersection Moats, a waypoint on victor airway one-three-six, twenty-one miles southwest of Raleigh. Still in the climb, cleared to flight level two-nine-zero."

"Twenty-nine thousand feet," the pilot clarifed. "I take it you've got the flight plan?"

"Yeah," Bill said. "They're on an IFR flight plan from Fayetteville to Harrisburg, Pennsylvania. Fayetteville via vectors to victor one-three-six to join victor one-five-five to Richmond to intersect victor one-five-seven to the ENO VOR, then radar vectors direct Harrisburg."

"What's the target?" Jed asked.

"The flight path takes them right by DC," Terry said, scribbling the last of the flight plan onto his pad.

"I didn't think you could fly directly over DC," Eli said, scooting in beside Jed.

"Well, that's true at low altitude. And this doesn't take them directly over DC. They'll pass a good fifty to sixty miles east of the city itself. But DC is the logical target. Also, they could veer off course."

"They won't need to," Nisha said. "It's a line-of-sight energy weapon, but at twenty-nine thousand feet, it's a buffet of targets inside a sixty-mile radius."

"Wait a minute," Bill said, his voice changing now. "What kind of weapon? I thought you were hunting for a plane. No one said anything about a weapon. What kind of energy weapon are we talking about?"

"I'll explain in a minute," she said, "but based on these parameters, the target could be anywhere. They'll pass within line of sight of a myriad of military bases including Navy Base Norfolk, Naval Air Station Oceana, Pope Air Force base, Fort Belvoir, Pax River . . . the list goes on and on."

"It's DC," Ben said and held up his tablet computer screen to show them. "The president, the vice president, and both the minority and majority leaders are all going to be together in the Rose Garden with a bunch of other senators, to make an announcement about a bipartisan proposal on trade."

"What? When?"

"Less than an hour."

Jed looked over at Terry the pilot. "Get us on an intercept course and check in with the fighters."

"On it," Terry said, hustling to the cockpit.

"We need to alert Secret Service," Bill said.

"I agree," Ben said. "But no announcements about a delay or cancellation. Not yet, at least."

"Won't all the VIPs and press in the Rose Garden become the targets?" Wanda asked.

"We'll stop the threat before then," Ben said and proceeded to read the non-Shepherds in the airplane in on the nature and capabilities of the Dark Ones' energy weapon.

"The whole thing is insane," Wanda mumbled when Ben had finished. "That someone would design such a thing . . ."

"The terrifying thing is that there is someone who would use such a weapon—and the answer to *who* is the terrorist group we're tasked to hunt," Ben said. "They want to incite a religious war . . ."

"Just like Islamic jihadists," Bill offered.

"Sort of. But imagine the statement here. Fire literally raining down on the leaders in Washington, DC—God's wrath against the people who have fallen from His grace."

"That would sure embolden the jihadists," Bill agreed.

"And ravage the faith of those who believe God loves us. What kind of

God would do—or even allow—such a thing?" Ben looked back over at Jed, their eyes locking and communicating beyond the words. "It's DC."

You're right.

I know.

"Can we work on confirmation?" Jed asked, finding his voice.

"Yes, but even if I'm wrong, we need to intercept that jet."

Jed thought about that, and it made sense, but could they get to them in time? The Boeing was already headed toward its target. Ben looked over the map, which Bill had zoomed out.

"It seems like their best targeting solution is here," he said, tapping a finger over the Chesapeake Bay, south and east of DC. "They'll be correcting northeast coming off the Pax River VOR." He indicated the red line now on the map, which showed the cleared course for the jet. "This is the best distance and then it only increases from there."

"If that's the target," Jed said.

"It is," David said, speaking for the first time.

Jed looked at him, and the fire in his eyes told Jed—well, maybe that it was true, but for sure that David believed it to be. That was his job, right? To be in prayer, seek out holy guidance. It wasn't that Jed didn't believe in that—he'd seen so much to prove it was true—but could David be sure enough to bet lives on it? Not theirs, but innocent lives?

He nodded to David.

"If we're sure, why not unleash the F-16s and take them out now?" Johnny asked from the back. "Problem solved."

"That risks a lot of civilian deaths on the ground," Ben said.

Jed was about to point out that there was not much else they could do, but Terry called out from the cockpit door, "We've got our fighter escort and we're diverting to intercept."

"What if we're too late?" Jed said.

"That old Boeing barely makes 0.77 Mach and that was clean and in her prime. We're gonna be making nearly Mach 1. I estimate we'll intercept them around the SVIL intersection on victor one-five-seven just north of Richmond. And we'll get ATC to slow them down right now."

"Can you get us behind them without them knowing we're there?" Ben asked.

"Easily," Terry said. "Why?"

"I have an idea," Ben said. "Just get us behind them tight and undetected."

"Will do," Terry said. "Might mean they make it another few miles—almost to TAPP intersection if you want to pull that up on the flight map. Still a good twenty to thirty south of Pax River."

"How long?" Ben asked.

"Two more minutes to altitude and then fourteen minutes," he said. "I'm squawking 7700, so I can maneuver at will. Sixteen mikes."

"What does that mean? The transponder code?" Nisha asked.

"It's the code to notify ATC that I'm a DoD authorized aircraft intercepting a hostile target. With the F-16s beside me, we'll get no questions asked. And Patuxent River approach will coordinate clearing the airspace."

"We don't want to tip them off," Ben cautioned.

"Colonel Mitchell took care of that for us with ATC," Terry said. "They won't notice anything. ATC is clearing flights off the route slowly and subtly."

"Man, that guy's everywhere," Eli said with an admiring smile.

"Yeah, you could say that," Terry said. "He's Red Devil One—the lead F-16 in the flight beside us, and the squadron XO is flying number Two." The pilot tilted his head right, toward the port side of the aircraft. Jed looked out the modern-looking window of the G700 just as sunlight glinted gold off the canopy of the F-16 climbing beside them a hundred yards off their left wing. With that Terry went back into the cockpit to get to work.

Ben fixed his eyes on Nisha. "Nisha, get on the horn with the TOC back home and bring them up to speed. Then see if any of our team can get eyes in the cargo hold. I want confirmation the weapon is inside. You know what kind of confirmation I mean."

"Roger that," she said and put on a headset.

"Jed, with me," Ben said. "You too, Eli," he added, striding down the wide aisle of the luxury jet toward where a mahogany door separated the main cabin from a conference room.

"Okay," Jed said, his already-knotted stomach twisting just a little bit more at the tenor of Ben's voice.

The Shepherd commander ushered them into the jet's aft conference cabin, shut the door behind him, and dropped into the chair at the head of the table.

"Oh no, I know that look," Eli said, shaking his head.

"What look?" Jed asked the veteran.

"*That* look," Eli said, looking at Ben but leaning into Jed. "It means he has an idea that is completely insane and we're definitely going to hate. Right, Ben?"

Ben flashed them a Cheshire cat grin. "Yeah . . . and I think you guys are probably gonna want to sit down for this."

CHAPTER THIRTY-ONE

Jed leaned against the narrow doorway as he peered over Ben's shoulder into the cockpit of the high-tech corporate jet. The control panel looked like something out of a science fiction movie, with brightly lit CRT monitors instead of dials and instruments. Gleaming stainless steel throttles were pushed all the way forward, and even the radio panels on either side of the throttle panel looked more like iPads, with touch screens and brightly colored icons. Terry sat in the left seat, his left hand on the joystick controller resembling that of a fighter jet, mounted beside his thigh instead of centered between his knees. The copilot was managing comms from the right seat, and Ben had taken a knee on the floor just behind and between the two seats.

"Here we go," Terry announced. He reached with his right hand to the twin throttles, pulling them back as he simultaneously moved the stick left. Immediately Jed's stomach rose as the jet began a steep, spiraling turn to the left. He pressed a shoulder into one side of the doorway and a knee into the other as he hunched his large frame over. He reflexively grabbed Ben's shoulder to steady them both as the g-forces ramped up.

"Pax River, Red Devil lead, flight of three, in a left turn descending," the copilot announced into the thin boom mic at his mouth.

"Roger, Red Devil. Maneuver your discretion for the intercept," came the reply over the speakers, the pilot having pulled his earpiece out to allow Ben and Jed to hear the traffic. "Your bandit—two miles southwest of Tappa level angels 21. Squawking 0427. Mode C indicates twenty-one-thousand-one-hundred-thirty-one feet. We will descend them again to target altitude in thirty seconds. Be advised, the airspace is yours from Tappa to Intersection Colin from angels 10 to angels 39. North of Colin you own the space from the surface to angels 39, but there could be VFR aircraft uncontrolled until the edge of Restricted Area Romeo-four-zero-zero-five with multiple primary contacts below six thousand."

"Red Devil One, roger," the copilot replied, then shot them a grin and thumbs-up. "Get 'em down when you can."

Jed clenched his jaw. Ben's plan was arguably insane—certainly crazier than anything he'd done as a SEAL or Shepherd thus far, and he'd done *a lot* of crazy. For the plan to work, they needed the target Boeing jet cruising at or below fourteen thousand feet. They also needed about a hundred other variables to behave reliably and predictably in their favor, something Murphy's Law had a nasty habit of making sure never happened.

"Can't they hear your radio calls?" Jed asked.

Terry shook his head. "No, we're on a secure DoD-only frequency now."

"Red Devil, your bandit twelve o'clock, dead ahead now inside three miles," the voice of the controller said. "Descending out of one-nine-thousand for angels 16. Call a visual."

A moment later, the gruff voice of Colonel Mitchell came over the radio, now designated Red Devil Two since the G700 had made his two ship a flight of three and assumed the lead as Devil One.

"Pax, Devil Two—visual contact. One—Two has a solution."

The words gave Jed a chill. He knew that meant the lead F-16, piloted by

Colonel Mitchell, had the target jet locked up with a missile, ready to shoot it down at a moment's notice if Ben's plan fell apart.

"Roger that, Devil Two," Terry said in a cool voice. Jed wondered what kind of fighter jet Terry had flown in his glory days before signing on with the spooks. "Devil One has visual contact."

"Roger, Red Devil flight. You have visual contact. You have control of the merge," the controller said. If he knew he was managing an intercept to shoot down an airliner over American soil, his voice didn't give it away.

Jed saw the Boeing, just a speck in the distance but growing rapidly in the windshield, just right of the sci-fi heads-up display on Terry's side of the cockpit.

Ben tapped the radio in his kit and made his own broadcast, which only the Shepherds team could hear on their dedicated frequency. "Watcher, Shepherd One," he said softly.

"Go ahead, Shepherd One," Corbin answered, sounding calm and collected. She was so good on ops; Jed would take her in his ear any day.

"Watcher, I need some help," Ben said, rising from the floor in the cockpit and turning to Jed and smiling. "I need to join you on our special frequency in just a second, okay?"

"Watcher, roger," Corbin said, her tone sounding a decade older than her years.

Ben turned back to the pilots. "Can you sneak us in close—low and behind so they don't see us?"

"For sure," Terry said. "I'll park right beneath them and in tight, keeping the fighters in our six and also out of sight."

"And you understand what I want to do next?" Ben asked.

"I do," Terry said. "It's not a problem. I did a stint with the Thunderbirds, so I can get you within a foot or even less. The hard part that comes next, however, is up to you."

"We've got that covered," Ben said, then motioned for Jed to join him in the plane's oversize galley.

"I'm still a little foggy on the *plan* part of the plan," Jed said in a hushed voice. "How does this work exactly?"

His mind went back to Corporal Alexander, the Nashville Metro PD officer who had died horribly after Ben had touched him. Did Ben intend to somehow kill or incapacitate the pilots from here? Was that even possible?

I healed Alexander, Jed, Ben said.

Uh-huh, right.

Ben smiled. "We can do this. It's all about harnessing the power of suggestion . . . with a little help from Corbin."

"And have you ever actually tried this before?" Jed asked, cocking a skeptical eyebrow.

Ben shrugged. "Sure, plenty of times."

"Let me rephrase: how many times have you tried it when it actually worked?"

"Once."

Wonderful . . .

Jed's mind went to the innocents on the ground—even if they could time it perfectly to splash the Boeing into the Chesapeake Bay, there were boaters all over the place. And of course, there was the loss of control over the weapon.

Father God, please be with us . . .

Ben stepped out of the galley and took a seat in the forwardmost leather lounger, sitting and crossing his legs at the knees. Jed watched him exhale and close his eyes.

"Ready, Watcher?" Ben asked softly, his voice just a whisper but much louder in Jed's earpiece a split second later.

"Yeah," Corbin said, sounding a bit more kidlike now. "What do you want me to do?"

"Get me on the thread of the man who looked out the airplane window on takeoff," Ben said. "Can you do that?"

"Pop in and I'll try," Corbin said.

Jed watched Ben's lips moving ever so slightly. The Shepherd commander was in the mind space now communicating with Corbin, making the radio irrelevant for the next few minutes. Jed turned and looked forward, through the open cockpit door and out the windscreen as the Boeing jet grew impossibly large ahead. Terry was working twin throttles as they appeared to be on what looked like, at least to Jed, a collision course. Jed had seen pictures and videos of the Navy Blue Angels and Air Force Thunderbird flight demonstration teams with their wingtips only inches apart and their cockpit canopies less than a foot from the jet above—but those were fighter jets and both pilots were coordinating. That thing in front of them was a Boeing airliner and its pilot was definitely not coordinating.

Feeling nauseated, he looked away and headed aft to join Eli and make ready for the terrible, terrible thing that was coming next.

CHAPTER THIRTY-TWO

"Roger, approach. November-six-six-seven-seven-Lima slowing to three-ninety indicated for spacing."

Captain Nate Wallace glanced over at his copilot, the quiet and always-angry-looking man who was just a few years his junior.

Yep, there's the scowl.

"They're slowing us again?" the copilot said, his voice more growl than anything else. The dude was so hot with anger, it seemed to almost make his eyes glow with rage.

"You got a date or something, bro?" Nate asked, pulling the throttles back and watching the speed drop from the already-snaillike four hundred and twenty knots down to three hundred and ninety—which was barely four hundred and fifty miles per hour over ground.

"Something like that," the copilot grumbled.

There was something off about this guy—a new hire who had come to them from UPS, supposedly. Sure, the Part 91 operations got less priority handling than the air carrier guys, but this was an easy gig with great pay and great hours. What was there to complain about? For Nate, this gig was just another chapter in a dream come true. He'd been working himself up the grinding ladder of commercial aviation—a grind for those without a military pedigree, at least—and now had an interview coming up in a couple of weeks with Delta. Slower just meant more pilot-in-command hours as far as he was concerned.

This guy, First Officer Smith or whatever, didn't seem to have the love of flying that all the other pilots at TransAmerica shared. Nate started to worry that meant he had a sketchy past that had kept him out of commercial cockpits, or maybe a less than honorable military discharge. He thought of those terrorists twenty years ago, and of Smith's filing their flight plan through the most overtrafficked corridor in the northeast, instead of around DC to the west.

He'd been eight years old when the planes crashed into the towers and the Pentagon. Was his copilot a zealot? A terrorist? A true believer with a score to settle?

He shook off the thoughts.

Don't be paranoid. This dude's an American.

Still, he couldn't shake the feeling that something was wrong with Smith.

"Never know when the next terrorist zealots will pop up, Nate," his dad, a retired postal worker, had said. *"They'll probably walk and talk and look like us next time."*

A chill chased down his spine, and he wondered how quickly he could get the Glock 43 out from beside his seat and whether he could point it at Smith and fire if the situation required. That thought made him suddenly claustrophobic, and despite being in the driver's seat doing what he loved, he was overcome by the compulsion to get on the ground and out of this plane.

"Hey, approach, any chance direct Harrisburg from here?" he said, calling ATC.

"Negative, seven-seven-Lima. Continue on victor one-five-seven. I might be able to get you direct a few miles north of Patuxent River. In the meantime, descend and maintain one-four thousand."

"Seven-seven-Lima—say again—fourteen thousand feet?" Nate said, then released the push to talk and glanced at Smith, wondering why he wasn't at least working the radios. The guy hadn't even asked to fly the leg, something every right seater asked as they tried to build their own hours toward the next job.

"Seven-seven-Lima, that's correct," the ATC controller came back. "Apologies, sir. We have activity in the special use airspace around Patuxent River Naval Air Station. We also need you at or below two-five-zero knots for just a few minutes, please—again, separation for military activity in the airspace. Crossing Pax River VOR, I can get you higher if you like and get your speed back up. We'll get you direct Harrisburg and higher sooner than that if I can. Working it now, so stand by."

"Seven-seven-Lima is now fifteen-five for fourteen thousand. Will stay between thirteen-five and fourteen for you. Like higher and direct when able."

He released the push to talk and glanced at Smith, who glared at him, and again a trick of the light made it look as if his eyes were literally glowing with rage, but then the illusion disappeared and the man's face relaxed.

"Man, they're jerking us around today, huh?" Smith said. For some reason he seemed to suddenly have a slight Georgia accent, but it might have been Nate's imagination.

"Yeah," he said, thinking again about the Glock in his flight case. Something was not right. "Once we cross Pax River, we're just twenty minutes out if he gives us our speed back. Probably more efficient at that point to just shoot on in. Certainly don't need more than flight level two-zero-zero. What do you think, Smith?"

"Maybe," the first officer agreed, flashing Nate a creepy smile. "Like to get back to twenty at least, I guess, if we can."

Nate nodded and said nothing, advancing the throttles slightly as he leveled at fourteen thousand feet, then letting the jet drift slightly down to thirteen thousand eight hundred. He set the speed at the two hundred and forty knots indicated, practically crawl speed for a jet like this.

They droned along the airway in silence, less than three hundred knots and at a fuel-guzzling altitude. They had plenty of gas, but the trip just kept getting more and more bizarre. First he had a new hire copilot he'd not even heard about; then they had a group of passengers—six of them no less—in the main cabin with the enormous box they were transporting. Supposedly they were scientists as well as security for some government tech, but only they knew why they would head to Harrisburg. And now, the weird redirects from ATC.

Nate blew air through his teeth.

Man, he'd be glad when this flight was over.

CHAPTER THIRTY-THREE

Eyes closed, Ben let out a slow breath and found Corbin in the ether. He wasn't a Watcher, but God had seen fit to gift him with complimentary skills. Like the ability to read another mind's emotional state and, through the power of suggestion, influence a target's thoughts and will. This was what he was going to attempt to do with the pilot.

But first . . . he needed visual confirmation of the weapon.

Okay, do you want to try to see it? Corbin asked.

Yes, Ben answered.

She towed him toward a dark thread. *This man is accessible. He's the one I stole a glance out the window from on takeoff. I never got a name . . . but he is on the plane.*

Great work, Corbin. He drifted toward the target and prepared himself to penetrate the dark servant's mind. He didn't know what it felt like for the kids when they popped into a target mind, but for him a good analogy was surfacing when swimming underwater. The ether was like the deep—sloshy, muted, and dark. The second he slipped through the bubble, his senses were flooded with the target mind's experience. In this case, the main cabin of the cargo jet materialized around him. The target was seated and looking at his phone.

Concentrating, Ben summoned the desire in himself to see the weapon and pushed that want into the target mind. He felt the idea take hold, and the target looked away from his phone and stared aft at the weapon, which was mounted on the port side, midsection. The design and appearance matched the description that Dr. Zhao had shared during the debrief sessions at Trinity Loop.

Well, that answers that question.

If he could compel complex behavior in this fellow, he might be able to sabotage the device and disable it. That would be mission accomplished without having to take down the plane. But the odds of that were extremely low, which was why he'd not even discussed it with Jed and Eli. For something like that to work, the target needed to already be disposed to the desired behavior and open to the power of suggestion. Very few dark servants were.

He pushed the compulsion into the target, but the man refused to get up from his seat.

With the clock ticking, every second wasted counted. It was time to abort. He slipped back into the ether and found Corbin.

Can you lead me to the pilot? Ben asked her.

Sure, follow me, she said, gliding along to another thread, this one bright and warm.

This man is no servant of the dark, he said.

No, he's not, she said. *I hope he's cooperative.*

He felt her hope and her smile. *Me too. You've been a great help, Corbin. Do you need me to wait here for you?*

No, you can head back to the Bullpen. I'll be fine.

Good luck.

Corbin's presence left the mind space. Ben slipped into the bubble of the pilot's mind and found himself in the cockpit, looking at the control panel through the pilot's eyes. He was in the left seat, so this pilot must be the captain. He could sense the anxiety and indecision rumbling around—and fear maybe. Not intense, but there. He scanned through the man's eyes, willing them to move across the cockpit panel, which they accommodated, and spotted his objective—the cabin pressure control subsystem.

Ben formed the compulsion, an intense desire in himself to manipulate the cabin pressure, and pushed it into the headspace he shared.

At first nothing happened; the pilot didn't react.

The cabin pressure is too high, Ben thought and pushed it hard.

The hand reached out, coming into view, but then hesitated. The eyes cut right, and Ben saw the copilot, arms crossed on his chest, staring down at a moving map on a tablet in his lap. He felt the pilot's fear and this time understood. The copilot was a Dark One and at some visceral level the pilot understood the danger and the malice.

Ben took a slow, deep breath with the pilot's body he occupied and tried again.

He saw the pilot's right hand reach for the panel and felt a sense of peace and satisfaction. The hand found the control panel and landed on the knob in the center of the panel marked Mode Select, currently pointing to Auto 2, and twisted it to Man, which transferred the pressurization to manual control.

"What the hell are you doing?" the copilot snapped.

The eyes ticked over and Ben saw the faint, amber glow in the other man's eyes.

"Resetting the cabin pressure," their voice said without needing prompting.

"Isn't it in auto?"

"Yeah," the voice said, "but this unit is finicky. I have to cycle in and out of manual sometimes. Why don't you put a note in the maintenance log for me?"

The copilot grumbled something but pulled a thin gray binder from beside him and took a pen from his short-sleeved uniform shirt.

Their eyes were on the panel again. The landing altitude was set to 310 feet and the cabin pressure indicator, the center dial on the row of three on the bottom, sat on the hash mark for 10—ten thousand feet. He needed to decompress the cargo hold for the plan to work, but Terry had explained that what mattered was differential pressure—the difference between the air pressure inside the plane and the atmosphere outside—which was indicated on the left bottom dial in psi, as the controlling parameter. It was okay for it to be slightly positive. In fact, that would make it easier to open the cargo hatch since the slipstream would be working against them. Too much positive differential pressure, however, would cause an explosive decompression, which would trigger alarms and a reaction from the flight crew and personnel in the cabin with the weapon.

Ben decided to go for as close to zero D/P as possible and compelled the pilot's hand to the middle dial on the top, spinning the dial from the neutral nine o'clock position to about the seven o'clock. Immediately the bottom-right dial ticked down, indicating a descent in cabin pressure. The change happened quicker than he thought and the pilot's hand then spun the dial back to neutral.

Thank you, Ben thought into the confused shared headspace. The pilot was a willing partner but had no idea what was actually happening to him.

I don't trust Smith. He's up to no good, the pilot thought and his eyes ticked back over to the man scribbling in the gray binder.

Ben affirmed the thought, imagining silent agreement to soothe the man's uncertainty.

I need to do something . . .

You just did, Ben pushed the thought, then pulled out.

When he opened his eyes, he saw the cabin of the G700 where *his* body was reclined in the same leather chair as when he'd left.

Jed, who was fully kitted up and waiting, stepped into view. "Well?"

"It's done," Ben said, sitting up. Then in a whisper he added, "The weapon is in the middle section of the main cargo cabin on the left side. Multiple tangos present, but I couldn't get a count."

Jed nodded. "All right, we'll get in position."

His head swimmy, which it always was after trips to the mind space, Ben took a second to steady himself after standing before walking to the cockpit.

"We're ready," he said, leaning his head through the open doorway. "D/P is equalized."

"How do you know?" Terry asked, a confused look on his face.

Ben smiled, wishing he could be more forthright. "We have some powerful tools at our disposal in our task force," he said, knowing that the familiar mantra of "special task force" would resonate with anyone serving since 9/11. "Trust me—it's done."

"All right," Terry said, right hand reaching for the twin throttles. "We're equalized here too, so let me get you into position."

In the windscreen, the Boeing seemed to rise above them, though Ben knew they had dropped a few feet lower in trail. Terry expertly maneuvered the jet slowly to the right, letting the nose begin to creep up along the side of the Boeing.

"Get ready," Terry said. "Thirty seconds and I'll have us stabilized in position."

"Do we need to be careful about discharging weapons inside the plane?" Ben asked.

"I mean, yes and no. From a decompression standpoint, holes through a wall or window won't cause an issue because pressure is equalized. But if you shoot the pilots or hit a hydraulic or fuel line, then you've got problems."

Ben turned back to where Jed and Eli stood on either side of the main cabin door, full kits, helmets, and assault rifles tight on their chests. That they both wore parachutes was a detail not lost on him.

"Ready?" he asked.

"We're not gonna get sucked out of this plane the second we open the door?" Eli asked. His tone suggested he meant to sound kidding, but Ben knew Eli well enough to know when he was nervous, even when no one else could tell.

"No, pressure is equalized with the outside," Ben said. "There will be several hundred knots of wind, however, so you're gonna wanna snap in."

He watched the two operators exchange glances and then snap the flexible bungees on the D-rings of their web belts into the handles beside the door. Ben leaned between them and looked through the window, seeing nothing but the worn paint on the side of the Boeing 717, mere inches away now that Terry had pulled their jet within "Blue Angels" distance from the rear end of the target jet. He checked that everyone else in the cabin was seated and strapped in before disengaging the door lock.

"Ready to open," he hollered to the cockpit.

"Okay," Terry called back. "Let me get a little separation. We're gonna yaw a bit to the left with the drag when you open the door, so give me a second to get stable and ease back in."

Ben acknowledged and looked at his two nervous Shepherds. "You got this, guys," he said, a last-second pep talk as he watched the adjustment maneuver through the porthole window in the door.

"Okay," Terry hollered from the cockpit.

"Is this door gonna tear off?" Jed asked, looking at the door with distrust.

"I doubt it," Terry called back. "It's pretty solid . . . but maybe, so I wouldn't hold on to it or anything."

"Here we go, guys." Ben turned the silver handle ninety degrees.

At first the door didn't budge, so Eli and Jed joined Ben in the pushing, Jed pressing a large shoulder into the stairs on the inside of the door. Then, once a tiny break in the seal formed, the three-hundred-mile-an-hour wind did the rest, pulling the door out and then down, the hydraulics of the door slowing the process enough to prevent the door from slamming and ripping off the frame of the aircraft as Jed had worried. The plane yawed left and Ben stumbled, but Terry quickly and expertly got control and seconds later the G700 began to drift upward until the side of the Boeing filled the doorway. As the pilots maneuvered the G700 doorway in line with the Boeing's cargo door, the wind whipping past the open cabin was loud but less intimidating than Ben had expected. Finally Terry had the plane stabilized, bobbing up and down six or eight inches at a time as if in a boat on gentle seas, in sync with the Boeing.

"Ready?" he asked Jed.

"Easy day," Jed said, smiling tightly and reached across the gap to the Boeing's external cargo door control panel, the wind whipping his heavily muscled arm around enough that he needed to steady himself with a shoulder in the doorframe. Jed's big hand found the rectangular vent door handle, which was recessed to sit flush with the skin of the closed four-by-six-foot cargo door behind it.

Ben heard Jed exhale, then watched him depress the twin buttons in the handle and turn the lever.

CHAPTER THIRTY-FOUR

The jet yawed suddenly to the right and a warning horn sounded. Nate reached for the yoke, but the autopilot corrected the yaw almost immediately.

"What have you done?" the copilot Smith screamed.

The aft cargo door warning light flashed red in sync with the *whoop* sound from the alarm blaring on the warning panel. Nate silenced the annunciator and turned to his copilot, where he saw two things simultaneously that stopped the breath in his chest. The first was a demonic red glow in Smith's eyes, and the second was the glint of silver from the knife in his copilot's right hand.

Nate reflexively tried to block the strike and felt the blade bite into his forearm, pain exploding like fire as it cut fast and deep. His middle fingers and pinkie suddenly released themselves from the fist he'd formed as the blade severed nerves and tendons. Blood sprayed the control panel and spattered the windscreen when Smith yanked the blade back.

He twisted in his seat, using his damaged arm like a shield to ward off the next attack, while going for his Glock in the flight case on the left side of his captain's seat with his left hand. His fingers managed to close around the butt of the Glock, but the four-point seat belt had him locked in his seat. Smith leapt out of his seat, the knife coming down fast. It ripped through Nate's hand, his mind registering with only passing interest how his pinkie finger now hung by the thinnest strip of remaining skin. Yet despite that, he pulled the Glock and brought it across his body.

A lash of fire seared his neck and he felt the blade cutting through his throat. He tasted copper in his mouth and blood poured into and down his severed windpipe. The world turned gray and crushing vertigo annihilated all sense of proprioception. Calling upon the last ounce of will he possessed, Nate squeezed the trigger with his left index finger twice.

His mind was only vaguely aware of the loud twin pops.

Smith fell backward off him and into the copilot's seat, then pitched over onto the center panel.

Nate glanced at the main panel, relieved to see the autopilot was still operating.

He felt the enormous rush of hot, wet blood on his chest.

He was aware, in a detached way, of the twin geysers of blood that arched up onto the ceiling and windscreen of the cockpit with each pounding beat of his heart.

He waited for Smith to lunge and finish him off, but the attack never came.

Maybe he didn't need finishing off.

I'm sorry, God. I tried to stop him. I hope I knew You well enough . . .

Unable to move, he slipped into a warm pool that seemed to engulf him mind, body, and spirit. Blackness took him and then the light . . .

CHAPTER
THIRTY-FIVE

Jed was surprised that the wind didn't tear his arm off when he reached for the cargo door control lever on the side of the Boeing. The geometry of the narrow gap between the two planes must have created disruptive eddies in the airflow, making the slipstream between a *manageable* cyclone of turbulence.

The cargo door opened on command, and Jed found himself peering inside the cargo hold of the Boeing. He looked back at Eli, who, in typical Eli fashion, summarized the situation with an economy of words.

"Well, ain't that a thing," the veteran said with wonderment on his face.

Jed took a deep breath, then pulled himself across the eight-inch gap, crossing the slipstream and into the Boeing. He landed painfully on his left knee but steadied himself in kneeling firing stance. Muscle memory in control, he loosened the sling to his rifle, brought it up to his cheek, and scanned the dark, windy cargo hold for targets. He felt the disturbance behind him, then a moment later the squeeze of Eli's hand on his shoulder. With Eli behind and to his right, they were up and advancing in the unlit and apparently empty belly cargo hold.

Jed snapped the NVGs on his helmet down into place in front of his eyes. The space came to life in green-and-gray night vision and he confirmed it empty. Ben had seen the weapon in the main cabin, which was configured to carry cargo in this transport configuration. However, there was no way that the cargo hold door ripping off the side of the Boeing had gone unnoticed, certainly not by the pilots or anyone sitting above them. Most likely, they would assume it was an aircraft structural failure.

Because operators sneaking from one plane to another in flight really isn't a thing . . .

Regardless, they'd lost some of the element of surprise and someone would be down to investigate any second.

"We're on board—sitrep," Jed whispered in his boom mic.

"Check," Ben said.

"We might have an issue. I can't find the pilot's thread," Corbin said on the line.

"What about the guy in the cabin?" Ben came back. "Go for him."

"On it," Corbin said, her reply sharp.

Jed and Eli had been briefed on the Boeing's design by the pilot spooks. In the passenger configuration, there was no access to the main cabin from the cargo bay—unlike what was frequently depicted in the movies. Some transport variants of this model had an access hatch installed between the cargo hold and main cabin at the rear of the aircraft. That was plan A. The backup plan, if they weren't so lucky, was to cut a hole in the forward bulkhead of the cargo hold to gain access to the electronics and environment compartment. From there, they could enter the cockpit via a hatch in the E&E compartment overhead / cockpit floor.

But everyone knew this was wishful thinking and would take more time than they had.

And if the Boeing made any move to fire the weapon before they could seize control, the F-16s would blast it out of the sky . . .

And Jed and Eli with it.

"Help me look," Eli whispered, flipping his NVGs up and turning on a powerful flashlight, which he aimed at the ceiling.

They crept aft, back toward the blowing air of the open cargo door, scanning the overhead for a hatch.

"There," Jed said, pointing at a ladder along the rear bulkhead with rungs leading up to the ceiling.

"Jackpot," Eli said, illuminating the underside of a hatch in the overhead.

"Sword One, Watcher," Corbin queried as they moved into position by the ladder.

"Go, Watcher," Jed whispered into his boom mic.

"I have good eyes," she said. "I count five tangos besides my host. One is standing by the weapon; the other four are all the way forward. They're pounding on the cockpit door and yelling. I think something happened to the pilots—that's why we can't find their threads."

Jed looked at Eli. "Think they're dead?"

Eli shrugged. "How would I know?"

"Are the tangos you see armed?" he asked softly, holding the rail of the ladder well now, picturing in his mind the tactical situation they would be bursting into.

"Three of the four are armed with assault rifles. My guy—I don't know. The guy by the weapon . . . he's armed too."

"Watcher," came Ben's voice in his ear, "tell me about the machine. Is there a hatch or doorway near it or anything?"

"No," she said. "But it's, like, connected to the floor of the plane right at the wall on the left side."

"Yeah, I remember that," Ben said.

"I see it," came Colonel Mitchell's gruff, low voice. "There's what looks like a black dome on the side of the aircraft right there. I saw it before but assumed it to be some sort of navigation or tracking system based on satellite. I thought it odd it wasn't mounted on top like usual."

"So that's . . ." Corbin's voice filled with dread.

"How they fire the weapon, yes," Ben said, his voice tense. "Corbin, if you get any sense that they're getting ready to fire, I need to know immediately."

"I gotcha," the teenager replied. "Sword One, I don't know if this helps you but inside the plane it's just open space, like the inside of that big Air

Force jet we took to Italy. There's a bench along the wall to sit on, but the entire floor is covered with black plastic boxes. That's what everybody is walking on."

"Those are the lithium-ion battery cells for the weapon," Nisha said, commenting for the first time. "Try not to shoot those, guys. They could catch on fire."

Jed looked at Eli and the veteran shook his head.

"Now they tell us," Eli grumbled.

"Copy all," Jed said through gritted teeth. He flipped his mic from VOX to PTT. "We're going to have to be quick, bro. There's no cover. And if Nisha's right, the plane is probably going to catch on fire because no way someone doesn't shoot the floor . . . Just saying."

Eli grinned and checked the security of his parachute. "If that happens, then we bail."

"Or if they fire the weapon before we kill them all," Jed said. "The F-16s have kill decision authorization."

"Yep," Eli said. "It's quite the party we've crashed."

"You ready?" Jed said, flipping his mic back to VOX.

Eli nodded.

"Here we go," Jed whispered to Eli and everyone else on the circuit.

He mounted the short ladder and a few steps later was hunched below the hatch. He glanced down at Eli, who crowded close at Jed's legs, but there was no way around the fact that Jed was popping out first and alone. Geometry dictated this was a single-file entry.

At least they're forward and distracted.

He pushed the flat, round detent beside the locking handle, which was flush with the panel, and it popped out with an annoyingly loud clunk.

He paused. *Did he hear me, Corbin?*

No. We didn't hear anything.

Can you keep your guy looking forward?

A silent pause.

I'm not sure how to do that. But you're good now. We're watching the commotion at the cockpit door.

Jed felt a chill at her use of the word *we*.

Eli, not privy to their private, in-head conversation, tapped Jed's hip. "We're running out of time," he whispered.

Jed nodded and spun the handle and felt the locking bolts disengage. He had to choose between exploding up through the hatch—which would be limited by the speed with which he could breach the narrow space—and easing the hatch open and sneaking into the cabin.

He chose the latter.

He felt more than heard a gentle click as the hatch snapped open. He pushed it a few inches, then a few inches more, depending on Corbin to let him know if at least the nearest bad guy heard something. He eased his head up into the gap and scanned the main cabin. The layout was just as Corbin described, with four men at the front of the wide-open cabin, shouting and pounding on the cockpit door with their hands. To his left, midway up, a man stood beside a machine straight out of a sci-fi movie. Corbin's tango was sitting on the bench seat at the forward starboard side.

Jed lifted the hatch slowly, mouthing a prayer that it didn't creak on corroded hinges. Once open, he gently eased it to the floor. Waist even with the floor, he brought his rifle up into a scan. As he took the next step on the ladder rung, rising out of the floor, the guard standing by the energy weapon turned and caught sight of him. Before the man could shout, Jed squeezed the trigger and dropped him with a single suppressed round to the head.

Accelerating into the action, he stepped out of the hatch and floated his holographic red-dot sight to hover on one of the men congregated at the cockpit door. Jed's target held a rifle in a vertical carry, beside another man who was pounding on the door with the butt of what looked like a Beretta AR90, an Italian iteration of the venerable M4. Somehow, with the roar of the wind outside the thinly insulated fuselage, the yelling and banging on the cockpit door, and Jed's suppressor, the other warriors had miraculously not heard the gunshot.

Jed drifted left, opening up a lane that would allow him to fire offset if needed, perhaps not killing the pilots if his rounds tore through the cockpit door. In his peripheral vision, he saw Eli emerge through the floor hatch and fall in beside him to starboard.

The fighter on the bench seat turned, his eyes wide in surprise.

"Leave him if you can help it," Jed said softly, knowing his voice would be amplified in Eli's earpiece. "Corbin's with him."

"Check," Eli said, but the choice was made for them when the man sounded the alarm by screaming at the fighters outside the cockpit, who turned to look aft en masse.

Jed squeezed the trigger, dropping his tango with a head shot.

"We have a gun!" Corbin screamed in Jed's head and his ear for Eli to hear.

Eli responded by firing three rounds center mass and dropping the guard.

"He's down. I'm out. Oh, it's horrible," Corbin said. "He's dying and he's so terrified . . ."

Jed moved left and forward, keeping his body much lower than usual as the man he'd shot slid down the cockpit door, leaving a trail of blood. He took a knee, hoping a low angle of fire might mean less likelihood of killing a pilot, moved his dot to the next tango, and fired. This bullet entered just under the fighter's chin, tearing his face off, as Eli fired two rounds into the chest of the third shooter, followed by a single round to the head as he fell.

They both advanced swiftly, in parallel, Jed glancing briefly at the mess that had been Corbin's man as they closed on the final tango, who was unarmed but standing with his head bowed in a strangely rigid posture.

"Hands in the air and get down on your knees!" Jed barked at the figure.

Instead, the man leapt into the action, moving toward them at super-human speed. The Dark One jinked right and spoiled Eli's first shot, the errant round hitting the top left corner of the cockpit door, which made Jed wince. The fighter's eyes glowed the color of flame, and he let loose an eardrum-piercing shriek as he kicked a booted foot off the fuselage wall, propelling himself upward and toward Jed.

Jed executed a reverse lunge, settling back onto his left knee, placed the holographic targeting dot in the middle of the man's forehead, and fired a three-round burst. The dark warrior's head evaporated in a puff of red, white, and gray, spattering the ceiling with gore—a gruesome image Jed's mind would not soon forget. Then the nearly headless body collapsed to the deck like a sack of wet cement. It twitched twice, hands and arms moving as if trying to push back up, then lay still.

Wordlessly, they converged on the cockpit door.

Jed took the left side and Eli the right, keeping some of his body behind the corner of the small galley. Offset as best he could in the narrow space, Jed pounded twice on the door, then pulled back and announced: "We are American operators. We have control of the cabin of the aircraft. Open the cockpit door immediately."

He rounded the corner by the edge of the door to the lavatory, expecting a barrage of gunfire to punch holes through the door any second. Instead, he was met with silence and steady, unaltered flight—no pitching, rolling, or altitude or speed change.

Jed gave Eli a nod, holding his weapon trained on the door.

Eli quickly pressed a tiny amount of breacher charge into the edge of the door beside the latch, pushed a detonator into the plastic pile, then unwound the attached cord and moved behind the wall of the galley as Jed pulled back behind the corner of the lav by the main cabin door. Eli gave a nod, connected the wires to the small device he pulled from his cargo pants, and a moment later there was a dull whump as the small explosion blew a hole where the door latch had been. Eli rounded the corner, pulling the door open toward him with his left hand, his right holding his weapon up at a forty-five so as not to tag Jed in the narrow space, while Jed surged forward to sweep the cockpit.

"Nice," Jed said, lowering his weapon as he surveyed the carnage in the pilot and copilot chairs.

"So that's a problem," Eli said in a soft, sarcastic drawl.

"Yep . . ."

The captain's throat had been slit nearly to his spine, his face white, eyes open, and features twisted in pain and fear. His shirt was soaked through in drying blood and the windscreen and control panel were caked in it. The copilot was slumped over the panel between them, facedown, with two large, bloody holes in the back of his white uniform shirt, evidence of two bullets fired right through his heart.

"Now what?" Eli's calm voice didn't match the tension on his face. "We can't just bail out and let it crash; we'd kill innocents on the ground."

"Maybe we can turn it around so it's headed out to sea?"

"Sitrep, One," Ben demanded, and Jed remembered they were on VOX, so their conversation was broadcasting on the comms circuit.

"Aircraft is secure," Jed said, realizing immediately how absurd that was. "All the tangos are dead, the weapon is secure, but we have a new problem . . . the pilots are dead. It's just us left on board now."

"That is a problem," came Ben's dry response.

"Yeah," Jed said. "I assume you want us to try to turn this beast around and point her out to sea before we bail out?"

His question was met with prolonged silence before Ben said, "One, I'm afraid we're gonna ask you to do one better."

"What's that, boss?"

"We'd like you guys to land that thing at NAS Pax for us. It's pretty important that we secure the weapon."

"Not it," Eli said without hesitation, shaking his head and raising his hands in surrender.

"I'm not a pilot, bro," Jed fired back, meeting Eli's gaze.

"Neither am I!"

"You're the veteran Shepherd. You've got more experience than me—you land it."

"I'm not landing it," Eli replied. "You're the lead; you land it."

"Dude, I can't land a commercial jet."

"Gentlemen, I understand your misgivings, but Terry tells me it's easier than landing a small jet," Ben said in his ear. "And it's going to take both of you. Now man up, get in the seats, and I'll get support on my end. We're going to have a pilot holding your hand every step of the way. Do *not* disengage the autopilot until then."

"We won't," Jed replied. "Like we even know how to."

"Dude, just don't touch *anything*," Eli said. "You Navy SEALS can be a little handsy sometimes."

Jed gave a snort at the comment; then they both started laughing. "Thanks, bro, I needed that."

"Anytime. . . . Let's get these dead guys out of the seats," Eli said.

Jed stepped into the cockpit and Eli followed. "Captain first," he said and unfastened the pilot's harness.

"Look, dude, full disclosure," Eli said, grunting as he helped lift the dead captain from the left seat. "I hate flying. I'm deathly afraid of airplanes."

"What are you talking about?" Jed said as they set the body on the floor inside the tiny galley. "You're a fully qualified Airborne Ranger, Special Forces Delta operator. You've jumped out of hundreds of planes."

"Yeah . . . 'cause I hate them. Ironically, it makes it easier to jump out."

"That's the dumbest thing I've ever heard," Jed grumbled, grabbing a shoulder of the copilot and turning sideways so Eli could fit in to help him.

"Well, it's the truth," Eli grunted.

A moment later, the second body was beside the first.

"We'll flip for it," Jed offered, wiping his bloody hands on his cargo pants.

"No." Eli shook his head and slipped into the right seat, ending the conversation. "We won't."

Jed sighed and slid into the captain's seat, using a rag to begin mopping blood from the windscreen. "All kidding aside, if you want to bail out when we're in range of Pax River, I can do this solo. Seriously, I got this."

"Nope," Eli said, wiping down the control panels and instrument clusters. He managed a tight smile. "You go, I go. We're in this together, brother."

CHAPTER THIRTY-SIX

Jed realized he was holding his breath and exhaled.

"You're looking great, Sword One," came the almost-annoyingly collected voice of the pilot in Jed's ear. "Right on course."

"Roger," Jed said, not sure what else to say.

"Sword Two, do you understand your duties here?" the ground pilot asked.

"Yep," Eli answered. His voice had taken on the more familiar, fatalistic tone Jed loved about his teammate. "I'm gonna work the flaps when you tell me, and I see how to do that. I'll lower the landing gear when you tell me, and I see how to do that also. Then I back up Jed on the yoke, and I put my hand on top of his on the throttles."

"You got it, Sword Two. Well done," the man said. "How about you, One?"

Jed sighed. "Do what you tell me and try not to die," he said. So far, it actually had proven to be pretty easy. He simply changed what the pilot directing him had called the "heading bug" on his main display and pulled the throttles back a bit until the airspeed settled on two hundred and twenty knots on the main display. It seemed like the plane was pretty much doing all the work.

He looked out the side window, relieved to see blue water of the Chesapeake Bay below them in all directions now. The controller and pilot told them they'd be approaching from the southeast, over the water the entire time until they made the runway, and no one had to tell him the reason for that. They were landing on runway 32, which the pilot explained meant they would be on a heading of 320 degrees on final approach.

"Okay, One, we're gonna try something here," the pilot in his ear said.

"What's that?" Jed asked, feeling his anxiety rise again.

"We're going to make a descent, but I want you to do it without the autopilot on this time."

"Why?" Jed asked, not thrilled. They'd descended to seven thousand feet and it had been simple—just dial 7000 into the altitude box on the autopilot and hit Accept. The plane had descended smoothly to the desired altitude, leveled off, and adjusted power to keep the speed at the preset two hundred and twenty knots. He'd begun to believe they might survive this insane plan.

"There's no auto-land feature on this plane," the pilot said calmly. "So we're going to line you up, walk you through power settings to manage the descent and speed, and give you little corrections, but at the bottom, you'll have to hand fly the plane to land. I want you to get a little bit of a feel for it now, okay?"

"Uh . . . okay," he said, shooting a glance at Eli, who tried to give him an encouraging smile but failed.

"One, put your left hand on the yoke—the steering wheel–looking thing—and your right hand on the throttles."

Jed did as instructed. "Check. Now what?"

"Two, I want you to turn off the autopilot," the pilot said, "and, One, you just hold her steady."

Eli mumbled a short prayer, then disengaged the autopilot.

To Jed's surprise, nothing happened at all.

The plane continued in straight and level flight, on heading, the speed constant.

"Okay, One, smoothly pull the throttles back. You'll feel the nose drop—which is fine, it's supposed to. You'll begin to descend. Once the vertical speed indicator—it's beside or beneath the airspeed indicator and probably labeled VSI—gets to about the five hundred feet per minute down hash mark, just ease the tiniest little pressure back in on the throttles."

Jed did it, his chest tightening when the nose dropped with the throttles coming back; then—when they didn't fall out of the sky in a gigantic fireball—he relaxed a little bit.

"Just keep the wings level with gentle pressure left and right if you need to. Look outside to do this—don't stare at the instruments and chase things around too much."

Jed concentrated on doing just that and again found it easier than expected.

"Okay, we're going to level now at two thousand five hundred feet, okay?" the faceless voice instructed a few minutes later. "Ease the throttles forward for me, slow and smooth, to somewhere about where they were when you were level."

Jed complied, and the plane bobbled a bit. He instinctively pulled on the yoke, but he found the less he did, the better the plane responded, and after a few tweaks on the throttles, they were level at two thousand two hundred feet.

"Sorry," he grumbled.

"Close enough," the pilot replied, but that felt wrong to Jed since being off by three hundred feet at landing would be a disaster.

"Autopilot on," the pilot said, and Eli complied. "Now I'll set you up on the ILS approach to runway 32 on your navigation radio. The autopilot will automatically capture the inbound radial and, if we set it up right, will even manage the glide slope. It will cut off automatically below five hundred feet, but we're gonna take it off sooner and walk you through the last few moments of landing, okay, One?"

"Okay," Jed said again, realizing how much he must sound like a scared kid.

Eli followed the detailed, step-by-step instructions, and moments later, the plane began a gentle left turn, scaring Jed until he realized it was doing just what it was supposed to do. Slowly the wings leveled, and Jed saw the airport, a sprawling field of crossing runways and taxiways on a peninsula stretching into the mouth of a river that dumped into the bay—the Patuxent River, he assumed from the name. They were lined up dead center on a runway that looked dangerously tiny from this height and distance. He'd been promised ten thousand feet, over a mile and a half, which sounded huge but presently looked like a driveway.

"Two, set the speed bug for one hundred and eighty knots," the pilot said.

Eli did and the throttles adjusted on their own, slowing them to exactly 180 on the indicator.

"Okay, good. Two, now I want you to put in thirty degrees of flaps and lower the landing gear in that order . . ."

Eli did, and Jed felt like someone had just lassoed the plane with a giant invisible rope.

"You'll intercept the glide slope in a second, guys. The plane will begin to descend on its own, and it will adjust power to keep the speed at one hundred and eighty knots. Keep your hands on the controls, One, and we will transition to manual on final, okay?"

"Roger," Jed said, just not willing to say "okay" again.

The plane flew smoothly in a slow descent, the altimeter winding down, the power staying constant, and the runway gratefully growing in both length and width in the windscreen.

"Eighteen hundred feet," the voice said. "Fifteen . . . At twelve hundred set the speed to one hundred and sixty, Two. . . . Set that now, please."

Eli did.

The plane slowed.

The runway grew.

"Eight hundred . . . Get ready, One. We're gonna go off autopilot in a second. Remember what to do?"

"Hold it lined up with the runway, wings level, and when you say, I start pulling slowly back on the yoke."

"Set speed for one hundred and fifty, Two. Let it settle in then, here we go . . . Okay, autopilot off . . ."

Jed felt little change at first; the beast of metal and electronics followed its angular momentum perfectly. The left wing dipped a bit, and he brought it back up.

"Five hundred feet . . ."

He remembered to put his right hand back on the throttles, resisting the overpowering desire to hold the yoke with both hands. He felt Eli's hand on top of his.

"Four hundred . . . Three hundred . . . Two hundred . . ."

Now the runway seemed to be rushing up at them, and Jed felt panic grow in his chest. He unconsciously pulled back on the yoke and the nose came up some.

"Not yet, One. Don't worry. I have a little extra speed in for you. . . . One hundred feet . . . Ease back a tiny bit on the yoke and keep your hand on the throttles. . . . Give a bit of power now; you have a slight headwind . . ."

Jed complied, working the throttles with Eli's hand on top of his.

"Get ready to come back off . . . Almost there . . ."

The runway filled the windscreen now, dark black marks on the approach end from all the other airplanes that had landed there before them.

"Nose up . . . nose up . . . That's it. . . . Throttle back a bit . . ."

Jed pulled back on the throttles as the nose came up and suddenly felt the plane drop.

"That's okay. . . . That's ground effect you feel . . ."

Indeed, Jed felt the plane waffle in a sort of cushion for a moment; then the tires hit the pavement, much sooner than he expected, and barked loudly, startling him. He made an embarrassing *"nuuuhhhh"* sound.

"Keep the nose up and let her roll; keep the nose up. . . . Pull straight back on the throttles now until they stop . . ."

Jed did, and the nose came down.

It hit the ground, not quite gently.

"That's okay, just a little quick on the throttles. . . . Remember, you're steering with your feet. . . . Bring the flaps back up, Two, and let's get heavy to get you stopped."

Jed didn't know what that meant. The flashing red lights of the crash trucks on both sides suggested that they had not been completely confident in Jed's ability.

"There you go. . . . Keep in on the center. . . . Let it roll; you have plenty of runway. . . . Let it roll. Use your feet . . ."

And the next thing Jed knew, they were stopped.

Jed looked out the side and saw he was right of the center on the wide runway and at the very end of the strip of cement, the plane's nose angled slightly left.

"Great job, fellas, you did fantastic," the pilot said and then walked them through the shutdown sequence.

Jed realized, as the blue Humvees tore toward them, that his forearms ached as if from a two-hour workout in the gym, and his legs were shaking. For a moment, he sat frozen, not sure he had the energy to crawl out of the seat.

"Awesome job, bro," Eli said. "You did it, man."

Jed turned and saw his teammate's eyes looked wet.

"We did it," he said. He squeezed his eyes shut, opened them, and looked up at an almost mural of blue sky, a few puffy white clouds dotting the canvas. "With some help, I suspect," he added and gave a quiet prayer of thanks.

"Amen, brother."

"Now," Jed said, feeling his energy return and his smile broadening, "can we please get out of this beast."

"Yeah," Eli said, laughing.

He followed Eli from the blood-spattered cockpit on still-quivering legs. "Next time you get to land."

"If there's a next time," Eli shot back with a grin, "I'm jumping."

CHAPTER THIRTY-SEVEN

Maria tapped a short fingernail on the plastic case holding the visitor's pass hanging from the lanyard around her neck. The guard looked at her with skeptical eyes as he spoke on the phone inside the main gate security building. She smiled, but he did *not* smile back, and she forced her eyes away. Her inner sentry was adamant that she keep her weapon with her at all times. Victor had big plans for today—big plans that he'd chosen *not* to read her into. The thought of being alone and inside the walls of the enemy's home complex without her weapon made her feel naked and exposed. Like when she was a kid, vulnerable and alone in a world full of—

A tap on the window snapped her back with a start.

"Very sorry, ma'am. I checked with my chain and I'm afraid you are not authorized to carry your service weapon onto the compound." His voice suggested he wasn't the least bit sorry.

"I see," she said, forcing a smile onto her face.

"I can secure it for you here," he suggested. "It will be locked in the safe and released to you, and only you, upon your exit from these grounds."

"I understand," she said.

"If you step inside, ma'am, I'll secure the weapon and generate a receipt for you."

She nodded and followed the guard inside. He led her past a large front desk where a female guard sat at a workstation. The woman nodded cordially at Maria, but her eyes held the same all-business suspicion of the guy escorting her to the safe. Maria's gaze ticked to the bank of monitors, each subdivided into eight windows, streaming security camera footage from what appeared to be dozens of cameras around the complex. She also noted a control panel for what she surmised were defensive countermeasures—invisible to the untrained eye—built into the access road, perimeter fencing, and this guard building.

"Your weapon, ma'am," the male guard said, calling her attention.

She said nothing, just pulled her Glock service pistol from the paddle holster on her belt, released the magazine, and then cycled the slide—expertly catching the ejected round in her free hand. With the weapon made safe, she handed it to him. He took it, cleared the chamber for himself and locked the slide back, and then dropped the magazine and extra round into a baggie. He opened the safe, slid the baggie and weapon onto the second shelf with a ticket, after tearing it in half, then handed the remaining half to Maria.

He smiled, but it looked like the smile one might program a robot to make, a trick to make it look more human.

"You have a good afternoon, ma'am," he said. "You can retrieve your weapon on your way out."

"Great," she said. "See you then."

She climbed back behind the wheel of her Charger and pulled through the gate after he lowered the thick steel barrier.

The compulsion to roam the compound and collect intelligence about the layout was overwhelming, but she knew better than to succumb. That security camera bank was proof that her movements were being monitored. This was her first entry into Trinity unaccompanied, implying, perhaps, that she'd elevated herself to a higher level of vetting—or a lower level of perceived security risk. Her conversation with Ben Morvant the night of the cookout had been cut short, but the man had seemed to consider her not-so-subtle expression of interest in joining the "Trinity Team," as she'd called it. And the perception that she was now Jedidiah Johnson's girlfriend probably helped as well. Maybe he had gotten her on some new list rating her unescorted access.

She surveyed the campus as best she could while sticking to the direct route to the neighborhood where the Yarnells lived. Minutes later, she pulled her unmarked cruiser into the Yarnells' driveway and parked. Rachel opened the door and met her on the stoop, pulling Maria into a hug that took her by surprise. She hugged back, equally surprised when the woman's affection stirred something warm and happy inside.

She promptly incinerated the feeling.

This woman is not your friend—she's an assignment. You have no friends . . .

She held the hug long enough that Rachel wouldn't see the conflicted emotions on her face.

"Come on in," Rachel said, holding the front door open. Despite the smile on her face, Rachel looked tired—exhausted in fact.

"Are you doing okay, Rachel?" Maria asked, playing the role to perfection. "You look tired, girl."

"I am, actually," she said, talking over her shoulder en route to the kitchen. "It's been a crazy week. David's been busy at work and there have been some . . ." She hesitated. "Some *things* going on. I'm alone most of the time . . . surrounded by plenty of people but alone nonetheless. When you called, I was literally picking up the phone to call you."

Maria held her smile, but her mind searched furiously for clues to what might be going on. What *things* could Rachel be referring to? And did they involve pursuing Victor? Had the Shepherds been tipped off about Victor's secret plans—plans he'd not seen fit to read her in on? But in her heart of hearts she knew. He was going to hit the Shepherds where it hurt the most. The only question was when . . .

"That's so funny—we're definitely on the same wavelength today." Then, probing for more information, she asked, "Do you think the guys will be back in time to join us for dinner?"

"I doubt it," Rachel said. "I think it's gonna be just us girls tonight. Which is fine by me. We can have the bottle of wine I bought all to ourselves."

"Amen to that," Maria said, feeling a little burn in the scar on her abdomen. "Should we open it now?"

"Honestly, if we did that, I'd probably fall asleep on you," Rachel said with a chuckle. "I know it's late for coffee, but I could use one, and we can save the wine for after I have some food in my stomach."

"Perfect."

"David bought this new, fancy machine, so I can make you a latte or cappuccino or anything you want. I even have the flavor syrups."

"Oh, that sounds great," Maria said and realized she meant it. "I would love a latte. Do you have low-fat milk?"

"Skim okay?"

"Perfect." She followed Rachel into the kitchen.

While Rachel made the coffee, Maria tried to make small talk, answering questions about what it was like back at work. She looked about the kitchen, searching for clues as to where David might have gone, but of course finding none. She would give anything to have Victor's ability to reach inside another person's mind. Her chest remained a tight band, her detective's gut telling her she better find a way to please him or her time on earth could be drawing to a close.

And any afterlife that may exist for me will not be good . . .

"So . . . how are things with Jed?" Rachel asked, grinning behind the frothy latte she'd just prepared.

Maria had already told her about their first kiss when they'd met for lunch the other day. Rachel's immediate reaction to Maria's gossipy confession had been a speechless, stone-faced stare—which had been telling in and of itself—but she'd seemed to warm to the idea. Maria sensed a torrid history existed between Jed and Rachel. Well, *torrid* was probably a gross exaggeration with these two Puritans. One step above platonic was probably more like it. The thought made her chuckle.

"That juicy, huh?" Rachel said.

"Hardly," she said with an eyeroll. "I haven't seen him since then . . ."

which is fine, I guess. I just wish I knew where he was running off to all the time."

"You and me both," Rachel said, taking a sip of her coffee.

"You mean David really doesn't read you in on what's going on? You don't have to pretend ignorance on my account. I'd never expect you to tell me anything if he did."

Rachel pursed her lips for a split second and said, "I know you wouldn't. But here's the thing: he *really* doesn't tell me anything. A part of me admires and respects him for that, but another part of me wants to smack him. I know he thinks he's protecting me by keeping me ignorant, but I don't see it that way."

"I totally get it, and I'd feel the same way. You're not a mushroom to be kept in the dark. Not some gossiping, social-climber housewife who can't be trusted. You're a valuable part of the team."

"Yeah, exactly."

"And you're on lockdown like everyone else here."

"It's so annoying . . . not being able to go outside."

Maria's heart rate picked up. She was so close now . . . if she played the innuendo card just right. "I know. Jed made me meet him at some random Starbucks in the lobby of a hotel. C'mon—is that really necessary?"

"I can't imagine how horrible it was to see it in person like Jed did. David saw the pictures and said they were horrifying, but I still think it's overkill. If they're going to vaporize me, they're not going to do it when I'm walking to the mailbox. It's going to be where people can see it. I mean, that's how these people operate . . ."

Maria nodded and maintained eye contact while Rachel was talking, but her mind went back to the Dark Horizon warehouse, remembering the refrigerator-size machine she'd seen on a wooden pallet. *It really was an energy weapon . . . Victor actually built a death ray.* So was that the plan . . . to vaporize Sarah Beth and the other Watcher children?

Rachel's expression abruptly changed, and for a split second she looked upset.

"What's wrong?" Maria said, her attention fully back.

"Oh, I just had a . . . a flare of heartburn." The other woman tapped the center of her chest with a closed fist. "Sometimes coffee does that to me."

"Yeah, me too, sometimes," Maria said, but the detective in her knew a lie when she heard it . . . Except why lie? She was the one who was talking.

I didn't say a thing, she thought.

"Hey, I have an idea," Rachel said, eyes bright and smiling broadly. "Let's sit outside on the back deck. It's too beautiful of a day to spend it inside."

"But what about the lockdown?"

"Screw the lockdown," Rachel said, defiantly picking up her coffee mug. "You and I certainly aren't a threat. They're not going to waste an attack on either of *us*. Wouldn't you agree?"

The little burning sensation in Maria's scar flared.

Something was off.

Something she'd done or said had triggered Rachel and now she was acting strange.

I need to let this play out. See if I can nudge her into making a mistake or until I figure out what's going on.

"Let's do it," she said, picking up her coffee. "After all, you know me. I prefer to live dangerously."

CHAPTER THIRTY-EIGHT

"You can't really be serious, Ben," Jed said, turning to the Shepherd commander, outrage threatening to boil over.

After tracking the energy weapon literally around the globe and repeatedly risking his life and the lives of his teammates, they were now expected to hand it over to the CIA, no questions asked. As far as he was concerned, that was the definition of insanity.

"I'm afraid the matter has been decided above your pay grade, soldier," Gayle's boss, Steve Schmidt, said, taking the liberty to answer for Ben.

Jed looked at the balding, middle-aged, potbellied man in his golf shirt, chinos, and boat shoes. "Yeah, well, I'm afraid you'll have to do better than giving us your word, since we're the ones who almost died recovering it and all," he said, his fists balled up and one rude comment away from punching the smug spook in the mouth.

"Jed, I'm afraid he's right," Ben said, but there was sympathy in his voice. "We've received direction from the ODNI that Mr. Schmidt will be taking possession of the weapon."

"Brilliant idea. That way the CIA can reverse engineer an exact replica and we can have two morally vacant governments in charge of weapons that turn humans into piles of smoldering ash from the sky. Until the tech leaks out—and then every terrorist in the world will find a way to get it. No way that's the plan, Ben."

"I'm not the enemy, Jed," Schmidt said. "I find this weapon as horrifying as you. It's a weapon of terror, with no real strategic application in any case. But we can't put this genie back in the bottle. The weapon exists in the world. They made one; they can make more, Jed."

The continued use of his name in the familiar was like spitting lemon juice in Jed's eyes, and on top of that, he didn't believe for a second that the CIA didn't see a "strategic application" for such a weapon.

"We have the man who invented it," Jed protested. "We pulled him out of China."

"And you think that means the team of engineers from the project, those still loyal to the CCP, can't and won't build another one? They have the plans, Jed."

"Here we go—another mutually assured destruction scenario to justify a new Cold War arms race with China," Jed said.

"Don't be so melodramatic," Schmidt said with a snort. "Those are two completely different scales of destruction. Nukes annihilate cities and blanket the planet in radioactive fallout. This weapon is nothing more than a glorified sniper rifle. Don't get me wrong; it's terrible, but with proper study we can develop appropriate detection and countermeasures for it so no one gets incinerated ever again."

"Somehow I don't believe you," Jed said, shooting a glance at Gayle, who looked at her hands.

"Jed," Ben said softly. "I've had my issues with CIA over the years, but we're on the same team. More importantly, you should know I have a great deal of trust and faith in the DNI, who is a close friend and benefactor of our task force. I don't know Mr. Schmidt here well enough to take his word at face value, but neither do I know him well enough *not* to trust him. What I *do* trust is the judgment of the DNI. It's time to let it go. Clear enough?"

Jed nodded, aware that his fists were still balled but also that both Gayle and Schmidt were staring at Ben with something that looked like reverence. His brain, still playing catch-up, zeroed in on the subtle but strategic comment Ben had made.

"I have a great deal of trust and faith in the DNI, who is a close friend and benefactor of our task force . . ."

So the DNI was part of the network that directly supported the Shepherds? Did that mean he was fully read in on the true nature of their work and their dark adversary?

"Mr. Schmidt, we appreciate your help and support. And let me add that Ms. James here is a gifted and capable case officer and liaison. We look forward to working with—" Ben stopped midsentence when the secure phone in his pocket chirped. "Excuse me, I have to take this," he said, checking the caller ID and pacing away from the group.

Jed, still simmering, turned and watched the large forklift driving up to the side of the Boeing 717, intent on removing the weapon and transferring it to another plane. He shook his head and, without a parting word to Schmidt, walked over to where Ben was taking his call. When Jed was at his side, Ben put the phone on speaker and held it between them.

"Corbin, please repeat what you just said," the Shepherd commander said.

"Sarah Beth saw a map. It wasn't a premonition or second sight through someone's eyes, but a memory, she thinks, captured from one of the men who helped load the weapon on the plane."

"But she didn't see it until now?"

"Yeah, and that part was weird. Maybe whoever has been blocking us kind of gave up once you guys had things under control. Everyone suddenly got a literal hurricane of images. But this one seemed very important."

Jed remembered the feeling at the hangar in New Jersey—like some sort of spiritual jamming system was keeping a dome of silence over the facility. Had that been Victor?

"So tell us exactly what you guys saw."

"The map had pins in it, and it labeled different sites. One was DC and underneath the flag it said *Rose Garden*—with the names of the president, the vice president, and a bunch of other people, like senators and stuff. Then there were other flags—in New York, Los Angeles, Miami, Chicago, and Denver. Each had names underneath. We're sending the names she can remember."

Ben looked at Jed, his eyes and face grim.

"Additional targets?" Jed said.

Ben nodded. "Sounds like."

"But we have the weapon."

"We have *a* weapon. What if there was more than one?"

"In which case those could be additional targets."

"That's my concern," Ben said. "Have Nisha get with the head shed at home and have a talk with Zhao to see if it's possible." Jed nodded and Ben turned back to the phone. "Send Jed and me everything you have, Corbin. And tell Sarah Beth good work."

Jed let out a long sigh through his teeth. He turned on a heel to jog to the hangar and get with Nisha.

"Jed," Ben called out after him. "You and the team get all your gear and get on board the C-130. Something doesn't feel right about this to me. We're heading home. I need to get back to Trinity with the leadership team. And I want Joshua Bravo as a QRF."

"But what about the other possible targets?"

"I'm mobilizing the other Shepherd units to every location the Watchers identified."

"All the units?" Jed asked, a chill running down his spine.

Ben nodded.

"I noticed Nashville wasn't one of the cities she named," Jed said.

"There's something bigger at work here. My gut tells me Victor is making a power move, but what that move is, I don't know," Ben said, fire in his eyes. "We need to be ready for anything and everything. The serpent only dies when we cut off the head."

Jed nodded. He felt eyes on him and turned to see Gayle staring at him from beside Schmidt, a pained look on her face. He jogged over to her, ignoring Schmidt and sticking out his hand to her. She took it, surprise on her face.

"Thanks, Gayle," he said, "for everything. We couldn't have pulled any of it off without you. We're in your debt and I personally hope our paths cross again."

She gave a nod, her eyes cutting over to Schmidt, and replied softly, "Thanks, Jed."

He nodded back, then took off for the hangar at a run to mobilize the team.

We should have seen this coming . . . I should have seen this coming, he thought, beating himself up. They'd stopped one attack, but Victor was the architect and he continued to stay one step ahead. *To be a leader, I have to stop simply reacting and start thinking proactively.*

To beat Victor, he needed to learn how to think like Victor, to anticipate his next move and be prepared with a countermove in advance. As a SEAL, that had never been his responsibility. As an operator, he'd been the club, not the hand swinging that club or the brain deciding where to hit.

To succeed as a Shepherd, he was going to have to learn how to be all three.

CHAPTER THIRTY-NINE

DARK HORIZON FACILITY

NASHVILLE

2040 HOURS LOCAL

Victor's mind was a chorus.

A chorus of fury and intent.

He had summoned many—as many dark angels as could be wooed to share his vessel—and he was full to bursting. The power was intoxicating, which was fortunate because the pressure was punishing. With so much rage to redirect, it was imperative that he keep them occupied, lest they turn on each other . . .

Or upon him.

And so occupied he had kept them.

To execute this mission, he'd needed tens of dozens to augment and bolster his intrinsic power. Keeping the Shepherds at bay and the Watchers in a fog of distraction while battle plans were being laid was beyond the skill of any lone warrior, even one knighted by the Dark Prince himself. To complete *this* mission required a legion.

And yet somehow, Ben Morvant and his new golden boy—Jedidiah Johnson—had beaten him once again. His own rage at being denied the victory in DC fueled the rage of the demons inside him. The plan to deploy the energy weapon had been perfection—a false flag operation that would be construed by faithful and faithless alike to mean that God had turned His once-loving face away from the spoiled child America had become. Tens of thousands, over time perhaps millions, of souls could have been kept from God's light. It would have been a triumph for the Dark Prince, and he blamed Jedidiah Johnson for his failure.

And that wretched girl . . .

He had always planned to use the chaos of his victory as a distraction to carry out a secondary, very personal mission. A mission that would ensure the success of many to follow. Now, with this latest defeat, it was his only remaining play. He would strike a blow to the Shepherds that would cripple them. He would damage the very nerve center of their operation.

So he'd made room for more demons and requested their presence to join the legion inside him.

His request had been granted.

For the mission to succeed, it was time to systematically unwind the deception of recent weeks and let the light creep in . . . but just a little. Just enough to serve the design. Just enough to scatter the Shepherds in every direction and leave their flock defenseless. Even now, Ben Morvant's knights were scrambling to protect the wrong targets from decoy weapons.

And when they return, they will find us bathing in the blood of their precious Watchers.

"Victor, I know you said not to be disturbed, but I have urgent news," the assault commander said, walking into Victor's chambers without permission.

Victor turned to face the man, deciding not to mete out punishment before he'd heard the report. "Tell me."

"The Shepherds have scrambled five teams and they appear to be en route to the target cities," the soldier said, unable to hide his distress.

Victor said nothing for a moment, basking in the other man's fear. There was nothing he reveled in more. Fear was a man's greatest weakness. If temptation was a lockpick to breach the soul, then fear was a sledgehammer. In the face of fear, intellect is abandoned for reflex. In the face of fear, solidarity crumbles. And in the face of fear, principle is traded for self-preservation.

Fear was, and always had been, his greatest weapon.

"It was inevitable. Inform the mission commanders of the threat," Victor finally said, "but their orders are unchanged."

"Yes, sir." The soldier lowered his head.

Victor sensed the man's fear ebb as he determined he would not be held responsible for the intelligence break. What the soldier did not understand and had no way of knowing was that Victor himself was responsible for the leak. Every element of the plan was compartmentalized at different levels of the hierarchy, and only Victor understood the endgame.

"Are the vehicles and your men ready for tonight?" he asked.

"We're locked and loaded."

"Very well," Victor said. "Do not disturb me again. I see everything . . . there is nothing you can report that I have not already seen."

"Yes, sir. It won't happen again," the assault commander said, bowing in deference.

"Leave me."

The heavily muscled mercenary departed, leaving Victor to his machinations. He settled into a squat, closed his eyes, and entered the mind space where the legion was deployed stymying the Watchers. For weeks he'd managed to keep them in the dark, masking his objectives and shielding even the weakest minds of soldiers from their snooping. Not even the most powerful among them—Sarah Beth Yarnell, with her gift of second sight—suspected he was coming for her.

PART III

Then Jesus asked him, "What is your name?"

"My name is Legion," he replied, "for we are many."

MARK 5:9

CHAPTER FORTY

Sarah Beth rubbed her temples and let her chin rest against her chest. She'd heard people say, "My head feels like it's in a vise," but she'd never truly understood . . . until now. She'd had to leave the Bullpen an hour ago when the headache started. The noise and frenetic pace down there, which at first excited her, eventually wore her down. Being in the TOC reminded her of swimming and playing in the ocean surf—it's fun and thrilling until it's not. Eventually the slamming surf, the tugging undertow, the chafing sand turns recreation into a chore.

A sudden wave of nausea twisted her insides and made her salivate. The subdued lighting in the Sanctuary was too bright. Even the once-soothing sound of the water bubbling in the fountain now was akin to fingernails on a chalkboard, grating her nerves.

Is this what a migraine headache feels like? she wondered.

"Are you okay, Sarah Beth?" Pastor Dee said, placing a gentle hand on her back. "You look like you're hurting."

"Yeah, I just have a really bad headache," she said.

"When is the last time you ate something, sweetie?" her Keeper said, kneeling beside her.

That's what Pastor Dee is now, right? My Keeper?

"I don't know," she said. "Lunchtime, I think. I had a banana."

"Oh, honey, you can't do that. What you're doing is hard work. You need to stay hydrated and eat enough to keep up your energy level."

"I know; you're right. It's just the Shepherds need us. We have to help them stop the other attacks."

"Yes, but we've got lots of Watchers on the job. You've worked hard all day without a break and now you're paying the price. It's time for you to rest. Head back to your dorm room and go to bed," Pastor Dee said. "I'll instruct your roommates to keep the lights out and no talking."

"I can't . . ."

"You and Corbin gave Joshua Bravo the support they needed to stop the attack in Washington, DC. You girls are heroes. Let the older kids take it from here. Your work is done for today. And if they send Joshua Bravo out again, they will need you rested."

Sarah Beth forced a smile and winced at the accompanying throb of pain. "Corbin needs me. I can't stop until all the Dark Ones are taken down."

"Listen to Pastor Dee, Sarah Beth," Corbin said, kneeling next to Sarah Beth's chair on the other side. "You've done enough. Michaela and I can handle it. We work well together. If Joshua Bravo goes out again, I'll come get you."

Sarah Beth smiled at her mentor and friend, noticing for the first time the heaviness in Corbin's voice and the dark circles under her eyes. The tired smile Corbin wore did little to hide the weight of the silent burden she carried. Sarah Beth realized she'd come to think of her mentor as an adult but she was barely old enough to drive. Her mind's eye flashed to the pages of Corbin's sketchbook and horrors recorded over her years of service. Did Watchers develop PTSD?

Is that my future?

"Are you sure?" she said, her voice weary but the thought of a break irresistible.

"I'm sure," Corbin said with a tender smile. "Take some Advil, drink a glass of water, and go to bed."

"Okay." Sarah Beth let Pastor Dee help her to her feet and escort her to the White Room. Pastor Dee rode the elevator down to the main level with her and opened the door for her. "You don't need to walk me back, Pastor Dee. It's okay."

"No, it most certainly is not. I am your Keeper now, girl . . . ," the woman said with a warm smile, mostly in her eyes, confirming Sarah Beth's thought.

I have a Keeper.

"And I am going to tuck you in and make sure those roommates of yours do not wake you up."

It was pointless to argue with Pastor Dee, so Sarah Beth surrendered and let herself be led to her dorm room—at the foot of the building's cross layout, with the girls on the west side and the boys on the east.

Pastor Dee gave her a glass of water and two Advil and tucked her into bed like a little kid. As much as the attention was embarrassing, secretly she kinda liked it. Pastor Dee was a good woman.

I'm glad she's my Keeper, she thought as she drifted off to sleep.

CHAPTER FORTY-ONE

"That's enough for me," Rachel said, waving off a refill as Maria tried to top off her glass of wine.

She suspected the detective was using the alcohol as a lubricant to loosen her lips. The question was why. She'd felt dark intent from Maria earlier in the kitchen—just a snippet, but it was enough to make her question her perception of the woman. Since that moment, Rachel's mind had been in overdrive, reassessing everything Detective Maria Perez had said and done since the day they'd first met.

Why did she turn up at our old house alone, without backup, the night the Dark Ones tried to kidnap Sarah Beth for a second time? When exactly did she enter the house, and which one of the kidnappers shot her? When and why did her romantic interest in Jed start? Why is she working so hard to kindle a friendship with me? And why does she ask so many questions about Sarah Beth and St. George's?

Am I being paranoid?

Maybe.

Probably.

But it felt right to be skeptical.

It felt right to be suspicious.

Sarah Beth had never warmed to the detective, and now Rachel was beginning to wonder if her daughter's misgivings were rooted in something deeper than adolescent jealousy and competition for "Uncle" Jed's very limited time.

"Are you sure you don't want any more?" Maria asked as she topped off her own glass. "If you say no, I'm apt to polish off the rest of the bottle myself."

"Yeah, I'm sure," she said with a laugh. "After two glasses I'm ready for bed."

Maria set the almost-empty bottle down on the table and checked her phone. "Still not a peep from Jed." She looked up at Rachel. "Have you heard from David?"

"Nope," she said without bothering to glance at her phone.

She felt a palpable uneasiness from the detective.

No, not unease . . . it's urgency. Maria wants something and wants it desperately.

Her daughter had reawakened a dormant gift inside her, a gift Rachel had tried to pretend away for nearly two decades. But the gift *was* real, and it wasn't just something that depended on Sarah Beth. For a while, that's how she thought it worked—that she was a passenger pedaling on the back of a tandem bicycle while Sarah Beth navigated from the front. She realized now that metaphor was wrong. They were both cyclists in this road race.

I've just been drafting off my daughter, taking it easy and pedaling with my head down while she did all the hard work, Rachel thought. *But not anymore. It's time for me to take control.*

Maria had been playing mind games during dinner and over dessert, and she was still at it now. The woman was good. So smooth and slippery. Like a seasoned stage actress, Maria delivered her lines with conviction and authenticity. Rachel had parried every question and attempt at intimacy as best she could, but now her gut told her it was time to go on the offensive.

Time to rattle the detective's cage for once.

"I've always been curious about that night you got shot at our house," she began, her gaze locked on Maria's face. "You know, the night the bad guys tried to kidnap Sarah Beth a second time."

The detective nodded and took a sip of her wine before responding. "Curious about what?"

"I'm curious why you decided to drop by so late and unannounced."

"We've been over this before, I thought."

"Have we?" Rachel said, cocking her head. "I don't remember."

"If you don't remember, that's fine," the detective said and took another sip of wine. "There's not much to it, really. I'd stayed late at the precinct that night because of everything that happened that day. I certainly didn't feel like I had closure on the case, what with Trinity's intervention and all. I was worried . . . so I decided to swing by on my way home."

"If you were so worried, why didn't you bring backup?"

"Because I was off the clock. Nothing had been called in. No 911 calls or anything, so why would I have? This was just me being a concerned citizen, who—if we're being honest—was feeling pretty guilty about her performance on your daughter's case." Maria let out a defensive laugh. "I thought I was the detective, but it sure feels like I'm being interrogated."

Rachel set down her glass and looked at the woman sitting across from her . . . *really* looked at her. And in that moment, she got the distinct and disturbing feeling that she'd let the proverbial wolf in a sheep's clothing into her home. No, not into her home, into her *life*—and into the lives of everyone she cared most deeply about. She was about tell the detective she was tired and ready to call it a night when a strange and disturbing flash of imagery came to her. A dark creature with a hundred demonic faces where there should only be one. It was snarling and chasing Sarah Beth through the halls of St. George's.

"Rachel, are you okay?" Maria said, leaning in with a concerned look on her face. "You just went pale. Are you going to be sick?"

"I . . . I don't know," she stammered, feeling suddenly nauseated.

The image flashed before her mind's eye again and she felt her daughter's terror as if it were her own. She tamped down the fear and reached out to Sarah Beth with her mind.

Sarah Beth, it's Mom. Are you okay?

When no answer came, she tried again, louder this time.

Sarah Beth, it's Mom. Answer me if you can . . . please.

"What's going on?" Maria said, screwing up her face.

"I have to go," Rachel said, popping to her feet and heading to the mudroom cubbies, where she kept her purse and keys.

"Rachel, wait . . . go where?" the detective said, chasing after her and grabbing her by the arm.

"Let go of me," Rachel said, shaking her arm free and whirling on Maria. "I can't explain it, but something is coming for Sarah Beth . . . something terrible. I have to help her."

"Wait!" Maria called, but Rachel was at the door, pulling on a jacket with her car keys clutched in her hand. She reached for the knob, then stopped.

I need a gun.

She turned and ran to the black gun safe next to the desk. Kneeling, she entered the code, the keypad beeping with each number and then double beeping as the bolts released. With Maria looking on, she pulled the compact pistol from the safe. She checked that a round was in the chamber, released the slide, and then grabbed an extra magazine, which she shoved into her jacket pocket on the left, the pistol going into the right.

"Where do you think you're going with that gun?" Maria said, blocking her path to the door.

"To St. George's," she said. "Now please get out of my way."

"Do you really think they're going to let you onto the campus, armed and raving like a lunatic about something coming for Sarah Beth that you can't describe?" the detective said, not moving.

Feeling flustered, Rachel stammered. "I'm her mom, and I have a right to protect her."

"They're not going to let you on campus in this manic state," Maria said, her voice and body the model of calm and confidence. "Believe me, this is what I do for a living."

"I don't care. I have to try," Rachel said, tamping down the panic and collecting herself.

"Then I'm coming with you," Maria said, reaching out and giving Rachel's shoulder a squeeze.

Rachel stared at the police detective—this enigma of a woman with an earnest, confident demeanor but muddy, unreadable intentions.

I wonder . . .

Using only her mind like she did with Sarah Beth, she reached out to the detective.

Are you with God or with the Dark Ones?

A long pause lingered between them, but Rachel's unspoken question was left unanswered.

"Look, I can see that you're upset," Maria said, dropping her cop voice and seeming to talk as her friend. "But why don't we call the school first? Let's start with that, okay?"

"It doesn't matter what they say," Rachel said, shaking her head. "I'm going."

"Then I'll drive," Maria said with a tight smile. "I've got lights and sirens and a radio if we need it."

Rachel considered the offer, her mind working at lightning speed, playing out the pros and cons. If she let Perez drive, she forfeited all the control; she would be powerless to help her daughter if the detective pulled something untoward. But despite her paranoia and sudden suspicions about the woman, she had no concrete evidence that Maria Perez was anything other than she claimed to be—a struggling, single detective who by fate, or possibly the hand of God, found her way into their lives.

What if Maria has some role to play . . . a role only God can see? Ben Morvant gave her unescorted clearance on campus. And Jed is dating her, for goodness' sake.

If they trust her, maybe I should too . . .

"Okay, Maria," Rachel said, unsure about her decision but committing anyway. "Let's go."

CHAPTER FORTY-TWO

Brandt Sanderson cupped his fingers around the top of his bottle of Coca-Cola to make an impromptu funnel, then dumped a third of a bag of salted Planters peanuts inside.

"Dude, what are you doing?" Vance, his fellow guard, asked.

Sanderson shot Vance a dubious look. "You've never had Coke and peanuts before?"

"Heck no, that's disgusting."

"Hey, don't knock it till you've tried it," he said, then took his first sip of the sweet and salty goodness, holding the floating peanuts at bay with his top lip.

"Must be a Southern thing," Vance said, scrunching up his face with disapproval as lightning flashed and the wind began to pick up outside.

Brandt had picked up the practice from his dad, who'd learned it from his grandpa, who'd learned it while working construction. And yes, it was a Southern thing—Texas, Georgia, Florida, Alabama—he'd seen fellas drink Coke with peanuts in all those places but never once up North.

"What do you do with the peanuts when you've drank down to the bottom?" Vance asked, unable to let it go.

"Well, you either eat 'em," Sanderson said with a wry, Texas-size grin, "or you don't."

"*Obviously* . . . what do *you* do?"

"I eat 'em."

"Don't they get soggy?"

"Yeah."

"Ah, man, that's disgusting," Vance said, getting out of his chair and throwing his arms up for dramatic effect.

Sanderson chuckled. He hadn't known Vance long, but he liked the guy. They were about the same age, late twenties, but Vance had a baby face and could easily pass for eighteen. Sanderson himself had made the mistake of misjudging the guy when they first met, assuming Vance was a rookie fresh out of high school. He'd been surprised when Vance told him he'd done not one but two tours with the Marines. They'd bonded immediately after that—shared service had that effect on people.

He extended the bottle to Vance. "You sure you don't want a swig?"

"Dude, get that disgusting thing out of my face," Vance said, his voice drowned out by a tremendous thunderclap outside.

"Looks like we're in for quite a storm," Brandt said, grabbing an iPad off the desk and opening a weather app. The app flashed with multiple warnings that appeared as a cascade of pop-ups over the current forecast:

SEVERE THUNDERSTORM WARNING
TORNADO WATCH
FLASH FLOOD WATCH

Vance, who was looking over his shoulder, whistled. "Looks like we're about to get pummeled, bro."

"Yep," he said, clearing the alerts and clicking to see the colorful radar map, which showed a monster thunderstorm heading their way from the northwest. "It's gonna be here in—" He stopped midsentence as the radio clipped to his belt crackled to life.

"Main Gate, this is Spotter—over."

"Go for Main Gate," Sanderson said, keying the mic clipped to his chest pocket.

"I hold multiple vehicles on approach, traveling in what appears to be a convoy," the spotter said. "It's got my antennae up. I don't like it."

"Their headlights on or off?" Sanderson asked.

"Off," the spotter said, "but they're still too far for me to make out the vehicle details."

Sanderson's heart rate picked up and a bolus of adrenaline flooded his bloodstream. With his free hand, he signaled for Vance to prep the defensive countermeasures. Tonight, Sanderson was the watch commander, and the safety of this school and all the kids inside was his responsibility. His time in the Army and later as a GRS contractor for the CIA had taught him the danger of inaction. In the security business, spinning up and responding to a false alarm was always better than doing nothing or reacting too slowly to a threat.

This was the first time in fourteen months that he'd been back at St. George's Academy to stand watch. After being promoted to chief of perimeter security at Trinity Loop, he'd been removed from the St. George's rotation. Trinity SG oversaw all the security for both campuses, but the Trinity Loop billets were way more coveted. Like moths to the flame, former operators ranked proximity to the action as their number one priority. And like Sanderson himself, most of the Trinity security staff had aspirations of being recruited as Shepherds. For him, it hadn't happened yet, but in his heart of hearts he was certain that day was just around the corner. He'd not been made privy to the reasoning behind the increased force at St. George's, but his instinct told him it was something important, and for Sanderson that meant he needed to be here.

He realized he might be about to learn why.

He acknowledged the spotter's report and switched his radio to VOX. "Alpha and Bravo teams, take defensive positions and prep for possible incursion. We have unknown incoming vehicles. I repeat, prep for possible incursion."

While Vance raised the retractable steel balusters on the access road, Sanderson unlocked the gun cage and pulled two Sig Sauer assault rifles from the rack. He checked the magazines and chambered rounds into both. Then he handed one to Vance, slung the other across his chest in a combat carry, and turned on the perimeter spotlights.

"Gate, Spotter—I have good eyes on the convoy now. Looks like three INKAS Sentry APCs," the spotter said.

Sanderson clicked his acknowledgment and cursed under his breath. He knew that vehicle well because Trinity had three INKAS Sentry APCs in its own inventory. Was it possible this convoy was a Shepherd team inbound to augment their presence? The coincidence seemed almost too much to ignore.

No, he told himself. *They would have radioed ahead. Technically those assets belong to Trinity Security Group and it would need clearance from me.*

The first gust of rain from the rapidly approaching storm spattered against the guard shack windows and roof, but his thoughts were focused on the inbound APCs. Built on a Ford F-550 platform, the Sentry armored personnel carrier was a SWAT infiltration unit. Equipped with armor plating and hardened everything, the all-terrain vehicle was capable of transporting up to ten shooters and resisting 7.62mm assault rifle rounds and grenades. There was no telling how many shooters were incoming, but he'd only brought five shooters with him to augment St. George's normal after-hours security force of four. To make matters worse, he had no hardware capable of damaging or even repelling an INKAS APC. On top of that, the academy's perimeter defenses were nothing compared to what was installed at Trinity Loop—no vehicle flipper, no remote-deployable tire-shredding chains, no hardened antiballistic guard shack, and no concealed heavy machine gun nest. The only defenses here were the retractable steel balusters on the access road and a very clever bit of landscape engineering where a "berm and moat" design had been used along the entire southern fence line. The only positive compared to Trinity Loop was that the school campus was heavily wooded on three of four sides, making the only possible vehicular approach from the south.

So we got that going for us . . .

"Inbound tangos passing my pos," the spotter said. "Do you want me to shoot their tires?"

Sanderson debated the question. His first inclination was not to engage unless the APCs turned down St. George Promenade, the entrance road leading to campus from the county road it intersected. But the sooner he engaged the enemy, the better. Trinity's Sentry APCs were equipped with off-road run-flats, but he didn't know if that was an INKAS standard or an upgrade.

"Spotter, Main Gate—shoot the tires," he said. "Alpha Three, you're overwatch on the approach."

"Spotter," the remote spotter said simply. "Engaging . . ."

"Three has good eyes. Three is now Archangel," his roving watch carrying the long gun with a long-range optics package said—the report indicating he'd taken a high ground position and was ready to serve as the team's sniper.

Fresh gunfire echoed, sharp and crisp, against the low and rolling rumble of thunder.

"Gate, Spotter—I put six rounds in tires with no effect," the spotter reported. "They're accelerating like mad now."

"Check," Sanderson said through clenched teeth. "Alpha and Bravo, stand by to engage."

"We're gonna stay in here?" Vance asked, the frown on his face telegraphing his thoughts on the matter.

"You mean so we can get blown up by an RPG?" Sanderson said with a crooked grin. "Nah, I was thinking we get wet outside with the rest of the team."

"Thank you," Vance said. "Which side you want me on?"

"West side," he said, picking up the desk phone. "I'm going to inform the headmaster what's going on and tell him to get the kids into the shelter."

"Check, and I'll radio Trinity Loop and let them know we need a QRF," Vance said.

"We are the QRF, remember?" Sanderson said. "All the Shepherds are deployed."

"So Morvant gambled and sent us here just in case, and now this happens?"

Sanderson nodded. "Man's got a gift. But let the head shed know—they'll think of something to do to support us." He had no idea what that might be, but hopefully God would provide.

Before he could press the speed dial to the headmaster's direct line, a loud boom echoed behind them and the power went out in the guard shack as all the perimeter spots went dark.

"Lightning strike?" Vance said, his eyes going wide.

"That was no lightning strike." Sanderson whipped around to catch the final seconds of an orange fireball belching skyward. "I think somebody just blew up the campus electric substation."

"You know what that means . . ."

"They're already here," he said, his voice catching in his throat as the words came out. He'd already split his force with the four-member Bravo team patrolling inner campus and the more experienced Trinity augments in Alpha team on perimeter and spotter duty. His guts went heavy and hot, like they were suddenly filled with molten lead as he said, "Bravo team, sound off and report your position."

"Bravo One, in a covered position at the main entrance," came the first reply.

"Bravo Two is in cover in the football bleachers, scanning the western tree line."

"Bravo Four is patrolling outside the dormitories," came the next voice.

When Bravo Three didn't check in, Sanderson tried again, but his query was met with silence.

"Three was patrolling the east perimeter. That's where the substation transformers and backup generators are located," Bravo One said.

Sanderson cursed and looked at Vance.

"I'm on it," Vance said, already heading to the door.

"Take the mule," Sanderson said, referring to the Kawasaki 4x4 ATV parked behind the guard shack that made getting around the sprawling 120-acre campus more manageable.

Vance nodded, grabbed one of the two Flir Scout III thermal-imaging NV scopes sitting on the table, and disappeared out the door into the rain. Sanderson's mind was racing at warp speed with all the things he needed to do and for some reason the execution of his list happened at a much slower rate than he needed it to happen. It had been five years since he'd seen real combat and he'd gotten out of practice. The whole thing felt like it was happening to someone else.

"Spotter, Gate—if you haven't started heading back this way, we're going to need you," he said, running down his list of coordinating actions.

"Roger that, I'm hoofing it back now. Gonna set up in flanking position to put those boys in a cross fire," came the reply.

Sanderson acknowledged the report and then rejiggered the call signs as he stepped out into the driving rain. "Gate is now Alpha Four, Vance is Five, and Spotter is Six. Bravo One, we lost phone comms. You need to let the Center know what is going on and secure the main building."

"Bravo One, copy," came the reply, barely audible over the howling wind and rumbling thunder.

What now, what now? . . . Phone it in to HQ, you idiot, he chastised himself as he pulled his mobile phone from his cargo pocket. How could he have forgotten to call it in to Trinity, and how was all this happening without anybody's knowledge? The Watchers should have seen this coming miles away. *I should be the one getting orders and updates, not giving them.*

Thanks to the pouring rain, the haptic touch screen on his phone would not react properly to his touch.

"Four, we've got incoming," an operator called in.

Nerves on fire, Sanderson stuffed his phone back into his pocket and raised his night-vision scope, looking down the access road to see three armored INKAS vehicles making the turn onto campus property. One of the APCs turned before the driveway, the second turned onto the driveway, and the third one held back. He understood the strategy immediately. The second APC was going to challenge the barricade and the first was going off road to attempt to circumnavigate the balustrades by driving through the moat and over the berm. In a few minutes, both sides would know which of St. George's countermeasures could repel a 4x4 Sentry attack vehicle. After they'd stress-tested the defenses, the third APC would charge in and take the path of least resistance.

He lowered his scope and scrambled to a covered firing position on the top of the berm to the right of the guard shack, beside where one of his Alpha team members had already set up shop.

"You know our seven six twos ain't gonna do jack against the armor on those APCs," the operator everyone called "Bags" said to him, sighting over his rifle.

"I know, but if the barricades hold, they're going to have to get out and then we can go to work."

Gunfire echoed behind them on campus somewhere, and he prayed that was Vance getting the jump on bad guys and not the other way around. Ahead, two of the three APCs were careening toward them at high speed, with the APC on the paved road leading the charge. Through the spotter scope, he saw it had a plow shovel on the front.

"Looks like we're about to answer that age-old question," Bags said.

"And what question is that?"

"What happens when an unstoppable force meets an immovable object?"

Sanderson looked at the speeding APC, then shifted his gaze to the row of steel balusters sticking out of the concrete and prayed the latter would prevail. Fifteen seconds later, they got their answer in a deafening collision of steel on steel as the armored truck slammed into the barricade at speed. The front plow broke off its mount and collapsed into the engine compartment, which in turn buckled into the passenger cabin. The back end of the APC catapulted eight feet up in the air—almost tipping the vehicle over—before crashing back down in a resounding thud.

"Thank You, God," Sanderson murmured as he scanned for cracks in the antiballistic windshield to shoot through.

Meanwhile, to the east, the driver of the APC taking the off-road approach still closed rapidly, clearly intent on driving up and over the hill. From most angles, the rolling grass-covered berm with its white three-rail fence on top and meandering rocky creek bed in front looked like something out of a storybook. In fact, it was so aesthetically pleasing, only a security expert would recognize it was a perimeter countermeasure designed specifically to prevent off-road vehicle incursion. But the geometry was deceptive by design and by the time the driver understood his mistake, it was too late. The incoming APC rumbled down the slope into the "moat" and crashed nose-first into the base of the upward-sloping berm. The impact stalled the vehicle in place, jamming it at a downward angle, making it impossible to maneuver out of the snarl because the front wheels had zero engagement.

"Take that, you dumbasses," Sanderson murmured and then in a loud clear voice into his mic said, "Alpha is weapons free. Shoot to kill."

At first, nothing happened. The infiltrators stayed inside the APCs while Alpha team scanned for targets from their prone shooting lanes atop the berm. But then, in a coordinated egress, Nomex-clad shooters poured out of the rear doors of the two APCs. The sound of Archangel going to work with his sniper rifle was music to Sanderson's ears as he and his team unloaded on the insurgents. Tracers zipped through the night as both sides traded volleys in the rain. Lightning flashed overhead and thunder crashed with malevolent fury as if the elements themselves had a stake in the battle raging below.

"Alpha Five, sitrep?" Sanderson called, checking in on Vance while he was sighting on the rear bumper of the wrecked APC at the gate.

"Engaged two insurgents moving from the substation toward the school. Both tangos are KIA," Vance said, his voice raspy.

"Copy. Reposition to front entrance and take command of Bravo element."

"Wish I could," Vance said with labored breathing, "but I'm not in the fight. Took a round in the gut just below my vest and my legs aren't working. Sorry, bro . . . I don't think I'm gonna make it. Too bad too, 'cuz when this was over, I was thinking about giving Coke and peanuts a try."

"Just hang in there, Vance. This is going to be over soon, and we're gonna get you a medevac," Sanderson said, gritting his teeth to fight back the raw emotion threatening to break the dam that was just barely keeping his head in the game.

"Roger that," Vance said. "Give 'em hell until then."

"Third APC incoming," Bags said.

Sanderson glanced down the road. Unlike the first two assault teams, this vehicle's driver was cruising slow and steady down the driveway. If the first two tries had taught them anything, it was that a brute force assault with their vehicles was not going to work. By Sanderson's count, they'd killed six insurgents and he estimated another four were still hiding either inside or behind the wrecked APCs. Alpha Six had not made it back yet to help set up a flanking cross fire, but Sanderson expected he'd be in position within the next few minutes.

"What's he doing?" Bags asked.

"Not sure . . . I'm wondering if they've got something heavy in there."

"That's what I was thinking too. Fifty cal . . . ?"

"Maybe, or maybe RPGs. We need to watch those rear windows."

"That's where my red dot is floating right now," Bags said.

The third APC pulled up behind the wrecked and smoldering one at the barricade and stopped. Several long seconds ticked by before all the doors opened and four black-clad shapes in helmets and Nomex body armor leapt out and charged the berms. They covered the distance with near-superhuman speed, eyes glowing the color of flame.

"Dark Ones!" Sanderson shouted on the open channel.

Alpha team unleashed a coordinated maelstrom of fire, riddling the possessed warriors with round after round, but the inhuman assaulters just kept coming. Emboldened, the regular human insurgents with whom they'd been trading bullets stepped out of their covered positions and began shooting. They strafed the top of both berms with brutal relentlessness, forcing Sanderson and his men to duck and shift. With Alpha's rhythm and fire lanes broken, the Dark Ones clawed their way up the rain-slicked berms.

"We're the first and last line of defense for this school," Sanderson yelled, looking right and left at his fellow shooters. "We must hold the gate, no matter what!"

"Aim for their heads," someone shouted.

"Get some!"

Gunfire popped as the battle for control of the berms raged all around him.

"Oorah, dropped one," someone else shouted.

"Three, look out—you got a Dark One on top of you," Archangel reported as sniper rounds echoed in the night.

Sanderson looked up and saw a black shape leaping through the air straight at Bags.

"Arrrrrhhhhhhh," Bags screamed—a war cry while squeezing the trigger again and again and again at the demon soldier.

Bullets riddled the Dark One's torso but it landed on Bags and drove him to the ground. With an inhuman growl, the dark warrior began to savage him with twin blades—one in each hand. Sanderson swiveled and put his red dot on the monster's right ear and squeezed the trigger. The possessed warrior's head jerked and then it collapsed on top of Bags.

Tracers zipped past as Sanderson crabbed over. Grunting, he pulled the dead thing off Bags's chest and looked down at his teammate. Blood gurgled from punctures in Bags's neck and chest, and he met Sanderson's gaze with terrified, helpless eyes. Then Bags's gaze ticked right. Sanderson spun, bringing his rifle up just in time to squeeze off a three-round burst into the face of a second Dark One who was already missing a chin but still coming at him. The salvo found its mark and the glowing-eyed creature dropped like a puppet whose strings had just been cut.

Breathing hard, Sanderson swapped magazines. He'd lost count, but he knew his current mag was almost out. Gunfire and thunder roared all around him. On the west berm, someone was screaming. Someone else reported something in his headset that didn't make any sense.

Hold on . . . Did Alpha One just say that Alpha Two shot himself in the head?

Sanderson had looked west to see what was going on with One and Two when a voice spoke to him with unfiltered, malevolent clarity.

You've lost. You're pathetic. You're weak . . . and every child in that school is going to die because of your incompetence.

He swiveled in the direction of where he perceived the voice to be coming from and saw a tall, dark figure walking—just walking—past the wrecked APC toward the guard shack. The figure was dressed entirely in black, with a hooded jacket that hid the face. It strolled between the steel balustrades, seemingly unconcerned about the tracers zipping past in all directions.

Sanderson raised his rifle and put his red targeting dot on the figure's forehead and squeezed the trigger . . .

But he didn't squeeze the trigger.

He'd meant to squeeze the trigger, wanted to squeeze it, but somehow his finger had been stayed.

Their blood is on your hands, Brandt. Just like the blood of your little sister . . .

His breath caught in his throat.

"What did you say?" he shouted.

That's right, Brandt, I know all about Ava. How your mom asked you to keep an eye on her for just five minutes while she put your brother down for a nap. How you decided to play your video game instead and how helpless, clueless little Ava walked out the screen door and into the pool. You didn't even notice she was gone. Your mom found her.

"Stop it!" he screamed. "I was six years old. That was an accident!"

If only you'd been a better brother. If only you'd cared. If only you'd loved her . . .

"Get out of my head!"

He tried to squeeze the trigger, to end that hooded son of a bitch, but his finger would not budge.

And now history is going to repeat itself. Over two hundred innocent children are going to die on your watch, because of your inattention, your incompetence, your apathy . . . so why don't you just end it now? Put yourself out of your misery. Let God sort it all out, because only God knows what should be done with a sinner like you.

He didn't see the Nomex-clad operator until it was too late—the one who'd snuck up the berm while he'd been distracted. He swiveled and fired at the same time as the insurgent. Both rounds found their marks. The enemy shooter pitched over backward and so did Sanderson. He felt his body rolling down the berm—his arms and legs tubes of jelly, useless and unresponsive. He came to rest looking up into the tempest.

Rain pelted his forehead, his cheeks, his eyes . . .

He tried to blink, but his eyelids ignored him.

Time passed and a hooded figure appeared, gazing down at him.

The figure's face was hidden in shadow, but twin rings of flame stared down at him from the void.

It spoke out loud this time.

"You see . . . God doesn't care about you. He doesn't love you. In your time of greatest need, He turned the other way and let mine be the last face you see."

"Go to hell," he said, but the words didn't come out, echoing instead in his mind.

The figure above him heard nonetheless.

"With pleasure," Victor said and slipped away into the storm.

CHAPTER FORTY-THREE

"St. George's is under attack!" Nisha shouted, running down the aisle from the front of the plane.

The proclamation hit Jed like a hot fire poker in the ribs. "What are you talking about?" he said, popping out of his seat.

"The front gate at St. George's is under assault. Multiple armored vehicles are attempting to breach the perimeter," she said, her breath coming in hard, fast pants.

"What?" David exclaimed, and Jed saw the terror in his eyes. "How?"

Sarah Beth, David nearly screamed inside Jed's mind.

Ben raised a hand but gave David a sympathetic nod.

"Tell me everything you know, and why am I just hearing about this now?" Ben said, joining her and Jed in an impromptu huddle in the middle of the aisle.

The plane jerked violently to port, knocking them all off-balance. The pilots had warned them to buckle in for what was looking to be a rough landing as they tried to beat the storm bearing down on the Trinity Loop complex.

"All comms with St. George's are down. I just got off the horn with the Trinity TOC watch officer. At first they thought it was because of the storm. The school lost power, but then Watcher Central went dark. The only reason we know about the attack is because the watch officer in our TOC picked up combat radio chatter via one of our campus repeaters," she said. "From the sound of it, the augment security team is being overrun."

Jed's mind instantly went to Sarah Beth. If St. George's was under attack, why hadn't he heard from her? Why hadn't she reached out for help?

Sarah Beth! Are you all right?

Nothing came back to him . . .

"What about main campus? Is Trinity Loop under attack too?" Ben said, worry on his face.

"Not as of this moment," she said, "but that doesn't mean Dark Ones aren't prepping to hit us there. It's what I'd do if I were Victor."

"That bastard set us up," Johnny said, falling in behind Ben and leaning around to join the discussion. "It was all a ruse! He scattered our teams across the country with that energy weapon horse pucky so we'd leave the flock vulnerable."

"It wasn't a ruse," Ben said with heat in his voice. "The energy weapon we recovered was real. We've seen firsthand what it does to a human being. And we don't know how many more he has out there. But you're right about one thing, Johnny: he definitely knew the chaos in the aftermath of the attacks, especially had they been successful, would provide an opportunity of vulnerability he just couldn't pass up."

"Nobody ever said Victor couldn't walk and chew gum," Grayson said, "and he's proved that tonight."

The plane dipped so hard Jed's feet momentarily left the deck and the crown of his head hit the ceiling. He cursed the turbulence, then, gripping a seatback in each hand, fixed his eyes on Ben. "We've gotta divert to St. George's and LALO in."

"Gimme a second to think," Ben said.

"We don't have a second. By the time we land this plane, off-load, and drive to the school, it'll be over," Jed snapped. "Those kids are completely defenseless."

"They're not the only kids we have to worry about, Jedidiah," Ben said, his voice rumbling in sync with a massive thunderclap outside that shook the fuselage. "Our only advantage is that Victor would have assumed we were all engaged because we just thwarted the first attack. He wouldn't have expected Joshua Bravo to be back here so soon. It's not much, but it's something."

Jed felt a tug and without trying he snapped into Ben's headspace. Like a water jet from a fire hose, the Shepherd commander's thoughts pummeled Jed. So many conflicting priorities and risk-reward scenarios were churning in Ben's mind, and Jed saw them all . . .

The decision Ben needed to make was not a simple "all in" or "all out" scenario. The calculus was so much more complex. St. George's was under attack, but what did Victor have in store for Trinity Loop? What if the Dark General was about to unleash a simultaneous attack on the Shepherds HQ? How would they rebuff that? Yes, the Shepherds' home base had more robust perimeter defenses than the Watcher academy, but that had already factored into Ben's original decision to send his most experienced security personnel to St. George's, which left Trinity Loop understaffed. The security presence at Trinity Loop right now was bare-bones—a skeleton crew not equipped to safeguard the hundreds of defenseless spouses, kids, and babies living on campus. And that figure didn't include all the unmarried support personnel who were not trained for combat. To make matters worse, the Trinity Loop complex was three times the acreage of St. George's. At the academy, the Watcher kids were concentrated in dormitories with quick access to a hardened tornado shelter that could serve as a protective bunker during the attack. At Trinity, defenseless families and employees were spread out all over the place. Rounding up and protecting everyone would be nearly impossible even if everything went perfectly . . .

"I get it," Jed said, jerking himself free from the vortex of Ben's mind. "We should split the team. I take half to St. George's; you take half to Trinity."

"I'll go with Jed," Johnny said, his eyes steady on Jed but his face saying so much more. "I'm with you, brother, to the end."

"I know you are," Jed said, meeting his fellow Shepherd's gaze.

"We're going with Jed's plan. Half of you are with me to secure Trinity; the other half LALO in with Jed to rebuff the assault on St. George's. Assuming Trinity is secure, we'll augment you as soon as possible. I wish it didn't have to be this way, but there's no perfect solution for this scenario," Ben said, addressing the group. Then to Jed, he added, "Pick your team."

"Johnny, Eli, and Bex, you're with me," Jed said, feeling this was the right combo.

A tight-lipped smile spread across Ben's face, and he clasped a hand on Jed's shoulder. "Go with God and be extra vigilant. Everything is muddy for me right now, Jed. I don't know how he's doing it, but Victor is blocking our Watchers' thoughts and I can't pinpoint his presence. If he's there, don't try to be a hero and face him alone."

Jed stared at his boss and mentor and asked the one question he couldn't get out of his mind: *What is his weakness? Does he even have one?*

Ben pushed a silent answer into his head. *Victor's only weakness is that he has turned his back on God and all those who might have loved him. Remember, even if he is surrounded by an army of dark warriors, he is alone.*

Jed nodded, not sure how exactly to turn that insight into a tactical advantage and hoping the answer would come to him should he face the Dark General in single combat.

Nerves on fire, Jed helicoptered a finger in the air. "My team, kit up and buddy-check your chutes."

"Gear's in the back; let's go, let's go, let's go," Eli shouted, his usual laid-back demeanor replaced with fervor.

"I need to brief the pilots," Ben said and bolted off for the cockpit.

"Check," Jed said and started toward the back of the plane to kit up.

"Take me," David said, grabbing Jed by the wrist and stopping him. "Jed, please, I have to come. She's my daughter."

"Brother, I get it. I do. But you have never done a LALO insertion, which is tricky as hell anytime but nearly impossible in this weather," Jed said, peeling David's fingers off his wrist. "You're becoming a real warrior, David, but in this scenario, you'd be a liability for us. I need you on the ground at Trinity with Rachel. My connection with Sarah Beth is not working right now, and I don't know why. Maybe Rachel can get through to her. She's going to need your strength and your prayers. We all do."

David opened his mouth, closed it, then shook his head. "I can't *not* save my daughter a second time, Jed. I just can't."

The plane's engines roared as it aborted the landing approach and banked hard to port. Jed caught and braced himself against one of the seats. He just didn't have time for David's angst right now, but he forced himself to keep his cool.

"You're saving her by letting the team do what it does best. We're more powerful this way—one body, many parts. I'll get her out safe—I swear," he added, a part of him screaming not to make such a promise. "And if Victor's there, I'm sending him back to hell once and for all."

Behind him, Ben's voice boomed. "Listen up, jumpers. We've got one shot at this. The pilots are looping round south of the lead storm cell and going to do a pass between it and the cell behind it. The LALO run will be southwest to northeast, with a jump at one thousand feet, angled off for chutes at two hundred. With this storm, it's impossible to calculate winds precisely, but the line *should* put you in on the chapel side of the main building if all goes well. Maps going now to your tablets."

Jed pulled his tablet out and opened the message, scanning the map. Then he looked up at his team, who'd gathered in front of him. "I'm not going to lie . . . what we're about to attempt will most likely be the most dangerous thing any of you have ever attempted. Out there we're going to face swirling and gusting winds. If you catch an updraft, you'll get dragged up into the storm and find yourself at twenty-five thousand feet being ripped apart and electrocuted in a thunderhead. Get hit with a downdraft when you pull the rip cord, and your chute will collapse and you won't have time to inflate the backup before you hit the deck. If any of you feel that you do not have the experience or gumption to attempt this jump, there is no shame in bowing out," Jed said, scanning Johnny's, Bex's, and Eli's faces each in turn.

"Count me in, boss," Johnny said with a crazy-eyed grin. "LALO-ing in a thunderstorm just so happens to be on my bucket list."

Jed nodded and turned to Bex.

"Have a feeling you're gonna need a medic, so I'm in," she said, her voice nothing but tight determination.

"Eli?" he said, looking at the veteran.

"You know how I roll," Eli said. "If today's my day to meet my Maker, then bring it on. I'm His, so I go home either way."

"All right, Shepherds. Let's do this," Jed said, grabbing a parachute pack. "I'm pulling at two hundred fifty feet; I recommend you do the same."

"Hooah," Johnny said.

Eli took a knee. "If there was ever a time to say a prayer, this is it."

Jed, Johnny, and Bex did the same and bowed their heads.

"Dear Lord," Eli began, "what we're about to attempt is probably insane, but there's a school full of kids down there who desperately need our help . . ."

CHAPTER FORTY-FOUR

SARAH BETH'S DORM ROOM

ST. GEORGE'S ACADEMY

In her dream, a faceless shadow creature—the size of a grizzly bear with glowing red eyes—was hunting her. The creature was relentless and untiring as it chased her through a misty forest. No matter how fast she ran or where she tried to hide, it somehow always managed to find her. But the demonic beast wasn't what shook her from her slumber.

A thunderclap, so powerful the boom rattled the windowpanes, woke her with a start.

She blinked, trying to make out the looming dark shape above her.

It took her a moment to remember where she was. Sarah Beth stared at the underside of Darilyn's bunk bed. She felt disoriented—decoupled from time and space. She turned her head toward Elizabeth's kitty cat–shaped digital alarm clock on the bedside table. With effort, she read the glowing red numbers: 9:29. The numbers didn't make any sense to her muddy mind.

9:29 would mean not even an hour had passed since Pastor Dee tucked her in, but she felt like she'd been asleep for hours and hours.

9:29 . . . Why does that seem important and familiar?

She made a *tsk* sound with her tongue. Her imagination was driving her crazy now.

A gust of wind blew rain against the window, beating out a snare drum snag.

Lightning flashed outside, turning the room electric blue for a fleeting instant.

She winced, her dark-adapted eyes rebelling against the brightness. Her migraine was back . . . or maybe it had never gone away. She groaned her irritation at being woken by the storm. Fresh thunder followed a moment later, not as loud or close as the clap that woke her, but it rumbled long, low, and ominous—like an approaching freight train. A heartbeat later another boom echoed, but this one didn't seem to match up with a lightning strike.

Strange . . .

The alarm clock went dark.

So did the strip of amber light glowing in the gap along the bottom of the door leading to the hallway.

"Hey, guys, I think we lost power," she announced and kick-crawled her legs out from under her blankets before swinging them off the side of the bed. Her bare feet touched down on the chilled, uncarpeted hardwood floor as she ducked out of her bottom bunk. A quick scan of her roommates' empty beds informed her that she was alone in the room.

Hmmm, she thought. *I guess Pastor Dee made good on her promise.*

She yawned, her weary body yearning to return to her still-warm bed and go back to sleep, but that wasn't going to happen. Her mind was up, alert, and fixated on getting an update on the mission. She padded to the door, depressed the lever, and pulled it open. Her across-the-hall neighbor Avery emerged from her room at the same time. They stood barefoot in their jammies staring at each other, but gratefully Sarah Beth saw Avery held a flashlight.

"Is that you, Sarah Beth?" the girl said, thankfully not shining the light in Sarah Beth's face.

"Yeah. Avery?"

"Yep," the eighth-grade girl answered.

"I guess the storm caused us to lose power," Sarah Beth said.

"Yeah, I'm surprised they don't have a generator or something."

"I thought they did . . ."

"What do you think we should do?"

Sarah Beth was about to suggest they find their dormitory RA when she heard the unmistakable sound of a gunshot.

"What was that?" Avery said, eyes suddenly wide with fear—suggesting she had a pretty good idea what the sound represented.

"I think it might have been gunfire," Sarah Beth said, her mind going to the active shooter training they'd had a few weeks ago.

"Everyone—into the tornado shelter. Hurry!" a male voice yelled. Mr. Baker, she realized.

Doors began opening along the hallway and kids trickled out. Like Avery, the new arrivals look terrified. Instead of running toward the shelter, most of them stood frozen in place, staring down the corridor.

"C'mon, guys," Sarah Beth shouted, "you heard Mr. Baker; we've got to get to the tornado shelter."

She grabbed Avery by the arm and pulled her down the hallway toward the shelter, the place they had trained to go for both tornados and active shooter situations—though in central Tennessee and especially at St. George's, she supposed, shooters were more likely than tornadoes. The shelter entrance sat smack-dab in the middle of the school, between the east and west halls. The room was long and windowless, with reinforced steel doors and a concrete ceiling designed to withstand an F5 tornado. It also was large enough to accommodate all the students and faculty and had battery lighting and self-contained ventilation, whatever that meant. Thirty feet ahead, Mr. Baker, the school's chemistry teacher and boys' dorm RA, waved his right arm and directed a river of kids toward the shelter.

Avery tripped, dropping her flashlight and almost taking Sarah Beth down with her.

"Ow, ow, ow," the girl howled, rolling onto her side and clutching her knee.

Fresh gunfire echoed, this time closer than before.

"C'mon, Avery," Sarah Beth said, grabbing her by the wrist.

"I got her," Mr. Baker said, scooping Avery up in his arms. "We gotta go now, girls."

All the kids in the hall were ahead of them now, running toward the shelter but also toward the sound of gunfire. As she ran beside him, Sarah Beth noticed that Mr. Baker was wearing a pistol in a holster on his lower back. He wasn't an operator like Uncle Jed, but hopefully the fact that he was armed meant he could defend them if necessary. They quickly reached the first door to the shelter, where a logjam of kids blocked the entrance as they pushed and shoved in a panicked frenzy to get inside.

"No pushing. Step in and clear the door," Mr. Baker barked, but then Sarah Beth saw his attention abruptly shift from the gaggle of kids to a dark shape with glowing eyes standing in the west hallway fifty feet away.

Lightning flashed outside, briefly backlighting the spindly, cloaked figure.

Gooseflesh stood up on Sarah Beth's arms and the back of her neck.

She knew this shape.

She knew those eyes.

Victor . . .

He was here, at St. George's . . . but how was that possible?

A chorus of screaming voices filled her head, so loud and shrill that her hands flew immediately to cover her ears. She looked at her classmates, assuming they were the ones screaming, but they all had their hands over their ears as well. Some of the kids had even collapsed to the floor and were writhing in pain. The screams were inhuman. Otherworldly. Demonic.

She turned to Mr. Baker, who, wearing an anguished look on his face, pulled his pistol and leveled it at Victor. But instead of squeezing the trigger, he just held the gun in midair, face tight with consternation.

"What are you doing?" she shouted. "Shoot him!"

Mr. Baker ignored her. She could see the cords in his neck straining and the veins on his temples puffing out. Then in horror, she watched him turn the pistol on himself. A tear ran down his cheek, and she understood what was happening. She looked away as he pulled the trigger and screamed as his body crumpled at her feet.

There you are, Victor said, his voice a parasitic worm in her mind. *Now we can finally finish what we started.*

Fear snaked around her chest like a python, making it hard to breathe.

Panic followed along with its twin sister uncertainty. This was it. The culmination of her nightmares. The sum of all her fears. There was no place safe from him.

Not even St. George's.

He had come for her, and this time there was no escape.

CHAPTER FORTY-FIVE

Maria braked to a stop halfway down the access road leading to St. George's Academy. Ahead, she spied multiple armored assault vehicles—of the same design and black paint scheme she'd seen in the Dark Horizon warehouse during her last visit with Victor. One appeared to have run off the road and crashed into the berm beside the front gate. The second and third were parked in front of the row of balusters blocking the road ahead of the guard shack, one of the vehicles appearing to have smashed into the barrier.

"What are those trucks?" Rachel said from the passenger seat beside her.

"They look like armored personnel vehicles," Maria said, squinting to see the all-too-familiar vehicles through the driving rain peppering the windshield.

"So the police are already here?"

"No, those don't belong to Nashville SWAT," she said, keeping her gaze straight ahead.

"How do you know?"

"Because I just know, okay?"

"Then why are they here?"

"I'm not sure," she lied.

"Well, what are you waiting for? We need to get in there!"

Maria shook her head. "No way. Too dangerous. We have no idea what's going on here. There's a high probability we'll be shot before we make it to the gate."

"We have to do something," Rachel said.

While driving over from Trinity Loop, the frantic mother had phoned the school no less than a dozen times, getting no response on each attempt.

"If those APVs delivered assaulters with automatic weapons, then there's nothing we can do," Maria said. "Just one shooter with a machine gun and we'll get cut to pieces. All we can do now is call for backup and wait for the cavalry to arrive."

She knew exactly what Rachel was going to do next, but the question on her mind was whether she should stop the woman. Did it even matter? Should she let Rachel run headfirst into the spray of bullets for a pointless, inglorious death? Or should she lock the doors and handcuff the woman in the car with her until her daughter and all the other Watcher kids were slaughtered by Victor's mercenary army? In her peripheral vision, she saw Rachel glance at her. A heartbeat later, Rachel went for the door handle, but Maria was faster, pushing the lock button.

"I'm sorry, Rachel, but I can't let you do that," she said, keeping her left index finger depressed on the door lock rocker switch on her side.

Rachel fixed her with a death stare that might have been chilling, had she not made a habit of convening with *real* evil. "Why are you doing this?"

"To keep you safe."

"Why don't I believe you?" Rachel said.

A strange compulsion washed over Maria, and she took her foot off the brake and pressed the accelerator. "Fine, if you wanna die, let's go die."

Rain pelted the winshield with such fury that even on max speed, the wipers couldn't keep up, giving her only fleeting glimpses of the road ahead as she accelerated toward the front gate. No sooner had she reached sixty miles per hour than she had to slam on the brakes to avoid crashing into the APV parked in the middle of the road in front of the gate. The Charger hydroplaned and fishtailed, causing Rachel to let out a panicked squeal while clutching the handle on the A-pillar.

Maria wrestled the big sedan under control at the last second and slid to a hard stop a few feet from the APV's rear bumper. Temper hot, she shifted the transmission into park and retrieved her spare service weapon and spare magazines from the lockbox under her driver's seat. She'd left her primary in the safe at the Trinity front gate, deciding the risk of being detained on the way out outweighed the benefit of having two pistols. She checked the weapon ready and slipped it and the extra mags into her waistband.

She waited for a five count, fully expecting the Charger to be riddled with bullets from an unseen shooter. When that didn't happen, she opened her door and stepped out into the deluge. By the time she reached the trunk, her clothes were soaked through. Rachel appeared at her side as Maria clicked the trunk release button on her key fob. The lid popped open.

"What are you doing?" Rachel said.

Maria grabbed her standard-issue body armor and handed it to Rachel. "Put this on."

"What about you?" Rachel said, taking the black antiballistic vest.

"I only have one vest." She grabbed a Maglite flashlight and closed the trunk.

"But . . ."

"I said put it on," Maria snapped, not sure why she was suddenly trying to protect a woman she intended to betray.

Rachel nodded but looked uncertain, wiping several tendrils of wet hair from her face with her left hand and holding the body armor in her right at her side.

"Put your arms out and I'll do it," Maria said.

Rachel complied and Maria helped her into the vest, fastening the Velcro cummerbund flaps for a snug fit. Before closing the trunk, she grabbed her spare drop holster, which she quickly put on before transferring her sidearm to it. Lightning flashed and a thunderclap immediately followed, the boom so loud for a fleeting instant Maria thought a grenade had been tossed at them. Quickly recovering her nerve, she waved for Rachel to follow her and marched through the gusting, swirling rain toward the front gate.

Thirty seconds later, she understood why no one had challenged them.

"It looks like a war zone," Rachel said beside her as Maria scanned the carnage around them. Bodies clad in body armor lay sprawled and unmoving on the berms on either side of the gatehouse. "What in God's name happened here?"

Not in God's name . . .

Maria knew the answer, but she didn't respond. Among the fallen dark warriors, one body was conspicuously absent . . . *Victor.* He was here, and he'd made it through the school's perimeter defenses. She could feel his presence. An overwhelming compulsion to run to him, to join him in battle washed over her and she started running toward the darkened school in the distance.

"Come on," she yelled at Rachel over her shoulder. "We need to get there before it's too late."

CHAPTER FORTY-SIX

Sarah Beth stared at the glowing eyes at the end of the corridor. A thousand voices screamed in her head, while Mr. Baker lay in a growing pool of blood at her feet.

Nobody is coming for you, Sarah Beth, Victor hissed over the din in her mind. *It's hopeless . . .*

A part of her wanted to run.

You're weak.

A part of her wanted to cry.

You're pathetic.

A part of her wanted to pretend that none of this was real . . .

But none of those things would help her defeat Victor. Twice before, Jed had swept in—her knight in shining armor—and rescued her from the clutches of the Dark Ones. But in her heart of hearts, she knew that wasn't going to happen this time. Jed was hundreds of miles away, and Victor was standing fifty feet from her. This time she was on her own.

This time she would have to face the monster alone. The monster and all the demons he carried with him.

9:29.

The image of the clock flashed in her head, some secret message her mind wanted her to see. *There's something special about that number . . .*

What is it?

Another image flashed in her mind, this one of the fountain in the Sanctuary, the sculpture of St. George slaying the dragon, and epiphany struck her. How could she have never put two and two together?

St. George's Academy . . . of course. This is the school where they train us to slay dragons.

"Certitude," she said and balled her hands into fists. A surge of something—energy, confidence, courage . . . she couldn't tell, but whatever it was flowed up through her core and radiated out to the tips of her fingers and toes. "This time I won't let you take me without a fight."

He laughed at this and the screaming in her mind increased to a roar.

A Scripture filled her head—from Deuteronomy, she remembered—and she felt certain that it was God who sent it.

"The Lord himself goes before you and will be with you; he will never leave you nor forsake you. Do not be afraid; do not be discouraged."

She pictured David, just a boy, before he was king, staring up at the giant. This would be her David moment.

Body electric, she fixed her gaze on the demon vessel before her.

"Quiet!" she commanded and the chorus in her mind instantly fell silent.

On the floor next to her, Avery sobbed, clutching her hands to her ears. Sarah Beth grabbed her schoolmate under the armpits, hoisted her to her feet, and shoved her through the still-open doorway into the tornado shelter. Then she locked eyes with a high school boy standing inside.

"Lock this door, and don't open it no matter what you hear outside," she said.

"But what about you?" he protested.

"Do it now," she barked.

With a strange, pained look on his face, he slammed the door. As soon as she heard the lock mechanism engage, she turned back to face Victor. To her bewilderment, he appeared to be alone. Why didn't he have an army of Dark Ones with him? Equally perplexing, why was no one trying to stop him? St. George's had a security team—where were they? Had there been a battle? Were they all dead on both sides except for Victor? Then she remembered what had just happened with Mr. Baker. She'd watched him try to engage Victor, only to turn the gun on himself. *There* was the answer to her question. Victor didn't need an army to defeat the security at St. George's. All he needed was his mind and the legion of demons who possessed it.

"You're powerless to stop me, little girl," he said, his voice slithering down the empty corridor.

"If you want me, come and get me," she shouted.

Lightning flashed and thunder crashed, as what had to be a massive thunderstorm bore down on the school. Wind howled like a tempest and rain battered the windowpanes, slamming the building in sheets. She wondered if an actual tornado was going to hit them at the same time a vortex of evil was ravaging the school from the inside.

Something hit her like a brick to the side of the head, and the world went black.

At first she thought she'd been hit by an actual piece of flying debris, but then she realized that she felt no physical pain. She was still standing. Her eyes were still open, but she was immersed in darkness. Then, slowly, a terrible, familiar setting began to materialize around her.

"No," she murmured, hugging her chest as she scanned a little girl's bedroom . . . the same bedroom where Victor had locked her up in the compound in the woods after she'd been kidnapped. The shag rug, the cushy bed with the pink-and-purple comforter, the troop of stuffies against the pillows . . . all back with stomach-churning authenticity.

"Oh, Sarah Beth," a woman's voice said. "Did you have another nightmare, sweetheart?"

Sarah Beth turned to find Fake Grandma in her apron standing at the doorway.

"What's happening?" she said, confused.

"Don't tell me you're dreaming about that silly school again . . . ," the old woman said with a hollow smile. "There's no such place as St. George's

Academy. No school for special kids with special gifts. It's time to stop playing make-believe, Sarah Beth, and grow up. This is your home now. This is where you belong."

Was it possible that she'd never actually been rescued? What if everything that she'd thought had happened to her since was some sort of delusion? Maybe because of the stress and abuse, she'd lost her mind and made all of this up to cope with the horror?

No, no, Jed is real. Everything that happened after is real. It's too much detail, too many people and experiences to make up, she told herself.

Anger flared hot in her chest. "You're trying to trick me. St. George's is real. *This* place," she said, backpedaling and gesturing to the cutesy little-girl bedroom decor, "is not. And you're dead."

"Stop being ridiculous and come get a hug," Fake Grandma said and opened her arms.

For an instant, she thought about calling out to Corbin, but then she realized what was happening and knew it would be a mistake.

This is an illusion. I'm in Victor's mind. He pulled me into the void so fast that I couldn't react. If I summon Corbin, he'll have us both.

Jaw clenched, she pushed as hard as she could. Not with her body, but with her mind—backward, out, and up. Away from the gravity. Away from the hate and the malice. Away from the treachery and the darkness of Victor's mind.

God, strengthen me . . .

She heard a pop and like that, she was free of him. She slipped out of her headspace, her vision returning to find him standing directly in front of her, reaching for her with his harpy hands.

She screamed and ducked, or maybe it was the other way around, barely slipping his grasp. Then she ran . . . ran with all the acceleration and speed she could muster. Her bare feet slapped the tile floor with every footfall as she turned down the closest connecting corridor to East Hall. She knew the layout of St. George's, which just might possibly give her an edge. Behind her, she heard rapid, pounding footfalls. He was chasing her, but she didn't dare look back.

If I can just make it to the Bullpen, I'll be safe, she told herself. *We can lock ourselves in the SCIF and he won't be able to get in.*

Then something strange and unexpected happened: she *projected* as she ran—her mind's eye zooming ahead to check each crossing corridor for hiding Dark Ones and glancing back to keep tabs on Victor as she ran. She'd never done anything like that before and it was both exhilarating and disorienting at the same time. As she began to tire, Victor began to gain. He ran not like a man, but like a thundering herd. It was as if she were being chased by a hundred Victors, all vying to occupy the same space and time.

Corbin? she called, needing her friend now more than ever. *Unlock the White Room!*

Oh, thank the Lord. I've been searching for you, but there's so much noise, Corbin came back, her voice dim and far away.

Victor's going to get me if you don't open the White Room right now!

Unlocking it now. As soon as you step in, shut the door behind you and the magnetic lock will engage automatically.

Check, she said, using one of Uncle Jed's operator words.

The hairs on the back of her neck stood up as she felt him closing on her. Victor's spindly and decrepit appearance was an illusion. He was powered by evil and much stronger and more lethal than he looked. She wouldn't be surprised if he was as strong as Uncle Jed. She'd once overheard Corbin talking about how the Dark Ones seemed to have superhuman strength and endurance. She stretched out her strides, pushing herself to the limit, but she knew it wasn't enough. He was going to catch her before she made it to the White Room.

Legs burning and lungs heaving, she made a split-second decision to juke left and take one of the connecting corridors leading back to West Hall. In a straight line, Victor was faster, but she was a kid and could change directions better than him. At least, she hoped she could. She rounded the corner without breaking stride. The one good thing about running barefoot on a waxed tile floor was it gave her incredible traction. Just before making the next turn north, she projected to look around the corner and check behind her—almost tripping in the process—but confirming first that the coast was clear and second that Victor had indeed followed her into the turn. Her projected self locked eyes with him. She felt his hunger and hatred burning, like the heat from being too close to a flame. More disturbing, she saw a ghostly demon visage swirling and morphing over his face, but not just one demonic face—a cascade of grotesque and hideous almost-human things that changed and twisted from one to the next to the next.

He was closing on her fast now.

I'm not going to make it . . .

Fear surged her adrenaline and she pushed herself to the limits of what her twelve-year-old body was capable of. She lengthened her stride. She increased the speed with which her throbbing feet slammed into the tile floor.

God, please . . . please let me make it. For me but also for my parents. And for all the other kids . . .

She could see the white door now, around the corner in her projected self. She turned and saw her physical body behind her, running with a speed that seemed impossible.

And behind her, Victor ran—not like a skeletal, frail man-thing but like an Olympic athlete.

She sucked back into herself, screaming out to Corbin as she did.

Open the door to the elevator! Be ready to close it right away!

It's open, came Corbin's tense voice.

She rounded the corner, the door already open.

She could hear him behind her, but far enough, she thought.

Sarah Beth leapt through the door, aware that it was closing already— Corbin in her headspace and seeing just when to close it.

The door seated against the frame, the magnetic lock clicked, and she exhaled with heart-pounding relief, letting her forehead rest on the cool floor. Then the door shuddered violently as Victor slammed into it and went to work pulling against the exterior handle. She heard the heavy wooden slab groan and creak as he tore at it with maniacal fury and superhuman strength, but the lock held.

For the moment at least.

There was a horrible, animal screech and Victor's pounding on the door, but already the little room-like elevator was moving up.

She had made it.

Thank You, Father. Thank You.

She was aware of the tears streaming down her cheeks and suddenly aware of the childlike sobbing from her throat. She wiped her face and held her breath to control the sobs as the elevator smoothly stopped.

The door opened and Corbin rushed in.

"Oh, thank our Lord God!" she cried, wrapping her arms around Sarah Beth, who couldn't quite find the strength to stand.

"I thought he had you," Corbin said, her voice cracking. "I'm so glad you're safe."

Corbin had pulled her to her feet, Sarah Beth's legs like jelly beneath her.

"Dude, that was close," Sarah Beth said, hugging the older girl and shuddering as the adrenaline in her system began to ebb.

Corbin let go and locked eyes with her. "That was a very brave and very stupid thing that you did. Why didn't you go into the tornado shelter with the others?"

"I don't know," she said. "I guess I thought if I could lead him away from them, I'd keep them safe. It kinda worked. I'm safe up here and everyone else is secure down there."

"Not everyone," Corbin said with a grimace. "While you were distracting Victor, we've been locating. Not every kid made it into the shelter. Some are hiding in their dorm rooms; others are in the common spaces, bathrooms, and locker rooms."

"What do we do?" Sarah Beth said.

"We have to help them," Josh said.

"Where are the grown-ups? I thought the school had a security team?" she asked.

"There was an attack at the front gate," Corbin said. "The Dark Ones brought armored vehicles and lots of soldiers. They broke through."

"But what about the teachers?" Michaela said. "Why aren't they helping us? And where are the Keepers?"

"They're probably trapped in the Bullpen," Josh said. "I know my Keeper is down there."

"And the rest . . . I think are dead," Sarah Beth said, practically choking on the words.

"What?" Michaela fired back. "What are you talking about?"

"I was with Mr. Baker in the hall when Victor showed up. Mr. Baker had a gun and he . . . he used it on himself," Sarah Beth said, feeling suddenly nauseated at the memory.

Corbin nodded. "That's Victor all right. He gets in your head, uses the power of suggestion . . . It's very difficult to get him of your mind once he's inside."

"Do you think he's going to do that to us?" Michaela asked, fear cracking her voice. "Make us kill ourselves?"

"He wants us all dead, that's for sure," Corbin said. "He's been tormenting me for months—Sarah Beth too. The Watchers are a big threat to him and his plans. I think tonight is his attempt to get rid of us and St. George's once and for all."

"Then we need to hide," Josh said, "and wait it out until the Shepherds come."

"I tried to reach out to Uncle Jed and tell him we need help, but he didn't answer," Sarah Beth said. "That's not like him."

"We can't count on the Shepherds coming," Corbin said, worry lines creasing her forehead. "They're busy and spread out all over the country trying to stop the Dark Ones. We're on our own."

"In that case, we definitely need to go down to the Center. It's way safer down there than it is up here," Michaela said.

"Why are you guys up here and not in the Bullpen anyway?" Sarah Beth asked. "They've got steel doors down there. Nobody could break in, not even Victor."

"We were up here praying and locating when the power went out," Corbin said. "We've been stuck up here ever since."

"Then how did the elevator work for me?" Sarah Beth said.

"I . . . I don't know," Corbin said, screwing up her face and looking back and forth between Josh and Michaela. "You needed it and I sent it."

"The power must be back on!" Josh said, his face lighting up with hope. "Let's go."

Corbin shook her head. "Josh, look around. There's no lights anywhere. The power is still off for the whole campus."

"But that doesn't make any sense! Are you suggesting the power came back just . . . just long enough for Sarah Beth to ride the elevator up?" he stammered, frustration and fear seeping through into this voice.

Corbin shrugged. "I'm not suggesting anything . . . all I know is what happened. The elevator worked for Sarah Beth when she needed it to, but it definitely doesn't have power now."

"It's like a miracle," Michaela said.

"I didn't say that," Corbin came back.

You didn't have to, Sarah Beth thought. *What other explanation could there be?*

Corbin looked at her and smiled and she smiled back as they shared their thoughts. The older girl's confidence and courage buoyed her own, and despite the risk, Sarah Beth knew what they needed to do.

"I hate to say it, guys, but it looks like it's up to us to save our friends," she said.

Michaela shook her head and took a step back. "No way. We can't stand against Victor."

"Sarah Beth is right. He's going to go after the kids who are hiding. They're all dead if we don't do something," Corbin added. "And don't forget, just because we're in the Sanctuary and the other kids are in the tornado shelter, it doesn't mean we're safe. Victor doesn't need to touch us to hurt us . . . The mind is his weapon of choice."

"Yeah, but he can't get into all of our heads at the same time," Michaela said. "There's only one of him, and more than two hundred of us, if you count the little kids."

"Um, that might not be entirely true," Sarah Beth said, wincing as the words came out.

"What do you mean?" Michaela snapped.

"When Victor was coming after me, it felt like—I don't know—like he wasn't alone. It was as if he had an invisible army running behind him. Or with him . . . At first, I thought maybe my mind was playing tricks on me because I heard dozens of voices and hundreds of footsteps. When I looked back, I saw only him, but his face was changing again and again. Corbin, is it possible for a Dark One to be possessed by more than one demon?"

Corbin pursed her lips in thought. "No one's ever asked me that before, but it explains a lot. Until now, I didn't understand how he did it."

"Did what?" Josh said, having finally stepped out of the elevator.

"How he evaded all of us. How he planned this attack and slipped into the school unnoticed, despite the entire campus being full of Watchers on high alert," Corbin said. "He must be using a legion of demons under his control to amplify and spread out his power. In the Bible, in both Mark and

Luke, Jesus confronts the demon-possessed man in Gerasenes. Jesus asks him his name, and the demon says, 'I am Legion, for we are many.' Remember, he casts them out and they go into a whole herd of pigs and the pigs jump into the sea and drown."

Sarah Beth looked at her in awe. Corbin shook her head.

"Don't be impressed," she said with a smile. "I learned it in New Testament class last year. So what if Victor is possessed by many demons?"

A terrible and crushing silence hung between them while they each considered Corbin's words and wrestled with the fear those words stoked inside.

Finally Corbin broke the silence and extended her hand like a team captain in a sports huddle. "Our brothers and sisters need us," she said. "We're the strongest. We have to help them."

Sarah Beth put her hand on top of Corbin's. "I'm in."

Josh nodded and clapped his hand on top of hers. "Me too."

When Michaela hesitated, they all turned to look at her.

"I'm afraid," Michaela said, trembling.

"We all are." Corbin smiled at her warmly. "But we're stronger together than we are alone."

Sarah Beth looked at her older schoolmate, her lip quivering. "It's okay, Michaela," she said, touching the girl's arm. "I'm afraid too. I was terrified when Victor came at me. But then a Scripture popped into my head—from Deuteronomy. Do you want to hear it?"

The girl nodded and wiped tears from her cheeks.

"It says, 'The Lord himself goes before you and will be with you; he will never leave you nor forsake you. Do not be afraid; do not be discouraged.' I think God put that verse in my head because I don't really remember learning it, but I sure know it now. Maybe we can believe it together? That God will go before us?"

Michaela gave her a tight smile and pressed her lips together, inhaling deeply through her nose. Then she slapped her hand on top of Josh's. "Okay, I'm with you."

CHAPTER FORTY-SEVEN

Jed and Eli performed buddy checks on each other's gear while Johnny and Bex did the same. After getting the thumbs-up from Eli, he tugged one last time on his rifle sling, snugging the weapon tight to his chest. He nodded at the veteran, who nodded back and gave him another thumbs-up.

"You guys all set?" he asked, his gaze shifting to Johnny and Bex.

"Check," they answered in unison.

"The radio chatter at the front gate has gone quiet," Ben said after putting on a set of headphones tuned to the same channel Jed's team was on. "And we have eyes on what looks like two vehicles caravanning on Route 70. There's nobody on the roads, so this could be a Dark One QRF en route, not sure, but either way it's not looking good down there."

"Any contact from St. George's at all?" Jed asked, desperately needing a ray of hope in what seemed to be a dismally deteriorating situation. He'd tried several more times to reach Sarah Beth and had gotten absolutely nothing back from her. As an experienced operator, he knew better than to play the what-if game, but his mind kept going there anyway.

What if she's unconscious?

What if Victor has her?

What if she's . . . ?

"I'm sorry, Jed, but the campus is dark and it's still radio silence." Ben clasped a hand on Jed's shoulder. "Are you sure about this jump?"

"We don't have a choice," Jed said, meeting the Shepherd commander's tortured eyes. "But don't worry. We'll make it."

"I wish I could come with you."

"I know, boss," he said. "But we've both got our jobs to do."

"Good luck and go with God."

"You too."

"Thirty seconds," the Air Force crew chief, now jumpmaster, said in his Peltor headphones.

Jed turned to David but found his friend on his knees—arms raised in fervent prayer—the wind from the open cargo ramp of the Hercules C-130 whipping his shirt and the legs of his pants. Jed felt a compulsion to interrupt, to ask David to try Rachel's mobile phone and find out if she too had lost her connection to Sarah Beth, but the time for that was over. Assuming he survived the jump, he'd learn the girl's fate himself just minutes from now.

"Twenty seconds . . . ," the jumpmaster said.

He chased the futile thoughts away, forcing himself into combat mode. This LALO was going to be the most dangerous jump of his life. The pilots were threading the needle between two massive storm cells. Under normal circumstances, they'd never take the risk—neither would Jed—but these weren't normal circumstances.

"Ten seconds . . ."

The plane hit a patch of turbulence and pitched hard right, knocking everyone off-balance. The pilots immediately corrected, bringing them violently back to level. Out the gaping hole in the back of the plane, lightning flashed in the near distance, illuminating an ominous, anvil-shaped thunderhead.

"Hooah! Light 'em up, baby," Johnny shouted, his voice the high-pitched, manic battle cry of a man staring down death and reveling in it.

Jed shook his head and shifted his gaze to the red light above the jump-master's head.

It switched to green.

"Go . . . go . . . go!"

Jed took three long strides and threw himself out into the night, noting the altitude of one thousand feet on the altimeter strapped to his wrist as he did. He had ten seconds until contact with the ground, roughly. So eight seconds to deploy his chute.

A wicked crosswind hit him the instant he left the plane and sent him corkscrewing.

Panic flared in his chest.

This wasn't a HALO where he had twenty thousand feet to get himself sorted. He had five seconds to orient, stabilize, and deploy his shoot. That was it. The SEAL inside instantly took control—vaporizing all fear, all uncertainty, all doubt. Two hundred and fifty kids were counting on him. Sarah Beth was counting on him. Tonight would *not* be the night he would meet his Maker.

Calling upon the muscle memory of countless jumps, he harnessed gravity and frictional aerodynamics to get into the proper form. Legs bent at the knees, arms out, he found the horizon. Like a bowlegged Superman, he leaned left and steered himself toward the dark campus below, which was getting closer and bigger at a ridiculous rate.

Seven seconds . . .

His right hand found the rip cord.

Lightning flashed.

Eight seconds . . .

He pulled it.

The chute jerked him upright in his harness. Thunder boomed and he waited to see if the blue serpent snaking across the sky had its fangs set on him, but thankfully the electric pain never came. He pulled sharply on the left riser, spiraling left before releasing it. He was coming in hot, *too* hot. At the last moment, he pulled hard on both risers, braking his fall and insane forward velocity. He felt the brick pavers under his feet, but as he released the risers, a powerful gust of wind dragged his chute violently to his right and then jerked him up again. Finding his Koch fittings, he released the parachute and dropped eight feet to the ground. On impact, he rolled out of the hard fall and came to rest lying on his back, staring up into the tempest.

He took a second to perform a self-check for broken bones and torn ligaments. Finding his body relatively painless, he thanked God and scrambled into a crouch. With practiced efficiency, he loosened his rifle sling with his left hand as he raised his weapon with his right. Then taking a knee, he dropped his night-vision goggles into place and scanned the grounds for threats. Seeing none, he searched the sky for parachutes.

He counted two—one released and skirting along the ground, the other attached to a jumper in the last moments of descent. The winds had scattered them, but they were all touching down within fifty yards of each other. He felt a squeeze on his left shoulder.

"That was a heckuva ride," Eli said with a grin. "I thought I was going to go splat there for a second."

"Tell me about it," Jed said, watching Johnny spiral in for a picture-perfect landing while Bex came in like Jed did, fast and fighting the wind, thirty yards away.

"Wooo-hoo," Johnny hollered into his mic. "Cross me another one off the bucket list. LALO-ing in a thunderstorm, baby."

"Little help here," Bex said, and Jed could see that she'd gotten tangled up and the wind was dragging her chute along the ground.

"I got her," Eli said and took off in a sprint.

Johnny fell in on Jed, breathing hard but smiling. "Man, when that lightning arced across the sky, I thought I was barbecued fer sure."

"Me too," Jed said, then keyed his mic. "Sword is on the ground and intact. Power is out. No targets or friendlies."

"Copy all," Nisha said. "We're still tracking two incoming vehicles—ETA eight minutes."

"Check," Jed said and swiveled to look back at the campus, where the main building stood completely dark and seemingly lifeless. He watched for muzzle flashes in the windows, but thankfully saw none.

"You're thinking about splitting the team?" Johnny said.

Jed nodded, hating both his options.

Johnny pursed his lips. "You're worried there are shooters in the building already, but you also know that two ain't gonna be able to take out a QRF of Dark Ones at the gate."

"That's right."

"You want my opinion?"

"I do," he said, and unlike most of the time, he meant it.

"If the first wave broke through, we're already too late," Johnny said, "but I don't hear any rifle reports or any fireworks inside. So I say we get to the gate and assess the situation. If Sanderson has everything under control, or if those vehicles don't turn down the access road, we infil to the school immediately. If not, we're going to have to kill this QRF one way or another. Either we fight them in the school or we do it at the gate."

Johnny made good points. Until he confirmed if the perimeter had been breached, learned the status of Sanderson's security augment team, and determined whether these incoming vehicles were heading for St. George's, he was operating with incomplete tactical information. In his peripheral vision, Eli and Bex headed in their direction, running in tactical crouches.

Here on the ground, he found himself in the same situation Ben had faced on the plane. Should he split his team? Where was the greatest threat, and how did he counter it while minimizing risk to innocents? Making the hard calls with incomplete information was what separated leaders from the rank and file. In the Teams, his first NCO had called this feeling "analysis paralysis" and warned Jed of the pitfalls of sacrificing precious time in pursuit of an optimal solution when the fog of war made predicting an optimal solution impossible.

He was the team leader for Joshua Bravo, but he was also the Shepherd commander on the ground at St. George's. By the time Ben arrived with reinforcements, the battle for the school would be over and the outcome of that battle would be decided by his choices.

Gritting his teeth, he made his decision and chopped a hand toward the front gate.

And as his team fell into a diamond formation behind him, he reached out to Sarah Beth one last time . . . Whether she could answer or not, she needed know he was here.

Hang in there, kid. Just a little bit longer . . . I'm coming to you.

CHAPTER FORTY-EIGHT

Sarah Beth looked at her three Watcher teammates and said, "There must be another way out of this room besides the elevator. I mean, *hello*, fire code."

"There are two alternate exits. One is a retractable fire escape ladder outside that window," Corbin said, pointing to a window on the south wall. "The other is a hidden staircase."

"I think it's obvious," Josh said. "We use the supersecret staircase."

"It would be easier, but my concern is that if things go bad and we need to retreat back to the Sanctuary, we don't want Victor to know about that entrance and block our escape."

"Hmm, that makes sense." Josh nodded. "Okay, we take the fire escape ladder and save the staircase for if we get in trouble."

As if in response, a flash of lightning filled the room with blue light from the window, followed by an enormous clap of thunder and a gust of wind pelting the glass with heavy rain.

"I don't know if I can do it," Michaela said, crossing her arms over her chest.

Sarah Beth watched Corbin put a hand on the other girl's shoulder. "You can do it, Michaela. I know you can."

Michaela bit her lip and nodded.

"What's the plan when we get down there?" Josh asked. "We're not Shepherds. I mean, what are we supposed to do—waltz up to Victor and say, 'Hey, we'd like you to leave and we're not going to stop asking until you do'? What can *we* do to him?"

"Taking on Victor face-to-face is not my plan," Corbin said. "Our job is to collect all the lost kids and get them to safety while avoiding Victor in the process."

"How exactly are we supposed to avoid him? And when we run into him—and we will—how will we survive that, Corbin?" Michaela demanded with a quivering voice.

A thought filled Sarah Beth's mind—one she felt sure came from outside herself.

"Actually, I have an idea how we might be able to avoid him," she said.

"Go on," Corbin said.

"I'm getting pretty good at projecting . . . I did it while I was running away from Victor."

"Hold on," Corbin said, her eyes going wide. "You projected *while* you were running?"

"Yeah," she said, unable to suppress a proud little grin, despite the fear she felt at what she was proposing.

"That's like expert-level stuff, Sarah Beth. I've never done anything like that."

"Thanks." After a beat, she added, "So what I'm thinking is that I project around until I find Victor and then I keep tabs on him. If I try to locate him the regular way, I think he can sense me, but it seems like when I project, he doesn't see it."

"You're projecting in the world, not getting in his head," Corbin said, nodding and rubbing her chin. "It makes sense, I think."

"So I find him on the campus, and then we go where he's not, always moving and escorting the lost kids to the tornado shelter. The room has two doors—one for East Hall and one for West Hall. We'll need to snapchat with somebody inside the shelter who can let us in. Getting the doors open and closed quickly is critical."

"My roommate, Trish, is in there," Michaela said. "We snapchat all the time. I can take care of that."

"Okay, good," Corbin said.

"And I'm good at locating," Josh said. "I can work on finding all the kids who are hiding."

"Perfect, and I'll work on masking our thoughts and intentions from Victor so he doesn't sense our plan and ambush us," Corbin said, nodding definitively as the roles for their four-person team were established. Sarah Beth felt some of her mentor's calm confidence infect her.

This might work. It has to work . . .

"Okay," Corbin said. "Let's get going, and, Sarah Beth, once we're on the move, find Victor so we can avoid him."

Sarah Beth nodded, saying a silent prayer she wouldn't choke when the time came.

"Hold up just a second." Josh jogged over to the fountain of St. George and the dragon.

With the power out, the water jets weren't running and it sat eerily quiet in the middle of the room. Sarah Beth watched, perplexed, as Josh climbed up onto the statue.

"What are you doing?" Michaela called.

"Arming myself," he said as he carefully slid the six-foot-long bronze spear out of their patron saint's marble hands. With a grin on his face, he jumped down clutching the weapon. "That's right, girls—now I'm a dragon slayer."

Michaela rolled her eyes, but Corbin seemed pleased and gave him a nod of approval before turning to open the window. Outside, the wind whipped violently and rain streaked past almost horizontal. A lightning strike illuminated a massive thunderhead in the distance. The effect backlit Corbin's head, making her look like a superhero with a crown of electricity for a fleeting instant.

"I'll go first," Corbin said and climbed out onto the fire escape balcony just as thunder roared.

Josh followed her without discussion, angling his spear awkwardly to finagle it out the window. Once outside, he popped his head back in and shouted over the wind, "Just wait there for a second while we get the ladder down. It's only big enough for two people out here."

Sarah Beth nodded and, while she waited, tried to project, but her mind's eye stubbornly clung to the inside of her skull. A loud *kachank, kachank, kachank* followed by an even louder *kaching* reverberated outside, making Sarah Beth cringe.

"Idiots," Michaela said under her breath.

"Sorry, that was the ladder," Josh said, poking his head back in one more time.

"If he didn't know we were coming before, he certainly does now."

Josh shrugged and waved for them to follow.

"Why don't you go next," Sarah Beth said to Michaela, sensing that if given the opportunity to go last, Michaela might chicken out and not come at all.

"No, that's okay; you go," Michaela said.

"Probably better if I go last; that way I can help talk you through it."

Michaela frowned but acquiesced. Sarah Beth watched as she climbed out the window, whispering the Lord's Prayer in a rapid-fire cadence as she did. As soon as Michaela was on the balcony, Sarah Beth heard her shout, "I can't do this," and then she tried to climb back inside.

"Yes, you can," Josh said, catching her by the arm. "Just don't look down."

"If I don't look down, how do I climb down the ladder?" Michaela snapped, panting hard, rivulets of rainwater streaming down her face.

"Good point. Okay, so only look down at the next step you're going to take. One rung at a time," he said. "Just go slow and be careful. The rungs are wet and might be slippery."

Sarah Beth saw the abject fear on Michaela's face and knew the girl was about to have a full-blown panic attack any second. Not knowing what else to do, she pushed a thought in Michaela's head.

I believe in you, Michaela. You have the power to do this. . . . Reach inside and gather your strength . . . Go now, and God will go before you.

"Okay," Michaela said, then murmured a soft prayer before looking up at Sarah Beth, a tight smile now on her face. "I can do this . . . I have the strength . . . I can do it."

"I'll be right below you, okay?" Josh said. "Just follow my lead and you'll be fine."

Sarah Beth smiled as she watched Michaela overcome her fear and climb down the fire escape ladder after Josh. Then gritting her teeth, she climbed out onto the fire escape balcony and into the rain. Within seconds, she was soaked through. With a resigned exhale, she began her descent, clutching the wet steel rungs with a death grip. Below her, she heard the others congratulating Michaela as she disembarked the ladder. This made Sarah Beth smile and without warning she felt a shift . . . and found herself in the transept corridor.

Oh, I projected, she realized. *So that's when my brain finally decides to work, while I'm climbing down a ladder. Nice . . .*

She was standing in front of the white door, looking at the nurse's office record room.

This was the last place Victor had been when I escaped. Interesting I came here.

She swept her surroundings, gazing east into the chapel first and then west into the wing that housed the cafeteria, gymnasium, and locker rooms. Finding herself alone, she crept on. Somewhere in the far, far distance she could hear people yelling her name. It took her a moment, but then she understood. Corbin, Josh, and Michaela were calling her name and shouting encouragement. To them, she was stuck midclimb, clutching the ladder.

They probably think I'm frozen with fear, she thought. *Well, you're just gonna have to hold on a minute, guys. I'm busy looking for Victor.*

Corbin had said there were kids hiding in the dorm rooms, common area, bathrooms, and locker rooms. She was closest to the locker rooms and bathrooms and decided to check those first. When she got to where her corridor intersected West Hall, she stopped short. Nerves on fire, she crouched low and peeked around the corner, looking south toward the tornado shelter and the girls' dormitory.

A chill rippled through her the instant she saw Victor—standing outside the tornado shelter door, his hands pressed against the steel slab. Mr. Baker's corpse lay sprawled at his feet exactly where she'd left him. She felt a stab of guilt as she flashed back to that gruesome moment.

There's nothing you could have done, she told herself.

But was that true? Could she have stopped Mr. Baker from squeezing the trigger if she'd jumped into his head? She'd pulled herself out of Victor's iron mental grip; could she do that for others? She boxed up the thought for another time. Now was no time for regret and second-guessing. She needed to be present, engaged, doing her job in the moment. She shifted her attention back to Victor.

What is he doing? No way he can get that door open. Unless . . .

Before she completed the thought, Victor turned to look at her.

His eyes flashed the color of flame and she gasped.

A profound sense of vertigo washed over her as she felt her actual body jerk in mirrored movement to her projected self.

Oh no!

Sarah Beth snapped back into herself, just as her left foot slipped off the metal rung. She grabbed tightly and then reset her foot on the next rung down. Taking a deep, shuddering breath, she descended to the ground.

"You scared me half to death there," Corbin said, hand pressed to her chest. "What happened?"

"I projected, that's what happened," she said, wiping rainwater from her eyes and smoothing a wet drape of hair out of her face. "I found Victor, and we have a problem."

"Where is he? What's he doing?"

"He's standing outside the shelter door in West Hall."

"Doing what?"

"Trying to get in." Sarah Beth turned her gaze to Michaela. "You've got to connect with your roommate and warn her."

"Okay, what do I tell her?" Michaela said.

"That Victor is out there trying to find someone inside the room whose mind he can penetrate and coerce to unlock and open the door for him. The senior Watchers in the shelter need to work in teams to guard the doors. All it takes is one person to give in to the fear and he's in."

"I'm on it," Michaela said.

"What do we do now?" Josh said, picking up the spear and holding it in a two-handed grip in front of his chest.

Corbin bit her lip with indecision for a moment and then said, "At least we know where he is. We stick with the original plan, with one major modification. We round up all the kids we can find and lead them to the secret staircase to the Sanctuary, since we obviously can't open the shelter doors with Victor standing there."

"Phew," Josh said through an exhale. "For a moment I thought you were going to say you wanted us to be bait to lure him away from the door."

Corbin flashed him a wry grin. "They always do that in movies, and it never works."

"Hey, guys, I got through to my roommate. Apparently two kids have already tried to open the doors and the upperclassmen stopped them. It sounds like Victor is trying to get in all their heads at the same time, just like Sarah Beth said. Trish said it's total chaos in there, with lots of arguing."

"And it's only going to get worse. We need to work fast. You guys ready?" Corbin said.

Sarah Beth nodded along with Josh and Michaela.

"Okay, then let's go." Corbin took off running toward the gymnasium, leading them on a mission that, in all probability, might cost them their lives.

CHAPTER FORTY-NINE

Jed took a knee beside Brandt Sanderson's unmoving body. He knew from the vapid eyes that the Shepherd security lead was dead, but he checked for a pulse anyway.

"It's worse than I thought," Eli said, checking another fallen Shepherd guard on the berm a few feet away. "This was a bloodbath."

"Mother, Sword One . . . ," Jed said into his boom mic, calling Nisha, who was essentially serving as their TOC on the C-130, which should have landed at Trinity by now.

"Go for Mother," she came back.

"The security augment team is dead. Took on a numerically superior assault force—a group like Dark Horizon from the looks of it. Assaulters tried to breach the front gate with three armored APVs. Unclear how many shooters got through," he said, bringing his rifle up to scan for movement among the bodies. Dark Ones were notoriously hard to kill and just because they appeared to be down didn't mean they were out of the fight.

"Copy all," Nisha said. "I've got good news and bad news for you. The good news is we have eyes in the sky with thermal-imaging capability. We just sortied a Predator and it's heading your way. ETA five mikes."

"That is good news. What's the bad?"

"The bad news is the second storm cell is about to be right on top of you and the pilot tells me the Predator will be very limited by the weather. And of course, there's no way we get air support to you in that. Also, those two vehicles on Highway 70 are still heading your way. ETA six mikes."

"Is the drone armed?"

She took several seconds to come back, probably querying the pilot to get the answer. "No."

"Check," he said, disappointed but not surprised by the answer. The tactical picture would have been immensely better if the drone had two Hellfire missiles, but despite all their capabilities, the Shepherds were not the US military. The fact they even had a Predator drone was beyond impressive.

"What's the plan, boss?" Eli said in his ear. "We could set up here to defend against the incoming on the high ground—pairs on each side of the road."

Taking covered positions on the berms was the logical choice, and yet he didn't want to end up like Sanderson's team, which from the look of things had done exactly that. He racked his brain for options. "We could set up an ambush for them."

"You thinking about using those abandoned APVs and set up a kill box at the gate?"

"Exactly. They're going to expect resistance. What if we don't give them any? What if we let them get past us and engage from the rear when they think the gate is undefended? We'll have cover inside the abandoned APVs and they'll be on foot out in the open," Jed said.

"It could work," Eli said. "Only problem is if we don't get them all, then anybody that squirts past will have a free vector to the school."

"We could leave a sniper on the berm," Johnny said, chiming in.

"All right, that's the plan," Jed said. "Eli and Bex, you're with me; Johnny, you're overwatch."

He got acknowledgments from all three of his teammates. Using hand signals, he directed Bex to the left, Eli to the right, and assigned himself the middle APV.

"Stay frosty—just 'cuz they look abandoned doesn't mean they are," Jed said, scanning over his rifle as he advanced down the berm in a tactical crouch to check out the abandoned APVs.

"Roger that," Eli said.

Jed's heart rate picked up as he closed on the imposing black armored personnel carrier, which had been left with the headlights on parked in front of the defensive ballusters. The rain had stopped, but he knew from talking with Nisha that wouldn't last long. As he slipped into combat mode, time seemed to slow, allowing his senses to collect and process every little detail as he scanned and listened for clues that he was walking into a trap. The driver's-side doors—both front and rear—were hanging wide-open with windows rolled up. Index finger tense on the trigger, he dragged his targeting laser over the windshield, looking for a shadow inside, then under each door looking for legs. Seeing nothing, he accelerated, keeping low in his crouch but legs churning to a sprint that set his quads burning.

He reached the driver's door, using it on the final approach as a shield, then whipped around the edge of the armored window frame to clear the front. Finding the front seats unoccupied, he cleared the back seats and empty rear cargo compartment, the latter requiring him to climb momentarily into the APV.

"Lead APV is clear," he reported on the open channel as he climbed out. Only then did he notice another vehicle parked behind the APV . . . a Dodge Charger.

That looks like Maria's car, he thought, dragging his targeting laser over and around the Nashville PD sedan.

"Right APV clear," Eli reported.

"Left APV clear," Bex added a moment later. "But the bad guys left some hardware in this one that could be useful."

"Like what?" Jed said.

"Like a box stenciled *MBDA Enforcer*—which I believe is a shoulder-launched missile system."

"Just one?" he asked.

"Yep," Bex said.

He circled the Charger, confirming that it was abandoned and belonged to Maria Perez based on her license plate number, which he'd committed to memory when applying for her unescorted visitor clearance at Trinity Loop.

What in the world is she doing here?

"What do you want me to do with it?" Bex asked.

"Pull it and run it back to Johnny."

"Hooah," Johnny said. "This day keeps getting better and better. Getting to shoot one of these bad boys is also on my bucket list."

Jed shook his head, but his lips curled at his teammate's bravado. "Two, what about you? Anything?"

"Nothing so exciting over here," Eli said. "Just a five-gallon fuel jug."

"Is it full or empty?"

"Hold on, let me check. . . . It's full," the veteran reported.

Jed nodded as a plan began to come together in his mind. "Grab it and we're gonna start moving bodies. I think I might have an idea . . ."

CHAPTER FIFTY

"Mother, One—sitrep on our incoming?" Jed said as he doused the inside of Perez's Dodge Charger with gasoline.

"Sword, Mother—the drone is on station. Incoming vehicles still heading your way. Two mikes out," Nisha reported.

"Check," he said and tossed the spent gas jug inside the car. Then pulling a lighter from his kit, he set his girlfriend's police car on fire.

Sorry, Maria, he thought as the inside of the sedan went up in flames, *but it's for a good cause.*

His mind still screamed with questions about what Maria could possibly be doing here, but there was simply no time to go down that path now . . .

He jogged back to the abandoned APV, avoiding the sprawled bodies he and his team had dragged down to the road. He hated using his fallen fellow operators as props, but he needed to recast the battlefield. He wanted to make the Dark Ones QRF team leader think the final battle had taken place on the driveway and draw their attention away from the berms, where Johnny was covering, and the crashed APVs, where Eli and Bex now hid. With a heavy exhale, he climbed inside the big armored 4x4 and closed the door. Kneeling on the rear bench seat, he looked out the back window down the access road toward Highway 70. The light from the burning Charger forced him to flip his NVGs up and scan with his unaugmented eyes.

As he waited for the enemy, his thoughts went again to Maria.

What was she doing here? Had she somehow heard about the attack, and if so, why had she come alone instead of calling Nashville PD?

Something didn't compute . . .

He wished he had his mobile so he could call or text her, but his cell phone was stowed in a duffel with his other personal gear back on the plane.

"Sword, Mother—two APVs are turning onto the access road," Nisha reported in his ear. Before he had time to ask, she added, "Five thermals per vehicle, ten tangos total converging on your pos."

"Well, that answers that question," he murmured. Then in a clear voice, he said, "Check. Sword, hold your fire until my mark."

Three acknowledgments came back from his teammates who were each covering in their assigned positions.

"Three, One—have you gotten that missile launcher figured out yet?" Jed asked Johnny.

"I think so. Just point and shoot—the missile does the rest," Johnny said. "Are you sure you don't want me to light up the lead vehicle on the approach?"

"I'm sure," Jed said. "I want them stopped with doors open."

"Roger that, boss."

The fire was already starting to burn out in Perez's car, with the most combustible materials quickly consumed along with the gasoline. The Charger's gas tank had yet to ignite, and he put the odds of that happening at fifty-fifty. Whether it did or didn't was irrelevant to his plan. The goal was to paint a picture of a failed last stand and draw the Dark Horizon shooters out of their vehicles en masse and into the kill box.

Reflexively, he slipped into four-count tactical breathing as the two enemy APVs cruised down the access road at a controlled, cautious speed. He felt uncharacteristically nervous and had to force his mind to stay focused on the moment, because the tug of the unknown behind him on the campus was doing a number on his psyche. It had taken all his willpower not to charge headfirst into the school in a frantic search for Sarah Beth after the LALO. The only thing that had stopped him was the knowledge that St. George's was no regular school. The staff trained constantly to safeguard their kids, and the school had robust shelter-in-place bunkers. Pastor Dee had once joked that you could drop a bomb on the school and the kids would be okay.

He prayed she was right.

"One, Mother—just wanted to let you know thermal sweep of the school in progress," Nisha said as if tuned in to his train of thought.

"What do you see?"

"Looks like staff and students are sheltering in place. We're only getting a half-dozen scattered singles and a cluster of four. My guess is these are kids who didn't make it into the bunkers. The school has a tornado shelter and the underground TOC. Both of those structures are hardened and too thermally insulated for the drone's sensors to penetrate, but that's the only place they could all be."

"Check. What about roaming shooters in the halls?"

"We're not seeing any . . . still looking."

"Thanks for the update, Mother," he said with relief.

He watched as the two incoming APVs slowed on the last half mile approach, assessing the battlefield. With ten shooters in this second wave assault force, Jed and his team were outnumbered. Against a ragtag group of militia or conscripted terrorists, that number wouldn't bother him, but these guys were trained operators. Worse, if they were all demon possessed, then the probability of Jed's team emerging victorious was terrifyingly low.

The lead APV braked to a stop twenty feet from the burning Charger and turned on its headlights and roof-mounted spotlights, illuminating everything in a fifty-yard arc. The dash-mounted radio in the APV where Jed was sheltering crackled to life:

"Razor, this is Stiletto—do you copy?" a gruff male voice said. When no reply came, the caller tried again. "Razor, this is Stiletto—sitrep."

Jed flipped his own radio to VOX and tightened his grip on his rifle.

Get ready . . .

The front passenger-side door of the lead APV swung open, and a single black-clad operator climbed out. Rifle up, he advanced on the burning Charger, scanning back and forth for targets. Jed watched as the dark operator surveyed the battlefield. Taking a knee beside one of his fallen cohorts, the man lowered his rifle and inspected the body, probing the dead warrior's neck with two fingers. The dark fighter's eyes flashed amber and he abruptly angled his chin up in a primal posture and appeared to sniff the air. Jed had seen this very vulpine behavior before from the Dark Ones, and he wondered just how fine-tuned their senses were.

The fighter stood and settled his gaze on the APV where Jed was hiding.

Jed stared back from the armored shadows of the enemy vehicle he occupied and resisted the urge to reach out and probe the enemy warrior's mind. After a long pause, the fighter turned and jogged back to his APV, climbed inside, and shut the door.

Then nothing happened . . .

With each passing second of inactivity, the compulsion to do something grew inside Jed, but he fought the impulse and held his team.

"One—want me to light them up?" Johnny said, his voice a strained whisper on the comms channel.

"Hold," Jed came back, noting that he wasn't the only one feeling the need to act.

He exhaled through pursed lips and forced himself to embrace the uncertainty.

They'll eventually do something. I just need to be patient.

Ninety seconds later, the call from Nisha came: "Sword, Mother—get ready, the fighters inside those APVs are prepping to step out."

He answered her with a double click and watched in unison as all the doors of the lead and trailing APV opened and a platoon of Nomex-clad operators stepped out onto the access road. The enemy fighters formed up into two five-man arrowhead formations, one taking the left and the other the right side of the road. Jed gritted his teeth as the Dark Horizon fire teams maintained good separation as they advanced. *Too good.* He wanted them more compressed so the missile explosion and shrapnel would take out as many as possible.

I need to wait for them to get into the kill box.

Then he remembered how fast Dark Ones could run.

What if they slip the ambush by sprinting through the gauntlet so fast we can't keep them pinned in cross fire? Once they get inside the complex, the battle is lost. No way we can take out all ten before they reach the school.

"Three, One—stand by," he said, modifying his plan. "When both fire teams are passing the Charger, launch the missile."

"Check," Johnny came back.

Heart pounding in his ears, Jed waited and watched as the two fire teams vectored around Perez's smoldering Dodge.

Now.

A rooster tail of flame lit the sky as the missile screamed through the night. The six-kilogram multi-effects warhead slammed into Perez's Charger and exploded, igniting the sedan's gas tank in the process and sending a massive fireball out in all directions that enveloped the Dark Horizon fire teams.

"Hooah," Johnny shouted in Jed's ear.

"Nice shooting, brother," Eli chimed in.

A tentative smile curled Jed's lips . . . Johnny had timed the strike perfectly and hit the target.

But the smile soon faded in lockstep with the rapidly shrinking fireball.

"No, that's not possible," Jed muttered in horror and disbelief as eight dark warriors—all on fire—got to their feet.

Despite the direct hit, the enemy was still in the fight. With eyes glowing the same color as their burning bodies, the demon warriors charged.

CHAPTER FIFTY-ONE

A prickle chased down Sarah Beth's neck as she crossed the threshold into the girls' locker room from the yard outside. She was already chilled from being soaked through by the rain, but this was something else.

This was the cold hand of evil.

All the gymnasium doors had been locked, foiling their first attempt, so Michaela had Watcher snapchatted one of the girls hiding in the locker room to unlock a door from the inside. Josh, who was the last one in, eased the heavy door closed against the frame. She heard his thoughts loud and clear as soon as he turned.

So this is what the inside of the girls' locker room looks like . . .

Don't be a perv, Josh, she fired back.

He whipped to look at her, and she shot him a *yeah, you heard me* look. He chuckled and shook his head.

"Where are the other girls hiding?" Corbin whispered to the girl who'd let them in.

April—the girl's name came easily to Sarah Beth—looked visibly shaken, her gaze flitting about like a prairie dog on high alert.

"I don't know. I was in a locker when you reached out. May . . . may . . . maybe they're hiding in lockers too?" April stammered.

Corbin nodded and closed her eyes. Sarah Beth heard the older girl's calm, confident voice in her head, silently but loudly beckoning any girls hiding in the locker room to come out. At first, nothing happened, but eventually two more locker doors opened and a pair of frightened young Watchers emerged. Hugs and reassurances followed, along with instructions for the girls to be quiet and follow them. Corbin led the way out of the girls' locker room and into the boys', where they picked up two more strays. From there, they advanced back into the north corridor, but Corbin held them well back from the turn to West Hall, where Victor had last been spotted.

Corbin waved for Sarah Beth to join her at the front. "Okay, you're up," she said. "Do your thing."

Sarah Beth nodded, closed her eyes, and projected on demand—her spiritual self slipping out into the hallway ahead of her body. The sensation was disorienting but also incredibly thrilling at the same time. She glanced back at her crouched and motionless body perched next to Corbin.

That's so weird, she thought and then turned her attention back to the task at hand . . .

Finding Victor.

Her ethereal self crept up to and peeked around the corner to look down West Hall. To her surprise and instant relief, the hall was empty. She exhaled—actually, *her body* exhaled—and then she sent a thought to Corbin.

He's gone. I'm going to go look for him.

Okay, came Corbin's reply.

She started creeping down the north corridor, but then her spirit self suddenly snapped to where she wanted to go—dematerializing and rematerializing at the intersection of East Hall.

Well, that's new . . . and very handy!

She peered down East Hall, which was basically the mirror image of West Hall just on the other side of the building. Seeing nothing, she zoomed past the classrooms, past the tornado shelter, and into the hall outside the boys' dormitories. She'd fully expected Victor to be here, but this side of the building was also completely vacant.

Where did he go?

She imagined herself standing in South Corridor, the transverse hallway that connected the girls' and boys' side in the dormitory wing and the farthest crossing hall from where she was, and snap—she was there in a crouch. She swiveled left and right and found herself alone yet again.

He knows I'm hunting him, she realized, not sure why or how she knew but certain that was the case. A scream from both far away and nearby broke her concentration and she slammed back into herself.

"I heard a scream," she said with her real voice, turning to look at Corbin with her real eyes.

Corbin didn't answer; her attention fixed straight ahead. Sarah Beth followed her gaze to find Victor—hooded, menacing, and reeking of death—walking around the corner from the north and opposite side.

"Get back," Corbin said, spreading her arms wide as if to shield the kids behind her.

Sarah Beth could feel the other girl's courage and power—pulsing, like a defiant heartbeat staving off primal, mortal fear. It was the same thing she'd felt at Uncle Jed's side when he'd rescued her from the compound in the woods. Josh must have felt it too because he stepped up on Corbin's other side, holding the bronze spear of St. George the dragon slayer. Even terrified Michaela joined their battle line for the final confrontation against a foe they had no business challenging.

Victor's eyes glowed like twin rings of flame, powered by the hate and malice of a hundred demons.

"Your kind is not welcome here," Corbin hissed. Then in a voice that seemed to be amplified by a dozen loudspeakers, she shouted, "I command you to *leave!*"

Victor shuddered as if Corbin's words had physically struck him. Then . . . quietly at first but steadily building to a crescendo, he began to laugh. It was a laugh with weight and judgment. With malice and intent. A laugh that wormed its way under her skin and made her feel weak and vulnerable and pathetic all at the same time. The experience was not new to her.

This was what he did.

This was how he fought . . .

She understood this now. She was not the clueless, helpless, unprepared little girl she'd been before. She'd gained skills and confidence. She had parents who loved her, a friend in Corbin who believed in her, and Uncle Jed, who would defend her to his dying breath. But most importantly, she had God on her side and an inner light that even the coldest, darkest, cruelest touch could not corrupt.

I believe, she told herself and turned to Corbin.

"Certitude," Corbin said.

"Certitude," she agreed.

Victor stopped laughing. "So naive . . ."

Shadow seemed to grow out of Victor like a dark halo consuming what little ambient light illuminated the hallway. Gooseflesh stood up on Sarah Beth's arms and neck and one of the kids beside her gasped.

"You can't hurt us if we don't let you," Sarah Beth shouted, surprised by the anger in her own voice.

"Oh, Sarah Beth," he said, his voice warm oil, "that's where you're wrong . . . so very, very wrong."

He moved swiftly, crossing the distance between them with inhuman speed, and she was his target. She scrambled left and almost got out of his way, but he caught her by the wrist. She felt his nails pierce her skin, like eagle's talons ripping into delicate rabbit flesh.

She shrieked and accidentally projected out of her body for an instant, to watch in horror from a detached point of view as he attacked her, before snapping back into herself. He raked her face with the nails of his other hand, and she felt a warm trickle run down her right cheek and under her jaw.

"Die," Josh screamed beside her, and she watched him ram the spear of St. George into Victor's torso.

The demon lord grunted and released his grip on Sarah Beth's wrist.

With a victorious battle cry, Josh thrust the spear deeper, the shaft sinking another foot into Victor, presumably coming out the other side. And yet despite being stabbed, Victor seemed almost unfazed. He backhanded Josh so hard, the boy's feet left the ground and he flew through the air, landing on the ground limp and motionless.

"No!" Corbin shouted, running to Josh's side and taking a knee.

"You dare think you can stand against us?" Victor said, his voice a strange chorus, grabbing the spear with his right hand and pulling it free. He held the solid bronze weapon out with ease, as if it weighed no more than a pencil, and looked at it. "Without your Shepherds, you're nothing. Who will save you now?"

He drew the weapon back and hurled it. The bronze javelin flew like a lightning bolt and found its target—piercing Corbin through the right upper chest. Wide-eyed, she looked down at the metal rod sticking out of her. With disbelief on her face, she turned to Sarah Beth while her tremulous fingers feebly pawed at her impalement.

"Your turn to die," Victor said, fixing his glowing eyes on Sarah Beth.

She gasped.

And he came for her.

CHAPTER FIFTY-TWO

FRONT GATE

Ablaze, eight demon warriors streaked toward the gap between the berms. They moved with preternatural speed, zipping past Jed's APV before he could even get the door open.

Johnny went to work immediately, firing from his elevated sniper hide on the berm. Eli and Bex joined the mix a heartbeat later, firing from inside their right and left side APVs through portholes in the rear windows. Jed, for his part, took cover behind the open door and engaged the dark fighters from behind. The Shepherds had the Dark Ones pinned in a perfect kill box, with gunfire pouring in from four axes. Under normal circumstances, against a normal adversary, the battle would have been over in seconds, but nothing about this engagement was normal.

Two demon warriors fell quickly from head shots, but the others scattered.

Jed saw a pair streak off toward the berm where Johnny was set up as overwatch.

"Three, you got incoming," Jed shouted, taking aim to drop the lead assaulter. They were running using an erratic and unpredictable zigzag pattern, making it difficult for Jed to get a bead. Despite having a laser target designator, his first three rounds missed.

"I see 'em," Johnny said. "Man, they're fast."

"And they're washing out my NVGs," Eli said.

"That's 'cuz they're on fire," Bex added.

"Yeah, I noticed," Eli came back, his voice interrupted by the staccato *crack, crack, crack* of his rifle.

"One, you've got flankers," Bex shouted. "Coming in hot at your nine and four o'clock."

"Check. Four, shift to cover Three," Jed said, shifting his aim from the assaulter closing on Johnny to the one closing on him.

He swiveled left, put his laser dot center mass on a flaming figure sprinting toward him, and squeezed off two rounds. The bullets found their target, but the possessed warrior kept on coming. Time slowed. Like a scene out of a horror movie, Jed saw the man's face twist and contort in slow motion as he charged—a silent scream of rage and pain as the flesh was literally being burned off his skull.

Pity, disgust, and fear all swept over him at the same time as he locked eyes with the thing charging to kill him.

His targeting dot found the inhuman assaulter's forehead.

Trigger squeeze.

The dark warrior's head split open, and Jed watched the demon hosted inside flee the body with a fiery snarl.

A metallic thunk reverberated from the APV behind him.

Someone screamed in Jed's ear—Johnny, he decided—at the same time someone else roared above him. He whirled and brought his rifle up just in time to see a smoldering black shape dropping on top of him from the roof of the APV. The second flanker had closed the distance faster than the first!

Jed flipped the fire mode selector switch from single to full auto and squeezed the trigger. His rifle burped and shook in his grip as he emptied his magazine into the shadow dropping on him from above. The Dark One slammed into Jed, and it felt like someone had dropped a house on him. Everything that happened next unfolded at reflex speed, a mortal combat between two feral gladiators. As the dark fighter savaged him with blows, Jed pulled his SOG Bowie from his kit and stabbed.

And stabbed.

And stabbed.

His arm was no longer an arm—it was a piston, pumping at redline and putting hole after hole into the beast on top of him until the fire in its eyes went dark. With a primal grunt, Jed heaved the massive fighter off him and scrambled into a kneeling firing stance. Sheathing his blood-drenched knife, his hands quickly found his rifle hanging from the sling around his neck. He ejected the spent magazine and reloaded a spare from his kit as he scanned for targets. He found one—a possessed warrior slamming its shoulder into the APV door where Bex was covering. Despite the armor plating, the dark operator had managed to buckle in the door to the point of collapse. Jed put his targeting dot on the back of the assaulter's head as it made to rip the door off the hinges to get at Bex.

Trigger squeeze.

The Dark One's head snapped forward and it sagged into a lifeless pile of flesh on the ground.

Finding no other targets, Jed popped to his feet and sprinted for the berm. Johnny was in trouble, big trouble—Jed could feel it, along with the calling to intervene. A shadow moving to his left drew a sideways glance, and Jed saw Eli on a converging vector to join him. They ran stride for stride up the embankment, passing a fallen Dark One as they did. At the top, Jed found the exact scene he feared—Johnny engaged in bloody, hand-to-hand combat with a demon warrior.

Jed and Eli unloaded simultaneous salvos at the smoldering black-clad shape on top of their teammate. The dark fighter shuddered and whirled to face them. It shrieked at Jed with a grotesque double visage as Jed put his next round through its glowing right eye. The dimming flicker of light in the remaining left eye immediately went dark and a flame-colored streak slammed into the berm, leaving a glowing stain behind as the demon retreated back to hell.

"Four, you better get over here," Eli said, kneeling at Johnny's side. "Three is an urgent surgical."

Jed scanned the grounds for targets and, seeing none, conducted a second sweep counting bodies in and around the kill box. "I think we got them all," he said, doing the math in his head—adding the ones he knew he'd killed to the count.

"My count was eight," Eli said as he pulled a blow-out kit from his cargo pocket. "Plus the two that didn't get up from the missile blast."

Bex arrived a few seconds later, panting hard.

"Dear God," she said, dropping in on Johnny's other side opposite Eli. Johnny tried to say something, but Bex shushed him. "Don't talk."

Arterial blood was spraying from the fallen Shepherd's throat where the Dark One had mauled him. Jed's stomach turned to lead as he watched Johnny bleeding out from a wound that he suspected was lethal.

Gooseflesh stood up on his neck and shoulders as if the cold hand of evil had reached out and touched him from behind.

"Victor's here," he said, turning to Eli. "Sarah Beth's in trouble."

"Go," Bex said without looking at him as she worked frantically to stanch the bleeding. "Both of you."

Jed locked eyes with Johnny and read his teammate's mind.

Don't worry about me. I finished my bucket list. Go save those kids.

Jed nodded and then turned to Eli.

"Let's go end this once and for all," the veteran Shepherd said, and they both took off in a sprint toward the school.

CHAPTER FIFTY-THREE

INTERSECTION OF NORTH CORRIDOR AND WEST HALL

Victor lunged for her and something primal and automatic took control of Sarah Beth.

She ducked.

She ran.

She didn't look back.

She'd managed to escape him once already today, and she could do it again.

Only the last time, I made sure all the other Watchers were safe first, her inner voice chastised. *This time, I'm abandoning my friends.*

Her legs didn't seem to care; they just kept churning.

She'd made it no farther than a few yards when something hit her in the back—something big and heavy—and it knocked her forward, sending her tumbling. She hit the ground and rolled—like her dad had taught her to do when she was learning to ride her bike as a kid—but it still really hurt. Strangely, the thing that had crashed into her also apparently got hurt because it yelped. Sarah Beth turned to find Michaela on the ground next to her, clutching her left forearm, which was bowed in the middle.

Did Victor really just throw another kid at me to take me down?

Whimpering, Michaela scrambled and kicked her legs wildly, scooting backward on her butt to get clear of Victor . . . who was charging at her with impossible speed. Sarah Beth's attention shifted from her injured friend to the ghoul-faced demonic attacker surging toward her.

She screamed and readied her legs to try to kick him—a defense she knew deep down would be futile. But before he could grab her, a pistol report echoed in the corridor and Victor's torso shuddered. A second gunshot followed, and black-red blood spatter puffed from his chest, spraying a cone of droplets on the white tile floor in front of her. She watched his expression morph from collective rage to surprise and back again as he whirled to see who had just shot him.

"Keep your hands off my daughter, you monster," the shooter said.

Despite not being able to see the speaker's face, Sarah Beth instantly recognized the voice.

"Mom?" she heard herself say. "Is that you?"

"Run, Sarah Beth," her mom shouted. "Get somewhere safe and lock the door."

"Well, well, well," Victor said, clapping his hands together. "Look who's all grown-up."

Sarah Beth scooted to the side so she could see around Victor to where her mom stood in a wide-legged firing stance, pointing a pistol at the demon lord. Beside her mom stood stone-faced police detective Maria Perez.

Seeing the detective standing beside her mom, fighting for good, flooded Sarah Beth with hope. If Perez was here, it meant the police couldn't be far behind. With help on the way, maybe they had a chance.

Then thoughts from inside Maria flooded Sarah Beth's mind—fear, uncertainty, and . . . *loyalty*. But not to Mom.

Loyalty to Victor.

Sarah Beth gasped as it all clicked together.

She'd had a bad feeling about Detective Perez for a while, but it was all crystal clear now. It was Detective Perez whose thread had connected her to the fallen Shepherd Nicholas Woland. She'd not understood how threads worked back then, but Perez was only one degree of separation from Woland, which meant they'd met face-to-face. And now it made sense why Detective Perez had been the police officer in charge of her kidnapping case . . . and why Perez had been the *only* police officer to show up at her old house when the Dark Ones had tried to kidnap her a second time.

She's been working for Victor the entire time.

Sarah Beth tried to scream, tried to warn her mom, but her lungs suddenly felt like they were filled with cotton—each breath a labor to get any oxygen at all.

I'm hyperventilating, she told herself. *I need to . . . I need to calm down . . . and focus.*

"The last time we played together, Rachel, was in Kenny's basement all those years ago," Victor said, his attention laser focused on her mom, "but it feels like yesterday."

Sarah Beth saw her mother's expression morph from one of fury to wide-eyed disbelief.

"Don't look so surprised," Victor hissed. "Surely you recognize *this* face?"

Her mom shrieked and began to backpedal, the pistol now wavering and unsteady in her two-handed grip.

What's Victor talking about? Sarah Beth wondered.

"As for you, Maria, my ever-loyal lieutenant," Victor continued. "An Oscar-worthy performance as usual . . . She's my Eve, that one, manipulating poor, hapless Jed from the beginning. We thought for sure, given your history, you'd sniff her out, Rachel, but no, you're as trusting and naive as you were the day of the bonfire."

Sarah Beth watched her mom turn to look at Detective Perez. "I trusted you. . . . How could you betray us like that?"

"I'm sorry," Perez said, looking down at the floor. "I didn't have a choice."

"We always have a choice," her mom growled and firmed up her firing stance. The muzzle flashed and another gunshot split the air, but Sarah Beth knew it was a miss by Victor's lack of reaction.

"Die," her mom said, firing and walking toward Victor.

As her mom fearlessly advanced on Victor and the legion of demons inside him, she squeezed the trigger again and again, her face a portrait of rage and strength.

Crack, crack, crack, crack . . . click.

With dismay on her face, her mom kept squeezing the trigger: *Click, click, click.*

Seemingly unharmed, Victor howled with laughter. "Just for that, your daughter gets to watch us savage you before we kill both of you," he said with a snarl and charged.

"Mom!" Sarah Beth screamed, clambering to her feet.

Victor tackled her mom and landed on top, his hooded jacket billowing out like demon wings. Meanwhile, Perez stood by and watched, her face a blank slate. Despite a stark warning from her inner voice, Sarah Beth ran to the police detective.

"Don't just stand there," she shouted, shaking Perez by the arm while her mother thrashed and screamed beneath a chorus of demons. "Help her!"

Perez looked blankly at Sarah Beth, then at Victor, then turned back to Sarah Beth.

Their pupils met and Sarah Beth felt a connection.

A bridge.

She heard a pop and she was in the police detective's mind. Not by sneaking, but by invitation. A torrent of memories streamed past Sarah Beth's mind's eye in a millisecond. Maria's memories from when she was a little girl . . . terrible memories of a gentle, good-natured child neglected by her mother and beaten by her father. Despite the misery and abuse, she found her inner toughness. Maria was a survivor. A fighter. Once she was orphaned, her *abuela* did the best she could but was not equipped to help the hurt and angry teenager. Maria rebelled and fell. Then her *abuela* died and she was alone again and felt abandoned by the God her grandmother had taught her about. Sarah Beth witnessed it all. Felt the pain as if it had happened to her. The turn to darkness to find strength and sympathy. She ran away from foster care and rose in the hierarchy of troubled kids until her circles intersected with rougher kids in other circles. She joined a gang at fourteen. The drugs, the crime, the violence and abuse that broke her to the core . . . She ran from God for a desolate, angry, lonely life of sin . . .

Sarah Beth felt her eyes go wet and a tear chased down her cheek.

Resentment . . . so much resentment. And anger . . .

It's not fair, a voice screamed in Maria's mind, a desperate refrain echoing over and over and over.

No, it's not fair, Sarah Beth said and pulled the other woman into an embrace—hugging her enemy's rigid torso until the tension finally evaporated. She poured all her love and compassion into the detective's mind. *I'm sorry. I'm so sorry for what happened to you.*

I am so ashamed . . . , Maria said, and Sarah Beth felt the woman's body begin to shake with sobs.

You have nothing to be ashamed of . . .

Yes, I do, and it's time I own my mistakes. It's time I make amends. I'm sorry, Sarah Beth, for what I let happen to you. I'm sorry for not having the courage to protect you.

I forgive you, Sarah Beth said.

Please tell Jed that I could have loved him . . . that I wanted to love him.

Sarah Beth felt a pop as Maria kicked her out of her mind. She released her bear hug and the detective flashed her a tight smile with tearstained cheeks. She pulled her service weapon and stepped between Sarah Beth and Victor.

"Victor, stop," Maria commanded, addressing the creature on top of her mom.

The animal sounds went quiet, and Victor turned his head, presenting the most horrifying demonic visage Sarah Beth could possibly imagine.

"What did you say?"

"I said *stop!*" Maria said, leveling her pistol at him.

A sneer spread across the presenting demon's face in sync with the sneer on Victor's own corporeal one. "You think God will forgive you? You think there's a place in heaven for fallen souls like yours? You chose your side years ago, my dear. Nothing you do now can change that. Your life is forfeit."

"I know," she said, "but I'm not doing this for myself. I'm doing this for the little girl behind me and all the little girls in this cruel world who need protection from you and monsters like you!"

He came at the detective in a flash and the detective did not flinch, emptying her magazine into the demon-infested thing that had once been a man. Bullets riddled Victor's torso, but they had little effect. He slammed into Maria and drove her backward until she slammed into the wall. Sarah

Beth watched in horror as he attacked, his body casting a colossal horned, winged shadow despite the dark. Maria kept firing until her magazine ran dry as he raked her face and neck with his talon nails. For a fleeting instant, time seemed to stand still. Victor's shoulder dropped low enough for Sarah Beth to make eye contact with Maria, who, despite her mauled and bloody face, smiled at her.

Then Victor broke the detective's neck, and she slid down the wall into a lifeless heap.

"Noooooo!" Sarah Beth screamed in horror as the now-dead detective tipped over onto the floor.

Victor whirled to face her.

Panic-stricken, Sarah Beth scanned the hall, taking in the horror show of misery and terror around her. Detective Perez dead. Corbin impaled and fighting for her life. Josh unconscious. Michaela whimpering with a broken arm. And her mom, battered and bloodied, crawling on the tile floor . . .

"That's correct, Sarah Beth. There's no one left to help you. And yes, this is all your fault," Victor said, verbalizing her thoughts.

Uncle Jed will come.

Uncle Jed will save me.

"Not this time," Victor laughed, eyes on fire. "Not this time."

CHAPTER FIFTY-FOUR

It is said that black holes possess gravity so powerful that not even light can escape their ravenous, insatiable appetite. They are the universe's great destroyers—eaters of planets and stars. Chaos collected, distilled, and concentrated to a form so pure and singular that all order and atomic substance is incinerated once ingested.

As he prepared to breach St. George's, Jed could feel the pull of a black hole—a force so violent and evil he could not possibly ignore it. To find it, he realized, all he had to do was let gravity lead the way.

"Can you feel that?" Jed asked Eli as he used the butt of his rifle to break an exterior window to a classroom on the west side of the building.

"Yeah, bro," Eli said, scanning their six while Jed breached. "I hope we're not too late."

"Me too." Jed stepped over the jagged row of broken glass still clinging to the bottom of the window frame.

Once inside the empty classroom, he cleared left and right, swiveling his torso in a combat crouch while sighting over his rifle. "Clear."

Eli landed with a crunch beside him. "I got a bad feeling about this, dude."

As if serving as an exclamation point to Eli's comment, gunshots echoed inside the school.

"Not good," Jed said, quick-stepping toward the classroom door leading out to the hall.

At the threshold, he crouched beside the doorframe and signaled he would clear left and go left. Eli nodded, his responsibility implicit. Jed counted them down, opened the door, and surged into the hall. Sighting over his rifle, Jed scanned for targets, his holographic targeting laser sweeping down the long, darkened cooridor.

"Clear," he said a moment later, his voice a near whisper.

"Clear," Eli echoed but immediately followed up with "I got a body, twenty-five feet away—down and not moving."

Jed swiveled for a quick look, needing to confirm with his own two eyes it wasn't Sarah Beth. "Looks like it could be a teacher. I don't think that was our shooter."

"Agreed," Eli said.

A scream from the other direction sent a chill down Jed's spine because it was a voice he'd recognize anywhere.

Sarah Beth!

Fresh adrenaline surged through his veins, and he took off in a sprint with Eli in trail. With every fiber of his being, he wanted to charge blindly around the corner, but nearly two decades of Navy SEAL training and muscle memory intervened. He stopped short of the intersection in a combat crouch and exhaled. Then sighting low and fast, he looked around the corner. What his eyes saw at first didn't compute—bodies sprawled everywhere, some moving, some not, and a towering dark malice closing in on Sarah Beth.

She was facing Victor alone.

Jed chopped a hand and surged around the corner, hugging the left wall while Eli advanced beside him, clearing right, then arcing wide left and falling in step. His immediate inclination was to flip his shot selector switch to full auto and cut the dark malice to ribbons, but the geometry didn't work. Victor was too close to Sarah Beth; there was no way to strafe him without hitting her.

Moving with preternatural speed, the demon lord leapt at a forty-five-degree angle, bouncing off the corridor wall like an air hockey puck off a rail directly at Jed. The blow came a split second later, Victor knocking Jed backward with so much force it drove the air out of his lungs before he hit the ground on his back. Not missing a beat, the dark avenger sprang at Eli. The experienced Shepherd managed to squeeze off a three-round burst, but belatedly, and the bullets slammed harmlessly into the opposite wall. Gasping for breath, Jed raised his head in time to see Victor grab Eli by the throat, lifting him in the air and flinging him like a rag. The veteran flew up and backward, slamming into the ceiling first and then the wall so hard his helmeted head went through the drywall, his neck twisting awkwardly. Eli's limp, unconscious body slid down the wall and slumped into a puddle on the floor.

With a deafening, inhuman shriek so loud and shrill it burned Jed's eardrums, Victor pounced from where he crouched ten feet away. Like a human-size jumping spider, he flew and landed on Jed's chest, pinning him to the floor. The demon lord looked down at Jed—eyes twin rings of fire, face morphing like a fun house mirror as a parade of demons showed themselves to Jed. Teeth bared, Victor grabbed Jed's assault rifle, jerked it so hard the sling broke, and flung the weapon clattering down the hall. Then with machinelike precision, speed, and power, Victor went to work. The blows came in a torrent and all Jed could do was raise his forearms in front of his face. But deflecting the strikes was like trying to block a jet of water from a fire hose—an exercise in futility.

Pain flared in a dozen places simultaneously, each blow from Victor feeling more like a gunshot than a punch. He tightened his core, shut down the fear, panic, and pain, and summoned his inner warrior. More than fifteen years of close-quarter combat training kicked in, and Jed maneuvered into the closed guard position—bringing his legs up, clamping them around Victor's torso and hooking his ankles in the back. As he scissored his legs, he was taken aback at the lack of mass and thickness between his knees—the thing attacking him was spindly and skeletal. He could manipulate the weight, but when he put a squeeze on with his powerful legs, it was like trying to compress a block of aluminum. He arched his back to get separation from the melee of blows still raining down from above. He could already feel the swelling from massive hematomas forming along his wrists, forearms, and shoulders. The handful of blows that Victor had landed on his face and head were also punishing. His left eye was swelling shut, a gash above his right eye was streaming blood, and his right ear throbbed and was ringing.

With a grunt, he extended his hips and pressed away with his knees to get vertical separation while maintaining control in the guard. For a brief respite, the maelstrom of blows stopped as his upper torso was now just outside the range of Victor's reach. But Victor adjusted quickly and began to savage Jed's midsection. An on-target blow to the solar plexus sent a volcano of hot pain through his insides, and alarm bells went off in his head that Victor might have ruptured his diaphragm.

Like previous Dark Ones Jed had been forced to fight gladiator style to the death, Victor was performing at a level far above what his human body should be capable of. And rage and adrenaline were not the reasons why. The demons within the enslaved warriors imbued them with inhuman strength, stamina, and resilience to pain. On his very first encounter with a Dark One in Nashville, an emaciated homeless man had fought with the tenacity and power of an MMA champion in the ring. And his hand-to-hand battle with Nicholas Woland in the tunnels under Vatican City had pushed Jed's NFL linebacker–size frame to the breaking point. But this adversary was different, as Jed realized Victor was augmented by not just a single demon, but a legion.

He felt a gash open in his right side below his kit.

A millisecond later, a stinger to his lower abdomen roiled his guts.

The blows from the demon horde were relentless.

He felt like he was being trampled by a herd of mustangs.

How can I possibly stand against so many? he thought in a panic.

You can't, Victor's voice taunted in his mind, and Jed felt his resolve begin to wane. *You have lost. You have failed. You are defeated.*

Stars danced in Jed's visual field, bright and sparkling against a backdrop of shadow smoke and raging black fire.

Is this how my journey ends? he thought as the creature on top of him sliced his forearms with talon-sharp nails. *Is this how I die?*

Yes, Jedidiah . . . this is how you die.

CHAPTER FIFTY-FIVE

Sarah Beth watched Victor maul Uncle Jed.

As she did, a cold, hollow helplessness enveloped her—as if a thousand slimy, cold leeches had latched on to every inch of her body and were sucking the life from her.

"I have to do something," she murmured. "I can't let him die without trying to help. Jed wouldn't quit on me, and I won't quit on him."

Finding her courage, she closed her eyes, exhaled, and followed the dark thread that led to the black hole that was Victor. As before with Maria Perez, she was sucked unwilling into his memories: *A colonial village . . . snow blanketing the ground. I'm cold, always so very cold. I'm a little boy. My mother hugs me and promises it will be okay. I can tell she is so hungry, but she gives me most of her every meal anyway. My father is dead . . . robbed from us by a bright-scarlet rash and a weeklong fever that made him shout at invisible intruders and shiver so hard he cracked his teeth. Now we're alone, and Mother must do secret, shameful things for money. People stare and whisper about us. When bad luck happens in the village, they start to blame it on her. Lots of bad luck happens that winter and eventually they come for her, clutching burning sticks. They call her a witch and drown her in an icy river in the name of righteousness. In the name of mercy. In the name of the holy Father. And so I curse them. I condemn them all to hell and they call me a child of Satan. And when the first demon comes to me, I welcome him. I am finally no longer cold inside. I am no longer weak. When a second demon finds me, I welcome it inside too. And then another and another and another. And when I'm strong enough, I make them all pay . . .*

I understand now, she heard herself say, her heart awash with pity as she began to pull away.

"You think you understand me?" a young Victor said, materializing before her eyes to stop her retreat.

"I am so sorry for what they did to your mother," she said, feeling hopeful that she might achieve a connection with him like she had with Detective Perez.

The boy smiled at her, his lips curling into a vulpine grin. "I don't need your pity; what I *need* is your soul."

A hundred pairs of flaming eyes opened in the ether all around her—devouring her with their hate and judgment. Fingers made of shadow and dark flame pawed and clutched at her ethereal body. And then they started to drag her down . . . down . . . down into the deep dark.

Come back to the light, Sarah Beth, a voice said in her head.

Mom? Mom, is that you?

A trembling but warm hand gripped her own, as her mother took her place at Sarah Beth's side. With sudden and great certitude, Sarah Beth severed the connection and snapped back into her body.

"I saw what happened to him. Maybe it's not too late. Maybe we can show him the light?" Sarah Beth said, turning to her mom.

"No, sweetheart. Victor is too far gone. He's chosen the darkness and he's never coming back from it," her mother said.

"You're right," she said and knew her mother's words rang true, "but I can't fight him alone. He's too powerful."

"But you're not alone. We'll stand against him together."

"The power of two," Sarah Beth said, a spark of hope glowing in her chest.

The power of three, Corbin said in Sarah Beth's head.

"The power of four," Michaela said, stepping up beside Sarah Beth and taking her other hand.

Uncle Jed screamed in pain as Victor continued to maul him.

A flashbulb memory of the clockface at her bedside table appeared in her mind. When the thunderclap had woken her, the time had read *9:29*.

The spark of hope in Sarah Beth's chest caught fire and she knew what she had to do. She finally understood. To battle a legion, it takes a legion. More than a legion, it takes a community. More than a community, it takes God.

"It's Mark 9:29," she shouted with certitude.

"What?" her mother asked.

"Mark 9:29 . . . Jesus is talking about a special type of demon. He says, 'This kind can come out only by prayer.' To defeat Victor, it's going to take everyone," Sarah Beth said. "All the Watchers, together, in prayer. We have to pray to cast out the demons."

Her mom nodded and Sarah Beth closed her eyes, and she was standing in the ether with Corbin, Michaela, and her mom.

What do we do? Michaela said.

We follow all the threads, until we're touching every Watcher, and we bring them together, Sarah Beth said.

And then what?

And then we pray for God to cast out Victor's demons.

Corbin, despite the pain, smiled.

Sarah Beth felt warmth, love, and gratitude *from* her friend . . . and also *for* her friend. That warmth, love, and gratitude radiated out from her, from Corbin, from her mom, and from Michaela. It lit up all the threads leading to all the Watchers who were crammed together in the tornado shelter— where they were huddled together and yet very much alone in their fear. A glow, like a winter morning sunrise, lit up the ether. In that moment, the entire student body of St. George's Academy was one mind, one spirit, one voice. And together, as one, they prayed . . . for God's love, for God's help, and for the demons to be cast out of the thing that once had been a boy called Victor.

CHAPTER FIFTY-SIX

Jed heard their prayer.

Despite the pain racking his body, the fog clouding his mind, and the ringing in his ears, he heard the Watchers' prayer loud and clear. And so did Victor, because the beating Jed was being dealt abruptly stopped.

Like a rabid, feral animal, Victor turned and lunged for Sarah Beth.

But Jed didn't let him go.

In a strange reversal of roles, Jed switched from defense to offense. Clutching his legs with all his might, he refused to let Victor's thin body wriggle free. As the demon prince strained Jed's muscles, tendons, and ligaments to the breaking point, Jed could see the demons abandoning him. With gritted teeth, Jed pulled out his SOG Bowie knife, crunched at the waist, and slammed it into Victor's abdomen. With a gladiator's bellow, he pulled the blade free and stabbed again.

And again.

Over and over he drove the blade home.

The demon master shrieked and knocked the blade out of Jed's grip with a powerful swipe that made Jed's hand go instantly numb from the wrist down. The blow was enough that his concentration faltered for an instant, an instant long enough for Victor to break free from his leg lock. With a frantic, arachnid-like gait, Victor scuttled across the floor toward Sarah Beth. Jed lunged and caught Victor's trailing foot by the ankle and jerked him backward. The demon host wasn't heavy, and he once again marveled at this strange fact. Movement in his peripheral vision drew his gaze and he saw Corbin, who, to his horror, had a metal spear sticking out of her chest.

Gray-faced, she stood on wobbly legs, clutching the spear with both hands.

Jed's mind did a quick battlefield trauma calculation. He'd seen many gunshot wounds to all parts of the human body during his time in the Teams. In Corbin's case, he was looking at a large-diameter puncture wound to the right upper chest, clean through the lung. If the entry was below the shoulder arteries but above the pulmonary arteries, the trauma was surviv-able. Likely tension pneumothorax and hemothorax. So long as she didn't pull the spear out and bleed to death before the paramedics arrived, she'd survive.

She flashed him a bloody grin.

"Corbin, don't!" he shouted but too late.

She yanked the spear out of her chest, her eyes reflecting the agony he heard as she screamed, then tossed it to him and promptly collapsed. He caught the weapon of St. George the dragon slayer in midair, just as Victor kicked and spun out of his grip. The demon keeper threw himself at Jed, but not before Jed got the spear tip in line with the fiend's charge. The weapon impaled Victor in the same place Corbin had been struck.

How's that feel, you demon bastard, huh?

Demons were fleeing in droves now, angry and shrieking at Jed as they slammed into the walls and floor all around him, leaving glowing, fiery residuals in their wake. Jed couldn't help but grin as the tide turned. He could see Victor weaken and seem smaller with each abandonment. With a powerful kick to Victor's chest, Jed drove him back and yanked the spear free. Flush with purpose, adrenaline, and light, Jed shifted his footing into a combat stance and thrust the spear repeatedly into his dark adversary.

For Corbin . . .

For Rachel . . .

For Sarah Beth . . .

For Johnny . . .

Jed set his stance one last time, watching the demons fleeing the bloodied body before him, the homicidal rage still twisting on the thin face.

And for me . . .

With gritted teeth, he rammed the spear upward—a mighty thrust powered by his arms and legs driving together. The point found its mark in the V under Victor's jaw and emerged a millisecond later from the top of the demon master's head. A pulse of dark energy knocked Jed backward and the spear from his grip. He backpedaled to catch his balance, then watched as what remained of the demon legion abandoned their general. Jed's breath caught in his throat at what happened next. Instead of collapsing in death, Victor's corpse decomposed before Jed's eyes—turning to shards and dust before hitting the ground. The spear of St. George, no longer suspended by the body that had now turned to dust, clattered to the floor.

He lingered, stupefied for a moment, before turning to the trio of Watchers holding hands—Michaela, Sarah Beth, and . . . Rachel.

Yes, Rachel's a Watcher too.

Epiphany struck. Like her daughter, Rachel had been targeted by the Dark Ones for elimination. What had happened in Kenny Bailey's basement all those years ago had been no accident.

"Are you okay?" he asked them, his eyes going from Rachel to Sarah Beth.

Sarah Beth nodded and ran to Corbin. Kneeling at the older girl's side, she felt tears begin to stream down her face. "Is she dead? Please tell me she's not dead, Uncle Jed."

He took a knee on Corbin's other side and checked the pulse in her neck, which was weak but detectable. Outside, he heard the unmistakable thrum of helicopter rotors, and he pushed a single thought out.

Hurry, Ben . . .

"Don't worry, Sarah Beth," he said, meeting her worried gaze.

"You promise?" she said, her eyes asking the other question on her mind.

"I promise," he said and, feeling a little woozy from blood loss himself, made sure to add, "We're *all* going to make it."

CHAPTER FIFTY-SEVEN

Jed left the building under his own power, his head swimmy. He walked across the pavers, his rifle at combat ready, scanning for threats through the one eye he could still open. Victor was defeated, but there could still be more Dark Ones out there, lurking in the shadows, waiting to strike.

I'm a SEAL and SEALs are never out of the fight, he thought. *I have to honor the legacy of those who fought before me . . . brave men who fought and died building the proud tradition and feared reputation that I am bound to uphold.*

But he was also a Shepherd—a guardian bound to protect and serve the innocent and the pure. He had done that tonight by facing off against the greatest evil he'd ever encountered. Despite the failed attempt to use the Chinese weapon to sell the lie that God had abandoned His children, the

Dark Ones had somehow still brought the fight to God's children anyway. In violating the Watcher sanctuary, Victor had crossed a line the Shepherds had believed uncrossable. By summoning a legion, he'd made the Watchers blind and deaf long enough for his army of dark servants to execute two missions at once while keeping the Shepherds off-balance with diversions, distractions, and misdirection.

And with God on their side, the Shepherds had thwarted both.

His mind turned to Maria, a woman he'd believed he could love. Victor's secret weapon. He'd watched them zip her into a body bag, his fist clenched with conflicting emotions he was struggling now to reconcile.

How could I have been so blind?

He walked behind the flight suit–clad medics who carried Corbin in a litter toward a pair of gray MH-60s with rotors turning at the edge of the courtyard. Behind him, two other litters borne by his teammates held the young teen boy who had not yet woken up and Eli, who was awake but still disoriented with head trauma.

Rachel was banged up with multiple lacerations, and Michaela had a broken arm, but both were ambulatory and would make full recoveries.

Not everyone had been so lucky. There had been losses . . . Besides the security team, a teacher and a nurse had died at Victor's hands, and he worried Johnny had made the ultimate sacrifice in the battle of the berms. He prayed there weren't others.

His scan complete, and finding no new threats, Jed jogged to Corbin's litter. She looked up at him, face pale and eyes still wide with fright. With a trembling hand, she reached for him, and he took it.

"That was a very brave and very stupid thing you did back there," he said, tears rimming his eyes.

"You're welcome," she said, a tight smile on her gray lips.

He looked at the medic managing the foot of her litter and asked the question on his mind with his eyes.

"She'll be fine," the medic said, his eyes telling the tale of numerous teammates who weren't fine over many years of service. "She has a pneumothorax, but she's still moving air. Sats are ninety. Her BP is okay, so blood loss is under control. We'll put a chest tube in en route."

He nodded.

"Put a tube in where?" Corbin asked, a glimmer of the kid she'd been, the kid she still should be, in her eyes.

"Not a big deal," Jed said, squeezing her hand. "I've had it done before—twice in fact. A little pinch and then you'll breathe easier."

"Okay . . . I'm not afraid," she said, raising her chin.

"I know you're not."

He gave her hand a final squeeze, and they hustled her off toward the closer helo. Eli's litter drifted past on his left, with Eli swearing at Grayson, who managed the head of his litter with Carl at the foot. The boy Watcher, Josh, came next, blinking his eyes as another pair of medics ushered him to the second helo. Jed grimaced, knowing the emotional scars these kids would endure for many years to come.

"You're a hero, son," Jed said to the kid and gave him a thumbs-up. "You guys saved a lot of people."

"Bet I get a date to the spring dance now," the boy said with a crooked smile.

"I bet he does," a voice said beside him.

Jed looked over at Ben, whose face was etched deep with worry.

"Where's Johnny?" Jed asked, his chest tightening at the words.

"Bex has him aboard the first helo," Ben said.

"It's bad . . . isn't it?" he asked, his voice a whisper. A week ago he didn't want the guy on his team; now the thought of losing Johnny was more than Jed could bear.

"It was," Ben confirmed, but his eyes conveyed something more, and in the weary fatigue of them, Jed knew what he had done.

Thank you, Ben.

Thank God, Ben answered in his head. *It wasn't his time.*

"I think I need to sit down," Jed said, suddenly dizzy.

"Yeah, do that," Ben said and helped Jed to a sitting position on the pavement.

Jed felt a strange, out-of-body sensation and realized Ben's voice sounded far away. He watched Ben wave at the helicopters, signaling for medics, he guessed. Sitting was difficult suddenly, and Jed allowed Ben to pry the rifle from his hands and help him recline until he was staring up at the night sky. He felt strong hands on his chest. A warm gush went through him. He blinked and his mind cleared.

"What did you do?" he asked, looking up at Ben, whose face came into sharper focus.

"What needed to be done," his boss said, looking down at him with an exhausted smile. "Like we always do."

"Uncle Jed!"

He turned toward the sound of Sarah Beth's voice, saw her tear-streaked face, arm wrapped around her dad and free hand clutching Rachel's pale, bloodstained hand. A pair of medics materialized beside him, rolled him on his side, then placed him on a litter of his own. With a grunt, they heaved him onto it and headed for the second helicopter, as the first was dusting off. They loaded him into the Black Hawk and locked the litter into the floor. The Yarnells and Ben climbed in after, quickly finding seats, with Sarah Beth jostling to claim the bench on the forward side of the cabin, beside him.

The doors closed.

The whine of the turbines soared and they lifted off.

"We're headed to Vandy trauma center," the medic announced loudly over the noise of the rotors.

Jed nodded and closed his eyes, feeling Sarah Beth's gaze on him.

"Are you okay, Uncle Jed?" she asked. "You don't look so good."

Yeah, I'll be fine, he answered in their headspace. *And so will your mom . . . I think all your friends will be okay, too. Even Corbin.*

I know, Sarah Beth said in his head. *I just snapchatted with her, and she tried to make a joke that her mom's going to kill her for getting her chest pierced before her ears. That has to be a good sign, right?*

Definitely.

A moment passed or maybe a few.

Victor can't hurt you anymore, Sarah Beth. It's over . . . it's finally over.

Maybe he never really could unless I let him.

Maybe.

And it's never over, Uncle Jed. There will always be another Victor. The devil will always find another lost person to empower and fight in this war.

Jed tried to think of something reassuring to say but came up short. He was again struck by the toll of this war—and make no mistake, it was a war—would have on these kids. That such a thought even occurred to such a young girl . . .

That's why God called us, Sarah Beth added. *That's why He needs Shepherds.*

And sheepdogs, Jed said with a chuckle that hurt his ribs.

I'm glad I get to be one of the sheepdogs with you guys. After a long pause, she added, *I feel sorry for Victor.*

Jed opened his eyes and looked at her young face, which stared at the middle distance.

What? Why? He doesn't deserve your pity, Sarah Beth, or anyone's. Victor was evil. Pure evil.

Yeah, she relented. *But he wasn't always. Before we prayed and cast out the demons, I slipped inside his mind and saw who Victor had been. I saw the scared little boy who had first been possessed so very, very long ago. He didn't deserve what happened to him. He didn't deserve the abuse and the abandonment, the pain and the suffering. He didn't deserve to watch his mom get murdered by people claiming to be righteous. He was so angry at God, but he didn't deserve the evil that Satan forced upon him.*

Jed wanted to say something, to argue that Victor could have made other choices, but he didn't have the energy.

In the end, he died that same scared little boy. I just think it's sad, because the boy Victor had been, the boy inside with all those demons, that boy was one of God's children too.

She turned to him, a sad smile on her face. In that moment, she looked so much older than he'd noticed before.

"You are an amazing girl, Sarah Beth," he said but probably too weakly to be heard over the whine of the twin turbines and the thrum of the rotors.

There's something else you need to know, she said. *Detective Perez tried to save us.*

She did?

Yeah, she turned on Victor. She died to save Mom. If it hadn't been for her, you wouldn't have made it in time.

I . . . I didn't know that, he said.

She wanted to love you, Uncle Jed, but she was afraid of love—afraid of it her whole life until the very end.

He wanted to hear more about Maria, to keep talking, but his eyes felt so heavy. He felt a jab in his right arm, where the medic was leaning over him. He tried to look to see what she was doing, but his eyelids were too heavy.

He started to pray—thanking God for their victory, for Sarah Beth and Corbin, for Rachel and David, for Eli and Johnny . . . for those who didn't make it . . . and for Maria and . . .

He couldn't remember the gate guard's name.

It's okay. I know your Shepherd's heart.

Unburdened and unafraid, Jed let the darkness engulf him like a warm blanket, hoping that it was the voice of God in his head and not the ketamine talking.

CHAPTER
TWO

Navy SEAL Senior Chief Jedidiah Johnson loosened the tie on his dress blue uniform and slid onto a barstool. He raised a hand to the girl behind the bar.

"Hey, Jed," she said and pulled a Corona from the cooler. She slid it to him across the counter. He caught it and then licked some spilled suds off the back of his hand. "Big day, right?" the girl said with a wink and a smile—the same pretty smile that earned her thousands in tips and hundreds of unsolicited phone numbers scribbled on cocktail napkins from the legion of Navy SEALs who called this bar their home away from home.

"Yeah," Jed said. "Big day." He took a long pull on his beer and looked around the bar. In minutes, the joint would be swelling with his teammates—*former* teammates, actually. He would have to get used to the word *former*: former teammate, former Navy SEAL, former senior chief. He sighed and smiled at the bartender. "Whaddaya say we get out of here? Run away to the Caribbean and drink Coronas on a real beach."

"Nuh-uh. No way, Jed," she laughed. "You're not getting out of this one. I promised the boys I'd lock the doors if I had to."

A resigned smile curled his lips and he shook his head. For a Navy SEAL, retirement was as difficult as it was inevitable. Being a SEAL was like being a professional athlete, and the human body, as amazing as it was, could only take so much abuse. At thirty-five, he would still be considered a young man in most professions. But in special warfare, seventeen years of hard service and a shattered hip had left him a bit long in the tooth. After taking a 7.26mm round to the left hip, the docs had said he'd walk with a cane for the rest of his life, but he'd proven them wrong and rehabilitated himself back into fighting form. And yet, it was important to be honest with himself. Could he still do his job? Yes. Could his brothers without chronic pain, scar tissue, and flaring arthritis in their hips do the job better? As much as it stung, the answer was also yes. Retiring with grace was not the same as being retired. Passing the torch was not the same as quitting. These were the things he'd told himself, and they were true . . .

But why didn't it feel that way?

"What's up, Senior?" A voice interrupted his rumination, and the slap on his back sloshed beer onto the back of his hand.

He looked up into the smiling face of a teammate ten years his junior—a lifetime in the SEALs. "Is this a party or a wake?"

"He's right, Jed," a familiar voice beside him boomed, and Jed felt himself reflexively straighten up at the sound of the Group Two Commander, Captain Mike Jared. He had served with the senior officer on and off his entire career. Jared was one of the SEALs Jed respected most, and he was confident the man would make admiral and one day command all of WARCOM. "You okay, Senior Chief? Not having second thoughts, are you?"

"No, sir," Jed said with a forced grin. "I'm good."

"Well," the officer said, "if you change your mind, let me know. I've got enough rank to make your retirement package disappear." Captain Jared smoothed his dress blues as he took the barstool beside his former platoon leader. Like the rest of the SEALs funneling into the room, Jared would be more comfortable in BDUs or blue jeans. In the Teams, the dress uniforms were little more than dust collectors in between funerals and retirements— more of the former than the latter since 9/11.

"I'm sure you could, sir," Jed said. "Like we made that bus disappear in Qatar that one time."

"Easy now," Jared said but laughed at the memory. "We agreed never to speak of that, shipmate."

Jed nodded and took a pull from his Corona. He loved his brothers more than anything in the world. Maybe he was making a mistake. What kind of life could he ever have apart from these men? Then a parade of faces marched past his mind's eye—the brothers lost and the lives he had taken. The same faces that harassed him in his dreams every night.

Jed sighed. *No, it's time.*

"What are you gonna do, Jed?" the younger SEAL asked.

"Still working on that," Jed said and looked away, not sure what else to say.

"My offer stands, Jed," Captain Jared said. "I have a lot of friends at the Agency and others working in contracting jobs. One quick call and I can have you in a six-figure job doing what you do best."

"I appreciate that, sir," he said, feeling uncomfortable now. "I may take you up on it, but I need to look around a little first. My whole life has been Navy. . . . I just need to see what else is out there."

Jared nodded. "Completely understandable. Look around and see what your options are. Just know I'm a phone call away if you need me."

Jed's phone vibrated and then rang in his pocket, giving him a perfectly timed out. He retrieved the phone and checked the caller ID but didn't recognize the number. Nonetheless, he'd take a call from the devil himself to get out of questions about what he planned to do with his life now that he was a *former* Navy SEAL.

"Excuse me a moment, sir," Jed said to Captain Jared and slid off his stool. He walked quickly to the door and stepped outside before pressing the green button on the screen.

"Hello?"

The relative quiet of the outside was shattered by the roar of an F/A-18 fighter jet screaming in from the ocean and then breaking in a ninety-degree turn directly over him before heading toward the runway at Naval Air Station Oceana a few miles away. When the vibration stopped and the ringing in his ears eased, he tried again.

"Say again," he began. "I couldn't hear you."

"I'm sorry. Maybe I have the wrong number?" The voice on the line sounded tight and strained. The owner was clearly under stress—maybe even duress—and Jed looked again at the screen, hoping the seemingly random string of numbers would become enlightening.

He put the phone back to his ear. "Who's calling?"

"Is this Jed?" the voice asked, and Jed suddenly felt something familiar about the voice, but he couldn't place it.

"This is Senior Chief Jedidiah Johnson," he said coolly. "Now who is this?"

"It's David," the trembling voice replied. He thought the man on the other end of the line might even be crying.

"David who?" he demanded.

"David Yarnell," the voice answered, and Jed felt the blood drain from his face. "I'm sorry to call, Jed. I know it's been a long time, but I need your help. I desperately, desperately need your help."

Anger, indignation, and a wave of other conflicting emotions swirled in his mind and made his guts ache.

"How did you get this number?" he asked and instantly realized what a ridiculous and inappropriate question it was. As far as he knew, his childhood best friend still lived in Murfreesboro and David's parents still lived three doors down from the house where Jed had grown up. Even if David had moved, he could still just call Jed's parents to get Jed's mobile number. It had been a long source of strain on Jed's relationship with his parents that they'd stayed in close contact with David all these years, despite his own bitter estrangement from his childhood friend.

"Please, Jed." David's voice choked. "You have to help me. They took her."

Jed felt his chest tighten as if he had just taken a blow to the ribs. "Took who—Rachel? Is Rachel okay?" he blurted.

"No, not Rachel," David said. "Sarah Beth—our little girl. They took my little girl. Please, Jed, you have to help us get her back."

Jed loosened his tie even further and started down the block, walking away from Hot Tuna, toward the corner where he could cross over to the beach side of the road.

"Take a deep breath, David," he said. "Start from the beginning and tell me exactly what happened."

He heard only uncontrolled sobbing from the other end of the line.

"David, listen to me. I can't help you if you don't talk to me."

His *former* best friend coughed and cleared his throat. "Okay . . . I'm okay . . ." David breathed, gaining his composure. "I didn't know who else to turn to. The police are looking for her, but so far they've got nothing. I know you're a Navy SEAL, and I . . . I just thought that if anybody could find my baby girl, it would be you."

Jed swallowed hard, but the lump in his throat persisted. None of the memories swirling in his head were pleasant. Old wounds reopened and the once-extinguished anger at the betrayal he'd suffered rekindled. And then there was the other memory—the one he'd been running from his entire adult life—that usurped all others and filled his mind with dread. He squeezed his eyes shut. How could he possibly go back to Nashville and face all the unresolved matters that awaited him there? And besides, he was a Navy SEAL, not a miracle worker, and he was certainly no investigator. What did he know about finding missing kids? Give him a target package and a location, and he and his team of SEALs could unleash the wrath of God, but what David was asking for was no counterterrorism operation.

"Are you there?" David said.

Jed let out a long, quivering sigh. He felt nothing but animosity toward the man on the phone, a man he'd vowed to never forgive. But this wasn't about David, was it? A little girl was missing. *Rachel's* little girl. And try as he might, he'd never been able to stoke a fire of anger toward Rachel. The connection they'd shared had been powerful and special. He'd never experienced anything like it with any other woman in the years since.

"Jed, please. She's only twelve years old. You have to help us."

The sound of a father weeping for his missing daughter eroded his defenses. No matter what had happened between them, no matter how painful unpacking the past might be, how could he walk away from the man he'd once loved as a brother?

"Okay," Jed said at last. "Tell me exactly what happened, and you have my word I will do whatever I can to help."

GLOSSARY

18 Delta—special operations medic

35 Foxtrot—intelligence analyst

APV—armored personnel vehicle

AR—augmented reality

BUD/S—basic underwater demolition/SEAL training

CAG—Combat Applications Group (First Special Forces Operational Detachment-Delta—aka Delta Force, the Unit), the Army's elite special operations force under operational control of the Joint Special Operations Command

CASEVAC—casualty evacuation

CIA—Central Intelligence Agency

CISA—conventional intelligence and signals analyst

CL or CTL—combat lead / combat team leader

CO—commanding officer

CONUS/INCONUS—continental United States / inside the continental United States

CSO—chief staff officer

DARPA—Defense Advanced Research Projects Agency

DNI—director of National Intelligence

DoD—Department of Defense

DS&T—CIA's directorate of science and technology

exfil—exfiltrate

FOB—forward operating base

HUMINT—human intelligence

HVT—high-value target

IC—intelligence community

indoc—indoctrination

infil—infiltrate

IR—infrared

ISR—intelligence, surveillance, and reconnaissance

JSOC—Joint Special Operations Command

JSOTF—Joint Special Operations task force

KIA—killed in action

MARSOC—Marine Corps Special Operations Command

MBITR—multiband inter-/intra-team radio

N2—the intelligence department in a military unit

NCTC—National Counterterrorism Center

NOC—nonofficial cover

NSA—National Security Agency

NSW—Naval Special Warfare

NVGs—night-vision goggles

OGA—other government agency; frequently refers to the CIA or other clandestine organizations

ONR—Office of Naval Research

OPORD—operations order

OPSEC—operational security

QRF—quick reaction force

PT—physical training

ROE—rules of engagement

RPG—rocket-propelled grenade

SAPI—small-arms protective insert

SCIF—sensitive compartmented information facility

SEALs—sea, air, and land teams; Naval Special Warfare

SecDef—secretary of defense

SF—special forces; refers specifically to the Army Special Operations Green Berets

SIGINT—signals intelligence

sitrep—situation report

SOAR—special operations aviation regiment

SOCOM—special operations command

SOF—special operations forces

SOPMOD—special operations modification

SQT—SEAL qualification training

SWCC—special warfare combatant-craft crewmen; boat teams supporting SEAL operations

TAD—temporary additional duty

Trinity Global—the official cover entity for the Shepherds organization

Trinity Loop—the headquarters facility for Trinity and operational command of Shepherds North America

TRP—thermoplastic rubber

TS/SCI—top secret / sensitive compartmented information; the highest-level security clearance

TSL—tactical spiritual leader

TOC—tactical operations center

UCAV/UAV—unmanned combat aerial vehicle / unmanned aerial vehicle

USN—United States Navy

ACKNOWLEDGMENTS

Since the launch of this series with book one, *Dark Intercept*, we have been overwhelmed by the support we have received for this new adventure. From our military partners and charities, to our media friends and podcasters and new connections we have made, to the staff and members of our churches, the support for these stories has been powerful. To say we are touched is an understatement. We've thanked our team at Tyndale House before, but your support is so amazing, it would be a crime not to say thank you again. Karen, Jan, Sarah, Andrea, Amanda, Elizabeth, Isabella, and Dean and the design department, thank you for all the attention and TLC you give us and this series.

Thank you, MacLeod Andrews, for narrating the audiobook and giving a voice to Jed, Sarah Beth, Ben, Eli, David, Rachel, and the rest of the cast of characters who feel as real to us as any.

Thank you, Tim Cruickshank, for being our friend and partner in copromotion. We love and admire your heart and passion—not just for coffee, wine, and service but for everything else you do to support the veteran community.

Thank you, Best Thriller Books, for your kindness, energy, and insight. We know you have hundreds of authors to read and support, and we are honored that you guys step up again and again to read and review our work (regardless of how many books we crank out a year). In no particular order we want to give a special shout-out to Derek Luedtke, Chris Miller, Sarah

Walton, Kashif Hussain, Todd Wilkins, Steve Netter, Stuart Ashenbrenner, David Dobiasek, Ankit Dhirasaria, and James Abt.

Thank you, authors/podcasters extraordinaire Sean Cameron, Mike Houtz, Chris Albanese, Jason Piccolo, David Temple, Kimberly Howe, Ryan Steck, Kris Paronto and Ian Scotto, Jeff Ayers, and John Raab for being overly generous with your time and praise. You guys are phenomenal at your craft—both on the page and on the air—and we are in your debt.

Thank you, fellow thriller scribes Joel Rosenberg, Don Bentley, Josh Hood, Mark Greaney, Marc Cameron, Jack Stewart, Ward Larsen, Chris Hauty, Hank Phillippi Ryan, Paula Munier, Jessica Strawser, Simon Gervais, Jon Land, James Tyler Brooks, José H. Bográn, Dawn Ius, J.B. Stevens, David Darling, Steve Stratton, Kerry Frey, J.T. Patten, Jared Macarin, Lawrence Colby, Benjamin Thomas, Joe Goldberg, Eric Bishop, and Jeff Clark. Your talent, creativity, and support inspire us every day.

Thank you, independent reviewers and vocal advocates of our work Andreas Tornberg, Abibliofob, Rellim Reads, Deep Reads, Jenny Jones, Robb McKeeganish, Colonel Steve, Tom Dooley, Steven Hendricks, Jen Wesner, Kean Bouplon, Josie Lanaker, Vikki Faircloth, Mark Elliot, Cynthia Williams, Nadeem, Merritt Townsend, Sara Wise . . . and everyone else who deserves to be mentioned but was not top of mind when we wrote this.

And finally, to you, our readers, from the bottom of our hearts, thank you for your patience, for your time, and for going on this exciting journey with us.

ABOUT THE AUTHORS

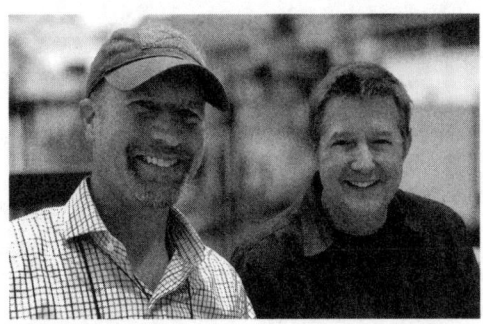

Andrews & Wilson is the bestselling writing team of Brian Andrews and Jeffrey Wilson—the authors behind the Shepherds series, the Tier One and Sons of Valor series, and *Rogue Asset*, the ninth book in the W.E.B. Griffin Presidential Agent series. They write action-adventure and covert operations novels honoring the heroic men and women who serve in the military and intelligence communities.

Brian is a former submarine officer, entrepreneur, and Park Leadership Fellow with degrees from Vanderbilt and Cornell. Jeff worked as an actor, firefighter, paramedic, jet pilot, and diving instructor, as well as a vascular and trauma surgeon. During his fourteen years of service, Jeff made multiple deployments as a combat surgeon with an East Coast–based SEAL Team. Jeff now leads a men's military ministry for a large church in Tampa.

To learn more about their books, sign up for their newsletter online at andrews-wilson.com and follow them on Twitter: @BAndrewsJWilson.

BOOKS BY BRIAN ANDREWS AND JEFFREY WILSON

THE SHEPHERDS SERIES

Dark Intercept
Dark Angel
Dark Fall

SONS OF VALOR SERIES

Sons of Valor

TIER ONE SERIES

Tier One
War Shadows
Crusader One
American Operator
Red Specter
Collateral
Scars: John Dempsey (a Tier One Origins novella)

W.E.B. GRIFFIN PRESIDENTIAL AGENT SERIES

Rogue Asset

THE NICK FOLEY SERIES (AS ALEX RYAN)

Beijing Red
Hong Kong Black

OTHER TITLES BY BRIAN ANDREWS

The Calypso Directive
The Infiltration Game
Reset

OTHER TITLES BY JEFFREY WILSON

The Traiteur's Ring
The Donors
Fade to Black
War Torn

PARTNER PAGES

Andrews & Wilson actively promotes and partners with veteran-owned small businesses that demonstrate a mission of giving. The organizations featured here donate and support the health and well-being of US service members as well as their families. We encourage you to learn about and support our partners and spread the word about the important and uplifting work that they do.

BONEFROG COFFEE/CELLARS

A veteran-owned and -operated premium, small-batch coffee roastery and vineyard located in the Pacific Northwest.

After serving twenty-five years in the Navy, former SEAL Tim Cruickshank created Bonefrog Coffee and Cellars as a tribute to the "brotherhood" of US Navy SEALs, the Naval Special Warfare community, and to all Americans who bravely served, or who are currently serving, in the United States Armed Forces. Each label they create tells a story to remind us of battles fought and great American heroes who answered the call, and proceeds from every sale support those who served in the Naval Special Warfare community and their families.

bonefrog-coffee.com
bonefrogcellars.com

ALL SECURE FOUNDATION

Founded by Army veteran and retired Delta Force Tier One operator Tom Satterly and award-winning filmmaker Jen Satterly, the All Secure Foundation provides resources, education, post-traumatic stress injury resiliency training for active-duty units, warrior couples workshop retreats, and family counseling for special operations warriors and their warrior families. They believe that every family member deserves tools to heal from war trauma and that no one is left behind on the battlefield or the home front.

allsecurefoundation.org

COMBAT FLAGS

Founded by US Army veteran Dan Berei, Combat Flags began as an idea to connect veterans and give back in a meaningful way. Combat Flags is dedicated to helping stop soldier suicide (stopsoldiersuicide.org) and Dan's personal mission is to leave the world a better place than he found it.

In addition to the store, Dan interviews veterans and talks leadership, life lessons, and service on the Combat Flags podcast.

combatflags.com

"The first time I heard Julie Meyer teach on singing the Scriptures, I was deeply impacted and activated the teaching immediately. It has resulted in ongoing faith-building devotional encounters for me such as I have never experienced before. You are going to really enjoy this book, and I am sure the teaching will impact and empower you greatly as it did me. I love this anointed teaching, and I love Julie Meyer!"

Patricia King, founder, Patricia King Ministries

"God created us with a voice to sing. What better way to sing before the Lord and see breakthrough than using His Word. *Singing the Scriptures* is a timely and helpful book."

Beni Johnson, author, *The Happy Intercessor*
and *Healthy and Free*

"Julie has spent the last thirty years singing the Scriptures back to Jesus. She has an amazing ability to help people to practically understand how to do what she has done so often—to read the Scripture and turn it into a real conversation with a real person—even singing the Word back to Him. Watch the Word of God come alive in you in a new way as you learn to sing the Scriptures and encounter a real person—our beautiful God, the Lord Jesus."

Mike Bickle, director, International House of Prayer,
Kansas City, Missouri

"Julie Meyer has an ability to connect others to the heart of God by simply singing. Julie's musical creativity will ignite your love and passion for God through singing the Scriptures. *Singing the Scriptures* will teach you not only the importance of the Word of God, but also the power of singing it over yourself. This book is a game-changer. Get ready to sing!"

Tammy Hotsenpiller, Women of Influence,
TammyHotsenpiller.com

"This book is so powerful. Singing touches the deepest part of us. David was a singer, a psalmist, framing Scriptures we sing today. Singing is a gift from God meant to express all the moods of God as well as ours. Julie Meyer has sung her way through life, from troubles, impossibilities, sickness and disease all the way through to amazing victories and miracles. Julie Meyer has become a song. Who better should write this book, *Singing the Scriptures*?!"

Barbara J. Yoder, lead apostle, Shekinah Regional Apostolic Center; Breakthrough Apostolic Ministries Network

"Want to grow in greater intimacy with God? Do you need a key to a breakthrough in your life? My friend and veteran prophetic psalmist Julie Meyer brings forth treasures from her life's experience just for you. Your heart will be encouraged and your stamina strengthened as you glean from the lessons contained in this revolutionary book, *Singing the Scriptures*."

James W. Goll, founder, God Encounters Ministries; author, *The Lifestyle of a Watchman*, *Praying for Israel's Destiny*, *The Seer* and many others

"In *Singing the Scriptures*, my friend Julie Meyer has penned a brilliant book that fills a gap in contemporary Christian literature by teaching the Body of Christ the power of singing God's Word. In this profound yet simple book, Julie combines powerful biblical insight with many dramatic testimonies of personal breakthrough and renewal. Julie has been leading the Body of Christ in prophetic worship and intercession for decades, and she can lead you into a new place of blessing and breakthrough. I highly recommend her book to every believer."

Joan Hunter, author and evangelist; founder/president, Joan Hunter Ministries

"Julie Meyer is an expert on singing the Scriptures. For over thirty years she has sung the Bible many hours per week. Her life in God is pure and deep, and through this book you can learn keys that will bring similar fruit in your own life. *Singing the Scriptures* will add joy and meaning to your personal walk with God. I love this book. And I love Julie Meyer!"

Stacey Campbell, co-author, *Praying the Bible: The Book of Prayers*

"This book is a tool from the Holy Sprit. If you have been seeking God for breakthrough, you are holding a huge key in your hands. Julie lives this book. What a gift to be able to glean from years of experience."

Rick and Lori Taylor, national directors, International Association of Healing Rooms, USA and Canada

SINGING
THE
SCRIPTURES

How All Believers Can Experience Breakthrough, Hope and Healing

JULIE MEYER

Chosen

a division of Baker Publishing Group
Minneapolis, Minnesota

Library of Congress Cataloging in Publication Control Number: 2017038733

ISBN 978-0-8007-9860-4

The personal testimonies included in this book are real; however, some names have been changed.

18   19   20   21   22   23   24   7   6   5   4   3   2   1

CONTENTS

Praise the Lord!
Sing to the Lord a new song.
Sing his praises in the assembly of the faithful.
O Israel, rejoice in your Maker.
O people of Jerusalem, exult in your King.
Praise his name with dancing,
accompanied by tambourine and harp.
For the Lord delights in his people;
he crowns the humble with victory.
Let the faithful rejoice that he honors them.
Let them sing for joy as they lie on their beds.
Let the praises of God be in their mouths,
and a sharp sword in their hands—
to execute vengeance on the nations
and punishment on the peoples,
to bind their kings with shackles
and their leaders with iron chains,
to execute the judgment written against them.
This is the glorious privilege of his faithful ones.

PSALM 149:1–9 NLT

Psalm 149 is the glory of every one of us as we lift our voice and sing the Scriptures. May each one of us take up our sword, which is the Word of the Lord in our mouths, and may our weapons be our very own melodies—then let us join Him releasing His light into every dark place in the earth.

I dedicate this book to Shiah Isaac and Sophia Grace, my two absolutely perfect grandchildren, and to all the grands that I shall have in the future but have not yet met.

May you grow up loving the Scriptures. May you sing the Word and let it be on your heart and in your mind at every moment of the day. May these words be life to your souls. May you be like some of our modern-day Levites, but mostly may you love the Word. And if you do not see the Word alive in those around you, then you *be* the Word to everyone around you. I love you, my sweet, perfect ones.

FOREWORD

God wants to be so close to us—He loves to hear our voices and speak directly to our hearts. He loves to hear each one of us pour our hearts out to Him in every moment with every type of emotion. I absolutely love *Singing the Scriptures*. It calls each one of us deeper into intimacy with God. I believe He wants to use this book to draw you closer to His heart of love for you, to help you understand what He feels for you and to bring restoration to your heart. God is singing over you, and He wants you to sing with Him and with all of creation in worship. God is fighting on your behalf; He is with you in every struggle, every painful moment and also in every victory. No matter where you go or what you do, you cannot escape the passionate love of God; He is pursuing you.

Julie shares how singing the Word of God allows us to remember, believe and live out these words of truth and life. It literally breaks fear off of our lives. It changes situations and brings breakthrough. God speaks and creation is birthed. He breathes and we come alive. He sings and our anxious hearts become calm in His peace. There is nothing in your life that God does not care about.

He is passionate for you, He is with you, He loves you, He has good things for you. Sometimes we can start to believe incorrect things about what God is like based on our own experiences or expectations. Singing God's Word realigns us with His truth; we sing until our hearts feel His love again. We sing until our emotions get the breakthrough. Julie shares personal experiences and testimonies from others who battled fear. Each time they began to sing the Word of God, their hearts softened and shifted, and perfect love cast out fear. Julie sang until her emotions changed. She knew God did not call her to be afraid, so she fought fear with the Word of truth. You can do the very same.

Julie is a dear friend of mine. We are both worshipers who love the presence more than anything else. We both love to worship and then respond with God as we minister His love to those around us, right out of that place of worship. We sing and receive His love, and then we pour out His love on everyone we meet, so that they will know Him, too. Julie is a powerful worship leader—she brings everyone willing right up into the presence with her as she sings straight to Jesus, her first love. It is in those deep places of worship where God encounters us and calls us to partner with Him in spreading His love and fragrance on the earth. Julie has a heart after God and a heart after people. She desires that we all know God more. That is why she wrote this book. Julie pours her life out for those around her, teaching people how to connect with God through song. She breaks into song about anything in any place. I love to hear her voice as she so readily loses herself looking at her King. It is easy to get caught up in the glory with her.

I encourage you not only to read this book, but to practice with Julie in singing the Scriptures. She provides many tools, including questions and even songs from Scripture to start practicing with. She teaches you how to start singing over any situation. It is so simple, yet so life-changing. Music is a key to our hearts that touches deep places we are not easily able to access. Song pulls us into a romantic dance with Jesus and allows us to be swept away by love. Don't wait. Start singing His Word today, and let yourself be captured again by His passionate love for you!

Heidi G. Baker, Ph.D., co-founder and CEO, Iris Global

ACKNOWLEDGMENTS

Thank you to my husband, Walt—who helped me so much by being the best spouse I could ever ask for and also doing the cleaning so I could write.

Thank you to Sophia Grace and Shiah Isaac—just because you are so amazing. I get to sing the Scriptures with you and you think that is cool.

Thank you to my amazing children, Isaac, Brit, Joe, Sarah, Jesse—just because you are all so amazing. This mom could not be more proud of any of her children. I love you.

Dad—I love you. You are the best dad ever. I am who I am because of you (and Jesus).

To my family, Penny and Jay, Jamie, Jeff and all my awesome nieces and nephews—it has been my joy to sing the Scriptures over all of you.

Heidi Baker—from the bush bush in Mozambique to the largest stadium filled to capacity, you, my friend, are always singing. Singing the Word, singing in the Spirit, everywhere you go, before every sermon, there you are on your knees singing to Jesus. Many in the nations are singing to the Lord because of your life.

God has surely picked you up like a paintbrush and painted His beautiful picture with your life. Love you much.

Thank you to my Into the River staff, Joseph, Isaac and Jesse. You have worked hours upon hours on videos, recordings, new ideas, social media, websites and new products. I am blessed to be able to work with such creative and inspiriational young men who also happen to be "my three sons."

Thank you to the amazing, kind, encouraging intercessor Kim Bangs. I believe your prayers over me brought this book about. You will never, ever know how much I felt your prayers and your email messages of encouragement. You are a star, Kim Bangs, a shining star in the heavens.

Thank you to Jane Campbell—for giving me this opportunity to shout out through the written word the amazing life-changing tool of singing the Scriptures.

Thank you, Patricia King—I love you so, so much. Thank you for being a champion to my heart and actually singing the Scriptures. You are one of my heroes.

Thank you to James Goll—for giving me feedback and helping me write this book. You will always be my big brother.

Thank you, Mike and Diane Bickle—for being who you are. Diane—you were the first prophetic singer I ever heard. In 1983, at our nightly prayer meetings, you would take up your Bible to pray, but you would sing it. You would sing your prayers, and you were my first teacher in how to sing the Bible. Thank you. And thank you, Mike Bickle. I love the House of Prayer. Thank you for loving the Word and encouraging all the singers to sing the Scriptures. It has kept me on the narrow road. I will always love you and the International House of Prayer in Kansas City.

Thank you, Stacey Campbell—I simply adore you. I love your walk in God. I love your passion for the Word. I am so glad we are now living blocks from each other, and we get to pray together and love Jesus together and pray for our kids together and pray for revival in California. You are an inspiration in my life.

Graeme and Sabrina—I am so thrilled that you are here. We are family. We are friends. We are piles and piles of mercy and grace, and I cannot even thank God enough for bringing some of my family here to Santa Maria, California.

And to some of my new friends.

Thank you, Rick and Lori Taylor—oh! I cannot believe I get to journey here in the Central Coast of Cali with you. Thank you for your prayers, your kindness and your encouragement. Thank you for your leadership, your "over the top" giving and blessing us. I am pinching myself that I get to do revival on the Central Coast with you.

And to David and Carol Kingsly—I love you both so, so much. I cannot imagine Monday nights without you. Look what God did because of our simple prayers—no more drought in California.

Jeff and Cindy Gough—I don't believe there will ever be a time that I can put into words how much you both mean to me. I simply adore you both. I love your honesty. I love your questions. I love that I get to do life with you.

To my amazing church—Crosswords Church in Buelton, California. Pastor Samuel and Sarah Keiser—I love our church, and I love the word in our church. I love doing life with you. I love your heart for the Word. This is my home. It is my family.

INTRODUCTION

I make it a practice to sing the Scriptures wherever I am and wherever I go. And I am blessed again and again by the response that I feel in my heart. In fact, it is so great that I began to think: *I cannot keep singing the Scriptures a secret. I need to tell everyone.* This is not about being on a worship team. This is an equipping tool, and it starts with personal use. But as you read through this book, you will see that singing the Scriptures works on a corporate level as well. To sing the Word is life changing; it is heart changing. It is my personal testimony. I have continued through many seasons to experience great breakthrough, hope and healing through singing the Scriptures. And you can, too.

Maybe you are one who will sing the Scriptures only in the privacy of your own home. That is wonderful—do it. Maybe you are one who will sing in public and shift the atmosphere. That is great—do it. Maybe you are one of the modern-day Levites who will take this tool and sing the Scriptures in the darkest places, at the very frontlines. That is amazing—do it. My prayer is that you will be so encouraged by this book that you will carry the Scriptures in song all throughout your day.

I want to shatter the mindset that singing is only for the trained ear, although that is really good for Sunday morning church services. We need to understand that singing the Scriptures is a powerful tool that each of us can use. It is important in our personal devotions, as it helps us remember the Word and keep it alive in our hearts, but it is also vital in the battle against darkness.

Sing the Word with all your heart, and watch as breakthrough, hope and healing are released in your own life and in the lives of all who hear it.

1

Sing

My heart is steadfast, O God,
my heart is steadfast;
I will sing and give praise.
Awake, my glory!
Awake, lute and harp!
I will awaken the dawn.
I will praise You, O Lord, among the peoples;
I will sing to You among the nations.

PSALM 57:7–9

Hemel Hempstead is a beautiful town in Hertfordshire in the east of England. It is located about 24 miles northeast of London. It is a town with shops, pubs and restaurants serving cream tea and sticky toffee pudding, which are some of my very favorite sweet treats in Britain. The cobbled streets and park are also some of my favorite memories.

But what I love most about Hemel Hempstead, besides the amazing people I met during my stay, is a very old church right in the center of town. The construction of St. Mary's Church started in AD 1140, and the people of Hemel will tell you it has its original spire built in the fourteenth century. The beautiful stained-glass windows and acoustics make it hard to stop singing as you walk through the church. I could imagine my voice right alongside the voices of all those who sang out in generations past, all those lifting their melodies and choruses of "Worthy is the Lamb who was slain." It has been more than a decade since my visit to Hemel Hempstead, and still I remember the sounds that arose from St. Mary's Church, and even sensing the *songs of the saints* from generations past that also arose in that beautiful church.

I was in Hemel Hempstead because I had been invited to be part of a worship school and teach about singing the Scriptures. It is simply singing the Bible to the Lord. He has our focused attention. He is our complete celebration. And suddenly we begin to experience 1 Corinthians 2:9–10:

> But as it is written: "Eye has not seen, nor ear heard, nor have entered into the heart of man the things which God has prepared for those who love Him." But God has revealed them to us through His Spirit. For the Spirit searches all things, yes, the deep things of God.

In the middle of our adoration and celebration of Jesus, the Spirit of the Lord does what the Word says He will do: The Holy Spirit begins to reveal the deep things of God's heart to the human heart. He reveals simple truths that set the heart free to love Him more and to feel His love in a personal, tangible experience. This actually helps us in loving God more, and in loving ourselves so that we can love one another more. It is a beautiful response that comes from praise, worship and singing the Word of God. It helps us obey what the Word of God says. It helps us to walk out forgiveness and walk out life here on earth.

Prophetic worship is a powerful part of our worship service. As a worship leader and singer, I made it a focused part of my life even when I was not at church or leading worship. If I was cleaning the house or driving to the store, I would sing the Psalms or the gospels or the epistles. I soon found that even without music playing in the background, I sang the words to simple melodies that I knew or that flowed from my heart as I went along. I discovered that when the Word of God is sung to our own melodies, it becomes a powerful tool that helps us walk out life and walk through life.

It became a passion of mine to encourage everyone to sing the Scriptures in worship services and in each one's personal life. I began doing simple workshops teaching how to sing the Bible. I would have everyone open his or her Bible to any one of the Psalms and begin to sing the Scriptures to a simple chord progression. The words are already written, so it is simply learning to make up a spontaneous melody and sing.

For years I mostly found myself teaching worship teams and musicians about singing the Scriptures. Which leads me back to the town of Hemel Hempstead, where I saw firsthand that singing the Scriptures is a tool for everyone—even those who are certain they cannot sing! We all need this tool in our tool belts as a weapon of warfare and breakthrough. Singing the Bible is for everyone, which I was blessed to witness firsthand as the Sprit of the Lord began revealing God's heart for an English grandfather who was at one of my singing the Scriptures clinics.

People of all ages had gathered to learn about singing the Scriptures, from teens to grandparents. They were not professional singers. They were also not necessarily on a worship team. They simply wanted to come and learn to sing the Scriptures. One gentleman caught my attention through most of the workshop. He was 82 years young and very quiet, sitting in the back of the room. But I noticed he was listening closely.

I began encouraging them to open their Bibles to Psalm 116:1–2, to make up their own melodies alongside the music that would be playing in the background, and to sing: "I love the LORD because He hears my voice and my prayer for mercy. Because He bends down to listen, I will pray as long as I have breath!"

In this part of the workshop, I asked them to take these verses and sing them as if God were singing directly to them. With a piano playing in the background, playing simple chord progressions to which everyone could sing, everyone in the room began to practice this musical exercise. I glanced at the gentleman in the back. He looked down at his Bible and I could see his lips moving. Then he looked up with his eyes closed and began to sing. As I watched, I could see a tear slowly drip down his cheek—and then another tear and another tear. At that point I looked away because I could see the Lord was touching him.

After a few minutes had passed I brought the music down. Then I asked for any testimonies.

"What did you experience when you began to sing the Word?" I asked. "Did singing the Word have more of an impact than reading the Word?"

The older man stood up and began to walk slowly to the front of the room. He still had tears rolling down his cheeks.

He said, "I was saved at a young age. I've walked with God my whole life, but I never felt like a true son. I looked at God as my Father, but I felt like a servant in my Father's house. I didn't feel worthy enough to belong in *His* house. I thought that at any time He would come to me and tell me to go back to the servant's house where I belonged. I didn't think He really heard my prayers. But today when I began to sing this Scripture, 'He bends down and listens,' I heard the Lord say to me, *Well, I have heard every word you have ever prayed.*"

This man looked at me and said, "I finally got it. I am eighty-two years old, and after all these years I finally understand. God has heard every single prayer I have ever prayed."

At this point, he had everyone's attention. With tears still rolling down his cheeks, he said, "God has heard every prayer. I now know that I belong in His house."

That memory is sealed in my heart as if it happened yesterday. I watched right before my eyes as someone found his place as a son of God. And it happened through singing Scripture. When he sang the Word, the Spirit of the Lord did what He loves to do: He revealed truth to this man's heart about who he was before the Lord. He was a true son. That simple song broke off decades of feelings of unworthiness.

Worship leaders and teams have experienced this for years. As they put the words of Scripture to song in worship, they receive personal breakthrough and freedom. But I have also watched those who would never consider themselves singers or musicians get incredible breakthroughs while singing the Bible. This is not just for those skilled in music. It is for everyone desiring a closer walk with Jesus, everyone needing to hear His voice, everyone needing freedom.

Plus, I believe it is the best way to retain the Word. We can meditate on the Word, pray the Word, speak the Word, declare the Word. But the best way to keep the life-giving Word in our hearts is to sing it.

Have you ever thought about the fact that you are able to remember songs from your childhood? I remember songs my Grandma Cook taught me when I was little. I remember songs from grade school and high school. I can pretty much remember songs from the different seasons of my life. And, on the other hand, I have no idea what homework I was doing when I was learning these songs, or what Sunday services I liked because the sermon was good.

When you enjoy a song, you will sing it over and over; it is a repetitive form of learning. The more we repeat something, the more it tends to stay in our minds. The songs that we have sung over and over stay with us over decades. Can you see that singing the Bible is not just for singers and musicians? Could singing the Bible be a powerful tool that everyone needs to use?

I saw a promotional piece online showing the power of music to help dementia patients. It records an elderly man named Henry sitting in a wheelchair in a nursing home. He is not responding to anyone. One of his family members puts his favorite songs that he sang throughout his life on an iPod. These were songs he had loved and listened to for years. We see as the nurse puts the headphones on his head and starts the music.

Immediately he comes to life. His face lights up. His feet start moving to the beat of the music. His eyes get big. There is excitement on his face. It is as if there is healing power in the music that his brain remembers. The doctor begins to interview Henry about the music, and he begins to sing and talk about some of the songs that he remembers from his past. This is powerful. When no one can reach him, this music is able to break in and actually enable Henry to have a conversation.

This reminds me of Colossians 3:16 where Paul writes, "Let the word of Christ dwell in you richly in all wisdom, teaching and admonishing one another in psalms and hymns and spiritual songs, singing with grace in your hearts to the Lord." Paul is encouraging the Colossian believers to let the Word of Christ live in them, to come alive in them.

John Wesley, in *Wesley's Notes on the Bible* (Zondervan, 1987), explains that we should let the word of Christ *dwell* in our hearts, "not make a short stay, or an occasional visit, but take up its stated residence," and let it dwell *richly*, "in the largest measure, and with the greatest efficacy; so as to fill and govern the whole soul." Regarding Paul's encouragement for us to teach and admonish one another in psalms, hymns and spiritual songs, Matthew Henry writes this in his *Commentary on the Whole Bible* (Revell, 1983): "Singing of psalms is a teaching ordinance as well as a praising ordinance; and we are not only to quicken and encourage ourselves, but to *teach and admonish one another*, mutually excite our affections, and convey instructions." Singing psalms, hymns and spiritual songs serves not only to teach but also to encourage and to warn.

Now maybe you are a singer or a musician; maybe you are neither. Regardless, the results are the same. Singing the Bible is a powerful means of breakthrough. As we put the living Word to simple melodies, we can all experience breakthrough just like the amazing grandpa who lived in Hemel Hempstead.

But here is an even greater reason to sing. Do you realize that God is singing over you? Look at Zephaniah 3:17: "The Lord your God in your midst, the Mighty One, will save; He will rejoice over you with gladness, He will quiet you with His love, He will rejoice over you with singing."

I think God loves it when we sing His Word. I have even heard recordings in which creation itself sounds as though it is singing. A friend of mine played a recording of crickets with their chirruping slowed way, way, way down—and it sounded beautiful. It seems as if everything praises in song—even crickets. You can find this on YouTube. There have been studies done with music on icicles and plants, showing how everything seems to grow better when the sound around them is beautiful singing.

Come with me on a journey of melodies and living Word. I believe you will find your song and your voice whether you are a banker, a homemaker, an artist, in the workplace or retired. The Holy Spirit will set your heart free to love God more and to feel His love in return. There is a song in you and Scriptures are waiting to be sung.

Lord,

I pray that You will help each reader begin the journey of singing the Scriptures. Let the Holy Spirit begin to shine His light into every heart revealing the truth about each word sung. I pray this journey of singing the Word takes us straight into Your heart with new passion to love You and new passion to love ourselves as You created us to be. Let every song awaken every heart as Your Word rides the beautiful waves of sound, coming from every believer.

In Jesus' name, Amen.

Questions

1. Can you think of a really old worship song that you may have sung years ago? Do you still remember the song?
2. When you read Colossians 3:16—what does this verse mean to you?
3. Have you ever read this verse and started singing the Psalms more because of reading this Scripture?
4. Are you willing to try? In fact, let's take the next five to six days and put a simple melody to Colossians 3:16. See if you begin to get excited about singing the Word from this Scripture that encourages us to sing the Scriptures.

Singing the Scriptures
How-To for Chapter 1

To help you begin practicing what I wrote about in this chapter, please go to www.juliemeyerministries.com/singingthescriptures and search for chapter 1. This short video offers practical instructions for singing the Scriptures.

2

Singing Your Way to Breakthrough

"O my dove, in the clefts of the rock,
In the secret places of the cliff,
Let me see your face,
Let me hear your voice;
For your voice is sweet,
And your face is lovely."
SONG OF SOLOMON 2:14

It was 1999. The International House of Prayer in Kansas City had just started.

Every Tuesday morning, I led worship, and I followed a young Misty Edwards. She would sing her songs straight from the Bible, declaring her devotion to the Lord as she played the keyboard. For two hours she sang like a little bird, unaware of anyone or anything around her—except Jesus. Word for word, straight from the Bible, with her tears rolling down her cheeks and dripping onto the keys, she sang of her unwavering love for Jesus. But she did not stop there; her theme and her song were also singing about His love for her.

I never wanted to interrupt her when her two hours of singing the Word were over. It seemed like a holy moment that one should not stop. Still, I would need to reach out and touch her shoulder to let her know the next worship set was starting. She did the same thing every single Tuesday morning. Misty would wipe her tears from her cheeks and move from the piano. Then, before I played a note, I would take a tissue and wipe each of her tears off the keys. Here was a young lady, just twenty years old, singing of her devotion to the Lord word for word from the Scriptures, and I never wanted to wipe away those precious tears.

But one Tuesday morning, as I wiped her tears from the keys, I suddenly came face to face with my own lack. I realized that I had never experienced a breakthrough in my heart where I could *feel* His all-consuming love. I *knew* the sermons about the love of Jesus crashing in over the human heart, but I had never actually felt His love for me—at least not the way Misty sang about it. I had the knowledge that He loved me; I also knew that He loved *everyone else*, but I did not feel His love for me in the depths of my heart. I always thought I could do much better and live much "holier." That was my focus.

After leading worship for years and years, after writing songs that stirred my heart for God, I realized that I did not fully understand how to embrace His heart for me—and it must work both ways. I was so focused on all of my lack and all of my stumbling that even in the place of worship, even though I loved God, I felt that I was a great distance from Him. I had not grasped the other side yet. I had not experienced His heart in the way the Song of Solomon describes it: "You have captured my heart, my treasure, my bride. You hold it hostage with one glance of your eyes" (4:9 NLT).

Love has to go both ways. It is not enough that we love God; there must be a meeting place, an awakening in the human spirit that God loves us. Our love for Him is actually a response to His heart: "We love Him *because* He first loved us" (1 John 4:19, emphasis added).

He picked us. He chose us and called us out of darkness. Because He loved us, Jesus came and died to break the power of darkness and death that holds us. This is why we love God. It is essential to understand and walk in this truth. We do not just love God: We love God because He first loved us.

This has to be more than head knowledge, and that was my dilemma. I knew it in my head, but I did not feel it in my heart. And this is one feeling that is necessary in walking out our day-by-day journeys with the Lord.

My Day of Freedom

I have a good idea why I kept this distance from God for so long. Most of my inability to feel His complete and total love came from growing up with a mother who was addicted to alcohol. She could never get free. And as her daughter, I heard things from her that no daughter should ever hear from her mom. My mother was amazing when she was sober, but that was not often. I had a great dad, who was a mother and father to all of us children. But there was something about the words my mother spoke that stuck in my heart for years. It was easy to believe the negative because I did not know the Lord until I was seventeen.

My mother gave her life to the Lord three months before she died, and it was a beautiful three months with her. I am grateful that she now has billions of years to say yes to Him. Years later,

I would find my story in the biography of Maria Woodworth-Etter when reading the first sentence of the first paragraph: "I was a drunkard's daughter." That describes me; however, *now* there is freedom, love, forgiveness and salvation when telling this testimony.

Still, every Tuesday morning I would wipe Misty's tears from the keyboard and feel great personal conflict. A good friend who was also the worship pastor saw my struggle.

He asked me, "Julie, what is happening?"

I said the very words I felt: "There is no way that God loves me as much as He loves Misty." I really did believe that in my heart.

Well, he did not miss a beat. He said, "You know, today we are going to sing from the first chapter of the Song of Solomon. Julie, for the next two hours the only thing that you can sing is verse five: 'I am dark, but lovely.' Let your heart know what this means: 'I am broken but beautiful. I am weak but God loves me.'"

At that moment, I did not feel beautiful. I felt weak, and in my weakness all I could feel was *I am weak.* And because I felt weak, I could not draw close to the Lord. I had a feeling of unworthiness because I did not feel His love the way everyone else was singing about it. My emotions were in great conflict with the words that I was singing. *I am dark, but lovely.* Yet I stepped out and began to sing Song of Solomon 1:5 for the next two hours. *I am dark but lovely. I am broken but beautiful. I am weak but God loves me.*

It is hard to sing something that you do not feel personally. Now if I had been told to go out and sing about how weak I felt, that I could have done. Singing is personal and is felt very deeply. I was not just singing Scripture; I was putting myself into the story—and that is even *more* personal. This is a great example of why we should not always go by our feelings, because my feelings were one hundred percent opposite of the way God felt about me. God loved me and was waiting for this moment in time when He knew I would be encouraged to sing Scripture over my heart. And He knew I would get one hundred percent breakthrough. He also knew I would tell everyone how I got free from thinking all the negative thoughts about myself.

I began that worship set with great personal conflict, especially the first couple of times I put those words to a melody. But the more I sang *I am dark, but lovely,* the more the raging emotions inside my heart began to still. It was as if my thoughts and emotions began to line up and agree with God's thoughts and emotions about me. The more I sang the more I believed, and the more I believed the more confidently I sang.

Those living words got inside me. They began resonating His truth within me. And truth literally found its dwelling place in my heart—just from singing five words of Scripture over and over: *I am dark, but lovely.* Suddenly my emotions about me were overshadowed by God's emotions about me, *and God's emotions won.* There was a winner—and it was God.

That Tuesday morning was my day of breakthrough. My heart rejoiced in the fact that He loves me and that He loves me all through my journey. He does not just love me when I have my act together; He loves because He loves. He does not love me because of what I do; He loves completely. I learned without a doubt that this tool of singing the Scriptures overpowers any and all negative words that penetrate the soul.

This "living understanding," this knowledge of His Word, right from Ephesians 1:17, came alive in my heart and it has never left. I went into that worship session with my negative thoughts and emotions overpowering me, and I came out with God's true thoughts and emotions living in me. I sang my way to freedom. The cloud of depression was turned to gladness. Personal failure was turned to triumph.

33

David's Strategy for Breakthrough

Singing the Bible, which is the living Word of God, is life changing. It is not just for Sunday services. It is not just for the great singers. Singing the Bible is a powerful tool of breakthrough that every single man, woman and child needs. Why should singers and worship teams get all the breakthroughs? This is for everyone. It is for you. All of us can do this within the walls of our homes or offices or life situations and experience freedom on every level.

Think of your voice as a weapon, the bow from which the arrow, the Word, goes forth to hit its target—even if the target is your own heart. With every note of your song you strike the enemy. It is your song, your breakthrough and your melody of triumph.

This is exactly what David did all through his life. He would sing and stir up his soul to hope in God. A great example of this is found in Psalm 7. David was pleading his case before God because someone in King Saul's service had accused David of treason. The introduction to this psalm says, "A Meditation of David, which he sang to the LORD concerning the words of Cush, a Benjamite." David meant this psalm to be sung. In it he declared that he took refuge in God. He wrote of his complete innocence. Then he asked God to *arise* on his behalf—to stand up so that his enemies would *see God* declaring David's innocence. David sang, "Judge me, O LORD, according to my righteousness, and according to my integrity within me. . . . My defense is of God, who saves the upright in heart. God is a just judge" (verses 8, 10–11). David was saying, *God is my defense, and He saves the upright in heart. He rescues and saves. He brings the victory to all who will reach out and call on His name.*

David made it clear that he would "sing praise to the name of the LORD Most High" (verse 17). This is not just poetic license but a significant strategy that David used to encourage his heart to trust in the Lord. We see over and over throughout the Psalms that David *sang* to focus his heart and mind on the deliverance and goodness of God—and breakthrough came.

David understood the power of singing the Word. His psalms were a reflection of his study and meditation on the Torah and other Hebrew Scriptures, which he says he did day and night, night and day. But he added one thing to his meditations: He added melodies. His meditations became his own personal song of deliverance. Generations of people, young and old, have read, prayed, sung and written songs from the Psalms, which mostly chronicle David's life. In all occasions, through every season, he had a song he could sing to encourage his own heart. He was his own chief encourager, and he did it through singing his meditations and his writings.

David used this great tool—singing his meditations to God, about God and for God. He sang his way to hope in God *before* he knew the outcome of whatever trial he was facing. He used his singing as conversation with God; it seems as if he kept an ongoing dialogue with God through his every waking moment. A number of verses indicate that the first words on his lips at dawn were the Torah, and the last words on his lips before he went to sleep were the Torah. He memorized those words. But he did more than memorize them; he sang them and used them as a foundation for the psalms he wrote.

Letting Your Song Arise

Every one of us can do what David did throughout his life. We can express our hearts in the words of Scripture and sing our way to breakthrough. God is always healing, always restoring, always removing the wrong mindsets that we have about Him or about ourselves.

Paul gives us a sense of this in Ephesians 5:18-19. Several Bible versions translate these verses just as the New King James Version does: "Do not be drunk with wine, in which is dissipation; but be filled with the Spirit, speaking *to one another* in psalms and hymns and spiritual songs, singing and making melody in your heart to the Lord" (emphasis added).

But I like the King James Version here. It reads: "[Speak] *to yourselves* in psalms and hymns and spiritual songs, singing and making melody in your heart to the Lord" (emphasis added). The word for *yourselves* in this verse is *heautou. Strong's Exhaustive Concordance of the Bible* (Riverside, 1980) translates this Greek word as "himself, themselves, yourselves, ourselves." It can mean "to come to one's self, to come to a better mind."

In many Bible translations, Ephesians 5:18 says, "[Speak] to one another," but we find in Strong's that most of the time when the word *heautou* is used, it means "himself." It is personal. So if we look at this verse based on the King James Version, it says, "Speak to yourself in psalms, hymns and spiritual songs making melody in your heart to the Lord."

We have this amazing command from Paul not to be drunk with wine but to be filled with the Spirit, and then to speak to ourselves in psalms, hymns and spiritual songs. I believe we should take this exhortation personally: You can speak to yourself, and do it by singing songs, hymns and spiritual songs, making melody in your heart to the Lord. If you want a "better mind," then sing the psalms, hymns and spiritual songs to yourself.

In his commentary, Matthew Henry states:

> To sing and to make melody in their hearts; not only with their voices, but with inward affection, and then their doing this will be as delightful and acceptable to God as music is to us: and it must be with a design to please him, and to

promote his glory, that we do this; and then it will be done to the Lord.

This totally changes the framework of Ephesians 5:18–19. Look again at this Scripture: Do not be drunk with wine, because that will ruin your life. Instead, be filled with the Holy Spirit, speaking to yourself in psalms and hymns and spiritual songs, singing and making melody in your heart to the Lord.

Could it be that Paul is actually inviting those struggling in life or struggling with addictions to sing the Psalms, to sing hymns, to let one's own songs arise out of singing the Word? Did Paul have an understanding of how these words come alive on the inside on the heart, and the breakthrough that happens when we sing the Word over ourselves?

I believe so. We already addressed Colossians 3:16 in which Paul writes, "Let the word of Christ dwell in you richly." This happens by singing psalms, hymns and spiritual songs. When we do this, our hearts become tenderized by the Word. In that place, true affection begins to stir in our hearts as we are singing truth. Jesus is the Word, and singing His words stirs them up on the inside.

David says this in a similar way in Psalm 57:7–8 (KJV): "My heart is fixed, O God, my heart is fixed: I will sing and give praise. Awake up, my glory; awake, psaltery and harp: I myself will awake early." David is singing this: "My heart—my inner man, my will, my mind, my thinking—is fixed. It is set; it is firm; it is certain. So wake up, be roused, be triumphant, O my glory, O my honor, O my abundance. Wake up guitar, harp and lute. For I will wake up, arise and stir up the morning, the dawn."

The introduction to Psalm 57 states that David wrote this "when he fled from Saul into the cave." Spurgeon, in his *Treasury of David* (Hendrickson, 1988), writes:

This is a song from the bowels of the earth, and, like Jonah's prayer from the bottom of the sea, it has a taste of the place. The poet is in the shadow of the cave at first, but he comes to the cavern's mouth at last, and sings in the sweet fresh air, with his eye on the heavens, watching joyously the clouds floating therein.

David composed his song from the darkness of the cave to the brightness of the day, from captivity to freedom, and from hiding to victory. It seems that these two verses from Psalm 57 speak to us in our own struggles, for David's battle was with Saul and our battle is with the darkness of this world. They also go hand in hand with Paul's admonition in Ephesians. David was singing his story through the Scriptures; then he wrote his songs—the very psalms that Paul invites us to sing. Instead of being drunk with wine and following worldly passions, here is what we do: Be filled with the Spirit. Sing the Psalms.

Lord,

For all those needing personal breakthrough, for all those who need to feel Your love upon their hearts, I pray that as they lift their voices and sing your Word, Your love will break through any wrong mindsets, any negative thoughts. Let them begin to have Your thoughts and Your heart for themselves and for all those in their lives.

In Jesus' name, Amen.

Questions

1. What are you currently walking through that you need freedom from or breakthrough in?

2. As you read through this chapter, can you identify any wrong mindsets that you also may have regarding God or how He feels about you?

3. Can I invite you to take the Bible verses used in this chapter or any of those listed in the appendix and sing them over yourself?

How-To for Chapter 2

To help you begin practicing what I wrote about in this chapter, please go to www.juliemeyerministries.com/singingthescriptures and search for chapter 2. This short video offers practical instructions for singing the Scriptures.

3

Singing the Word from Your Heart

In 2015 I met a young woman named Eli Rose. I met Eli after a worship service during which she burst into a song that told her life story. Some of this song was sung and some of it was a literal rap. Now, *rap* in our context means taking Scripture or personal testimony and mixing it with melodies and syncopated rhythms.

Hers was a journey from darkness to light and from captivity to freedom. Through her testimony, you will learn how to take the first steps of singing the Scriptures. Eli experienced an amazing breakthrough—and you can, too.

During worship, she began rapping and singing about the way Jesus suddenly broke into her life, and about His power that healed her of HIV. I learned later that she had crafted this song in her personal devotional time right in the middle of singing the Scriptures. I still remember her words based on Psalm 103. Declaring that "God heals everything," she sang out, "He healed me of HIV!" When she poured out those words, the room erupted into shouts. We were all in tears and cheering at the same time. Eli did exactly what David did: *She sang about it.* And an explosion of joy hit the room.

I listened as Eli told her whole life story in song. Through the message that "God heals everything" and through the vehicle of song, she offered hope for personal breakthrough to everyone in the room that night. The Lord had set her free by healing her body. As she sang, everyone began to believe that if God did this for her, He will do it for me.

Later Eli told me more of her story. In 2012 she found the Lord, or I should say He found her. She lived on the streets and ran with a rough crowd for years. She was at the end of everything and was going to end her life if something did not change. She believed in God, but she did not know if God believed in her. That night He showed her that He did.

As God's divine providence would have it, she happened to walk into the Healing Rooms in Santa Maria, California. The Healing Rooms Apostolic Center (HRAC) provides regional and global resources for people to receive healing, to pray, and to be equipped for spiritual growth and personal ministry. The Center is home to the Healing Rooms of the Santa Maria Valley, where thousands have come for healing for nearly two decades.

The worship team was singing praises to God from the Word, and the Word of God went out. In that atmosphere Rick Taylor was given a word of knowledge, revelation of information given him by the Holy Spirit. "Somebody here has been in a really dark place," he said. "Please don't take your life. I promise, God has already begun to heal you."

That somebody was Eli, and her life was changed forever. It started with worship, singing the Word. Then it was as if the Bible came alive, stirring up a word of knowledge for her. In that moment Eli gave her life to Jesus. She continued to grow in the

Lord by singing the Scriptures, and that is what is so powerful about her testimony.

I got to know Eli more in 2016 when I moved to the Central Coast of California. She invited me to come to Redemption Center, which is a walk-in refuge for the homeless that she founded. She had asked me to lead a music class and teach about singing the Scriptures.

The first time I went to teach, I brought my boom box and put on a CD to use as background for singing Psalm 116: "I love the LORD because he hears my voice and my prayer for mercy. Because he bends down to listen, I will pray as long as I have breath!" (verses 1–2 NLT).

Let me say that there is no right melody or wrong melody for singing the Scriptures because it is *your* melody. To get started, you can sing along to your own tune, or you might want to sing along with an instrumental CD. Either way it begins as simply as opening your Bible, picking out a psalm and beginning to sing the words to whatever tune you choose.

The CD I played that night had seven different musical progressions or musical styles. I hoped that the different selections might appeal to those new to this idea.

I said, "I want everyone to turn to Psalm 116, the first two verses. We are going to write songs today, and they can be raps that you speak or songs that you sing." I handed out paper, pencils and Bibles. Then I pressed the Play button on the boom box.

The music began to get their attention almost instantly. I looked around the room and saw Bibles open, eyes focused and pencils moving over the sheets of paper. Smiles began to spread across their faces and many began humming along. Part of this engagement was the music, but a big portion of it was the Word.

For some reason I kept looking at a young guy in the back. His name was Matthew, and from the time he had entered the room he had not looked at anyone. He was sitting with his head down. I could not tell if he was writing. After about ten minutes, with him in mind, I began to walk around the room with a microphone and ask if anyone would like to sing his or her song from Psalm 116.

Eli held the mic and began singing the words of the psalm. But she took it one step further; she made it personal. She used the words David wrote and applied them to her own story. Oh, that we would all learn from Eli and apply each word of this psalm to our own journeys and our own stories!

This is how Eli's song progressed. She summarized the first and second verses and then began to sing her own story. And freedom along with joy broke into the room. People stood to clap and there were yells of "Yes, yes!" as each person understood what it felt like to make mistakes and then cry out to the Lord for help in making better choices.

Eli rapped these words:

> I love the LORD
> I love the LORD
> Because He bends down to listen.
> I made mistakes in the past
> But now, today, I make a better choice, a better way.

Then she began to sing out loudly:

> He hears my prayer!
> He hears my prayer!
> He hears my prayer!

When the Word of God is declared, it does not matter who does the singing or declaring. It is powerful. And hope came alive in that room from her very first words. Why? Because truth was being spoken. God *does* listen. He *does* hear our prayers.

Slowly other people began to say, "I'll sing my song. I'll rap." The room came alive with words spoken to the beat of the music and choruses set to melodies. Faith started to rise in their hearts as they sang, "I love the Lord; He bends down and listens to my voice."

Then after a few minutes I looked at Matthew and said, "Matthew, will you sing?"

He nodded and began to rap these words:

> I love the Lord
> I love the Lord
> Because He listens.
> Put your hand in the hand of the One who listens.

He sang softly. I asked him if he would sing again, which he did, a little louder.

Then I went with the mic to another young woman, and she sang these words:

> I love the Lord
> I love the Lord 'cause
> I was a child catching a buzz
> Didn't know who Jesus was
> But now, I'm saved! A new day, hurray
> My battles are fought on my knees
> Brother, pray.

Another gal sang:

> I love the Lord; I love the Lord
> I love the Lord because He hears my voice

> He loves me; He loves you
> No matter what I say, no matter what I do

Then I went back to Matthew and said, "Will you sing your rap again?"

The Redemption Center was alive with new sounds, new melodies and new songs as Psalm 116 filled their hearts. Then I saw that Matthew was speaking to others, encouraging them. It was almost as if he were prophesying over them; right there we had church.

Eli told me when I saw her a couple weeks later that the people who attended the session that night were still walking around the Center singing Psalm 116. She said that around every corner you could hear someone rapping or singing:

> I love the LORD
> I love the LORD
> I love the LORD
> Because He hears my voice.

This is what the people in the Center experienced. This Scripture came alive within them. It was not sitting dormant and forgotten; it was resonating and bubbling up from the inside. David wrote, "Your words are the theme song of my life" (see Psalm 119:54). Psalm 116 became the theme song that they continued to sing for weeks. The more they sang this theme song, the more it found a home in their hearts. Those songs got into people. Those living words from the Psalms made the way for hope.

And it can be the same for you.

For all of us, as we grow in the Word we come to understand that the Word is something we want to cling to. We want God's Word in us, changing us, speaking life to us. But it also works the other way. When we sing the Word, it does not let us go. It stays with us. As Paul said, it "dwells within us richly."

The next time I visited Redemption Center, I was amazed. As soon as I walked in, I could hear the echo of voices down the hall. I heard the singing of "I love the Lord. I love the Lord. He hears my voice."

As we gathered for the teaching session that afternoon, I saw the excited faces of those who had experienced the awakening that happens when Scripture comes alive. There were also some new faces. I passed out Bibles and asked them to turn to Psalm 23. This time instead of a boom box, I had brought a small band with me to play as they sang. We had an electric guitar, bass and percussion.

The Holy Spirit highlighted a man sitting near the front on the sofa. He was not showing much interest in singing; mostly he was looking at his phone. His name was Raymond. There was something about him; I wanted the Lord to break into his heart with the Word.

I asked the band to start playing as people picked up their pencils and began to write. I loved the sounds of rap, humming and melodies all floating together in the room as each person wrote a song from Psalm 23.

After a few minutes, I started walking around with the mic asking if anyone would like to sing.

I was so hit with the Lord's heart for Raymond that I began quietly to ask the Holy Spirit to break in. I remember hearing Heidi Baker storm heaven for someone with these words: "Get him, God. Get him." So as I walked around the room, that was my prayer for Raymond: "Get him, God. Get him. Help him sing the Scriptures and find his worth today. Help him see who You are today. Get him, God. Get him."

"Who would like to sing?" I asked. "Who has finished a song?"

As a couple of people began to sing, I noticed that Raymond had put down his phone and picked up his pencil. He began to write. It is a wonderful thing to see the process of the Word of God awakening the human heart. I continued to walk around the room encouraging people to share their songs and their raps. Then I asked Raymond if he wanted to sing. At first he shook his head no. But I asked again and he took the mic.

He began to sing these words very softly:

> The LORD is my Shepherd
> I have all that I need.

As the band was playing, he sang his chorus and one verse, and then handed the mic back to me. But then he stayed engaged, watching and nodding as others sang. So I asked Raymond to sing his song again. This time he sang with more confidence; then he quickly handed off the mic. I always ask people to sing their songs four or five times so the Word really gets into their hearts. The more they sing, the more the words begin to replace wrong mindsets. That day you could see each person, one by one, come alive.

Then I noticed Raymond beginning to fidget. He looked as though he could not hold in his feelings any longer. He jumped up and took the mic. This time there was boldness in his demeanor—new joy seemed to bubble up within him. Everyone saw it.

He went to the front of the room, holding his paper with the words he had written, and confidence overcame him. Divine might on the inside began to well up within him. Raymond sang loudly and strongly. He had been awakened. He had come alive as the words he was singing came alive within him.

I had gone to the Redemption Center that afternoon to reach out to those beautiful people whom Eli Rose and her incredible staff touch every single day. They feed people, love people and help them with every need. But that afternoon I was the one who was touched. I was the one who was blessed by inviting people to write songs from the Word and then sing them out. I simply stood back and watched the Spirit of God awaken each heart that sang:

The Lord is my Shepherd
I have all that I need.

Could this be the secret weapon for all people who need personal breakthrough? For encouragement? For hope? I believe it is. It is not just my testimony. It is also the testimony of many, many people.

Eli's Testimony

Eli Rose wrote me to share her story in this chapter. She wanted to say in her own words how singing the Scriptures was a turning point for her. Here is her personal testimony.

My name is Eli Rose, and I am the founder of Redemption Center in Grover Beach, California. We are a nonprofit organization, a walk-in day Center that serves our community and offers full-service advocacy. We also go to the trenches, the highways and the byways to look for the lost and to love those society often deems as unlovable.

I never thought I would start up a nonprofit—or do anything with my life for that matter, as I was just like those we love and serve today. I had pretty much seen it all by the time I was a teenager. I had been deeply strung out on drugs for fifteen years. I'd been raped, homeless, almost murdered multiple times, kidnapped, shot at, involved in prostitution, and part of a very dangerous group in Los Angeles that operated heavily in the crime world. By age 28, I had been hospitalized more than twenty times for suicide attempts, mental breakdowns and poor health. My heart was damaged from shooting heroin and getting a horrible infection that had caused two of my heart valves to deteriorate. Plus I had been diagnosed with HIV. I had also developed quite a "career" going in and out of the jail system.

I had been locked up around sixteen times, but, quite frankly, I had lost count. The end of my rope came when I began to have PTSD seizures. Yes, that's right. I had no idea that even existed. But sure enough you stuff pain for too long and it's going to seep out or completely explode out of you. I could no longer stuff in even a speck of more pain; my body would drop and have a seizure.

So in 2012 my greatest plan was to take my life in my storage unit in L.A. And though I was not on good terms with God, I did believe He existed. I remember thinking to myself, *Well, at least I'm finally going to do something right for God. I will take one more loser off His list.* But by a series of absolute miracles and God directing me without my knowing it, I ended up at the Healing Rooms in Santa Maria.

The first moment I walked in, I heard music playing. Immediately, I began to feel something tingle around my heart, but I had no idea what it was. I sat down pretty suspicious about what the heck I was doing there. I began to feel hot. After the music, a person I guessed to be a pastor came up to the front. He said with tears in his eyes, "Wow, somebody here has been in a dark place . . . so dark."

As he spoke and I saw the emotion in his eyes, an overwhelming hot tingling began to turn in my chest. I became heavy with emotion because I knew he was talking about me.

He then looked out into the crowd and said, "Please don't take your life. I promise, God has already begun to heal you. He's healing you now."

Needless to say, I was absolutely blown away. I began to realize that God didn't think I was a loser at all . . . and this pastor was talking to me.

That night I finally and truly turned my life over to God. That was the first time in my life that the torment and the anxiety began to go. To my shock, about a month and a half later I found out that I was completely healed of HIV and that I have a perfectly brand-new, undamaged heart. I am also off all psych medication.

Worship and singing the Scriptures became my saving grace every morning as I stayed in rehab that whole first year. I played my guitar to Jesus and began writing songs from the Psalms. Then in 2014 I met Julie Meyer when she came to minister in Santa Maria. She showed us how to literally open up our Bibles to the Psalms or wherever and sing the Word over any circumstance—to put ourselves right in the words.

I not only sing and worship daily, but I also rap the words. I took the entire chapter of Psalm 119 and translated it into rap, which I sing and declare often. My friends and I are talking about producing an audio Bible all in rap. It's fun, and I feel the Lord's absolute delight.

Since that day I have stayed clean and sober, off drugs and alcohol. I started giving local homeless friends a ride to church with me and my friend Karen. That ended up growing to five vans, a team and a Center that gets involved in the good, the bad and the ugly to all those who are hurting and in need of help. Sometimes the greatest need someone has is for a friend. We love no matter what. We bring them into the Center and include worship and singing the Scriptures as part of every service.

When Julie is able to come to the Center to do music group, there is nothing like it. We get the word out on the streets and the people are excited for days before. What Julie didn't know about Raymond beforehand was that he slept in the streets and had lost his entire family. He battled with a serious addiction that was constantly destroying all the progress he would try to make. He had long given up and stopped fighting this demon. He spoke in a soft and muffled voice and was hard to understand.

Well, that day there was Raymond, singing like someone born to be a rock star! He was holding the mic, and in the most beautiful raspy and hard rock voice he was belting out the Word of God. To this day that memory blows me away. Raymond's confidence has since remained alive and free. He is now out of his shell and taking an active approach to getting his life together.

We see it again and again. Singing the Scriptures helps even the people from the most hurting and broken places explode with laughter and joy.

Wow! I love Eli's testimony. We have seen that this is the very thing that happened to David when he wrote and sang, "Awake, my glory." This is the very thing that Paul was talking about when he said, "Sing to yourself."

Will you give it a try? Maybe you can start with Psalm 23, just like Raymond.

> The LORD is my Shepherd
> I have all that I need.

Lord,

I ask that You will help these readers turn to Psalm 116:1–2 and find themselves in the grand storyline of God hearing our cries and prayers. Let them find comfort in knowing they are never alone, and that You, Lord, even at this very second, are bending Your ear way down to hear their cries. Let this knowledge turn into the grandest love for Jesus, and then let the whole theme be played over and over in their hearts and minds. "I love the Lord because He hears my voice and bends down to listen."

In Jesus' name, Amen.

Questions

1. Have you ever been in a place like I was where it was hard to feel and experience the Word of the Lord?

2. If you answer yes to this question, how did you break out of that negative thought pattern?

3. Some of you reading may be in this place now. Can you go to the back of this book, and among all of the Scriptures listed for talking and encountering God, can you find one that you can sing over yourself for these next five days? Don't get in a rush—for the more you sing, the more these words will sink in.

4. After you sing this one verse over your life—can you write down your thoughts? Are you finding it easier to break through negative mindsets when you sing?

5. Don't get in a hurry with this part. Sing it and let it soak in.

Singing the Scriptures
How-To for Chapter 3

To help you begin practicing what I wrote about in this chapter, please go to www.juliemeyerministries.com/singingthescriptures and search for chapter 3. This short video offers practical instructions for singing the Scriptures.

...ipt

..s that you checked out

Title: Checking in : how getting real about depression saved my life-and can save yours
ID: 31172099110837
Due: Saturday, August 28, 2021

Title: This close to okay : a novel
ID: 31172099509655
Due: Saturday, August 28, 2021

Total items: 2
Account balance: $0.00
8/7/2021 11:34 AM
Checked out: 20
Ready for pickup: 2
Messages:
OK

Thank you for using the 3M™ SelfCheck System.

4

Singing and the Brain

Deep calls unto deep at the noise of Your waterfalls;
All Your waves and billows have gone over me.
The LORD will command His lovingkindness in the daytime,
And in the night His song shall be with me—
A prayer to the God of my life.

PSALM 42:7–8

I was sitting on a United Airlines flight awaiting takeoff. It was my first trip to Israel. This had been a dream of mine for years. I had prayed the Bible, sung the Bible, meditated on the Bible, and now I was going to walk down some of the very pathways of the Bible. I would see many places where Jesus lived, where He taught and where He prayed. I would be in places where Jesus healed the sick and spoke the Beatitudes. It was the dream of my heart.

My first stop in Israel was a conference for 130 young Arab women where I would be one of the speakers. I had my notes completed for my sessions. I had Scriptures and personal stories ready to encourage the women who would attend. But as the plane began to back out of the gate, a thought passed through my mind: *What if it's not enough? What if my notes and stories are not enough to encourage these women?*

In that one moment I went from pure excitement at the thought of walking where Jesus walked to complete, utter fear at the thought of the conference. This was the very spot where a song *should* have started. I *should* have thought, *Start singing the Scriptures. Pick out a psalm and sing it until it overshadows every fear.* Right there, in that moment, had I opened my Bible to any one of the Psalms and begun to form an easy melody, if I had sung the Word, faith would have found its place in my heart. That fleeting thought of doubt *should* have pointed me in the direction of singing the Scriptures.

But in a weak moment I leaned in the other direction and fell right into fear. My mind started racing. I started thinking, *What do I have to offer these young women? Our worlds are so different.*

This is a great testimony because there are times when all of us get caught off guard. Darkness never rests; we should not rest either. If we are not taking ground, we are losing ground. The enemy is constantly looking for struggles in our walk of faith. He is continually looking for a gap in our armor through which to fire those flaming lying arrows described in Ephesians 6.

In my excitement my song stopped. Here I was on my first trip to Israel with the opportunity to minister the Word of the Lord. My song proclaiming the Scriptures should have been foremost on my mind. The battle does not wait until you land; it starts before the plane even takes off.

I had my walls down, and I gave fear an opportunity to make its entrance. Because there was no song arising in my heart, those lying spirits stirred up negativity and doubt in my mind. A flaming arrow headed straight for me, and it hit the target. Looking back I am shocked at how fast those dark thoughts gathered and seemed to take up residence.

I had boarded the plane thinking I could just enjoy my flight; I was not thinking that I needed to be on the offense. Because I failed to extinguish that flaming arrow with an immediate verbal response and a declaration of faith, fear and anxiety positioned themselves firmly in my mind and heart. Those thoughts were determined to stay and lead me on a continuing downward spiral.

Until I began to sing Scriptures. Once I realized what was happening, I began fighting back against the overwhelming negativity. I chose several verses from the Psalms and sang them to a simple melody, quietly, right there on the plane. I will be honest. Because fear had found a landing spot I had to do some pressing. I knew, however, that I could break through. I was determined that faith would have its way. So I sang, and I sang the Word already written by David.

Once I began singing, the war in my head subsided. The melodic song of Scripture quenched the flaming arrow and settled peacefully in my mind and heart. In fact, the song played and replayed in my thoughts throughout the whole flight. It "took hold" and helped me maintain the victory I had won against darkness.

Singing Scripture helped me remember what was true. It stirred up my faith. I knew that God would help me at the conference to say what He wanted me to say. God would put His words on my heart; I would simply be the messenger delivering those kind, powerful words to beautiful Arab women. In fact, this lesson was the very thing that I began to teach about when I finally arrived at the conference. We can learn from every trial we go through, and this trial became a teaching point. Never ever stop singing the Word.

Emotions Join the Battle

One of the Scriptures I sang on that flight to Israel was Psalm 13:5–6: "I trust in your unfailing love; my heart rejoices in your salvation, I will sing to the LORD, for he has been good to me" (NIV1984).

Psalm 13 describes how David had to remember the Word and then sing his way to faith. He started this psalm in a distressed state of mind. This is the "How Long?" psalm. Four times David cries this out from his heart: "How long, O Lord? Will You forget me forever? How long will You hide Your face from me? How long shall I take counsel in my soul, having sorrow in my heart daily? How long will my enemy be exalted over me?"

David wrote Psalm 13 when he felt that God was slow to answer his prayers. He felt alone, even though he was never alone. There was a fight within David to find hope and faith in God in the midst of wrestling with his emotions. This was a perfect psalm for me to use in my battle because I was right there struggling with my own emotions. Was God leading me? Would my part in the conference be a disaster? Would I have no real help for those women? Had God forgotten me? This is a good lesson for us because many times our emotions are not an accurate gauge of the truth.

Then David began to sing: "I will trust in Your unfailing love. I will sing to the Lord, for He has been good to me."

It is as if his song began to stir up hope. He thought about all the times that God had been good to him. He also began to take control of his emotions instead of letting his emotions control him. David sang and wrote his statement of faith: "I am going to trust in Your unfailing love. Right now, it settles everything."

Psalm 13 is a perfect example of the breakthrough we can get by simply singing the Scriptures. David started off being honest about his struggles, all that he was thinking and feeling. And then he determined to find God right where he was. Somewhere as he was writing and singing, the truth landed in his mind and overpowered all doubt and fear.

I love this quote from Spurgeon:

> There is not half enough singing in the world. . . . I remember a servant who used to sing while she was at the wash-tub. Her mistress said to her, "Why, Jane, how is it that you are always singing?" She said, "It keeps the bad thoughts away."

Never again on that trip did I have to fight with my thoughts or try to rein in my emotions as I did at the beginning. I had my weapon, and my weapon was singing the Scriptures.

Why It Works

When I got home I began to ask myself about this. We can read a Scripture or declare a Scripture and receive great benefit. But when that Scripture is sung to a simple melody, it is as though the words make their way to our hearts and stay there. It is like hitting a home run every time we come up to the plate. David used this for his benefit, as he was always singing, and I found myself doing the same thing. But I had no idea why it worked so well.

I wanted some information about the brain that would help explain what happens when we sing, and why it is that singing the Word of God can suddenly break through emotions of depression, fear and anxiety. I knew that in my personal walk with the Lord—the times when I was being stretched to the nth degree—singing the Scriptures was the quickest way to peace.

I decided to find out a little about how our brains work in this regard. Now I am not a scientific person at all, but I wondered,

What is it in our brains that clings to songs? Why is it that a song will stay in our minds and play over and over and over? Why does music touch our emotions so powerfully? It became my mission to seek this out.

I started reading about the power of music and the brain. Book after book, website after website said the same thing.[1] When you listen to music or play an instrument, the activity causes different parts of the brain *to work together.* Adding words to the music strengthens the mix. Words come from the left side of the brain; applying those words to music happens in the right side of the brain; the joining of them rhythmically in song comes from the back of the brain. The front of the brain contributes the emotional reaction to music.

This working together is what makes instrumentation or song so memorable. I even found a word for those tunes that get in your head and stay there: *earworms.* If you cannot get a song or melody out of your head, that is an earworm.

Several scientific articles I read explained that singing helps calm your nerves even as it lifts your mood. It is believed that singing causes certain hormones to be released that actually lessen anxiety; other hormones seem to be released that have to do with feelings of pleasure.

A number of studies also showed the healing power of music. Doctors are now using music to help stroke victims recover and to help patients deal with pain. Music helps with everything from migraines to postpartum depression because it has such a strong and healing effect.

There are many studies of music being used with Alzheimer's patients. When these individuals cannot remember their families or any past memories—when all they do is stare at the wall—doctors can play their favorite music and suddenly these patients come back to life. Many YouTube videos show the powerful effect of music and singing. Doctors are finding new ways to reach patients with dementia, patients struggling with depression, and patients with mental illness.

I found again and again that doctors and patients alike are seeing the benefits on the human body when people actually *sing*. Open a search engine or go on Amazon and type in *singing and the brain* or *music and the brain*. There are so many books and articles that I could not begin to read them all before finishing this chapter.

Do you see why Scripture set to music is such a powerful tool? Scripture set to a melody will stay in your mind and not leave. The brain takes hold of it and fills your thoughts and heart with the life-giving Word of God. Melodies combined with Scripture can stop you from going down anxious paths of fear, depression and doubt.

Changing Our Focus

We are not just making music; we are welcoming Jesus to take first place in our thoughts and drive out doubt and fear. I believe this is why singing the Scriptures is such a powerful tool for us to use. Remember, different parts of the brain work together with words and music to calm and heal. The immense added benefit of putting Scripture to song is that God's truth stirs up our faith. No flaming arrows can penetrate a mind flowing in a unified expression of the Word. It is a one-two punch.

Think back to the earworm. It can get frustrating to hear some songs or melodies playing endlessly in our heads. But when earworms are songs of Scripture, the effect is just the opposite. As the Word replays in our minds, it begins to come alive in us. These are the earworms we want—we *want* these verses and choruses to play over and over and over.

The Word of God needs to get on the inside. Adding a melody is the very tool that keeps our brains engaged and stimulated so that the words have their full effect on us—heart, soul and body. *This is genius.* If we sing the Word it becomes alive on the inside of us so that we actually "do" the Word. It works for our benefit.

This is the exact thing that happened to me on the flight to Israel. When my own thoughts and emotions were leading me down a dangerous path of fear and doubt, I took the Word of God and began to sing it. This singing began to stimulate my brain in the right direction. It took the focus off the negative thoughts and emotions and put the complete focus on truth. Everything in my brain began to function in unity. Suddenly the melody and Word of God overcame every fear that had positioned itself in my heart. Negativity simply evaporated and faith took up residence.

I believe this is what David experienced in Psalm 13. He was fighting a battle with doubt in his mind. At the beginning of the psalm, his emotions seemed to be leading him. It was as though his circumstances were voiding his knowledge of God. "How long? How long?" he cried. But then he began to sing truths from the Torah. He put himself in the middle of his meditations, and his song broke through. David encouraged his heart that day by singing his way to hope and faith, remembering that God is good and that God had been good to him.

Using Your Tools

How amazing is God? God created the brain with the capacity to use words and music in order to help us stay steady in life. King David might not have understood medical science, but he knew the battles the heart faces. Is this why he was always singing? Is this why Paul taught the Colossians to sing and encouraged the Ephesians to sing psalms, hymns and spiritual songs?

Music is powerful. Singing is a tool. This is our weapon of warfare in the earth—"for we do not wrestle against flesh and blood, but against principalities, against powers, against the rulers of the darkness of this age, against spiritual hosts of wickedness in the heavenly places" (Ephesians 6:12). Singing the Scriptures can help you break cycles of despair and find faith. It can help you overcome fear and have peace. It can help you shed illness and find healing. We can all use this to fight messengers of darkness, the drug lords that entice us with lies every single second of the day and night.

Testimonies

Now let's take this scientific information and make it personal: How does this help me in my life? Here are testimonies of people who simply sang the Scriptures in their everyday lives. I believe it will encourage you to sing the Scriptures in your life. Let me add, *this is not singing silently to yourself*. Your singing needs to be out loud. It is when you sing and actually make a sound that the different areas of the brain work together. You do not get the same effect in the brain if you are listening to someone else sing or you are singing silently.

One of my Facebook friends sent me a message. I had asked on Facebook Live if anyone could share a testimony about the change of heart and mind that comes from singing the Word. Linda Thomas from San Antonio, Texas, wrote back that she is a hospice nurse. She said she always sings the Scriptures over those in her care. This is a difficult occupation but a beautiful one at the same time. Linda's is sometimes the last voice people hear before they pass away.

I asked if she would send me some of her testimonies of singing the Scriptures over people. This is her reply. As she sings from the Word, God begins to touch each patient—and it shows us the "why" behind singing the Scriptures. These testimonies show us the reason we want to sing the Scriptures.

I've been in the nursing field since 1973. I believe people hear while in comas, in different mental states, etc. I often sing the Scriptures regarding God's love, His plan of salvation, our hope for a future in heaven. God's presence and peace come into the room and truly change the atmosphere. Sometimes I sing softly, intending for only the patient to hear, yet family members from other parts of the house will somehow hear and thank me for caring for their loved ones and for singing the words of the Bible to them.

I have found that singing the Scriptures opens doors for me to talk with people who would never otherwise talk about God. I have seen emotional healing take place as I put comforting and life-giving verses into song. People tell me, "I've never thought about it like that before."

I had one patient who was in a coma; he had four adult children. When one son opened the door to his father's house that morning, I wasn't sure how my day would progress. It was a bad part of town. This young man was wearing a muscle shirt that exposed his tattoos (before they became so popular). He had a long braid going down his back, a bandanna on his head and many earrings in his ears.

He led me to his father's room. When I gave the patient a bath, I had the door shut for privacy. I then began to sing hymns, Scriptures and spiritual songs. When I opened the door, all four children were standing there listening. I was surprised and they were embarrassed.

The son who had met me at the door came to talk to me privately. He wanted me to sing the songs to him. As I began to sing, he closed his eyes and listened. He then shared with me that he used to keep a journal. I was able to encourage him in the Lord to begin again and write what he felt God was speaking to him. He wanted to know how to hear God speak. What a precious time!

His brother told me later that he had never heard anyone sing like that before outside of church. "It was so beautiful," he said.

I told him it was not my voice but the beauty of the Lord's presence that he felt and experienced. He actually put his head on my shoulder and wept. There seemed to be purity in his heart toward God.

That afternoon the brother brought his sister into the room for me to sing over her while she sat in a chair at the bedside of her father. She and I were able to talk afterward. I could sense God pouring His love into her as she told me about a difficult situation she was in.

Later that day about fifteen family members showed up at the house, and the son asked if I would sing to them. There was such a strong sense of God's presence in the room that I asked if I could pray. God gave me the opportunity to bless them in prayer and share God's love with them.

The day I had wondered about turned out to be one of my most memorable days. I was deeply touched by God's love and acceptance.

I once had an Alzheimer's patient who spent six hours one day glaring at me while saying, "I hate you. I hate you. I hate you!" She would try to kick me, punch me or spit on me when I was sitting across the room or taking care of her. By midday I was honest with God and told Him it was hard not to take this personally; it was hard for me to love her. I asked Him to please give me His love for her.

I then felt impressed to hum quietly and then sing a hymn. She looked at me, and I could see her soften. She asked me to sit next to her at her bedside. She then wanted me to hold her hand. She opened up with me and sang a song her mother had often sung to her. As we held hands for the next hour we talked about God and His love. We even sat quietly while God ministered His healing to our hearts. I could have sobbed but did not have a tissue and did not want to let go of her hand. During that hour I also received healing in my own spirit and soul—and love for my patient.

That evening her son came to visit and as he was turning to leave, she called out to him, "I love you!"

He turned back full of surprise, knelt by her wheelchair and said he loved her also. He later told me that he had not heard her say those words for a very long time. I was glad to tell him that she and I had been singing and talking about God that afternoon.

The Word of God does not return void but accomplishes what He desires. Oh, praise God! He is marvelous!

I asked my friend and "older brother" James W. Goll to write out his testimony of what happened when he sang the Word during times of attack from darkness. Through seasons of pain in his body and unyielding grief, one thing pulled him through, and it was singing the Scriptures.

Over the past several years, I have been walking through some rather difficult times in my own personal life. A brief synopsis includes the enduring of nine years of non-Hodgkin lymphoma cancer but eventually by grace beating down that dark foe. But in the midst of my own cancer battle, I ended up becoming a single parent to four kids as my amazing wife lost her hard-fought struggle with cancer herself and graduated to a much better place. My story for some time has sounded more like a whiny country song with the loss of income, strained relationships, lots of misunderstanding and even my dog dying!

I have often been asked, "How did you persevere and not give up?"

Want to know the truth? I had to tell my heart to sing again! I took old hymns filled with the Word of God and sang them loudly over myself. I let songs that point to Scripture—songs like "It Is Well with My Soul," based on the book of Lamentations—wash over me. Singing part and parcel of the Word of God, particularly as it is expressed in old hymns, renewed and refueled me with faith, hope and love.

I sang over and over, "We bring the sacrifice of praise into the house of the Lord!" On and on it went. I would not give up. I sang my way through the valley of the shadow of death (see Psalm 23).

Some sit in the valley and never make it out. I determined to sing my way through the valley and out to the other side. As for me, singing and declaring songs of salvation—songs filled with the "Wonderful Words of Life"—brought comfort and solace to my weary soul. If it worked (and still works) for me, it will work for you also.

Wonderful Words of Life

I remember singing that hymn—the one James refers to—way, way back in the second grade when I lived in Belvue, Kansas, and attended the Methodist Church: "Wonderful Words of Life." When I sang this song, even as a young child, I always thought of the Bible as "the wonderful words of life." I thought of the Scriptures.

Now, many years later, I see how powerful this hymn is and how powerful singing these words is—for that which I sang about in the second grade is literally what I *do* every day. I sing the wonderful words of life.

> Sing them over again to me,
> Wonderful words of Life;
> Let me more of their beauty see,
> Wonderful words of Life.
> Words of life and beauty,
> Teach me faith and duty:
>
> *Refrain:*
> Beautiful words, wonderful words,
> Wonderful words of Life;
> Beautiful words, wonderful words,
> Wonderful words of Life.
>
> Christ, the blessed One, gives to all,
> Wonderful words of Life;
> Sinner, list to the loving call,
> Wonderful words of Life.
> All so freely given,
> Wooing us to heaven:
>
> Sweetly echo the gospel call,
> Wonderful words of Life;
> Offer pardon and peace to all,
> Wonderful words of Life.
> Jesus, only Savior,
> Sanctify forever:
>
> **PHILIP P. BLISS, 1874**

As we come to the end of this chapter, let me encourage you to pick up your Bible, turn to Psalm 13 and sing it. Learn with me; go on this journey with me to personal breakthrough. You have the tools. Try this. Let God's Word flow out in a melody. Then let the Holy Spirit push the Replay button over and over until that Scripture is firmly planted in your heart.

Lord,

> *I thank You for Your Word. Help me to keep Your Word in my heart. When life begins to crash in, like wave after wave, help me remember to sing Your Word. And let the peace of God still my troubled soul as Your words of life arise in my heart and my mind. Jesus, help me to sing.*
> *In Your name, Amen.*

Questions

1. Is there a hymn you sang as a child that still has meaning in your life today?
2. In your life, how have you persevered and not given up? May I ask you, now, to add singing the Scriptures in times when you must persevere? I believe this tool will strengthen your heart.

How-To for Chapter 4

To help you begin practicing what I wrote about in this chapter, please go to www.juliemeyerministries.com/singingthescriptures and search for chapter 4. This short video offers practical instructions for singing the Scriptures.

5

Sing—Make It Personal

Make a joyful noise unto the LORD, all ye lands.
Serve the LORD with gladness: come before his presence with
    singing.
Know ye that the LORD he is God: it is he that hath made us,
    and not we ourselves; we are his people, and the sheep of
    his pasture.
Enter into his gates with thanksgiving, and into his courts
    with praise: be thankful unto him, and bless his name.
For the LORD is good; his mercy is everlasting; and his truth
    endureth to all generations.

PSALM 100 KJV

Psalm 100 is a psalm of praise. The word *praise* here means
"confession or thanksgiving in songs." It is a hymn of confession. And David is instructing us how to enter the presence of

the Lord. He invites us to make a joyful noise with gladness. This word *noise* means "to shout, to raise a sound or cry out, to overcome." We are invited to come into His presence; the word *presence* also means "come before His face, come before His Person" and when we come, come with singing. *Singing* also means "triumphing."

It is as if Psalm 100 is giving us a command to sing when we come before His Person, His face and His presence. They are all one and the same. David is writing down the instructions for entering the presence of the Lord. We are invited to come before the all-wise God, the ever-living God, the transcendent One, and the Creator of the universe; and when we come—come with joyful singing.

Matthew Henry's commentary tells us:

> We must come before his presence with singing, not only songs of joy, but also songs of praise. Enter into his gates with thanksgiving. We must not only comfort ourselves, but glorify God, with our joy, and let him have the praise of that which we have the pleasure of. Be thankful to him and bless his name; that is, 1. We must take it as a favor to be admitted into his service, and give him thanks that we have liberty of access to him, that we have ordinances instituted and opportunity continued of waiting upon God in those ordinances. 2. We must intermix praise and thanksgiving with all our services.

We have access to the King of kings, the omnipresent God, and it is not only for our benefit, meaning we come only when we need deliverance or help; we come also to praise His glorious name because He is good.

We make a joyful song telling God who He is and what He has done. We make a sound declaring His worth because He is great.

This is not something to keep to ourselves; this is something to shout to the earth. And every one of us can do this. Make a joyful noise. Make a singing sound. Sing the Scriptures.

We find a similar invitation in Psalm 33:1–3. David writes: "Rejoice in the LORD, O you righteous! For praise from the upright is beautiful. Praise the LORD with the harp; make melody to Him with an instrument of ten strings. Sing to Him a new song; play skillfully with a shout of joy."

This psalm is also an invitation to *everyone* to praise the Lord. There is a command to praise Him, for He is good. He is kind. He is great and greatly to be praised. Praise Him because He wants all our praise. David goes on to say, "Sing to the Lord a new song," by which he means, sing something new and fresh. Open your mouth and sing from the overflow of your heart because you have seen the goodness of God and encountered His goodness today. Sing to the best of your ability because He is worthy of all your sound, and He is listening to you.

When I looked up *praise* in biblical Hebrew, I found that it means "to boast, to celebrate." I noticed also that it is related to another word, which means *to shine*. What if we pictured *praise* through this lens? When David writes, *Praise the Lord*, I believe he means, "Everyone, boast in the Lord. Celebrate the Lord. Shine forth to the Lord." We shine, which means, "to beam, radiate, gleam, glow, glimmer, sparkle, glisten and shimmer." When we sing the Scriptures and the Word gets within us, it is as if the Word comes alive in our hearts and in our minds, and we actually begin to look and shine like Jesus. Our countenances begin to shine before the Lord and those around us begin to notice. A beautiful picture of this is in the Song of Solomon where the young maidens say of the Shulamite: "Who is this that appears like the dawn, fair as the moon, bright as the sun, majestic as the stars in procession?" (6:10 NIV1978).

As we sing to the Lord, as we celebrate Him and boast in Him, we shine forth as our new song arises. I believe God loves this. God loves the sound of our voices. Have you ever considered that our voices are beautiful to God? That He likes the way we sound, that He listens to every word and melody line? He bends over to hear every tiny sound we make. He hears every chorus, every melody, and He takes great delight in our unique sounds.

In our personal times of devotion or in the middle of public praise services, the God of the entire universe is our fascinated audience. He does not check to see if we are singing on pitch. He does not check to see if we are on the worship team. Over and over there is a cry from heaven of "Let Me hear your voice." He wants to hear our sound. He longs to hear our voices: "My dove in the clefts of the rock, in the hiding places on the mountainside, show me your face, let me hear your voice; for your voice is sweet, and your face is lovely" (Song of Solomon 2:14). And again, "O my darling, lingering in the gardens, your companions are fortunate to hear your voice. Let me hear it, too!" (Song of Solomon 8:13 NLT).

When we go to church, we want the singers on the worship team to be in tune and sound great. If we attend a church that has a choir, we want the choir to sound amazing. That is good. When we buy CDs, we want the singers to sound great with harmonies and vocals. When we go to concerts, we expect that what we came to hear will be beautiful. There is something amazing about a truly gifted musician, one who knows how to bend the tones of his instrument to enhance the music.

But in this book I am talking about a completely different type of singing. This is the singing that we can all do even if we did not make the team, even if the only people who like our singing voices are our mothers—because mothers like everything about their children's singing.

David's Legacy Can Be Our Legacy

Let's take a look at David's life. His life has always inspired me to reach for singing the Word in every season.

Mike Bickle writes this in his book *After God's Own Heart* (Charisma, 2009):

> David was born in Bethlehem, the youngest of eight sons of Jesse and the lowest in rank and privilege in the family structure. In his early years, he became a shepherd. . . . [K]eeping the sheep in that society was not a distinguished occupation. If the family could afford it, they delegated this dirty task to the servants. But in Jesse's family, the job fell to David. So, like other shepherds, he stood around all day on the hard rocks, alone under the hot sun with the sheep as his only companions. We like to imagine David sitting in the shade on the hillside with lush, green grass and sheep gathered around him like fluffy cotton balls. . . . But that's not how the story went. David lived for several years in what amounted to solitary confinement in a desert environment. His flock was small, so he was the only one needed to do the tiresome work (1 Sam 17:28). He was very much alone in harsh terrain. . . . The only portrayal we find of him during this time is of him keeping the sheep (1 Sam 16:11). We might think of him as a gas station attendant or a janitor. His life was filled with menial tasks nobody wanted to do, yet he did them with a spirit of devotion toward the Lord.

Bethlehem is a desert. I have been there, and I have seen it with my own eyes. There is nothing beautiful in the place where David would have been tending the sheep. It was not an oasis of beauty; it was the dry, extremely hot desert.

This is a quote from C. H. Spurgeon when he preached at the Metropolitan Tabernacle, Newington, on a Sunday morning, July 9, 1865.

> He had sung the praises of Jehovah in the wilderness where he had led his flocks, and by the waterside he had tuned his harp and made the rocks echo with the sweet music of his grateful soul. . . . [H]e sang God's praises as the nightingale will sing in the dark when no human ear is listening and no eye is admiring.[1]

In this season of David's life, he did not sit around and sulk because he got the lowest of jobs; instead, he turned his eyes to the Lord. In this place of hiddenness in the harshest of environments, God put within David a heart that would sing, and he began to lift his voice at every opportunity. As we see from the quotes above, no one was near enough to hear except the sheep. But that did not stop him, because he was not singing for others; he was singing to the Lord. He was singing for God, and all his passion was for Him alone. Mike Bickle calls this season in David's life, "singing before the audience of One." This was David's devotional time, and it connected his heart on every level to God.

David sang when no one was listening or watching, and in this place of hiddenness he developed his skills. He developed his skills as a singer, a songwriter, a musician and a warrior. He let every aspect of life move his heart, and we know that David moved the heart of God. David was not entirely alone when tending his sheep. The God of all creation was listening to every song, melody, rhythm, beat—and paying attention to every sound he made.

These songs that David cultivated in hiddenness later became the very thing that got him noticed by King Saul's court when men also began to take note of David. He went from the lowest job, to serving in the king's court as a minstrel before King Saul. When a distressing spirit from God would trouble the king, David would be called to play. Matthew Henry writes that David most likely sang over Saul, too.

> Only his instrumental music with his harp is mentioned in I Samuel 16:16, but it should seem, by the account Josephus gives, that he added vocal music to it, and sung hymns, probably divine hymns, songs of praise, to his harp. David's music was Saul's physic. Music has a natural tendency to compose and exhilarate the mind, when it is disturbed and saddened. Elisha used it for the calming of his spirits.

Sing As David Sang

Throughout my life the thought of David's heart for God and God's heart for David has moved me. God even called David "a man after His own heart" (I Samuel 13:14). David studied and understood the emotions of God's heart, and he ran *to* God instead of *away* from Him. David wrote psalms during every season of his life. He went to war with a song on his lips. In the depths of despair, he was singing. In the midst of a storm, he was praising. Whatever the situation, he sang from his heart to God. Singing to the Lord was David's way of life. It was his conversation with the Lord. It was his heart connecting to the Lord in every season.

David wrote down what he sang, and thousands of years later we are still blessed to be singing his songs. Can you imagine writing down your prayers and songs that people of every nation will sing and pray thousands of years later?

We know from Psalm 1 and Psalm 119 that throughout David's life, he meditated on the Word, on God's commands, the Law of the Lord; so David would have sung from the Torah and whatever books of Scripture he possessed. David began to encourage his own heart through singing the Word.

I decided to adopt David's lifestyle, and I began singing Scripture word for word. For instance, I would sing Psalm 116:1–2: "I love the LORD, because He has heard my voice and my supplications. Because He has inclined His ear to me, therefore I shall call upon Him as long as I live."

Immediately I made a wonderful discovery: Singing Scripture is the easiest and quickest way to remember it. Since then, I have used this exercise around the world in my Prophetic Singing Workshops.

I then began to do for myself during all my personal devotions that which David did. He prayed his prayers through song, and I began to do the same. It helped me remember the Word better. One thing I noticed was that I began to have a new understanding of what I was singing. When we sing the Scriptures, we tend to linger. This is not "fast" reading or simply reading about someone else's life. As I sang through the Psalms or the gospels, I took my time. I turned the words into choruses, and as I sang the words I went suddenly from reading words of Scripture to feeling the Holy Spirit tenderize my heart. I began to experience these words as if they were my very own. Suddenly the Scriptures I was singing become my own heart cry to God.

Singing the Word caused me to linger to the point where Ephesians 1:17–19 began to work in my heart. I call it "the linger factor," for in the lingering the Lord gave the Spirit of wisdom and revelation to my heart. I began to experience and understand Jesus in a deeper way. I had "living understanding" (meaning we understand what we are singing and who we are before Him) for today and deeper knowledge of Jesus, which caused my heart to love Him more and hunger for Him more.

It is a wonderful circle—and each part stirs up the next. Singing the Word is the easiest way to meditate on the Word, to let it nourish and impact the soul.

Sing It, Pray It, Own It

This is an easy way for all of us to learn to sing the Scriptures. It is not complicated, but it is impactful. Let me put into words how I sing the Word. There are basically three ways I like to sing through the Bible. I take one or two Scriptures at a time, and I stay on those two Scriptures for a while. I sing around the house. I sing in my car. I sing in the store. I sing everywhere. Two Scriptures are my total focus, and I simply make up any melody that comes to my mind.

Remember, your ears need to hear your sound. This is what makes the difference. This is not about praying the Scriptures silently or listening to someone else teach or pray the Word; you have to hear the sound of *you* saying and singing these words. There is something about the reality of our voices that greatly impacts our hearts and minds, and we literally begin to own and live out the words we are singing out loud.

As we look at the three ways I sing the Word, let's take one of my favorite Scriptures, Psalm 116: "I love the LORD because he hears my voice and my prayer for mercy. Because he bends down to listen, I will pray as long as I have breath!"

The first time through, I sing the Scripture exactly the way it is written, word for word. It does not matter what translation you use, but use a translation that you understand. Now you need music to go with the words. Make up any melody that comes to mind. If you can hum only two notes, then sing Psalm 116:1–2 to those two notes. If you have a guitar or piano, play simple chords. I like to start with a couple of simple chords and sing my own melody; whatever comes to my mind, I simply sing it out. There are no wrong melodies, and the words are already written out for you. I sing this over and over. One Scripture can last a month. You do not have to move on quickly; in fact, it is better if you do not. Just sing this and linger.

Then I take the same Scripture and turn it into my own prayer. As I am still singing and using a couple of chords, or even without accompaniment, I sing it using my own words as if it is my prayer: Maybe the prayer would go something like this:

Lord, I love You. I know You hear my voice. I know, right now, You are listening. You love the song that I sing. You are not too busy to hear this simple cry and song from my heart. I know that even now You are bending down just to hear my song. You love to hear the sound of my voice. So I will pray, I will sing forever.

The words can change every time. This is what makes Scripture so personal because we are suddenly not just reading or singing about David's heart encounter with the Lord: We are singing about our own. We are not trying to remember a melody—although sometimes we will—it is simply taking the words that David wrote and singing them to God in our own way.

Then I take the same Scripture and sing it as a prophetic word over my heart. I sing the words as if God were singing them over me. *I love this part!* It teaches you to prophesy in song and sing out God's Word over your soul; I even sing out my name so that my heart and mind feel the impact of these words—for right as I am singing, these are *my* cries and these are *my* words. As I set my heart to receive these words as if God were singing over me, it may sound something like this:

Julie, I hear your voice. I hear everything you say. And your voice is very lovely to Me. I love to hear your song each time you sing.

Let me see your face and let Me hear your voice. I created you.
I created you with sounds and melodies in My heart, and I love
it when you sing out. I love to hear your songs. Every time you
sing, I am bending down to hear every word. Not one word is
unnoticed, and not one word is unheard. So sing again and
sing aloud. Let Me hear a fresh new sound, for I love the way I
made you. You are Mine and I am yours.

Every day I have a song in my heart. I am singing God's Word while I am cleaning, cooking, driving. Whatever I am doing, I have that song in my heart with the Word.

Birth Your David

I want to share an amazing dream. During this dream, I felt as if I were alive in King David's day. I saw his passion to be skilled musically and his passion for God's Word.

In the dream I was walking beside King David, and music was everywhere. The sounds of stringed instruments filled every room. The music was beautiful and varied, with many different musical themes and scales. There were rehearsal areas where musicians and singers practiced. The training and polishing was nonstop. The sound in the atmosphere was amazing and filled every hall I walked through. I recognized that these men and women, both young and old, had devoted years to studying their instruments.

The singers and musicians were also studying the written Word—the Torah. There were small rooms where they would study with a teacher. They studied the Law with as much passion as they studied their instruments.

In the dream King David walked from room to room and became involved, as a mentor, in both their study and practice sessions. Study of the Torah, musical lessons and practice sessions continued all day long.

Then in the dream David turned and looked into my eyes and said, "When you have excellence of heart [which I knew referred to the study of God's Word], combined with excellence of skill—you get a David."

Oh, that we would long for God's Word! That we would have His words on our lips. That no matter who we are or what we do in life, we would be skilled in the Word and use the tool that David used: "Sing it."

Oh, Lord,

Thank You for Your beautiful, powerful words that bring life and release hope. Oh, that I would sing Your Word every single day, and that my song would be a blessing to all who are around me! Lord, let my simple singing of the Scriptures change the whole atmosphere around me. Thank You that my simple song combined with Your powerful Word always brings a shift, and it always brings freedom.

In Jesus' name, Amen.

Questions

Before you answer these questions, spend a couple of weeks singing Psalm 116:1–2.

1. Have you ever considered that God loves the sound of your voice?

2. What is your "life verse" that you can begin to sing in the three different ways we discussed in this chapter?

3. As you sang through Psalm 116:1–2, did it make this Scripture more personal to you?

4. Did you have a deeper understanding of God's love for you?

Singing the Scriptures
How-To for Chapter 5

To help you begin practicing what I wrote about in this chapter, please go to www.juliemeyerministries.com/singingthescriptures and search for chapter 5. This short video offers practical instructions for singing the Scriptures.

6

Sing—Get the Word on the Inside

Blessed is the man
Who walks not in the counsel of the ungodly,
    Nor stands in the path of sinners,
    Nor sits in the seat of the scornful;

But his delight is in the law of the Lord,
    And in His law he meditates day and night.

He shall be like a tree
    Planted by the rivers of water,
    That brings forth its fruit in its season,
    Whose leaf also shall not wither;
And whatever he does shall prosper.

PSALM 1:1–3

I still remember the little chorus my Grandma Cook taught me, and I can also remember right where I was when she taught it to me. I was on the swing set on her front patio as she was rocking in her glider and she began to sing:

> A peanut sitting on the railroad track,
> Its heart was all a-flutter.
> Around the bend came number ten—
> Look out, peanut butter!
>
> A bullfrog sitting on a lily pad
> Looking at the sky.
> The lily pad broke and he fell in—
> Got water in his eye.

The fact that I can remember these silly rhymes even now shows the power of a song to stay with us.

A couple of times when my sons had history tests, we would make up a melody to remember all of the people and dates. One son even got a detention for "singing in class." And detentions are never good, but I did ask to keep the slip for his scrapbook. When you are a worship leader who loves to sing, and your child breaks out in song during class—okay, I must admit—it was a proud moment for me. Sing, children, sing. I apologize for that statement if a teacher is reading this; however, any time I heard of my children singing, I was elated.

Why does singing work? Here is another interesting study showing why singing works for learning and remembering words. This research study was conducted by Dr. Katie Overy.

Researchers took 60 adults and randomly split them into three groups of 20. Then they gave the groups three different types of "listen-and-repeat" learning conditions.

Researchers had one group simply speak the words. They had the second group speak the words to a rhythm, or beat. And they asked the third group to sing the words.

All three groups studied words from the Hungarian language for 15 minutes. Then they took part in a series of language tests to see what they remembered.

Why Hungarian, you ask? Researchers said they chose Hungarian because not many people know the language. It does not share any roots with Germanic or Romance languages, such as Italian or Spanish.

After the tests were over, the singers came out on top.

The people who learned these new Hungarian words by singing them showed a higher overall performance. They did the best in four out of five of the tests. They also performed two times better than those who simply learned the words by speaking them.

Dr. Katie Overy supervised the study at the university's Reid School of Music. She says singing could lead to new ways to learning a foreign language. The brain, it seems, likes to remember things when they are contained in a catchy, or memorable, tune.[1]

So my question to you would be, if *singing* is the factor that makes the difference in memorizing and keeping these words in our minds and hearts, why not sing the Word? There are no better words to have in our brains and to have on "repeat."

Let me give you another example. Take brothers Charles and John Wesley. These brothers along with George Whitefield were three voices at the forefront of the Great Awakening throughout Britain and the American colonies in the 1730s and 1740s.

John Wesley was known as a preacher, a theologian and a writer. Charles was known for writing thousands of hymns. Many, such as "O for a Thousand Tongues to Sing," "Jesus, Lover of My Soul," and "Love Divine, All Loves Excelling" are still sung in churches today. The brothers might have realized that people could remember a song more easily and longer than they could remember a sermon.

Charles began composing hymns based on John's sermons. Charles seemed to be stirred as frequently with a new hymn as John was with a new sermon. . . . John had the gift of touching people with God's presence through his sermons and Charles through his hymns.[2]

"John is considered the organizational genius behind the founding of Methodism. But without the hymns of Charles, the Methodist movement might have gone nowhere. As one historian puts it, 'The early Methodists were taught and led as much through [Charles's] hymns as through sermons and [John's] pamphlets.'"[3]

Charles wrote "Hark! the Herald Angels Sing" in 1739, and we still sing this Christmas carol every year, word for word. It is as though this song is implanted in our brains as a Christmas song. I am sure that every person reading this chapter right now can put this book down and sing the first verse of "Hark! the Herald Angels Sing."

Though it was written in 1739, we still sing it—our children even sing it. I actually learned this carol without looking at the music; it was the song we sang at Christmas. Now we want this very same thing to happen with us every day as we sing the Bible.

The point is, songs stay in our heads. As we sing the Scriptures, they can become the prayerful and prophetic words that feed our hearts and minds.

In this chapter we will take the next step. We will learn that the things we focus on and remember affect our everyday lives. Do you want to prosper? Then let's see how singing the Scriptures, keeping them in your thoughts and on your tongue, helps you actually do the things that you are singing about. Let's empower ourselves with the written Word of God. Our guide for this study is Psalm 1.

New Life in Jesus

When I am studying a psalm or portion of Scripture or getting ready to sing it so that it stays in my mind, I love using Strong's concordance, because just as in the English language, we can find several different words to describe the word we are interested in. Using this amazing concordance we have more language to sing as we unwrap the Scriptures and discover new words from the Hebrew and Greek meanings. When we study, sing and meditate on the written Word, we grow in our passion, our love and our knowledge of Jesus Christ. It all points us to Jesus.

John 1:14 tells us that "the Word became flesh and made his dwelling among us. We have seen his glory, the glory of the One and Only, who came from the Father, full of grace and truth" (NIV 1984).

And I love how the New Living Translation says it: "So the Word became human and made his home among us. He was full of unfailing love and faithfulness. And we have seen his glory, the glory of the Father's one and only Son."

When we sing the Scriptures, we are singing about Jesus—who came in human form (see Philippians 2:6–7 NLT), God incarnate, the Word made flesh— it is another way for the Word to be alive on the inside of us. We are also making a way for His living Word to fill us, "for the word of God is living and powerful" (Hebrews 4:12).

We will see that singing this psalm helps us do what it tells us to do. Many believe, in fact, that Psalms 1 and 2 lay out the instructions for reading through the book of Psalms. The very foundation of Psalms is the teaching to get the Word on the inside of each of us. And when we do, then in every minute of the day or every waking moment of the night, our thoughts are invaded on every level with these words of life.

Psalm 1 is an invitation not only to living righteously but also to letting the Word come alive on the inside of us. We become consumed with this Word, longing, craving with a constant hunger for it. When the Word is alive on the inside and we are thinking about it and singing about it, then we actually begin to do as it says.

Now, you ask, what does singing have to do with this passage? Psalm 1 offers the instructions for living a life in God, the complete directions on how to be successful in life and even prosperous. This is the exact reason we want to sing Psalm 1. In fact, the syllabus for "Singing the Scriptures 101" could be Psalm 1 because here David lays out the basic rules of life.

We want these truths to be on our hearts day and night. If you want to remember something, then sing it. It will get in your mind and never leave. In fact, singing can be so powerful that you can sing your song to others, and most likely they will leave singing the very song that you were singing.

Walking Carefully

Verse 1 of Psalm 1 tells us that we are blessed if we do not follow the guidance of those who dishonor God. David Guzik unwraps these words in his commentary on Psalm 1.

> *Blessed* translates the Hebrew word "esher," which has the idea of happiness or contentment. *Esher* comes from the Hebrew word *ashar*, which in its root means "to be straight" or "to be right." *Blessed is the man* speaks of the happiness, the blessedness, the contentment in the life of the man or woman who is right or "straight" with God. The righteous man will be a blessed man, a happy man.[4]

But it is more than just being happy and content. *Blessed* has the meaning of being "supremely happy or fulfilled."

Notice that the psalm shows a progression. If you *walk* in the counsel of the ungodly, or guilty, then you will *stand* in the path of sinners. If you *stand* alongside sinners, then it follows that you will actually *sit* at the seat of the scornful. Those who scorn are those who boast and mock others, who laugh at and make fun of others. It is a horrible thing to be a mocker, to join with those who make fun of and bully others. This is happening all over social media right now with devastating results. High suicide rates are being reported among youths because of the mocking and scorning they endure from media contacts.

There is a counter to ungodliness: We must not walk or stand or sit with the mockers. We must make it our chief aim to be focused on the Law of the Lord, the testimony of God, His beautiful Word.

We find this teaching in the New Testament also. Jesus' words in Matthew 7:13-14 say the very same thing in a different way.

"Enter by the narrow gate; for wide is the gate and broad is the way that leads to destruction, and there are many who go in by it. Because narrow is the gate and difficult is the way which leads to life, and there are few who find it."

Delighting in the Word

There is another reason that David speaks of his love for the Word. He states in Psalm 1:2 that delight comes from this practice of meditating on the Law of the Lord.

That word *delight* means "your pleasure, your purpose, your desire, your longing, that which is most valuable to you." The word *meditate* does not mean just quiet contemplation; it means actually making a sound. According to Strong's concordance, it means "to speak . . . to [make] a sound, like the sound of a harp when struck, the sound of cooing of doves, let your tongue celebrate it, actually roar his Word. . . . We are jealous for this Word. We are fighting for this Word to be ours, to be alive."

This verse gives us completely new insight as to what it means to meditate on the Word. We are to spend time with it, to chew it as a cow chews. I have read that in order to digest its food properly, a cow spends nearly eight hours out of every day chewing its food a second time—chewing its cud. You take the Word and chew it and chew it and chew it.

We find the same thing in the book of Ezekiel: "Moreover He said to me, 'Son of man, eat what you find; eat this scroll, and go, speak to the house of Israel.' So I opened my mouth, and He caused me to eat that scroll" (3:1-2). This kind of meditation on the Word is accomplished as we sing it.

Let's pause here. I want to encourage you to take these verses, make up your own melody and sing them. Watch how they stay in your mind. And then watch how this will remind you to be careful about whom you spend time with and what you are listening to. This is an amazing psalm to get into your mind and never ever let go of. This psalm will keep you on the narrow road. Your delight will come from this meditation on the Word of God.

Why not practice with my paraphrase of Psalm 1:1-3 below?

> Blessed is the one who does not take counsel from the guilty
> But his delight, is in the Word of the Lord
> It's in the Word of the Lord.
> Blessed, happy, supremely content is one who
> Meditates day and night
> Singing it out loud
> Praying it out loud
>
> And this is how we stay on the narrow road
> And this is how we stay on the path of Life

Delighting in Your Word—meditating
Singing it out
Praying it loud
Having conversation with God

The Promise

Reading the Word is totally different from meditating on the Word. If you simply read it, you run the risk of forgetting it. But to sing it is to meditate on it. And then comes the rest of the promise in Psalm 1:3 for living life. The one who walks carefully to stay on the narrow path and who meditates on God's Word can be assured of a wonderful promise: "He shall be like a tree planted by the rivers of water, that brings forth its fruit in its season, whose leaf also shall not wither; and whatever he does shall prosper."

You shall be like a tree with your roots deep in soil right beside rivers of water. These are not stagnant waters but free-flowing clean waters. There is always refreshment. You will never dry up and wither because there is a constant stream of water right beside you. Even in the winter months when there is no fruit on your branches, the roots of the tree are going deeper and deeper and getting stronger and stronger. Even when you cannot see this with the natural eye, you are getting stronger. And you will always bear fruit in season.

The Passion Translation states it like this:

Their pleasure and passion is remaining true to the Word of "I Am," meditating day and night in his true revelation of light. They will be standing firm like a flourishing tree planted by God's design, deeply rooted by the brooks of bliss; bearing fruit in every season of their lives. They are never dry, never fainting.

Then—and this is an amazing promise—whatever you do shall prosper. The word *prosper* means to "break out, succeed, be profitable, make progress, advance and experience prosperity." This is how to live. This is how to stay steady for many, many years. This is how you walk out life and never ever see burnout. You sing this and know this and have it in your heart in every season of life.

I have written out a chorus for you to sing based on Psalm 1. You can practice putting a melody with it. Make it personal. Put yourself in the psalm.

> We shall be like a tree planted by rivers of water
> That brings forth its fruit
> In every season, whose leaf shall not fade away.
> And whatever we do will prosper;
> And whatever we do will bring forth and break out
>
> Feeding our soul on His Word—
> The testimonies of God,
> The Commandments of God—
> By meditating on Your Word,
> Day and night, night and day,
> By meditating on Your Word.
> It's my chief delight.
>
> And whatever we do will prosper;
> And whatever we do will bring life.

The whole purpose of singing Scripture is for your heart and mind to be thinking about it every waking moment. If you sing it, it will stay there. This is something that you will discover as you try this. Give yourself a month—it takes more than just a day. You will see the amazing breakthrough of understanding that comes from having Scripture on your mind and in your heart at all times.

If you want to grow more in singing the Word, I want to invite you to join my online "soaking" community called "Into the River." You can "soak" in the ministry of the Psalms set to music. I offer this because singing the Scriptures has completely changed my life. It has kept me in the river of God and has kept me steady in all seasons. My heart's desire is to teach people how to go deep in God's river—and the way to do this is to *sing the Scriptures.*

Lord,

I pray that every person reading this chapter and reading this book will feel empowered and excited to be on this amazing journey of singing the Scriptures. I pray that You will do for these readers what You did in David's life. I pray that You will give them the spirit of wisdom and revelation so that as they sing, they will know You more and love You more. Help them grasp a clearer understanding of Your Word and of Your love for them.

In Jesus' name, Amen.

Questions

1. What songs can you remember from your childhood or high school days?
2. Can you sing "Hark! the Herald Angels Sing"?
3. Try singing choruses from Psalm 1 in this chapter. Do this every day for two or three weeks and see if you begin to live life differently. Watch as you begin to make wiser choices simply because you are singing Psalm 1.
4. After you answer question 3, ask yourself this: What began to prosper in your life? What breakthrough did you experience?

Singing the Scriptures
How-To for Chapter 6

To help you begin practicing what I wrote about in this chapter, please go to www.juliemeyerministries.com/singingthescriptures and search for chapter 6. This short video offers practical instructions for singing the Scriptures.

7

Sing—The Song of the Steadfast

In the Lord I put my trust;
How can you say to my soul,
"Flee as a bird to your mountain"?
PSALM 11:1

There were many pivotal moments in the life of David, times when singing the Word opened doors of favor—including, as we saw in the last chapter, a call to service in King Saul's court. But singing the Word helped him other times as well, such as when those doors of favor slammed shut. In this chapter we explore another experience with King Saul, and see how the king's envy and jealousy sent David on a path of trusting the Lord and finding God as his only help and defense. We learn this through his song.

Psalm 11 is the writing of a young David. Some commentaries suggest this was written as David began to feel the resentment, bitterness, envy and anger of Saul toward him.

And it happened on the next day that the distressing spirit from God came upon Saul, and he prophesied inside the house. So David played music with his hand, as at other times; but there was a spear in Saul's hand. And Saul cast the spear, for he said, "I will pin David to the wall!" But David escaped his presence twice.

1 Samuel 18:10–11

Apparently, as Saul's mistrust of David and his rage toward David began to surface, those who were closest to David told him to run. He described in this song how he responded to those who pressed him to flee to safety.

"How can you say this to me?" David said. "How can you tell me to fly away like a bird to the mountains?"

They were comparing David to a defenseless bird that was being hunted for the kill. They warned him that the wicked "make ready their arrow on the string, that they may shoot secretly at the upright in heart" (verse 2). They encouraged David *not* to rely on his confidence in God this time; instead they reminded him of the genuine threat on his life.

A Safe Place to Hide

Why did David not run from Saul? We know later in the story, he did flee. In fact, he spent a good portion of his life running from Saul. Did his recent victories in battle help him stand in unwavering faith? Was he remembering the boldness that came upon him as he faced Goliath with a stone and a sling? Was he thinking that God protected him then and believing that God would protect him now?

Spurgeon, in his *Treasury of David*, calls this psalm "the song of the steadfast" and tells us why David might have been insistent on staying put in the face of great danger: "It may be . . . he was advised to flee at a time when this flight would have been charged against him as a breach of duty to the king, or a proof of personal cowardice."

So rather than run David set forth his statement of faith in the first line of his song: "*In the Lord* I put my trust," he declared. "*To Him* I will flee for protection. I have made *God* my refuge."

David began to sing of his faith in God though his friends compared him to a helpless bird. He put into words the complete opposite of himself. He was the one with the steadfast heart. He began to sing of his present state of danger, yet reminded himself that God alone was His hiding place. "Don't they know, Lord, that I have made you my only Hiding Place. Don't they know that I always trust in you?"[1]

David had a fixed resolution to make God his confidence. There was no changing his mind at this point. He was not going to turn and run from the danger. He would stay in his position. He sealed this declaration with a song that affirmed God as the only place of protection he would run to.

As he remembered the greatness of his God, it was as if his heart became even more steadfast.

Yet the Eternal One is never shaken—he is still found in his temple of holiness reigning as Lord and King over all. He is closely watching everything that happens. And with a glance, his eyes examine every heart. For his heavenly rule will prevail over all. . . . But remember this: the Righteous Lord loves what is right and just, and every godly one will come into his presence and gaze upon his face![2]

David was affirming, "God is my safe place. In the midst of danger He is my hiding place. God is watching and He is reigning.

And in *this* place, though being hunted like a bird, if I stay and do not run, this is where I will be in His presence. This is the place where I will gaze upon His face in the middle of this trouble."

Most probably, as David began to sing this song and declare it over his situation, great faith began to arise in him. He stayed because his hiding place was God, and God was there. There was no place to run.

The Word for Today

As we begin to understand this psalm, we can also bring it into our "today." We are not merely learning *about* the psalms that David wrote and sang; we want to use them in the same way David did and sing them in the midst of our circumstances. We want to sing them in the midst of trouble because we know God is our hiding place.

First Peter 1:25 tells us that "the word of the LORD endures forever." This means that the Word of God continues; it remains and it stands present; it is without end. There is also no time limit of strength for the Word of God.

Just as the Scriptures stirred David's heart to believe, so do the Scriptures have power to stir our hearts to believe—and help us overcome our personal fear in times of danger. We find our hearts empowered just as David's was. This breakthrough power is available to each, and it produces the same results.

Let me give you an example of how we can take Scripture and bring it into our lives today.

Sending the Word Out

In September 2015 my husband and I, along with two of our friends, had been traveling in Israel for two weeks. One morning during breakfast we began to talk about our day and the places we would visit. Our first stop would be the Church of St. Anne and our second would be the Pool of Bethesda. Both of these are located near the Lions' Gate in the Muslim Quarter of the Old City of Jerusalem.

A friend of ours who lived in Israel had offered to show us around. After we all piled into a van for the short drive to the Lions' Gate, he began to pray: "Lord, we give this day to You. As we make our plans, we ask that You direct our steps."

Little did I realize that this prayer based on Proverbs 16:9 and singing the Scriptures would have such an impact on our safety in the hours to come.

As we stepped through the Lions' Gate we were met by a group of Israeli Defense Force soldiers. They let us continue on, but the feeling in the atmosphere was quite heavy. There was a sense of great conflict from the religious war between Muslims and Jews. Everyone there was walking in the presence of deep conflict. But *this* morning there was a feeling of danger that I had not experienced before. It was right about then I began to sing a song under my breath from Psalm 11: "I have made You, Lord, my only hiding place. I always trust in You."

We turned a corner and followed our friend through another gate. This gate of solid wood was attached to thick wooden walls that went up maybe twenty feet high, completely surrounding St. Anne's Church and the Pool of Bethesda. We had walked about ten steps past the gate to St. Anne's when suddenly chaos broke out. We heard explosions, yelling and screaming. It was like the sound of the Fourth of July in America with multiple M-80s firing at once.

I had never been that close to such danger. In the midst of my song, I thought, *Am I going to die here?* There was the fear of death right where we were standing. From the sound of the blasts I guessed that the firing was within fifty feet of us. Suddenly, right outside these walls surrounding St. Anne's, a riot started. The cries of *Allahu Akbar* were coming from every direction, anger and fear mixed together within ten feet of us. People were running and screaming.

We were ten feet from a war zone. We could feel the vibrations from the blasts just beyond the tall wooden walls. There was the sound of dirty bombs being thrown from the Temple Mount and stun guns being used by the IDF. Then Israeli soldiers closed the heavy wooden gate, shutting us in.

We could hear the shouts, the cries, the blasts and the firing of stun guns. The five of us were the only ones locked within these walls. Everyone else was on the outside in the middle of the chaos and the rioting.

My mind was going in one hundred different directions yet the song of Psalm 11 remained constant. The theme of strength and confidence played with unwavering certainty in my mind; *I have made You, Lord, my only hiding place. I always trust in You.* The truth of the Scripture I was singing, even though under my breath, began to stir my heart more strongly than the sounds of rioting, shouting, dirty bombs and gun blasts outside the walls. Singing the Scripture actually brought me back to reality: *God is my refuge; God is my hiding place.* It was as if this Scripture took hold of my very being.

I thought, *Our song can shut down this riot.*

I shouted to the others, "We have to worship! Let's get to the sanctuary!" Now I have no idea why we could not just start singing right where we were, but it was as if the Holy Spirit was drawing me to the center of St. Anne's church. I had never been there before, yet I knew to run right through the main doors and right to the center of the sanctuary. It was an empty church with a beautiful sanctuary just waiting for the sound of the human voice to lift up the power of praise.

Not all of us were singers or worship leaders, yet not one of us kept silent. This was not a scheduled worship service; it was not a Sunday morning praise service. This was the frontline of battle and every voice was needed. We literally turned our bodies to the sound of the rioting. We aimed our voices in the direction of the blasts and screaming. We all began to sing a song we knew: "How Great Is Our God!" We sang with all of our might.

Our confidence became our song sung straight in the direction of the riot. We sang loud. We sang strong. We sang of the greatness of God, and we sang of the worthiness of the Lamb from Revelation 5. Our voices singing the Word of God broke through the sounds of stun guns, dirty bombs, screams and blasts.

Somehow in the middle of our worship, as we were declaring who God is from His Word, I knew that the sound was going out past the walls of the sanctuary and past the thick wooden walls surrounding St. Anne's. I believed that this sound of praise as we sang the Scriptures went to the core of the riot.

As we lifted our voices that morning I felt as if I was a soldier in God's army. I felt as if I was carrying a weapon right in my body. The ammunition I fired was the sound of the living Word of God being sung out and declared loudly. I knew that the Word of God going out on the wings of our voices was able to overpower anything.

As we turned toward the sound of chaos, the sound coming from our mouths acted like a big fire hose with the water turned on full blast—putting out the strongest of fires. No one can stand if this hose is pointed in his or her direction. Our bodies were that hose and our sound was the water of the Word that went out and shut down the rage and rioting.

After about twenty minutes of singing, we stopped to listen. There was complete silence. The blasts and the screams had subsided. We all stood in amazement at the power of God's glory sent forth through a song of Scripture.

I give all the credit for the faith that arose in us to singing the Scriptures. Somehow the act of lifting those words in song began to stir up greater faith to believe what we were declaring. It stirred up in us possibly the same thing it stirred up in David when he wrote and sang Psalm 11—for as we sang of the greatness of God, as we sang the Word, fear was replaced by faith.

That morning God invited five worshipers to do what David had done: to lift our voices in praise and sing the Word. David wrote this in Psalm 11: "The godly ones will come into His presence and gaze upon His face." And that is the very thing that happened. We witnessed the power of almighty God at the release of a simple song with powerful words.

I took the words of David from Psalm 11 and put them with my own melody. I wanted a song of remembrance from that morning in Jerusalem, the day God became my hiding place.

> Fly away like a bird
> Fly away in the mountains
> Fly away like a bird
> Fly away, fly away
> Hide away
>
> When darkness and shadows plan to overtake me
> When friends begin to say, "Run away and hide away"
>
> I have made the LORD my only Hiding Place
> He has become my song, in Him alone I'm safe
>
> It's the song of the steadfast one with the steadfast heart
> I'm the one with the steadfast Heart and this is my song.
>
> You are never shaken seated on Your heavenly throne
> Reigning as LORD and King over all

So I lift my eyes to the Lᴏʀᴅ and here is faith
And confidence in times of trouble
Here I see His face

Lord,

I pray that should I find myself weary, help me to lean on Your Word, find strength in Your Word and run to You. You are my help, and with You I am never shaken. Let this be my song. I lift my eyes and look to You.

In Jesus' name, Amen.

Questions

1. Have you ever found yourself in the middle of unexpected danger?
2. What did you do?
3. Has there ever been a time in your life when you felt surrounded by fear and began to sing the Scriptures? What did you experience?
4. Do you think you are ready to try this?

Singing the Scriptures
How-To for Chapter 7

To help you begin practicing what I wrote about in this chapter, please go to www.juliemeyerministries.com/singingthescriptures and search for chapter 7. This short video offers practical instructions for singing the Scriptures.

8

Sing—The Battle Weapon of Song

"Thus says the LORD to you: 'Do not be afraid nor dismayed because of this great multitude, for the battle is not yours, but God's. . . . You will not need to fight in this battle. Position yourselves, stand still and see the salvation of the LORD, who is with you, O Judah and Jerusalem!' Do not fear or be dismayed; tomorrow go out against them, for the LORD is with you."

And Jehoshaphat bowed his head with his face to the ground, and all Judah and the inhabitants of Jerusalem bowed before the LORD, worshiping the LORD. Then the Levites of the children of the Kohathites and of the children of the Korahites stood up to praise the LORD God of Israel with voices loud and high.

So they rose early in the morning and went out into the Wilderness of Tekoa; and as they went out, Jehoshaphat stood and said, "Hear me, O Judah and you inhabitants of

Jerusalem: Believe in the LORD your God, and you shall be established; believe His prophets, and you shall prosper."

And when he had consulted with the people, he appointed those who should sing to the LORD, and who should praise the beauty of holiness, as they went out before the army and were saying: "Praise the LORD, for His mercy endures forever." Now when they began to sing and to praise, the LORD set ambushes against the people of Ammon, Moab, and Mount Seir, who had come against Judah; and they were defeated.

2 Chronicles 20:15–22

~~

In the last chapter I mentioned that a friend of ours who lives in Israel offered to show us around. He is a friend, historian and Bible teacher—and he and his family are simply amazing people who love God, love His people and love the beautiful land of Israel. Every place we were taken was not just part of a tour; it was a history lesson, a Bible lesson and a heart lesson.

I love how he described the community of Tekoa during our visit there. We were told that Amos the shepherd was from that area. *Tekoa* means "the very breath that is expelled from the shofar." As we stood overlooking the valley, we could see in the distance the mountains of Moab and then even farther away the mountains of present-day Amman, the capital of Jordan.

This valley is mentioned in 2 Chronicles 20 as the place where King Jehoshaphat was instructed by prophetic word to go face a great army coming against him.

It happened after this that the people of Moab with the people of Ammon, and others with them besides the Ammonites, came to battle against Jehoshaphat. Then some came and told Jehoshaphat, saying, "A great multitude is coming against you from beyond the sea, from Syria; and they are in Hazazon Tamar" (which is En Gedi).

2 Chronicles 20:1–2

The armies were crossing the desert and following a passageway through the valley, hoping to capture Jerusalem.

Some men saw the armies and went quickly to tell Jehoshaphat of the great multitude coming against him—announcing that the troops were already in En Gedi. En Gedi, which means the "fountain of the goats," is an oasis west of the Dead Sea, a place of running waters; water flows freely twelve months out of the year. It is a very fruitful place where David hid from Saul. The armies were likely storing up water and dates in preparation for the siege against Jerusalem.

This was a dangerous time for Jehoshaphat and his people. The king's response was to proclaim a fast throughout all of Judah as he set his face to seek the Lord. A powerful military force was approaching with the intent of destroying them, yet they took time to seek the Lord. I love that! This is one of those places in the Bible just to ponder. A marching army was headed in their direction with intent to kill the population and take the city, yet still they bowed down. They looked to the Lord. They waited for His instruction. They did not jump into war mode. They did not run into hiding. They bowed low.

As the people assembled in Jerusalem from every town in Judah, Jehoshaphat stood in the front of the courtyard of the Temple and began to pray, seeking God, reminding Him what His Word says. Jehoshaphat lifted his prayer before the Lord saying, "God, we are standing before You. You have given this land to us, the descendants of Abraham. We worship in Your house and in Your presence, so please hear us and help us."

As the armies of Moab with the people of Ammon marched toward them, Jehoshaphat and all of Judah stood before the Lord reminding Him of His promises. They were crying out to God saying, "Lord, if You do not save us, who will? We cannot do this in the natural."

Then the Spirit of the LORD came upon Jahaziel . . . a Levite of the sons of Asaph, in the midst of the assembly. And he said, "Listen, all you of Judah and you inhabitants of Jerusalem, and you, King Jehoshaphat! Thus says the LORD to you; 'Do not be afraid nor dismayed because of this great multitude, for the battle is not yours, but God's. Tomorrow go down against them. They will surely come up by the Ascent of Ziz, and you will find them at the end of the brook before the Wilderness of Jeruel. You will not need to fight in this battle. Position yourselves, stand still and see the salvation of the LORD, who is with you, O Judah and Jerusalem!' Do not fear or be dismayed; tomorrow go out against them, for the LORD is with you."

And Jehoshaphat bowed his head with his face to the ground, and all Judah and the inhabitants of Jerusalem bowed before the LORD, worshiping the LORD.

2 Chronicles 20:14–18

They had been given a prophetic word from the Lord, and now they had to act upon it. They arose early in the morning; they did not tarry. They had heard the word and got up early to obey it. As the men left the safekeeping of Jerusalem and began to march about seven miles south to Tekoa, they could have thought it would be safer staying in the city behind the thick walls. But they did not stay. God had told them to go out from the safety of their houses and meet the enemy head on. They obeyed the word of the Lord.

As they went forth, Jehoshaphat "appointed those who should sing to the LORD, and who should praise the beauty of holiness, as they went out before the army and were saying: 'Praise the LORD, for His mercy endures forever'" (2 Chronicles 20:21).

This is actually mind-boggling. The singers who went out praising the Lord were on the frontlines. They were leading the way. If the enemy began to throw spears, they would be the first ones hit. They were placed at the front between both armies.

But they had the promise of the Lord: "This battle is not yours; it is the Lord's." The singers, most likely Levites, began to lift their voices, marching in front of the multitude, singing their declaration: "Praise the Lord, for His mercy endures forever." They did not carry swords and did not wear heavy armor; their armor was their song and the words were their weapons, bringing a complete victory.

I wonder if they were thinking about the song that Moses and the children of Israel sang after the Lord had delivered them out of Pharaoh's hand: "The LORD is my strength and song, and He has become my salvation; He is my God, and I will praise Him; my father's God, and I will exalt Him. The LORD is a man of war; the LORD is His name" (Exodus 15:2–3).

Was the purpose of the singers singing because God wanted them to understand the all-encompassing power of the song to overtake every emotion? This song that becomes sealed in the brain? They would possibly have sung that song for hours as they headed toward Tekoa. Did their song get louder as they went and more confident? Were they thinking of Joshua when he said, "Be strong and of good courage; do not be afraid, nor be dismayed, *for the LORD your God* is with you wherever you go"? Were they remembering David who also appointed singers to give thanks to the Lord—"for His mercy endureth forever"—as the Ark of God was safe in the tent David had pitched for it?

This is one of those passages one could ponder and ponder; we know only that the weapon of warfare for that battle was their song.

An interesting thing about the valley of En Gedi is that it creates a natural echo. It is possible that as the men approached with their song, the opposing armies heard their voices echoing through the valley and thought more soldiers were approaching than actually were. They did not know what to do, so they somehow turned on themselves and began to kill each other. God had set up ambushes against the people of Ammon, Moab and Mount Seir, and they were defeated.

As the singers lifted their voices with the words, "Praise the Lord, for His mercy endures forever," God did a great work. Perhaps He sent His mighty angels to fight on their behalf. In any event, Jerusalem was victorious that day and the weapon of war was their song echoing through the valley.

When the men of Jerusalem and Judah reached the spot where they would have met the opposing armies head on, all they saw were dead bodies lying all over the ground. Jehoshaphat was able to collect the spoils—more riches and jewels than they could carry away. It took three days for them to gather the plunder.

Then they blessed the Lord and "came to Jerusalem with stringed instruments and harps and trumpets, to the house of the Lord. And the fear of God was on all the kingdoms of those countries when they heard that the Lord had fought against the enemies of Israel" (2 Chronicles 20:28–29).

The Battle Today

My friend brought this biblical experience into present-day reality for our group when he began to describe some of the attacks on Jerusalem that his family has endured. We were particularly moved by their struggles when he told of Saddam Hussein's launching SCUD missiles into central Israel in January 1991, hoping to draw Israel into the war being waged between his Iraqi forces and the Arab and Western coalition opposing him.

My friend said his family and friends had some of their greatest prayer meetings in the midst of that danger. They prayed the Word and sang the Word right in the middle of a war zone. They turned his house into a house of prayer as they cried and sang out to God continually, reminding Him of His Word.

Israel was struck by 42 SCUD missiles during the six weeks of that Gulf War. Because government officials feared that the missiles might contain nerve gas, the residents were given gas masks along with instructions to prepare "sealed rooms" for their protection. The code word for wearing the gas masks was *Nahash Tsefa* ("Viper Snake"), and it was broadcast frequently. Two Israelis were killed by the missiles; dozens of others died from suffocation and heart attacks, a result of the fear and panic. Property damage throughout Israel was extensive.

The prayer meeting in the home of my friend was right in the middle of Jerusalem, and it kept going all through the bombing, all through the sirens, all through the fear and all through the calls of *Nahash Tsefa*. In the midst of alarms giving notice for citizens to put on gas masks, there was also a song rising. As these faithful believers prayed and sang the Word, their hearts were secure. Though there was war on the outside, they experienced peace and safety on the inside.

My friend also told us of his family's experiences in Jerusalem when missiles were launched at the city during the 2014 Gaza War. He said they saw the contrails and "rebuked the devourer" as their house once again became a house of prayer. He explained how the family watched as missiles missed their targets repeatedly and detonated harmlessly in the desert. Other times the family stayed in their shelter (an inner room) and heard the explosions.

He said, "Living in Jerusalem means that you have continual conversation with the Lord, continual prayers for protection and safety, and continual worship from the Word."

As we listened to my friend give this testimony of great deliverance, I looked out into the valley and thought also of David. This was his place of hiding described in 1 Samuel 24. When Saul was informed that David was hiding in En Gedi, he took three thousand of his choice military troops and set out to hunt for David like a bird of prey.

Matthew Henry writes:

[Hearing that David] is in the wilderness of En-gedi, [Saul] draws out 3000 choice men, and goes with them at his feet in pursuit of him upon the rocks of the wild goats. . . . [In a cave, Saul] turned aside to cover his feet, that is, to sleep awhile, it being a cool and quiet place, and very refreshing in the heat of the day; probably he ordered his attendants to march before, reserving only a very few to wait for him at the mouth of the cave.

A. W. Pink, in his *Life of David* (Baker, 1981), writes:

In that section of Palestine there are large caves, partly so by nature, partly so by human labor, for the sheltering of sheep from the heat of the sun; hence we read in the Song of Solomon 1:7 of "where thou makest thy flock to rest at noon." In one of these spacious caverns, David, and some of his men at least, had taken refuge.

As David and his men pressed their bodies against the chilly walls of the cave in hiding, David began to write Psalm 57, possibly singing these very words under his breath, with an audience of One hearing the melody: his beloved Lord. David wrote and sang these words before the deliverance and before the rescue: "My heart, O God, is steadfast, my heart is steadfast; I will sing and make music. Awake, my soul! Awake, harp and lyre! I will awaken the dawn" (verses 7–8).

From Spurgeon's *Treasury of David* we read:

> This . . . is probably that celebrated cave where David with his six hundred followers lay concealed when Saul entered and David cut off the skirt of his robe. The king, accompanied by three thousand followers, chased him to the loftiest alpine heights—"to the sheepcotes," where the cattle were driven in the hottest summer months only—to hunt him in every hiding place. . . . Such caves in Palestine and the East are frequently enlarged by human hands, and so capacious that they accommodate thousands of people. This song of complaint was written during the hours of suspense that David spent there. . . . His life was really suspended by a hair, if Saul or any of his attendants had espied him! *Agustus F. Tholuck.*
>
> It should alarm the wicked that they are contending with a people who sing and shout on the battlefield. Yea, they never sing louder than when most distressed and afflicted. Whether saints conquer or are conquered they still sing on. *William S. Plumer.*

The history lesson for our group on that hot September afternoon was to understand the magnitude of singing the Scriptures. God used the power of singing the Word and delivered His servants from certain death—and He did it over and over again; from David to Jehoshaphat to a modern-day family facing SCUD missile attacks.

We looked out over the vast valley and mountains extending as far as the eye could see. And remembering our own harrowing experience in the Church of St. Anne, we lifted our voices in new words of praise in the very place where the powerful weapon of song had been used to bring about great deliverance.

I will never forget standing there and declaring the praises of God. We prayed that God would pull down the hatred, the evil, the curses, the spirit of murder, the taunting voices appealing to other gods. We asked God to set ambushes again so that good and not evil would prosper. We spoke and prayed and sang His Word back to Him that afternoon as our voices echoed through the valley with the timeless words of Scripture: "Praise the Lord, for His mercy endures forever."

A Shaking and a Song

I had a dream.

> I was standing in the heavens. I began to hear a sound like many melodies, all of which were wafting upward like a fragrance. I saw a mist rising from the earth, and it carried the melodies right up past me to the throne of God. The melodies were beautiful, and beautiful voices were singing in major and minor keys. I was captivated by the sound of the voices.
>
> These voices caught my attention because when I looked down I saw blackness and darkness and confusion. But in the middle—*in the middle of it all*—was the beauty, the sweet perfume of prophetic song rising up.
>
> I heard one song that seemed like a great light in the midst of shaking and darkness; it was refreshing like water in the desert. In the midst of the shaking came direction,

comfort and hope. This was released through the prophetic songs. As I looked down and saw the earth, I noticed that this fragrance began to lift up from every place. It was not coming from just one area; it was rising from every nation. This sweet fragrance, this beautiful sound, had authority in it even as it rose.

The dream shifted and I saw a great army arising. It was the army of Judah and of the Levites—an army of prophetic singers and skilled prophetic musicians standing on the earth to sing a new song to the Lord and to declare His song to the nations. It was powerful. It was loud. It was a new sound; it had authority.

This army was getting ready to be dispatched across the earth. I understood that where darkness abounds, a new song will arise. Instead of hopelessness, fear and destruction, a new song will be sung with the anointing to bring hope, direction and comfort. I saw people in many nations begin to run to this sound, as it was a sound of hope. And *in the midst of the sound*—just as in 2 Chronicles—the Lord was setting ambushes against darkness. The Lord was sending the message through prophetic song that the battle is His; He will fight for us.

Suddenly the dream shifted and I heard a voice declare, *I am getting ready to release the Jehus.* The Jehus are the fearless ones. They are the ones who set their hearts to serve the Lord, and they do not stray. They lay their lives down for the purpose of God's plan—and in that place, they accomplish everything God wants them to do.

The voice continued: *Their weapons will not be weapons that they carry in their hands; their weapons will be their voices. I am going to anoint their voices to speak as one. The breaker is coming upon the voice.* I knew this meant that at the sound of their voices, breakthrough will come. The voices will be the weapons of warfare that will bring about great breakthrough and freedom.

These are the ones who speak in boldness and authority. They do not shrink back but speak with precise wisdom and speak the mind of Christ in authority. Just as Jehu arose in all boldness and zeal to fulfill the will of the Lord, so will these Jehus strike the principalities of darkness and evil. They will not stop until their mission is accomplished.

I noticed that at the sound of the voice, everything seemed to stop. Everything seemed to listen. Nature itself seemed to become quiet and lean into the sound of declaration coming from above. The voice penetrated the very core of my being; it almost made the bones inside my body shake. This is the voice of many waters, the voice that breaks the cedars in two—and He declared that the Jehus are arising.

Your Invitation

Maybe you are reading this right now and feel a stirring of the Lord on the inside. I believe this is the Spirit of the Lord inviting you to be trained in His army—to eat the scroll, to meditate on His Word, to have His Word written upon your heart, to sing His Word, to pray His Word, to memorize His Word. To sing the battle weapon of song to the ends of the earth.

Look at these words from David:

Blessed be the LORD my Rock, who trains my hands for war, and my fingers for battle—my lovingkindness and my fortress, my high tower and my deliverer, my shield and the One in whom I take refuge, who subdues my people under me. . . . I will sing a new song to You, O God; on a harp of ten strings I will sing praises to You.

Psalm 144:1–2, 9

In this psalm David declared that the Lord is a Man of war. The word *rock* is the Hebrew way of expressing strength: The grand old language is full of such suggestive symbols. Here David praised God for training him in the art of war. The Lord was his rock, his teacher and his strength. David was a fighter. He was a man of war. And to a fighting man the education of the hands is of far more value than book learning could ever be; he who has to use a sling or a bow needs suitable hands-on training. In this psalm he shows that "education" extends to the smallest members of our frames: The Lord teaches fingers as well as hands; indeed, it sometimes happens that if the finger is not well trained the whole hand is incapable of activity.

Spurgeon notes there are three qualities of a valiant soldier who serves Christ: boldness in attack, skill in defense and steadiness in conflict.

> Singing of the Word is a weapon. . . . And to those who accept the invitation, God shows up as teacher and trainer. He always leads in a different way, but one thing stands firm in the middle of crisis, when worship starts, when Singing the Word arises, there is salvation, there is healing, and deliverance.

God is inviting you to be part of this great army of Levites that He is raising up. It is in the middle of shaking that the song will begin to arise in great passion, in great beauty and in great authority. We praise the Lord, for His mercy endures forever.

Lord,

Let my voice carry the sound of victory as I sing Your Word.
Let me never keep silent but sing the beauty of Your holiness.
For every battle, let my song from the Word arise declaring Your
truth, declaring the victory.
In Jesus' name, Amen.

Questions

1. Have you ever been in a place where you felt great danger and people looked to you for help in resolving the danger?
2. What did you do? What was your response?
3. Have you ever felt that something you sang or said actually brought peace to a situation that could have been very volatile?

How-To for Chapter 8

To help you begin practicing what I wrote about in this chapter, please go to www.juliemeyerministries.com/singingthescriptures and search for chapter 8. This short video offers practical instructions for singing the Scriptures.

9

Sing—Taking It to the Streets

I waited patiently for the LORD to help me,
 and he turned to me and heard my cry.
He lifted me out of the pit of despair,
 out of the mud and the mire.
He set my feet on solid ground
 and steadied me as I walked along.
He has given me a new song to sing,
 a hymn of praise to our God.
Many will see what he has done and be amazed.
 They will put their trust in the LORD.

PSALM 40:1–3 NLT

This chapter is full of testimonies to encourage you to sing the Scriptures wherever you are. Take a melody and become skilled at this. You will find that you can literally change the atmosphere wherever you go. Your song can be loud or soft, but when you begin to do this you will see change happening.

I want to share about some modern-day Levites who take their instruments as their armor and their songs from the Word as their weapons. Some go alone, some with their families, and some choose to stay and live among the hardest places. But one thing they all carry with them is their song from the Word.

What is so powerful about singing the Scriptures is that it does not just affect you personally; it touches, changes and gets inside of everyone around you. Let me start with two examples of when I joined a team simply to sing the Scriptures at places where the Word is not normally sung.

Singing in a Pub

My husband, Walt, and I have friends in San Diego who have a passion for worship rising on the streets of the Gaslamp Quarter. This is an area with a lot of clubs; young people favor it as a hangout. In San Diego it is the place to be on the weekends.

Our friends approached us about bringing a worship team to San Diego and offering an evening of worship and spontaneous singing of the Word. They wanted to pour out an offering to the Lord for San Diego, so they found a pub in the Gaslamp Quarter that was interested in the idea.

Our friends brought in a couple of worship teams, and we spent the whole evening playing worship music and singing the Word. They also asked some of their friends to come and mingle with the people who might show up that evening and give them words of encouragement.

Now, let me say, it is not in my comfort zone to sing in a pub or bar. But we set our hearts to sing to the Lord and encounter the Lord for the people there. We got a good sound check and simply began to worship and sing psalms to the Lord. People were surprised, but they were actually enjoying it. Not one person I met was angry or mad that we were singing about Jesus. I did not see people leave because they were mad at the worship music; in fact, it was the complete opposite. Everyone really seemed to enjoy it.

The more we sang, the more we noticed changes in people—particularly the people who were sitting at the bar. Several of them who said they had come to drink and forget their problems actually began humming and singing along with us. We had chosen a variety of familiar worship songs, brand-new worship songs and Scripture songs with easy choruses and melodies so anyone who wanted to could sing along. As we sang throughout the evening, we could feel the atmosphere of loneliness and sadness begin to shift; people began to have joy.

Because San Diego has a warm climate most of the time, a lot of the clubs in the Gaslamp Quarter have outside dining areas. Many clubs can open the front of their buildings by a sliding door or window, and these big openings let new customers hear the sound coming from the club. People who were at other clubs began to come over to the "songs with life on them." We had college students come up to us and say, "This is so much better than handing out tracts or preaching sermons on the corner."

Then people began to open up. The team that was mingling and offering words of encouragement engaged in many conversations with young people who said they had grown up in church and had had a relationship with the Lord, but it had slipped away. More than one said, "Tonight made me think about those times." They began to talk of wanting to find a church or Bible study at their college campuses.

That night I saw the Spirit of God begin to touch broken hearts and hard hearts at a bar in a popular pub. It was evident that many people who came inside to block out their hurts for an evening left having thoughts about God and feeling loved. All because we began to worship and sing the Word.

Who would have thought that God would touch so many lost hearts that night? There was no preaching; there were not even any testimonies. But there was the power of the Word going out. And the sound began to touch people in a way no sermon could. The Bible going forth on the vibrations of music began to have its perfect way in the hearts of those who listened.

The worship team had the best seat in the house. We were at the front of the stage simply worshiping the Lord and singing His Word. We saw firsthand each time the Spirit of the Lord seemed to "land" on someone. It was as though the Word we were singing suddenly found its way into their hearts, and dark faces came alive with hope.

I remember at one point catching the eye of a young woman sitting at the bar. I began to sing the Word over her, though she was not aware of it. I sang something like, "The Lord is your strength and your hope. He will be your song in the night, your champion and your friend in this life."

I shall never forget watching as hope entered her heart and light came into her eyes. I did not know her and she did not know me, but the words I began to sing were the words she needed to hear. Those verses set to music made their way into her heart.

We all saw hope come alive in the people there that night. It was not the singers who made it successful, nor the band; it was the power of worship, simply singing the Scriptures. All night I picked out different people and sang the words of life straight at them, and I watched the same thing happen over and over again.

Oh, the night that hope found its way into hopeless hearts! Many people were prayed for and encouraged because a small group of worshipers went into an unlikely place to fight darkness with our weapons of warfare—our voices and the Word.

Come and Dine!

The next year our friends wanted to bless people again at a particular restaurant, also in the Gaslamp Quarter. The restaurant was known for its great food and live music. It seemed like a perfect location.

Our friends asked the manager if they could provide music for one evening and also "buy out" the club, purchasing three hundred meals for anyone who came in. The management was quite surprised because this had never been done before and gladly said yes. They prepared an amazing buffet to serve that night.

When the night came, a whole group of our new friends got together and went up and down the streets of the Gaslamp inviting people to come. They said, "We are celebrating the goodness of God, and we want to invite you for a free meal."

Some of God's favorite people were just waiting for an invitation: the homeless. Those on street corners, those sleeping under tarps, those carrying all of their belongings in a grocery cart said yes. And the beautiful restaurant was filled mostly with the poor.

As I watched, a number of regular diners from the business world came into the restaurant. Though surprised at first at the offer of a free meal, they soon joined the homeless in the buffet line. Two different groups of people who would normally not be eating together—the wealthy and the poor—were gathered in the same room sharing the same meal. Men and women dressed in their business suits were sitting right alongside the homeless and the poor.

It seriously looked just like the wedding feast of Matthew 22:2-3, 9-10.

> "The kingdom of heaven is like a certain king who arranged a marriage for his son, and sent out his servants to call those who were invited to the wedding; and they were not

willing to come. . . . [The king said,] 'Therefore go into the highways, and as many as you find, invite to the wedding.' So those servants went out into the highways and gathered together all whom they found, both bad and good. And the wedding hall was filled with guests.'"

Every worship team singing that night combined songs of worship with songs of Scripture. And the Word went forth on the winds of sound touching every heart. We were simply doing what Ephesians 5:19 asks us to do—"speaking to one another in psalms and hymns and spiritual songs, singing and making melody in your heart to the Lord." We were singing to each person the powerful truth of the Word.

I am not one who gets emotional, but that night as I watched people piling their plates with food, it was hard to hold the tears back as I watched peace, joy and calmness take over the room.

I saw faces of fear, faces of anger, faces of agitation melt into expressions of peace as Scripture settled in their hearts. Their stomachs were full, but so were their spirits. The door was opened for many to begin to tell their stories and get prayer.

We were doing what King David wrote about in Psalm 40. He wrote of singing a new song: "He has put a new song in my mouth—praise to our God; many will see it and fear, and will trust in the LORD" (verse 3). David apparently experienced the glory of God touching people as he sang and worshiped with new songs. When the presence of God fills the atmosphere, people can feel and see that something good and new is happening. It makes them crave more of it.

As we played and sang to the Lord, people sitting and talking at the bar and the tables began to quiet down. Some began to listen intently. At one point as I began to sing the Word that was in my heart, an amazing chorus began to unfold. Our family band picked up the chords, and one of my favorite songs, "Alabaster Box," was written.

Only heaven knows all the miracles that happened that night. Our friends who mingled with the "guests" were the real worker bees in this story for, as the worship went forth and the Scriptures were sung, they walked around hearing testimonies, encouraging everyone and praying for people all night long. Every one of us who came to help with the ministry surely remembers that night as being remarkable.

What also is amazing is the way the restaurant staff remember it. They began to refer to it as "the miracle night." They said it was the only night they could remember without various problems at the bar or the tables. The staff said they called it "the miracle night" because they always had arguments and spats, but that night they did not. There was peace in every corner of the building. It was as though a cloud of peace came over everyone.

Psalm 22:3 tells us that God dwells in the praises of His people. You could say that God showed up to hang out with His people, the wealthy and the poor side by side in unity that night. The Scriptures went out through song, landing in many hearts. Jesus was the good Shepherd who went out of His way to go after the "one" lost sheep. That night a whole lot were found. And they were filled in spirit and in body.

It truly was a miracle night.

Worship 24/7

In May 1999 Mike Bickle founded the International House of Prayer–KC, which is dedicated to outreach, prayer and fasting. It is a 24/7 worship and prayer missions base. It began with intercessors and worship teams praying and singing the Word together thirteen hours a day. Just a few months later, it became the 24/7 base for worship and prayer that it is today.

I was blessed to be a part of this ministry as a worship leader and prophetic singer from the first day the doors opened. One of the principles for the House of Prayer is praying and singing from the Word. During our intercession sets, we would invite people to come up and pray straight from Scripture, the very language of God's heart, as we interceded for cities and nations.

It is Mike Bickle's passion that every singer, musician and intercessor know the Word, love the Word, sing the Word and pray the Word. I learned that as you sing the Word, you remember it. It gets on the inside, and you start to believe it. The Word makes an entrance into your heart and actually takes up residence there. The Word becomes more than a passing thought in your mind; this Word that you sing every day is alive and directing you from the inside.

We began to call IHOPKC the "Singing Seminary," for the more we sang the Scriptures and prayed the Word, the more these Scriptures began to consume every thing we did, every decision we made. The Word began to invade every single part of our lives because that is what the Word does.

I wanted to show you the heart of the International House of Prayer–KC because God has begun to raise up thousands of prayer ministries all over the world, and many have moved outside the walls of their buildings. We began to see prayer ministries and Houses of Prayer go into the dark places of the world where great tragedies had happened; people began taking the House of Prayer to the streets. There are thousands of prayer ministries in the earth all using the same foundation of praying and singing the Word.

Sean Malone is one of those people. His ministry, called Crisis Response International, goes right in with the Red Cross and the

Federal Emergency Management Agency (FEMA) to cities facing devastation. Several years ago Sean began to set up a mobile House of Prayer. He has many testimonies of response workers going into the prayer tent and being ministered to simply by listening to someone sing the Scriptures. Singing the Scriptures is for personal breakthrough, but now God is using this tool across the world to make room for His light and truth to break in.

Singing the Word in Africa

Three years ago I traveled to Pemba, a port city in Mozambique. I went to work with Heidi Baker at Iris Global and "love on" all of the amazing children she has in her "Village of Joy," the Pemba base for Iris Global. The Village of Joy is home to many programs, including Mercy Ministries, which supports a large number of women and their families. These women are either widowed or abandoned single moms facing the challenge to sustain their families of three to eight children on their own. They live in mud huts with no means of support. Iris aims to meet one of their biggest needs by supplying their families with one meal a day.

On Thursdays and Fridays, the Bakers or some of their staff go deep into what Heidi calls the "bush bush," not only to take food but also to preach the Gospel of Christ and to heal the sick.

Every outreach begins by showing the *Jesus Film*. Many of these villagers have never seen a movie, so when the lights go on and the movie starts, the whole village shows up. The Iris team shows the *Jesus Film* in the local dialect of each village, so every tribe not only sees a movie but hears it in their own tongue.

When we went to the bush bush on this trip, we had to take the Iris plane to reach a particularly isolated village. We landed and began to set up camp. Heidi always puts the movie on first thing, and then when the movie is at the part where Jesus is hanging on the cross, she stops the movie and begins to preach the Gospel. Generally this is well received. This night, however, when the movie was paused and Heidi started to share the Word, the crowd turned angry. It was clear they wanted to see the movie. I did not know their language, but I could tell by their faces they were not happy that the movie had been shut off.

Then to build more tension that night, the electricity going to the movie would not turn back on. Someone yelled, "Start the worship!" Jason Lee Jones, a powerful worship leader, was trying to get the keyboard set up and working, but there was no electricity going to the keyboard either. You could feel the tension mounting.

Well, it got worse and worse. I was almost panicking. Now, I knew from my last visit to Pemba that when villagers get angry, their first response can be throwing rocks at you. So this situation needed to be resolved quickly. I was feeling, *This is not good.* I thought, *Hurry, hurry!*

I was expecting someone to step up and make everything okay; I never thought that God might be considering me. My head swiveled back and forth between Heidi, Jason and the guys working frantically with the generator and the sound system. The villagers were getting angrier by the minute.

I looked around thinking, *Who is going to help now?*

I turned toward Heidi, who had the only working microphone in her hand. She pushed it right into my face, her eyes locking with my eyes, and with great authority she said, "Sing!" It was not a suggestion; it was a command.

In that moment there was no time to think. There was only time to sing.

I took that mic, and I began to sing the only song I knew in Portuguese, thinking there might be a similarity of language. I sang with all my heart there in the middle of the bush bush with a very angry, frustrated group of people.

I sang from Psalm 86: *Obrigado, Senhor. Aleluia.* Which in English is, "Thank You, Lord. I will praise You."

I sang this over and over until I heard the generator's supply of power to the keyboard begin to work. Jason jumped in and began to worship from the keyboard. We continued to sing *Aleluia* over and over.

And somewhere in the middle of singing that Scripture over and over—because it was the only song I knew to sing—the Spirit of God began to defuse the volatile atmosphere. Peace and calmness came upon the crowd.

I never thought I would be in a situation like that. But I did witness firsthand the powerful tool of singing the Word. I did not need a lot of verses; I needed only those three words and the angry crowd turned into a singing crowd. Finally the generator's supply of power to the movie began to work again, and the crowd turned its attention to the message.

Then before Heidi got up to share the Gospel, Jason began to sing in their own tribal language the parables of Jesus. He was telling the stories of Jesus through song. It was as if he was a singing preacher in the middle of the bush bush, declaring who Jesus is through singing the Scriptures. There was a hush upon every person there. He set up a perfect ramp for Heidi to come and preach the Gospel in power.

That night in the bush bush singing the Scriptures saved the day. And anyone could have done what I did. With Heidi's direction to sing—well, sing I did. And as I sang Scripture, peace descended on us all and doors for the Gospel to go out were opened.

There were many, many baptisms the next day.

Obrigado, Senho. Aleluia.

That became the theme song of our trip. And I was truly thankful to the Lord, and I did wholeheartedly want to praise Him. It was a personal lesson in the power of God to release peace in the midst of turmoil.

God had a remedy, and it was three words from the Bible set to music.

"Meet Me in Ferguson"

I first met Jonathan Tremaine Thomas—many call him J. T.—at a conference in Kansas City several years ago. J. T. has a passionate heart for spiritual awakening in the black community. The cry of J. T.'s heart was answered in a way he had not expected when one day, after fasting and praying, he heard the Lord say, *I am going to Ferguson. Meet me there.*

I share this story as an example of how singing the Scriptures had a positive effect in an American city—and the same influence would be evident in any given situation where a need might arise anywhere in the world. Though there has been a raft of similar incidents since this one I am about to relay, this one struck a fiery spark of renewed racial unrest in the United States.

Michael Brown, an unarmed black teenager, was shot and killed on August 9, 2014, by Darren Wilson, a white police officer, in Ferguson, Missouri, a suburb of St. Louis. The shooting prompted protests that roiled through the area for weeks. After a grand jury decided not to indict Officer Wilson, tension escalated.

When J. T. arrived in Ferguson, he was shocked to see armored tanks patrolling the streets; it looked like a war zone. Along with the military presence, he saw worldwide media attention and various ideological groups such as the New Communists Revolutionary Guard and the Muslim Brotherhood, along with many others. Everyone was descending upon this city with various agendas, and they actually had camps set up in the city. The FBI and all the different governmental agencies had tent cities.

J. T. walked around looking at all these camps and began to say, "Where is the camp of the Lord?" He quickly joined other prayer warriors in a 21-day fast for the region.

He told me, "We felt an invitation from the Lord to create a 'couch' in Ferguson for Him to come and sit upon." So they rented a former Kentucky Fried Chicken building that had closed down and turned it into Healing Rooms and a House of Prayer. Then they pitched a three-hundred-person tent in the parking lot behind the building.

The urgent need for prayer was evident among Christians living in Ferguson. Soon close to eighty churches had partnered together to offer worship and intercession in the tent for ten to twelve hours a day, every day. They prayed the Word, sang the Word and then went out and shared the Word.

The days passed but tension did not lessen. October 22 was declared "a night of resistance against police brutality" with eight hundred protestors from all over the world taking part. They planned to march from the street where Michael Brown was killed to the police department. J. T. told me that activism in and of itself is not sinister, but there were anarchistic agendas and ideological factions embedded within the activism that had great impact on the spirit of the demonstration.

As the angry activists marched toward them, forty people— J. T., area pastors and mature intercessors—took their posts in front of the police station, which was *in between* the police and the arriving protestors. And they prayed. There was one guy playing a djembe and one guy playing an acoustic guitar, and the other 38 people stood with their Bibles, praying. All the while, worshipers in the tent, the House of Prayer, were singing the Word and praying the Word.

J. T. was declaring and praying verses from Isaiah 42, that God would bring justice to the nation, when suddenly he heard the protestors approaching. A number were carrying weapons. They were chanting:

No justice, no peace! No racist police!
Mike Brown means we shut **** down!

Then God answered the prayers being offered to Him. The forty worshipers saw something like an Old Testament manifestation of His glory. As the angry crowd came to the forty worshipers standing in front of the police, it was as though a cloud of confusion came upon them. Suddenly, the chant broke up and everyone looked confused.

Then the chant leader came up to J. T., completely livid, and said, "I know you all are out here trying to pray, but not everyone out here is Christian." He said, "You are either for us or against us. Whose side are you on?"

J. T. answered, "We are on the side of Jesus. We are on the side of the Lamb. We are not on your side. We are not on the police side."

"No," the man said. "You can't be in the middle; you have to choose a side."

J. T. then replied, "We are on the side of righteousness."

J. T. told me, "Another chant leader who had a megaphone kept trying to start another chant, but nothing would take. It was as if no one could hear her. So she stopped and handed her megaphone to *me*! Stunned, I took the megaphone and began to chant:

"There is no justice without Jesus,
The police need Jesus;
We need Jesus.
Turn your life over; He's the One who frees us!"

The moment J. T. said the name *Jesus*, more than half the crowd turned around and ran in every direction. And the rest of the people were paralyzed and could not move.

He said those words came by the Spirit, and it turned into a prophetic rap—as if the Lord released a chant.

"Meanwhile," J. T. said, "we began to witness the power of God falling upon individuals. Person after person began to respond to the manifest presence of God. Even officers in their riot gear were moved by what they were witnessing. Without any human interaction, people were getting delivered from rage and bitterness, and they were beholding Jesus.

"Meanwhile," he added, "many of the folks who ran from us ran up the street directly into the Healing Rooms and House of Prayer tent only to be greeted by the power of God. Many were saved, delivered and experienced the love of Jesus.

"From that night on," J. T. said, "we gained a reputation as 'the Jesus people.'"

Reports after that night confirmed the work of God.

"There were miraculous healings and deliverances, a couple of major protests were turned into prayer meetings, a few violent situations were defused through supernatural intervention . . . ," says Pastor Jeff Riddering.[1]

"An unlikely coalition of conservatives and liberals is coming together in a way that only God can orchestrate," said [civil-rights activist Dr. Alveda] King, niece of . . . the Rev. Dr. Martin Luther King Jr.[2]

The City of Ferguson has commended the "Jesus People" for their efforts and said, "We don't know what you're doing, but when you do it the atmosphere changes . . . thank you!" The Missouri Highway Patrol offered their thanks as well."[3]

God's hand came upon Ferguson. Since that time J. T. Thomas has been keeping the fire on the altar burning, keeping worship and prayer going, and carrying the ministry and message of reconciliation forward.

When we sing the Word and pray the Word, there is always a response from heaven. God breaks in powerfully when we simply show up and begin to sing the Scriptures. "He lifted me out of the pit of despair, out of the mud and the mire. He set my feet on solid ground and steadied me as I walked along."

Lord,

I pray that You will raise up many, many modern-day Levites. Strengthen the ones who are already out there on the front lines, strengthen them with Your Word. Help them to sing Your Word—and as they do, Lord, break in powerfully. I ask that as Your Word goes forth, a mighty move of God will arise in the earth. We say, "Yes, Lord!" We will meet You anywhere, and we will follow You everywhere.

In Jesus' name, Amen.

Questions

1. Are you familiar with Psalm 40?
2. Can you remember a time when you felt the Lord lift you out of the pit of despair?
3. Were you ever in danger or in great emotional stress and God put a new song in your mouth?
4. Can you take Psalm 40:3 and memorize it by putting this Scripture with your own melody?

Singing the Scriptures
How-To for Chapter 9

To help you begin practicing what I wrote about in this chapter, please go to www.juliemeyerministries.com/singingthescriptures and search for chapter 9. This short video offers practical instructions for singing the Scriptures.

10

God Sings, Creation Sings—It Is Time for You to Join In

> The Lord your God in your midst,
> The Mighty One, will save;
> He will rejoice over you with gladness,
> He will quiet you with His love,
> He will rejoice over you with singing.
>
> **ZEPHANIAH 3:17**

I want you to have a big picture in your mind of our big, big God singing over you. And not just singing over you, but twirling with all of the strength of Himself. This is the awesome God that we serve.

We know from Zephaniah 3 that God sings over us. And the word *sings* in this verse is actually *singing*. He is singing with a melody over you and over me. He is the glad-hearted singing God.

When you sing the Scriptures, I pray that you have a picture in your mind of God singing right back to you. He is not only listening but also singing over you. Oh, what an amazing God who takes so much delight in us that He sings!

We need this picture of God in our minds. This is what actually helps us step out of great brokenness: that in our weakness and in our addictions and in our failures, this is our testimony. God is singing over us because He loves us, and He will get us to the place we need to be. This is the glory of our amazing God. We must know and believe that right where we are, He loves us. This is a perfect picture of the passion that God has for us. David says this another way in Psalm 18:19: You deliver me *because* You delight in me.

God sings over us. He loves us all through the brokenness, all through our weakness, and He delights to save us and set us free. I promise you that if you will find yourself in the storyline of the Book, you will get free from whatever is tripping you up because God will demand it. He will demand in His twirls and songs that darkness let you go. When we are weak, He clothes us with *His* amazing strength, and then we are strong together. The passion of His twirls around us reveals this very thing.

> What kind of beautiful God gives beauty for ashes?
> What kind of beautiful God gives joy for mourning?
> What kind of beautiful God loves dancing and singing?
> What kind of beautiful God delights over me . . . ?

Zephaniah takes this one step further and declares, "He is singing, yes . . . He sings over us. He does not, however, just sit and sing. He actually gets up and then He begins to dance around us, *spinning around us like a top*."

This is beautiful. We are singing to God and God sings right back to us, but His song goes through us; His song is all around us. And God dances; He spins all around us.

When we unwrap this Scripture—and I love using the Strong's online version—it gives even more language for us to see in our minds and to sing. It helps us see this with the eyes of our hearts and sing right back to God.

Strong's begins to unwrap the words in Zephaniah 3 as:

> For the Lord, The Self-Existent One, The Eternal, Jehovah, He is among us, He is within us, He is right in the middle, and He is Mighty, He is Strong, He is valiant. He is the Champion. He is the Chief. He is the mightiest. He is the strongest.

Oh, I just want to stop writing right now and start singing! This is how we get the amazing truth of who God is and how He feels about us into our hearts and minds. We sing every word. I encourage you right now, as you are reading, just take some time and sing this out with your own melody. Sing who He is, and then sing it over and over. Oh, you will hunger for more if you will sing all that He is!

> He will save. He is a Savior. He will deliver me. He will help me. He will avenge me. He will rescue me. He will keep me safe and He will give me victory. And He will rejoice, He will show His joy over me. He will greatly be glad. He will have joy over me—and not just a little joy, but great joy.
> He will give us peace. He will keep us. He will show us His love. His passionate fiery love; He will be glad and rejoice over me with singing.
> He will shout over me. He will have a proclamation of joy over me. He will sing songs over me.

Strong's tells us that the word *joy* here means "to spin round (under the influence of any violent emotion)."

God has great emotion for us. He is not stoic. He is not uncaring. He is passion. If passion looked like something, it would look like God. He sent His only Son, *His only Son*—we need to grasp this love our Father has for us. He sent Jesus, His only Son, because He loved the world. This is how much He loves us, and this is the passion that He sings with and that He dances around us with. He is passionate. He is passionate that we be free.

I love what the Matthew Henry commentary says about this Scripture:

> Thou hast ravished my heart, my sister, my spouse, with one of thy eyes . . . The great God not only loves his saints, but he loves to love them, is pleased that he has pitched upon these objects of his love. [This means: He sings over them—that is the "pitch."] He will joy over them with singing. He that is grieved for the sin of sinners rejoices in the graces and services of the saints, and is ready to express that joy by singing over them.

The last line of this Scripture is amazing. He will joy over you with singing. He will *joy* over you; that actually means, "He will *spin* around you. He will dance around you like a spinning top."

He will joy over you with singing. Think of the great Jehovah singing! Can you imagine it? The commentary continues:

> Is it possible to conceive of the Deity breaking into a song: Father, Son and Holy Ghost together singing over the redeemed? God is so happy in the love He bears for His people that He breaks the eternal silence, and sun and moon and stars with astonishment hear God chanting a hymn of joy. Here, by the pen of inspiration, the God of love is pictured

as married to His Church, and so rejoicing in her that He rejoices over her with singing. If God sings, shall not we sing? Here He spent eternal thought, and drew up a covenant with infinite wisdom. Here He gave His Only-begotten Son, and put Him to grief to ransom His beloved ones. When all was done, and the Lord saw what became of it in the salvation of His redeemed, then He rejoiced after a divine manner. What must the joy be which recompenses Gethsemane and Calvary! "He shall rejoice over thee with singing."

Oh, but there is more! Creation sings, the heavens sing, all of the earth sings. If all of the earth is singing, should not we join in the celestial chorus? Do you know that the stars actually sing? We have it in the Word in Job 38:4–7 as God begins to talk to Job.

"Where were you when I laid the foundations of the earth? Tell Me, if you have understanding. Who determined its measurements? Surely you know! Or who stretched the line upon it? To what were its foundations fastened? Or who laid its cornerstone, when the morning stars sang together, and all the sons of God shouted for joy?"

God is telling Job that the morning stars sang together and shouted for joy when the foundations of the earth were laid. Now, with the scientific information NASA gives us, we are finding out that stars actually do "sing." They are making a sound, a vibration. (To learn more about this, I encourage you to go to YouTube and view "Louie Giglio Mashup of Stars and Whales Singing God's Praise." I think you will enjoy listening to this over and over.)

We see this again in Psalm 148:1–5:

Praise the LORD! Praise the LORD from the heavens; praise Him in the heights! Praise Him, all His angels; praise Him, all His hosts! Praise Him, sun and moon; praise Him, all stars of light! Praise Him, highest heavens, and the waters that are above the heavens! Let them praise the name of the LORD.

NASB

We need to join in. We need to join in this great chorus of praise because God is so amazing, and He is singing right back. All creation is singing. God is singing. The stars are singing. The sun is singing. Space is singing. The moon is singing. Why are we not singing? Children are singing. The whole of creation, the deep-sea creatures are singing—they are lifting up their sound. Why are we not singing? It all comes together in Psalm 150: "Let everything that has breath praise the LORD. Praise the LORD!" (verse 6).

We have a command here to sing. Could it be that the very foundation of the earth started with a song? Many believe that when the Word spoke at the beginning of time He actually sang.

Oh, reader, I ask you, I ask you to sing through the Scriptures in this chapter. Take any melody you want—there is no wrong melody—and begin to sing Zephaniah 3:17 and Psalm 148.

Oh, my friend, let's try this. Let's do this. If God is singing, and creation is singing and the deep-sea creatures are singing and David sang and Paul told us to sing—then we actually need to sing. Sing on the way to work. Sing at Walmart. Sing at home.

I think of that old song, "Ain't gonna let no rocks out-praise me!"

Beloved—it is time to sing. . . .

Oh, Lord,

I pray that You will stir in every single heart the joy, the freedom of singing Your praise. Holy Spirit, remind each reader every single minute to sing the Scriptures. Remind all of us that You sing, too, God. You sing, too. Remind us that the universe is singing. God, You created everything with sound. Jesus, help us to make a sound back. Help us to sing Your Scriptures— help us to sing as the stars sing, the moon sings, all of heaven sings. Thank You, Jesus, for revealing Yourself to the human heart through something as easy as singing the Word. Remind us every day to sing the Scriptures.

In Jesus' name, Amen.

Questions

1. Have you ever thought about and pondered Zephaniah 3:17?
2. Have you ever felt that God is mostly mad at you? Or mostly delighted with you?
3. List three Scriptures showing that God is for you.
4. Will you take the Scriptures and sing them over your heart for the next month and write down the results?

Singing the Scriptures

How-To for Chapter 10

To help you begin practicing what I wrote about in this chapter, please go to www.juliemeyerministries.com/singingthescriptures and search for chapter 10. This short video offers practical instructions for singing the Scriptures.

APPENDIX

Here are forty Scriptures to help you jumpstart this new adventure of singing the Word. We start with the Psalms, as it is easier to sing from the Psalms because they are already written as songs. You want to find Scriptures that you can sing "to" God and not just "about" God. This makes singing the Scriptures even more personal. I have included here Scriptures from both Old and New Testaments. There are promises, prayers, Scriptures that declare who Jesus is, and Scriptures about how we should live. Some of them are a little long, but, oh, what glorious words to come alive on the inside!

> But you, O Lord, are a shield around me; you are my glory, the one who holds my head high. I cried out to the Lord, and he answered me from his holy mountain. I lay down and slept, yet I woke up in safety, for the Lord was watching over me.
>
> Psalm 3:3–5 NLT

God is my shield, saving those whose hearts are true and right. . . . I will thank the LORD because he is just; I will sing praise to the name of the LORD Most High.

Psalm 7:10, 17 NLT

O LORD, our Lord, your majestic name fills the earth! Your glory is higher than the heavens. . . . When I look at the night sky and see the work of your fingers—the moon and the stars you set in place . . . O LORD, our Lord, your majestic name fills the earth!

Psalm 8:1, 3, 9 NLT

I will praise you, LORD, with all my heart; I will tell of all the marvelous things you have done. I will be filled with joy because of you. I will sing praises to your name, O Most High.

Psalm 9:1–2 NLT

I trust in your unfailing love. I will rejoice because you have rescued me. I will sing to the LORD because he is good to me.

Psalm 13:5–6 NLT

Keep me safe, O God, for I have come to you for refuge. . . . I will bless the LORD who guides me; even at night my heart instructs me. I know the LORD is always with me. I will not be shaken, for he is right beside me.

Psalm 16:1, 7–8 NLT

The LORD is my shepherd; I have all that I need. He lets me rest in green meadows; he leads me beside peaceful streams. He renews my strength. . . . Even when I walk through the darkest valley, I will not be afraid, for you are close beside me.

Psalm 23:1–4 NLT

The LORD is my light and my salvation; whom shall I fear? The LORD is the strength of my life; of whom shall I be afraid?

Psalm 27:1

I waited patiently for the LORD; and He inclined to me, and heard my cry. He also brought me up out of a horrible pit, out of the miry clay, and set my feet upon a rock, and established my steps. He has put a new song in my mouth—praise to our God; many will see it and fear, and will trust in the LORD.

Psalm 40:1-3

God is our refuge and strength, always ready to help in times of trouble. . . . "Be still, and know that I am God! I will be honored by every nation. I will be honored throughout the world." The LORD of Heaven's Armies is here among us; the God of Israel is our fortress.

Psalm 46:1, 10-11 NLT

Have mercy on me, O God, because of your unfailing love. Because of your great compassion, blot out the stain of my sins. Wash me clean from my guilt. Purify me from my sin. . . . Restore to me the joy of your salvation, and make me willing to obey you.

Psalm 51:1-2, 12 NLT

When I am afraid, I will put my trust in you. I praise God for what he has promised. I trust in God, so why should I be afraid? What can mere mortals do to me? You keep track of all my sorrows. You have collected all my tears in your bottle. You have recorded each one in your book.

Psalm 56:3-4, 8 NLT

O God, You are my God. . . . My soul thirsts for You; my flesh longs for You in a dry and thirsty land where there is no water. . . . Because Your lovingkindness is better than life, my lips shall praise You. Thus I will bless You while I live; I will lift up my hands in Your name.

Psalm 63:1, 3–4

A day in Your courts is better than a thousand. I would rather be a doorkeeper in the house of my God than dwell in the tents of wickedness. For the Lord God is a sun and shield; the Lord will give grace and glory; no good thing will He withhold from those who walk uprightly.

Psalm 84:10–11

Those who live in the shelter of the Most High will find rest in the shadow of the Almighty. This I declare about the Lord: He alone is my refuge, my place of safety; he is my God, and I trust him.

Psalm 91:1–2 NLT

If you make the Lord your refuge, if you make the Most High your shelter, no evil will conquer you; no plague will come near your home. For he will order his angels to protect you wherever you go. They will hold you up with their hands so you won't even hurt your foot on a stone. . . . The Lord says, "I will rescue those who love me. I will protect those who trust in my name."

Psalm 91:9–12, 14 NLT

Come, let us sing to the Lord! Let us shout joyfully to the Rock of our salvation. Let us come to him with thanksgiving. Let us sing psalms of praise to him. . . . Come, let us worship and bow down. Let us kneel before the Lord our maker, for he is our God. We are the people he watches over, the flock under his care.

Psalm 95:1–2, 6–7

Oh, sing to the Lord a new song! Sing to the Lord, all the earth. Sing to the Lord, bless His name; proclaim the good news of His salvation from day to day. . . . For the Lord is great and greatly to be praised.

Psalm 96: 1–2, 4

Let all that I am praise the Lord; with my whole heart, I will praise his holy name. Let all that I am praise the Lord; may I never forget the good things he does for me. He forgives all my sins and heals all my diseases.

Psalm 103:1–3

Your word is a lamp to guide my feet and a light for my path. . . . Your laws are my treasure; they are my heart's delight.

Psalm 119:105, 111

O Lord, You have searched me and known me. You know my sitting down and my rising up; you understand my thought afar off.

Psalm 139:1–2

Where can I go from Your Spirit? Or where can I flee from Your presence? If I ascend into heaven, You are there; if I make my bed in hell, behold, You are there. If I take the wings of the morning, and dwell in the uttermost parts of the sea, even there Your hand shall lead me, and Your right hand shall hold me.

Psalm 139:7–10

How precious also are Your thoughts to me, O God! How great is the sum of them! If I should count them, they would be more in number than the sand.

Psalm 139:17–18

I saw the Lord sitting on a throne, high and lifted up, and the train of His robe filled the temple. Above it stood seraphim; each one had six wings: with two he covered his face, with two he covered his feet, and with two he flew. And one cried to another and said: "Holy, holy, holy is the Lord of hosts; the whole earth is full of His glory!" And the posts of the door were shaken by the voice of him who cried out, and the house was filled with smoke.

Isaiah 6:1–4

He is despised and rejected by men, a Man of sorrows and acquainted with grief. . . . He was despised, and we did not esteem Him. Surely He has borne our griefs and carried our sorrows. . . . But He was wounded for our transgressions, He was bruised for our iniquities; the chastisement for our peace was upon Him, and by His stripes we are healed.

Isaiah 53:3–5

"For you who fear my name, the Sun of Righteousness will rise with healing in his wings. And you will go free, leaping with joy like calves let out to pasture."

Malachi 4:2 NLT

In the beginning was the Word, and the Word was with God, and the Word was God. He was in the beginning with God. All things were made through Him, and without Him nothing was made that was made. In Him was life, and the life was the light of men. And the light shines in the darkness, and the darkness did not comprehend it.

John 1:1–5

And the Word became flesh and dwelt among us, and we beheld His glory, the glory as of the only begotten of the Father, full of grace and truth.

John 1:14

"I am the true grapevine, and my Father is the gardener. He cuts off every branch of mine that doesn't produce fruit, and he prunes the branches that do bear fruit so they will produce even more. . . . Yes, I am the vine; you are the branches. Those who remain in me, and I in them, will produce much fruit."

John 15:1–2, 5

I pray that from his glorious, unlimited resources he will empower you with inner strength through his Spirit. Then Christ will make his home in your hearts as you trust in him. Your roots will grow down into God's love and keep you strong. And may you have the power to understand, as all God's people should, how wide, how long, how high, and how deep his love is. May you experience the love of Christ, though it is too great to understand fully. Then you will be made complete with all the fullness of life and power that comes from God.

Ephesians 3:16–19 NLT

Now all glory to God, who is able, through his mighty power at work within us, to accomplish infinitely more than we might ask or think.

Ephesians 3:20 NLT

You must have the same attitude that Christ Jesus had. Though he was God, he did not think of equality with God as something to cling to. Instead, he gave up his divine privileges; he took the humble position of a slave and was born as a human being. When he appeared in human form, he humbled himself in obedience to God and died a criminal's death on a cross. Therefore, God elevated him to the place of highest honor and gave him the name above all other names, that at the name of Jesus every knee should bow, in heaven and on earth and under the earth, and every tongue declare that Jesus Christ is Lord, to the glory of God the Father.

Philippians 2:5-11 NLT

If then you were raised with Christ, seek those things which are above, where Christ is, sitting at the right hand of God. Set your mind on things above, not on things on the earth. For you died, and your life is hidden with Christ in God.

Colossians 3:1-3

Long ago God spoke many times and in many ways to our ancestors through the prophets. And now in these final days, he has spoken to us through his Son. God promised everything to the Son as an inheritance, and through the Son he created the universe. The Son radiates God's own glory and expresses the very character of God, and he sustains everything by the mighty power of his command. When he had cleansed us from our sins, he sat down in the place of honor at the right hand of the majestic God in heaven. This shows that the Son is far greater than the angels, just as the name God gave him is greater than their names.

Hebrews 1:1-4 NLT

Therefore we also, since we are surrounded by so great a cloud of witnesses, let us lay aside every weight, and the sin which so easily ensnares us, and let us run with endurance the race that is set before us, looking unto Jesus, the author and finisher of our faith, who for the joy that was set before Him endured the cross, despising the shame, and has sat down at the right hand of the throne of God.

Hebrews 12:1–2

We love Him because He first loved us. . . . And this commandment we have from Him: that he who loves God must love his brother also.

1 John 4:19, 21

And standing in the middle of the lampstands was someone like the Son of Man. He was wearing a long robe with a gold sash across his chest. His head and his hair were white like wool, as white as snow. And his eyes were like flames of fire. His feet were like polished bronze refined in a furnace, and his voice thundered like mighty ocean waves. He held seven stars in his right hand, and a sharp two-edged sword came from his mouth. And his face was like the sun in all its brilliance.

Revelation 1:13–16 NLT

And I looked, and behold, in the midst of the throne . . . stood a Lamb as though it had been slain. . . . Then He came and took the scroll out of the right hand of Him who sat on the throne. . . . And they sang a new song, saying: "You are worthy to take the scroll, and to open its seals; for You were slain, and have redeemed us to God by Your blood out of every tribe and tongue and people and nation, and have made us kings and priests to our God; and we shall reign on the earth."

Revelation 5:6–7, 9–10

And I heard, as it were, the voice of a great multitude, as the sound of many waters and as the sound of mighty thunderings, saying, "Alleluia! For the Lord God Omnipotent reigns! Let us be glad and rejoice and give Him glory, for the marriage of the Lamb has come, and His wife has made herself ready." And to her it was granted to be arrayed in fine linen, clean and bright, for the fine linen is the righteous acts of the saints.

Revelation 19:6–8

"And behold, I am coming quickly, and My reward is with Me, to give to every one according to his work. I am the Alpha and the Omega, the Beginning and the End, the First and the Last." . . . And the Spirit and the bride say, "Come!" And let him who hears say, "Come!" And let him who thirsts come. Whoever desires, let him take the water of life freely.

Revelation 22:12–13, 17

NOTES

Chapter 4: Singing and the Brain

1. Here are links to just three of the countless fascinating articles and books available online about music and the brain: http://www.cnn.com/videos/health/2016/01/29/your-brain-on-music-sanjay-gupta-orig.cnn; and http://goodmusicbrighterchildren.com/?p=2740; http://ideas.time.com/2013/08/16/singing-changes-your-brain/?iid=sr-link1.

Chapter 5: Sing—Make It Personal

1. Charles H. Spurgeon, "Who Are the Elect?," *Spurgeon's Sermons*, vol. 11:1865, http://www.ccel.org/ccel/spurgeon/sermons11.xxxi.html.

Chapter 6: Sing—Get the Word on the Inside

1. Anna Matteo, "Brain Remembers Language Better If You Sing It," *VOA: Health and Lifestyle*, May 26, 2015, http://learningenglish.voanews.com/a/brain-remembers-language-sing/2776476.html; copy provided by learningenglish.voanews.com.

2. Roberts Liardon, *God's Generals: The Revivalists* (New Kensington, Pa.: Whitaker, 2003), Kindle edition, chapter 1.

3. "Charles Wesley: Greatest Hymn Writer of All Time," *Christianity Today*, 2017, http://www.christianitytoday.com/history/people/poets/charles-wesley.html.

4. David Guzik, "Study Guide for Psalm 1," *Blue Letter Bible*, 2006, https://www.blueletterbible.org/comm/guzik_david/studyguide_psa/psa_1.cfm.

Chapter 7: Sing—The Song of the Steadfast

1. Brian Simmons, *Psalms: Poetry on Fire, and Proverbs: Wisdom from Above: 2-in-1 Collection with 31 Day Psalms & Proverbs Devotionals,* The Passion Translation (Savage, Minn.: BroadStreet, 2015), Kindle edition, Psalm 11.

2. Ibid.

Chapter 9: Sing—Taking It to the Streets

1. Christian Newswire, "Miracle Breakthroughs Reported at 'The Ferguson Response,'" *Charisma News,* November 11, 2014, http://www.charismanews.com/us/46102-miracle-breakthroughs-reported-at-the-ferguson-response.

2. Mark Andrews, "Prophetic Prayer Meetings in Ferguson See Deliverance," *Charisma News,* October 27, 2014, http://www.charismanews.com/us/45912-alveda-king-joins-campaign-restore-the-dream-2014.

3. Kingsley Walker, "God Is Using His Worshippers," *Breaking Christian News,* November 20, 2014, http://www.breakingchristiannews.com/articles/display_art.html?ID=14991#.

Julie Meyer spent more than fifteen years in Kansas City, Missouri, working alongside Mike Bickle to help establish the International House of Prayer–KC. She was part of the leadership team overseeing the Global Prayer Room. She is a worship leader, songwriter, author and has also been a faculty member at Forerunner Music Academy, teaching vocal lessons and pouring into the next generation's worship leaders, singers and musicians. Julie is currently serving on the staff at the Healing Rooms Apostolic Center of Santa Maria Valley, continuing to help build the House of Prayer.

She attended Kansas State University and studied music. Julie is ordained by the Healing Rooms of Santa Maria, California. She is a popular conference speaker and singer. Author of two books and many CDs, she travels internationally, ministering at churches and conferences, leading worship, and sharing on Revival, God's Heart for Raising Up the House of Prayer and Worship. Her recent CD titled *Christmas* was nominated for a Dove Award in 2014.

Julie leads an online worship community called Into the River, which provides an epic collection of soaking worship, weekly Bible studies and edifying interactive classes via Facebook Live. Since June 2016, she has been adding one hour's worth of soaking worship as she sings through the Scriptures each month. Additionally, Julie hosts a class, also through Facebook Live, offering the opportunity to interact in real time with Julie and select panelists, including Stacey Campbell, Ray Hughes, James Goll and more!

Julie Meyer Ministries and Into the River
www.juliemeyerministries.com

Facebook:
www.facebook.com/juliemeyerministries

Instagram: @juliemeyerministries

Twitter: @juliemihopkc

You Tube:
Search for "Julie Meyer Ministries"

1/21/20